Apex Predator

J.A. Faura

Barola Press
DALLAS, TX

To my wife and children, you are my life.

Whoever fights monsters should see to it that in the process he does not become a monster. And if you gaze long enough into an abyss, the abyss will gaze back into you.
—Friedrich Nietzsche

We don't protect our young, and we tolerate predators of our own species.
—Andrew Vachss

Prologue

LOS ANGELES, CALIFORNIA

Les Martin sat in the lavish waiting room and looked out the window at the San Fernando Valley through the haze of rush-hour smog. This was his fifth appointment and Les knew better than anyone else that he was a new man.

He had been referred by the CEO of his company who had in turn been referred by the chairman of the board of a major movie studio in L.A. Like his CEO, Les had been wildly successful in his professional life, rising to his current position of executive vice president of global operations for a major technology company, but he had been a disaster in his personal life.

He had been an awkward child, in spite of having parents that were supportive and loving, and he had continued to be awkward through high school, college and into his career.

He had absolutely no sense of fashion or style and his posture and countenance reflected his almost constant anxiety. He had always been an introvert and unable to maintain any relationship socially.

Before seeking counseling, he had always believed that his inability to form relationships was a result of his intellect; he had tested well above the genius level in every standardized test he had ever taken.

All that had changed six weeks ago when he first came to this office and met the man who had given him his new life.

Now, as he sat in the waiting room, he stood and walked over to the big mirror that hung on one of the waiting room walls. With a smile, he straightened his tie and plucked at his hair, making sure it was just the way he wanted.

It was remarkable, really, he had gone from being someone with dated and ill-fitting clothes and a horrible bowl haircut, a nerd if he was to be honest, to a man sporting a two-thousand-dollar Hugo Boss suit and a Piaget watch worth more than most people's cars.

He had handsome Nordic features and was just under six feet tall, which combined with his new look attracted a fair share of female attention. Les had been a virgin until four weeks ago when he had met a woman at a bar and ended up spending the night with her.

He smiled at the memory. Everything had indeed changed for him the day he came for his first appointment. His therapist had listened to him share his most intimate thoughts and fears, allowing him to go on until he felt like he was drained.

He had told Les to share everything with him, no matter how awful or horrible he thought it might be, and he had let him know he would not pass judgment or think any less of him. He did as he was told and shared everything with his therapist, even the dreams and ideas that had seemed to haunt him since childhood.

Before seeking help, Les had thought there was something wrong with him, that his intimate thoughts and impulses were the product of a sick human mind.

Over their time together, his therapist had let him know just how wrong he had been. He explained why it was that Les felt the way he did and had let him know that there was nothing wrong with him.

Spending as long as he needed to, he had slowly revealed to Les the real reason that he'd had so much trouble fitting in. It had truly been a liberating experience for Les.

He finally understood who and what he was. Les had always believed there was something fundamentally different about himself, but he had thought those differences were an indication that he was simply inadequate. Now he knew different.

As he thought back over the last six weeks, the door behind the receptionist opened and his therapist, a neuropsychologist, appeared with a smile on his face, "Are we ready, Mr. Martin?"

Les stood, "Ready, doc." The therapist turned and Les followed him into his office. He lay down on the small sofa in the office and the therapist sat in a chair facing him. "So, how have things been since we saw each other last?"

Les put his hands behind his head and looked up at the ceiling, "Well, doc, I have to tell you, it's getting easier and easier for me. I can't believe how easy things are now. To be honest with you, I find myself looking for ways, nothing big you understand, but just little ways, to make things more challenging."

The therapist nodded thoughtfully and took a few notes, "I see. You need to be careful with that. We don't want to go too far too fast with this. It's the type of thing that can derail everything we've been able to accomplish."

Les looked at the doctor and then back at the ceiling and shook his head slowly, "I know, I know, it's just that it feels like I wasted the first 35 years of my life. I can't tell you how many things come to mind that make so much sense to me now, things that would give me the shakes before.

"It's hard, doc, it's like a kid not being able to ride a bike and then suddenly finding out he can not only ride the bike, he can do backflips on it. That's what you've done for me, doc, and it's hard not to do flips all day long, you know what I'm saying?"

The doctor chuckled, it was not the first time he'd heard such thoughts, "I'm sure it is, but you are right in the sense that for a great part of your life you lived an existence of confinement, which kept you from evolving naturally. Now that you understand how things are, it's understandable that you want to spread your wings and you want to test yourself, it's only natural.

"This is precisely when you have to be most careful, because this is the time when a lot of individuals like yourself make mistakes and end up in an even more confined existence. As you grow and continue to understand your own capabilities, you will learn that there will be plenty of opportunities to be challenged and to test yourself.

"Understand, Mr. Martin, that the world is full of opportunities for those like you, and if you are patient and continue to hone your skills, you will find many ways to grow further, but you must be patient."

Hands still behind his head, Les responded, "I know, doc, it's just hard. It's just incredible to me that the world is so unprepared, it really is. They walk around, completely oblivious to their surroundings, to the millions of tiny shifts going on around them. I just can't believe I didn't see it before, that it was all around me and I didn't notice.

"Honestly, now that I know better, now that I know the truth, dealing with those around me is like a game. It doesn't matter who it is or what it's about, I get what I want when I want. It's too easy, almost unfair if I'm being honest."

The therapist nodded, "I know exactly how you feel. It is a very common experience among those like you, but like I said, it's also this type of situation that can lead you to make a mistake that could prove to be disastrous. Now, tell me about your last experience."

Les smiled and took on a faraway, wistful look, "She was beautiful, doc, and I don't just mean her looks. She was smart and quite funny. We met at a bar on Sunset. There's dozens of girls like her in those bars, all looking to make it in Hollywood. She was different, though, educated and very well traveled. That's why I picked her, I thought she'd provide a bit of a challenge.

"But it was like you said in our second, or was it our third, meeting…anyway, it was like you said, once I knew her soft spots, her vulnerabilities, she was putty in my hands, and after that it was, like I said before, just too easy. That's what I mean, doc, they are just clueless."

The doctor took some notes and then looked at his patient, "I understand. Today, why don't we talk about different ways you can continue to grow without taking unnecessary risks? Don't try to rush this. You have a lifetime ahead of you, a lifetime to test yourself in a variety of ways."

Les sat up, "I guess you're right, doc. I'll work on being more patient."

He lay back down and the doctor proceeded with the session, "I assure you we will find a way to make sure you remain engaged." The doctor was pleased with his latest patient. He never grew tired of witnessing as one of nature's wonders blossomed before him.

Besides personal satisfaction, his unique practice had made him a wealthy and resourceful man, and it was that wealth and those resources that had allowed him to establish and grow his practice in the United States and around the world.

The neuropsychologist also knew that it wasn't just wealth and resources that had allowed him to accomplish what he had. Power and influence had always been a key part of his objectives early on, and he was absolutely certain that he had attained both.

He was pleased with his last project and wanted to ensure Martin was on track before leaving for New York. The therapist smiled at the thought of a potential new project waiting for him there. Another soul waiting for his guidance, waiting to be led into the light.

Chapter 1

Manhattan, New York

It was a cool night, not quite cold, but just at the point where people were beginning to think about wearing their scarves. Christmas season was just around the corner and the streets of New York were packed with early Christmas shoppers.

Not that anyone would be able to tell the difference, New York streets were always packed. People here never needed a reason. Trinity was just beginning his stroll.

He always liked to start at Central Park. He loved picking up the scents that so many people just took for granted. The dewy grass, the perfume of any one of thousands of women walking by, the mustard on the hot dog vendor's cart, so many delights that it could be overwhelming.

Never overwhelming enough for the scent he truly craved, the one he actually allowed his nose to hunt for. Children. Like everything else, children gave off a distinct smell and Trinity could pick up that scent for miles.

Here at Central Park, however, he never needed to wait too long to pick up the scent. The smell of children's shampoo, candy, ice cream smeared on a sweater, he could smell each and every one almost immediately. During his evenings of indulgence he did not like to stay around the park for long, lest someone get a clear look at his face.

That was another of New York's gifts to his purpose, no one looked at anyone else past a cursory glance, and if they did it was more out of annoyance than curiosity.

Still, he wouldn't take the risk when it was so unnecessary. On nights like tonight, it would not take him long to find what he was looking for. In fact, in the time it took for him to form that thought, he found exactly what he was looking for.

A mom, walking along with two children and a stroller, was just rounding a corner. And as if luck was truly smiling down on him tonight, they were headed for the ice rink.

Marybeth Loomis had a long day by any standard. After doing what early Christmas shopping she could do, she ran errands that had been on her to-do list for over a week.

It was just bad luck that the sitter had cancelled on her tonight, because she had planned on being home by noon, making dinner and waiting for her husband to come home. Christopher was also starting to get cranky.

She really couldn't blame him after three hours of sitting in a stroller. Tracy, all of six now, wanted to stop at every window and tell her mother what she would be asking Santa Claus for, but Bethany had shown remarkable restraint in the things she had asked for the entire day.

So when the two girls asked to go skating, even just for a little while, Marybeth could not bring herself to say no. As usual, Bethany, unable to control her excitement, ran far ahead to the rink in order to 'pick the best skates.'

Marybeth did her best to keep up, but pushing Chris along slowed her down. Trinity watched from across the street and saw all the things he needed to see. He made note of exactly what the mother was wearing, the names of the children, listening for the names of the girls as she called after one of them when she was running ahead. His van was not ideally parked, but it was hidden by a dumpster and near an intersection, which would allow him to do what he needed to and to get out of the area quickly.

As he watched, the expected scenario unfolded in front of him almost exactly as he had predicted. Mom, pushing Christopher and running and calling after Bethany, would glance back every few minutes to make sure that Tracy was following along, which she was, but at a farther and farther distance from her mother. She was stopping at every other store window to look at dolls or toys.

The group crossed the street to Trinity's side and began making their way back toward the rink, still in their disorganized procession. As mom rounded the corner, Bethany tripped and cried out.

Her mother rushed to catch up to her, leaving Tracy around the corner. Distracted by Bethany's skimmed knee and Chris's crying, she did not realize Tracy was not with them.

Trinity made his move, "Did you see how pretty that doll's dress is when it lights up?"

Having been taught not to talk to strangers, the six-year-old hesitated for all of half a second, "No, which one?"

Trinity now covered her with his own form as he answered, "The one in the blue, like the one I have in my van."

Tracy looked suspicious, "You really have one like that in your van?"

He smiled a disarming smile, "Yes, and many others with other dresses. Would you like to look at them? The van's just right there."

Tracy had been warned at school and by her parents about bad men, men who would hurt little children. Like almost every child who heard the stories, Tracy thought of monster-like creatures that would come and steal them in the night.

The man in front of her was wearing a suit like her father wore, his hair was combed and he wore glasses like her mother. She looked her mom's way, but Trinity knew how to seal the deal, "Don't worry about your mom, she's wearing that bright blue coat, so we'll be able to find her and we'll be right along. Besides, she's probably just catching up to Bethany right now and you know how hard that is, pushing your little brother along."

Tracy smiled at that, "Yeah, she gets really upset. Okay, but only for a minute."

And in just a blink of an eye they were lost in the New York bustle, walking to his van hand in hand. He knew not to look hurried or nervous and instead looked down at Tracy as a father might look at his daughter, with care and concern.

To anyone who might have seen the two, it was simply a father and daughter out for a stroll. When they got to the van, Trinity made sure no witnesses were around and opened the back where there were indeed many different dolls with pretty dresses.

Tracy's eyes lit up as she saw the dolls, but Trinity stopped her, "Oh, honey, you have a runny nose. Here, let me wipe it." Completely unfamiliar with chemical odors, Tracy never recognized the chloroform he used to put her to sleep. The whole process had taken just under three minutes.

He looked around and, seeing no one, put her in the van. He taped her ankles and wrists and bound her mouth, although she shouldn't be waking up for another few minutes. Now that she was accommodated in the van, Trinity could take pleasure in the fact that he could begin working on his true mandate, his calling, just like he had done time and time again.

Marybeth did not notice Tracy was not behind her until she had caught up with Bethany. Expecting to turn and see the bright red overcoat as always, enthralled, looking at windows. Failing to find her sent off the first of many red flags in Marybeth's head. She hoped she had walked close to a window that had flagstone around it, which was why she couldn't see her.

Her next instinct was to yell out her name several times to make sure she didn't just happen to be standing behind someone. In spite of having gone through these rituals like all mothers who could not spot their child right away, Marybeth knew something was seriously wrong. She had never lost sight of her little girl for this long, and looking at the sea of people strolling the streets of New York, she felt a sense of helplessness.

The first thing she did was to look for a policeman, luckily finding one at the far corner. "Excuse me, excuse me, officer, but I can't find my little girl!"

It was most definitely not the first time Officer Allen heard this from a frantic mother, especially at this time of year. Most of the time it turned out the little girl went into a store or was with another relative, so Officer Allen remained calm and asked all the pertinent questions. Was there another relative with them? Had she lost her before? Was there a favorite place the little girl might want to go to nearby, an ice cream stand, a toyshop?

Having gotten a negative on all pertinent questions and seeing the true panic on the mother's face, Allen put out a "be on the lookout," or BOLO, call on his radio for the missing little girl, giving her physical description, her last known whereabouts and her possible locations.

After two hours of not locating the girl, an all-city bulletin went out over the police band turning this from a lost girl into an actual missing person report with a possible kidnapping involved.

Every officer out there looking for the little girl had the same thought, but none dared speculate about it. There had been six other little girls, same description, same M.O., that disappeared in the past three weeks, and although no one wanted to think it, most were already counting her as number seven.

Trinity pulled his van into his rented warehouse and workshop. He had been careful to rent it in an industrial area where waste was dumped and processed at all hours of the night, negating the need to soundproof his space or bother with the odor.

Walking into it, one might think they were walking into a movie set. Behind plastic curtains was what could almost be called an operating room, complete with IVs, surgical instruments, an operating table of course and a cabinet full of drug vials.

Next to this was a curtain that separated the "clinical" part of the space into what anyone seeing it would describe as a typical little girl's bedroom, a small bed with four posts and a white frilly cover on the top, a dresser and two nightstands with small lamps. Then the observer would most likely notice that there were dolls, dozens of dolls, arranged all over the stands and the dresser in the middle.

Nothing strange about dolls in a little girl's bedroom, except these dolls were in various stages of disassembly. Some had the eyes cut out, others had no arms, and yet others were nothing but a torso with a head. Each had been carefully arranged to fit in with other dolls in a similar state. The dolls with no eyes were all arranged together, the ones with no arms likewise, and so on.

Another vast difference between this and any other little girl's room was the handcuffs attached to every one of the four posts, each pair having left bloodstains on the part of the bed it was on and on the post it was attached to.

The final part of this make-believe world was also divided, but by plastic curtains only. It could only be described as a chamber of horrors.

In the corner of the space near the entrance, there was an actual workshop with a table saw, various tools hanging on the wall, and a carry pack with various forms of cutting instruments as well as tools for machining fine parts.

Even the best crime profilers in the business could not have imagined a more disparate and sick space.

He headed over to the cabinet with all the drug vials, selected the appropriate vial and loaded a syringe, not too much though, she must be compliant but not fully unconscious; no sir, it would not do at all for her to pass out or worse, stop breathing, like the one before her.

He already knew what he would take, those eyes, those sparkling blue eyes now looking at him in sheer horror. After he applied the injection, Tracy's eyes took on a faraway look and she stopped struggling.

Gently, he picked her up from the van and placed her on the bed where he cuffed her hands and feet. Tracy would indeed be the seventh, and although she didn't know it yet, she would leave this world in a haze of horror and fear that a six-year-old mind would not be mature enough to comprehend.

Trinity walked over to the van, lifted her from the floor and placed her on the operating table, whispering, "It will all be over soon and you are being so good. I hope you know how much you are helping me, helping us, really," and with that he started an IV line on her.

To anyone who knew him, Donald Riche had been as average a child as there could be. He never picked on other kids and he never did anything that might cause his mother to be angry with him.

Had anyone been paying close attention, they might have noticed that young Donald was *too* average. He never showed interest in toys or comic books like other boys his age. What Donald did have an intense interest in was small animals. He would catch them and then, as best he could, he would take them apart using tools he found or knives from the kitchen. He didn't torture them, he simply wanted to see how they worked.

Donald knew he was not like the other kids, knew he didn't think the same way. He knew of adults who took children and did things to them, but rather than fear, such thoughts engendered curiosity in the young boy.

His mother had been decent enough, but she'd met a man, had left Donald with relatives when he was nine and had never returned for him.

His relatives gave him as much love and support as they could, but never as much as they gave their own children. Still, they encouraged him and showed him they were proud of his small accomplishments. His childhood should have been filled with happy memories of holidays and school events where he was treated like the other children in the family, but it wasn't.

Even in his early childhood, he'd understood that his interests were not normal for his age and that some of the things he did might attract unwanted attention; therefore, he was always cautious and meticulous in everything he did. As he became an adolescent and a young adult, his interests grew in intensity and he found that he had to be even more careful now that he was an adult.

Through high school, he participated in some student organization, never in a leadership role, but just as a member, a fly on the wall. He began to recognize that the more he adhered to the rules and the more he did what was expected, the less attention he was likely to draw to himself.

When he went away to college, he took his required course work, but he also always took electives in physiology, anatomy, biology and anything else that could assist him in his activities.

He began to dress better and take better care in his appearance. He bought stylish clothes and glasses and began grooming himself with more care. He also began to realize that there were people out there who had nothing and no one to care for them or to even know they were alive.

He trolled neighborhoods where he found such people simply lying on the street or against a doorway. It had not been too difficult for him to lure them with the promise of a meal or more alcohol. He was, as always, very careful not to go to the same place more than once, and he never did anything near where he lived.

Never curious about religion, he was nevertheless interested in the concept of the Holy Trinity. One individual, but three entities, he found it fascinating and decided that he too was a Trinity, one made up of intelligence, purpose and destiny.

By the time he graduated from Wisconsin University, Donald Riche had made more than 18 people disappear. He was never considered a suspect nor even questioned.

He moved to New York where he worked as a runner for a Wall Street firm, was well liked by his coworkers, had a nice apartment, which he kept in meticulous order, and he dressed the part to perfection.

After he began taking care of himself, he became not a bad-looking man. His suit and his poise attracted a fair share of female attention, but he had no sexual inclination whatsoever.

He had gone on a couple of dates, but more out of curiosity than because of any real sexual desire. He wanted to learn, to study, to see if he got the same sense from grown women that he got from the girls. In his mind, he believed women and adults were too far gone, too imperfect and could not be corrected, but still he wanted to test his theory for himself.

Both dates had been pleasant enough. After dinner they had gone for a nice stroll to let their food settle, and as they approached Donald's van, he had made sure no one was on the street and overpowered them with the chloroform.

During one of these episodes, Donald had come dangerously close to being spotted, when a young couple happened to be walking by as he held the woman's arm around his neck and pulled her to the van.

But it was New York, and when the couple looked, he simply said, "She couldn't hold her Chardonnay..." The couple smiled and kept on their way, as they could relate to having a bit much at a wine tasting.

Donald went through his process. He took the women to his workshop and did his work, and as he suspected, it was not the same; they were too far gone, too far into a life of excess and waste and worry.

There was none of the innocence and purity that a child had, none of the opportunity to fix what had been done wrong.

The two women had never told anyone who they were going on a date with, and Donald had been careful enough to use a false name in any case.

They had both come from completely different parts of town and from different online dating services, so Donald thought they would most likely be added to the long list of women who disappeared from the streets of New York without a trace. He had been correct in that assumption and had never been questioned about either woman.

◆

Steven Loomis had a long day. Meeting after meeting kept him from returning calls or emails all day long. As he walked out of the building, he saw he had eight missed calls from his wife. He would call her back as soon as he got into a cab, which during that time of year in New York at that hour could be quite a while.

Steven worked as a risk consultant for one of the largest security firms in the world. His job often took him to distant locations, where he would assess the risk situation of any number of companies or foreign government organizations before putting together a proposal on how to best address those risks.

It was a perfect fit for him after having spent 20 years in the Navy, the last 10 as a Navy SEAL. His travel now did not compare to those long tours of duty he would have to go on where he wouldn't see his family for months. Now he would be gone for two weeks at the most, and while it still felt like a long time to be away from his wife, girls and his little boy, he considered himself lucky to have a job he loved and which he was exceedingly good at.

He was 48 years old and had dark brown hair, cut neatly and peppered with slight spots of grey. He had bright hazel eyes that reflected calm and intelligence, even from a young age. He was six feet tall and carried a solid 195 pounds of well-toned muscle on his frame.

He had played football in high school and received several offers to attend good universities, not because of his size but because of his speed and ability to come up with the big plays when he needed to. He had chosen Annapolis. His dream had been to become a Navy pilot, but a knee injury playing football kept him from that.

So instead, he had decided to go into the investigative branch of the Navy, where he spent his first 10 years in the military police and eventually moving into the sensitive investigations unit, often liaising with the better-known NCIS.

Longing for something more adventurous and which would test him in a more rigorous way, he applied for the Navy SEALs. He'd been old by SEAL standards, 31, but he was in supreme shape and he had honed his mental toughness during his time at the investigative group. He made it through the infamous SEAL training program with no problem at all.

Within his first year he was assigned to the Special Warfare Development Group (DEVGRU) team, one of the most elite units in the program. SEAL Team Six, as it had been commonly called, was the team called when the missions were critical and difficult. Most people would be surprised to find that SEAL Team Six was made up of men in their mid- to late thirties. No one could be considered for the team without years of experience in the field.

In spite of exemplary evaluations throughout his career, Loomis had only risen to the rank of lieutenant commander. He knew that higher rank meant more likelihood of having to sit behind a desk, and that was not something he'd signed up for. He enjoyed the camaraderie and sense of accomplishment that came with being an operator.

After showing his mettle once and again and participating in hair-raising operations, it was time for Steven to retire. He had a fulfilling career where he made lifelong friends and learned more than he had ever imagined.

He raised a family along the way and understood that his priorities had changed. He could no longer go charging into whatever a situation demanded without regard for his safety. He now had people who depended on him, people he loved more than life itself.

That's when Lieutenant Commander Steven Loomis knew it was time to hang it up. After leaving the Navy, he'd dedicated himself to helping veterans coming home from 'the sandbox' of Afghanistan and Iraq, men and women who came home injured or depressed, most suffering from posttraumatic stress disorder.

He procured exercise equipment and therapy from a number of companies wanting to help and had taken a few men under his wing to help them to get back into a normal life. He'd also helped organize events to raise money for wounded veterans.

It was during one of these events that he had caught the attention of the CEO of an international security and intelligence firm. After their first meeting, Steven knew he'd found a place and the CEO knew he'd found the man that would eventually take over for him.

The air felt cold but good on his face. After sitting in meetings all day, it was good to feel the fresh air. It was early Christmas season, just after Thanksgiving, and getting a cab at that hour was going to be a nightmare. He stood on the corner of Madison and 52nd waiting for 20 minutes, allowing an older woman to take a car that had stopped for him along the way.

Finally he saw a couple coming out of a cab and ran before anyone else could snag it. He entered the cab, gave the cabbie his address and shook off the cold. Now in the comfort of the cab and with the noise significantly reduced, he could finally call his wife back.

He dialed the number and she picked up immediately, she was hysterical and Steven knew instantly that something was wrong. "Why the hell haven't you been answering your phone?"

He tried to calm her, "Beth, Beth, calm down, what's the matter, what's wrong?"

Beth had to take a couple of breaths before she could answer, "Tracy, it's Tracy, she's gone, I can't find her! She was right with me and now she's gone!"

Steven took this in and had his mind racing to think of possible answers to where Tracy could be, "Maybe a cop found her and she's at some station or maybe someone else found her and they're taking her there."

But she could not be consoled, "Steven, she's been gone for hours. The police have an alert out, they've checked with every precinct, every hospital, she's just gone!" Beth was sobbing on the other end of the phone.

He could tell she was barely functional and knew he had to get to her immediately, "Beth, where are you?"

At that point Beth continued to sob and could not speak or answer Steven's questions, "Beth, if there is a police officer around, let me talk to him, pass him the phone, Beth!"

On the other end Steven could hear the phone rustling and then a male voice came on, "This is Detective Mullins, Mr. Loomis. We're here with your wife and your other children. They're fine. We're at the precinct closest to Central Park. It's the…"

Steven interrupted, "I know where it is. Where is my daughter?"

Mullins answered, "Well, that's what we're trying to find out. We have all units notified of a missing child and we have the missing persons unit notified already. There are three detectives at the park interviewing people and retracing your wife's steps. We're doing about as much as we can right now, Mr. Loomis. I would suggest you come and pick up your wife and your children. We will stay on this and let you know as soon as we have something."

After hanging up with the policeman, Steven gave the cab driver the new destination.

When he got there, Steven Loomis could see that this was indeed a serious situation. The level of activity, the number of people on the phones with copies of a picture his wife had given them told him this was not a simple lost girl situation, something else was going on.

He looked around for his wife and his children and found them sitting on a wooden bench in the middle of the precinct. Marybeth was a total mess, her face streaked with makeup, her eyes still full of tears.

As soon as she saw Steven, she launched into his arms and began weeping, "I'm sorry, I'm so sorry, it's my fault! But she was right with me and we were going skating, and she was gone, just gone!"

Steven tried to calm his wife down in order to get a more cohesive story, but it became clear to him that he was going to need to take his wife to an emergency room to be sedated because she was on the verge of a complete breakdown.

"Beth, breathe, breathe, just relax, baby, and breathe. That's it, slowly, just calm down and breathe, honey, that's it." Slowly Beth began to calm down.

Steven spoke softly to her, "I spoke to the police, honey, and they are doing everything they can."

Beth looked up at him and began crying again, "But it's my fault, she was with me and…and I let her out of my sight…it was just a minute…Bethany fell…"

She couldn't finish her sentence before she broke down again. "Honey, it's nobody's fault, it happens, children break away from their parents all the time. Let's not think the worst yet. She is probably somewhere with someone who is trying to get her back to us."

Beth looked up again, "You really think so?"

Steven kept his composure and answered his wife with a lie, "Sure I do, honey. Now just relax and make sure Bethany and Chris are okay. They must be scared."

Feeling a bit calmer, Beth went back to the bench and started comforting her other two children. But Steven Loomis was certain there was something else going on, something serious. His business was security and risk assessment, and he spent 20 years in the Navy doing nothing but investigating and learning how to notice things other people did not notice, and something was going on here, something he intended to get to the bottom of.

He asked around and finally found Mark Mullins, the policeman he had spoken to on the phone. "Detective Mullins? I'm Steven Loomis. We spoke on the phone."

They shook hands and Mullins told Loomis, "I sure am sorry about this. I have two girls of my own and I can't imagine what you are going through."

Steven appreciated the man's sentiments, but at the moment he just wanted to get as much information as he could, "I appreciate it, detective. It is incredibly difficult. I'm still trying to process everything."

Mullins nodded in understanding, "So what can I do for you?"

Steven needed to be careful how he approached this if he wanted to get as much information as possible, "Well, I wanted to get an update on what's going on with my daughter."

Mullins responded without much preamble, "Nothing new to report. We have had a couple of sightings we followed up on, which unfortunately turned out to be dead ends. Every patrolman has a physical description of Tracy and we have detectives building a file."

Loomis listened to Mullins telling him all of this, all of which he already knew, but he also knew there was more. "See, that's the thing, detective, I was an investigator in the Navy and I work in security now, and I can't help but notice that there is a lot of activity for a child that's been missing for a few hours."

Mullins immediately got defensive, "Listen, Mr. Loomis, we take missing persons very seriously, especially when it is children. Actually I'm surprised. Most people never think we are doing enough. I've never had someone complain that we are doing too much."

Steven raised his hands trying to appease the officer, "I apologize, I didn't mean to come across as complaining. I just noticed that for the time she has been missing there is a lot of activity. It seems as though a case has been already developed and like it's much further along than I would think if it was just a missing girl at Central Park."

Mullins looked at Steven's eyes and could tell the man was not lying; he had the look of a cop, of an investigator. He knew if he lied to him he would see through it, and having the parent of a missing child not trusting the police during an investigation was no way to investigate anything.

Mullins considered it for a moment and then told Steven, "Alright, you did not get this from me. It could mean my job, do you understand?" Steven nodded.

Mullins went on, "You need to speak with Detective Grady, Robert Grady. He's on the floor above. He should be able to give you more information."

Steven looked back at his wife and kids and once he made sure they were okay began to make his way to the floor where Grady was. After a few inquiries, he was asked to wait until Detective Grady could see him. Steven sat down and again observed a lot more activity than he would expect for a case like this.

After 20 minutes, a short and stocky man came out to talk to him, "Can I help you?"

Steven stood up, "Yes, I'm looking for Detective Grady and I was told he worked on this floor."

The man looked him up and down and responded, "I'm Grady, what can I do for you Mr. …?"

Steven stuck out his hand, "Loomis, Steven Loomis."

As they were shaking hands, Steven saw a sign of recognition in Grady, who became extremely uncomfortable at the same time.

"Detective, to be honest with you, what I'm trying to get at is what's going on here. My daughter is missing and I appreciate everything your department is doing, but I'm in the business, in the security and intelligence gathering business, and there is clearly something more going on than just my daughter missing.

"I just wanted to get the full update, I'm sure you can understand this is my daughter we are talking about and I want to know everything there is to know that is pertinent to my little girl."

Grady considered Loomis. He could also tell the man wasn't lying, he was in the business.

He also thought about his own daughters and what he would do and what he would want if one of them went missing, "Follow me."

They went past the rows of desks manned by investigators and other detectives and went into an office at the far end of the floor. After they were both in the room, Grady closed the door behind him, "Have a seat, please." Steven sat down across from Grady and waited for what the detective had to say.

"Mr. Loomis, I'm about to share something with you that has not been released for public consumption and I am going to trust that you will keep it that way. It is not something that is easy for me to tell you, and I imagine it will be even more difficult to hear it."

Steven was now losing his patience, "Can you just tell me what's going on?"

Grady leaned back in his chair and went on to tell Steven, "We have been working on a number of missing person cases over the past three weeks. At first no connection was made because the missing people came from completely different areas, but we are fairly certain now that all of the cases are related."

Steven was puzzled and did not quite understand, "What does that have to do with my daughter?"

Grady was clearly uncomfortable with what he had to say next, "Mr. Loomis, without going into too many details, the reason we are fairly comfortable that the cases are related is because all of the missing persons are little girls, between four and seven years old.

"The M.O. is exactly the same in every one of the cases, the little girls were there one minute and gone the next, always with a parent nearby, always without a trace, no witnesses and no clue as to where they went. We have a task force working on this, but we have not yet gotten anything significant."

Steven Loomis was speechless, he thought there was something else going on, but he never imagined that there might be a serial kidnapper or worse, a murderer, on the loose in New York. "Let me get this straight. You guys have known there might be someone out there snatching little girls off the streets and you've decided to keep it from the public?'

Now it was Grady's turn to lose his patience, "What exactly would you have us do, Mr. Loomis? Huh? Tell the public we have a serial kidnapper on the loose when we haven't fully developed a firm connection between the cases? Create a mass panic only to find out that the cases are unrelated?

"So far, everything we have is based on speculation, we do not have one single iota of physical evidence to go on, and let's not forget that we are still speculating about these being kidnappings. Everything points to that being the case, but again, we do not have a single shred of concrete evidence that someone took these kids. So I ask you again, what would you have us do?"

Steven held his head down as he listened. He knew the detective was right; they were doing the right thing by keeping this an internal matter until they had something else. "How many girls have gone missing?"

Grady answered, "Six so far. We are scouring the system to see if there are any other cases whatsoever that could be related. Nothing's come up so far."

With his hands interlaced on the back of his neck, Steven asked, "And you think that my daughter might be the seventh, is that it?"

Grady knew how hard this must be for the man, so he tried to soften the blow, "We're not counting her as the seventh. Like you said, she has only been missing a few hours, so it could be that it is completely unrelated."

Steven looked up at the detective with a knowing look, a look that said, 'You think she's the seventh one and you think the rest of those girls are dead,' but he didn't say anything. He stood up and thanked the detective for his time and for his honesty.

Grady tried to reassure him, "I will keep you posted on anything we get as soon as we get it. I'm really sorry about this, Mr. Loomis, I really am."

Steven nodded and left the office. On his way back down he had to decide whether this was something he would share with Beth. He decided that if he did share it with her it would not be until she was much calmer. Right then, she was teetering on the edge and he knew something like this would just push her over.

He also had to decide what he was going to do. He just couldn't imagine himself going back to live life as if nothing had happened with his little girl missing. For the time being, he had his kids and his wife to take care of.

Chapter 2

Trinity was finished with Tracy and was still enjoying the bliss of the experience. Those eyes had been sublime, and he had found the proper place for them and for the other beautiful parts he had harvested from her.

Like every other time, however, he knew the feeling would not last long. He had started to notice that the feeling was in fact lasting less and less, so as much as he wanted to bask in the feeling he was still enjoying, he had to begin planning his next hunt.

This last experience had also gotten Trinity thinking that he may have to do his work with more than one subject at a time. It would definitely make his work harder and he was aware that it might be more difficult to keep his activities under the radar, but the work demanded it. And who was he to deny the universe, destiny itself, of what was to be?

For the next week, he went hunting every night and just couldn't find the right opportunity. On Friday, when he went to work, his coworkers could see a distinct change in him. Donald had always been meticulous in his appearance and in his work, and today he was clearly out of sorts. He was clearly sleep-deprived and had been withdrawn all day.

Had any of his coworkers been able to gain insight into what he was feeling, they would have realized that he was feeling like a drug addict without his drug of choice.

As he was winding up his day and cleaning up his desk, Nancy Hunt, one of the administrative assistants at his firm, happened to be walking by with a girl of about seven.

She was in her early twenties and had the typical look of a young, single woman in New York. Not unlike many of the other administrative assistants at the firm, she enjoyed having a good time and was on the constant prowl for "the one." She had always been friendly to Donald and often wondered why such a nice man still found himself alone. He was not a bad-looking guy, dressed well, although he definitely was a little quirky.

In the three years they had worked together, he had always been courteous and helpful to her. "Hi, Donald. Wrapping it up for the day?"

He looked up from his desk and smiled, "Yeah, it's been a bit of a rough day and I am ready to go home. And who is this young lady with you?"

Nancy smiled and brought the little girl forward to say hello, "This is Mia, my niece."

Donald smiled at the little girl, "Well, hello, Mia, you sure are pretty."

Mia looked at Donald in the way of little girls her age but did not respond to the compliment. There was something about the man and the way he was looking at her that she didn't quite like.

Nancy turned to her and prompted her, "Mia, don't be rude, say hello and thank you to the nice man."

Mia complied, "Hello and thank you."

Donald smiled as he looked back to Nancy, "No worries, she is just a little shy, that's all. So I heard some of the girls are going to *The Lion King* tonight, are you going to be joining them? I am sure it will be wonderful."

Nancy exhaled in frustration, rolled her eyes, and with as much tact as she could muster she answered in a whisper, "No, I promised my sister I would watch Mia and her friend over at my place. She's having a sleepover. My sister and her husband are off for the weekend to Niagara Falls. Second honeymoon and all that."

Donald was looking at Nancy and nodding, but in the deep recesses of his mind Mia enthralled him. Her curly dark hair, her perfect skin, it was almost as if destiny had brought her into his path, and now the perfect opportunity had presented itself. "You know, Nancy, if you want to go with the girls, I can babysit for you."

Nancy was a bit taken aback by the offer. Had she been older and had children of her own, perhaps there would have been red flags going off, but she was young and had really only agreed to babysit because she owed her sister.

"Jeez, Donald, I don't know, I mean, they can be a handful and I'm sure you probably have other plans."

Donald put on his most vulnerable and sympathetic smile, "No, I don't have any plans tonight. I was planning to go home and work on some puzzles and watch some DVDs, and I can do that as easily at your place as I can at mine. Besides, I have plenty of experience with little girls. I have watched my nieces more times than I can count."

Nancy hesitated for a moment, but she really did want to go to the theater and hearing that Donald had nieces and that he had watched them gave her a bit more confidence. Besides, it would only be for a couple of hours, just so she could watch the show and maybe have a drink.

She smiled, "Well, if you're really sure and you don't have any plans, then I would really appreciate it. It would only be for a few hours, just to see the show with the girls."

Donald's smile broadened, "Sure, have some fun. I will bring some DVDs for Mia and her friend and I am sure we will have a great time, won't we, Mia?"

The child looked at Donald with caution. In her child's mind, she could see something wrong with this man but she didn't know what, and he looked like all the other men her aunt worked with, so maybe he was not really that bad.

Donald went on, "Mia, what movies do you like to watch? I will bring some so you and your friend can watch them. I'll even bring the popcorn."

Tentatively, Mia, still standing behind her aunt, said, "I like *Beauty and the Beast* and *The Little Mermaid*."

Donald nodded and said, "Well, *Beauty and the Beast* and *The Little Mermaid* it is. What time would you like me to come over to your place?"

Nancy thought for a second and responded, "By six thirty would be great. Thank you so much, Donald, I really have wanted to see that play."

Donald waved her off, "Don't mention it. Like I said, I was just going to watch movies and do puzzles. I'll see you at six thirty. Bye, Mia." The little girl looked back and waved, but her eyes still held a hint of fear.

As Donald watched them disappear, he was in utter bliss. He didn't have any nieces and had never had the chance to spend extended periods of time just observing his subjects, the material for his creations.

He knew he had to be careful and that regardless of how strong his desires were he would have to play along. The time would come for him to do what was needed, but for now he knew he would savor this experience, an experience he had not had the opportunity to enjoy. He would take the time to study them, to hone his craft to decide what he would take from them when the time was right.

◆

Drew Willis had just finished a 12-hour day at his law office, if you could really call it an office.

In reality, it was storefront with a small desk for a receptionist, a room for a few paralegals, an office for him and one for his only associate, a sharp young woman two years out of law school.

Willis had graduated from Yale Law School and had his pick of corporate jobs the day he graduated. He thought he knew what he wanted, the big office, the expensive car and house, and the prestige of working at some of the most prominent law firms in New York.

The only problem with Drew's aspirations was that they required that he conform to a strict set of billing policies, political wrangling, and virtually no social life. After spending some time as a corporate attorney, Drew Willis knew he had to get out, go out on his own and do things on his terms.

He was deceptively intense and hard, given his physical appearance. He stood a lean five foot ten but would tell anyone who would listen he was six feet, and the way in which he said it was so matter of fact that even people that were clearly six feet and taller did not challenge his claim. He had intense brown eyes and a mane of unruly, curly, dark hair that he sometimes put in a ponytail.

He had ventured out on his own as a "ham-and-egger," someone who took any and all kinds of cases. As a general practitioner, he took on husbands trying to short their wives in divorce cases, insurance companies refusing claims, and criminal defense cases, with some wills and trusts thrown in for kicks.

To start his small law office, Drew had used the inheritance he had gotten from his grandfather, and after paying school loans there was not much left for a fancy office. He found that the ability to take on the cases he wanted to and to run his business his way was far more satisfying to him than all the trappings of the corporate firms.

To make ends meet, Drew also took on assigned cases from the court. These cases were all criminal defense for which he was paid a flat fee per case, cases that the public defender's office could not handle because of conflict of interest or because of overflow. Almost every case ended up with a plea deal and the defendant copping to a lesser crime in exchange for considerations from the court in sentencing, so what he got paid for those cases wasn't much.

It was rare that an assigned case would go to trial, but when it did Drew held nothing back; he used every resource at his disposal to defend his clients to the end.

He had only tried seven murder cases, and the truth was that the clients had flat out confessed to him and asked him to try and get the best deal possible. Drew explained that in order to do that, they would have to put on some sort of defense to motivate the prosecutor to offer some sort of deal.

In the end, the cases usually went on for three or four days before the prosecutor made an offer of second-degree murder with a minimum of 25 years in prison, which was not at all bad considering his clients had been looking at anywhere from 40 years to a life sentence without the possibility of parole.

His persistence and performance in the courtroom had also garnered him some high-profile felony cases, mostly involving drugs and gang activity.

Drew was also the type of person one couldn't help but like, even when he was the opposition. He had good relationships with most of the assistant district attorneys (ADAs) and judges with whom he worked, in large part because even when dealing with the most uptight and dry personalities he was able to keep a semblance of levity in the situation.

His practice was doing well, as well as a small firm in New York could expect to do, but truth be told, Drew wanted more. He wanted to get something to really sink his teeth into, and he knew in order to do that he would have to keep his ear to the ground and use every relationship he had with the judges' clerks, court clerks, district attorney's office, and the public defender's office.

As was the case with every attorney, he could not out and out solicit cases, but he could certainly position himself to catch better cases, cases that were not going to just walk into his office.

◆

Detective Robert Grady stood in his office looking out the window. Had anyone walked in, they would have most likely made the observation that he looked like a character out of a Dick Tracy comic. He was just shy of 250 pounds and just north of five foot six. He was clearly overweight, but he was one of those men on which the weight looked solid. He had thick, powerful forearms and hands that conveyed his strength every time he shook someone's hand. He wore his hair in a crew cut, now more salt than pepper, and always seemed to have a five o'clock shadow, even when he had just shaved. The suspenders he wore to hold up his pants were legend around the office, but only his closest friends ever mentioned them in jest, and his tie was never done up all the way. His eyes were narrow, the color of steel and wrinkled beyond his years. The crap he had dealt with over the years and the cruelty and violence he had seen human beings capable of inflicting upon one another had left him with a heavy dose of cynicism and, to a certain extent, bitterness.

These latter qualities were not unlike those of most of the detectives in the homicide bureaus in almost every precinct. You just knew someone with a twinkle in his or her eye and a bounce in their step hadn't been homicide detectives for long.

As he looked out the window, Grady was thinking about the Loomis girl, wondering what her fate might be, knowing what was most likely the case.

There was nothing concrete to tell him she had been the victim of a serial killer, just like there wasn't anything to tell any of the other detectives working the other cases involving missing little girls that they had also met a similar fate. But 20 years working homicides had also developed in him a kind of sixth sense about things like these. And this one felt wrong, really wrong.

He supposed that seven girls gone in three weeks, all taken in broad daylight, usually in front of dozens of people, could be a coincidence. It could be, but he knew it wasn't. One of the first things to go after working some years in homicide was the ability to believe in coincidences.

Where to go from here, though? It was just a matter of time before one of the local beat reporters put two and two together or until someone in the department let something leak and then they would have a serial kidnapper/killer story on their hands with every jackass, talking head news anchor speculating on what might be going on in the darkness of New York City, all accompanied by the usual calls from crackpots and false confessions.

Whoever this guy was, he had to be good to be doing this the way he was. He had to blend in perfectly and not raise any red flags. He had to have impeccable timing to know just when to strike and at least some rudimentary knowledge of police response in order to have a ready way out.

There was nothing to go on, though, no witnesses, no physical evidence, no trail to follow.

As hard as it was to acknowledge, he knew that there would most likely be another girl missing before long, and as callous as he knew it was to think, he knew that to catch this guy they would have to be waiting for it to happen and for the guy to make some sort of mistake that would give them something, anything, to go on.

In most cases, Grady was able to distance himself from the families of the victims. After years of delivering the worst news anyone could get and of seeing some of the worst things man was capable of, he had been able to build a wall around his emotions, but talking to Steven Loomis that night had done something to him. In a sense, he had seen what he himself would look like if one of his girls had been taken.

Loomis had the hard eyes of someone who had more than a nodding acquaintance with death, someone who had overcome it and who in spite of hoping for the best knew and was prepared for the worst.

So, in spite of his best efforts to look at this as just another case, Detective Robert Grady felt closer to this one than he was comfortable with. Loomis had gotten to him because he had given Grady the impression that he wasn't planning on just waiting on the police to do something to find his little girl, and the detective knew that an obsessed parent could compromise a case. While Steven Loomis didn't appear to be an obsessed parent, he certainly appeared to be a parent that, in spite of his best intentions, could get in the way.

As he was lost in thought, Mark Mullins walked into his office, "Hey, Bob, did a Steven Loomis come talk to you?"

Grady looked back from the window, "Yeah, he did. How exactly did he know to come talk to me?"

Mullins hung his head sheepishly, "I know, I know, but you met the guy, he would have detected bullshit in half a second and he would have gone on to do something on his own.

"Hell, I don't know he still won't go do something on his own, but I know that if I had lied to him, we would have lost his trust and this shit is getting deeper. So maybe I blew it by sending him to talk to you, but I would rather take the flack for that than have a guy with access to intelligence resources not trusting us and more than likely getting in our way."

Grady smiled a sardonic smile, "Yeah, I know, I would have probably done the same thing, and you're right, he probably is going to do some of his own digging. The trick is going to be to keep him informed enough to try to keep him out of our way as much as possible.

"Let's not kid ourselves, the guy was in the business at some point and he isn't just going to sit with his arms crossed, but it will be better to keep him in check by keeping him in the loop than by giving him pat answers he'll see through anyway."

Mullins scratched his head in response, "I get what you're saying, but do you think it's a good idea to let a civilian get that involved? I mean, he could leak some info and then we'd really have a shit storm on our hands."

Grady came around his desk and plopped down on his chair while he looked out over the city, "No, he strikes me as a pretty cool customer and to be honest with you, this one feels bad to me.

"I don't know what it is, but it just feels wrong and maybe having a different perspective, someone to keep us in check, might not be a bad idea on this one."

Mark Mullins thought he knew Bob Grady as well as anybody, and in all of his years of working with the man, he would have never expected to hear him say what he just did.

Mullins didn't respond to Grady, he just nodded, turned around and walked out of the office. Truth be told, though, this one felt wrong to Mullins, too, and when something felt wrong to seasoned homicide detectives in New York, they tended to take their gut feelings seriously.

♦

After taking his wife to the emergency room to get her sedated, Steven Loomis brought his family home. Their SoHo condominium was nothing spectacular, but it was modern, spacious and tastefully decorated. It was a good balance of SoHo modern style and décor more typical in a house from the suburbs. It was full of family photos and mementos from recitals, along with the requisite smattering of toys on the floor that a home with three children would have.

He had to carry his wife up the steps while the doorman opened the door. After walking in and telling his kids to get ready for bed, he took her straight to bed.

After getting some food into his and his kids' stomachs, he put his son and daughter down to sleep, reassuring them that their little sister would be coming home soon while choking back the tears from knowing that it was a lie.

Steven Loomis had been in the business of killing, of getting intelligence to plan assassinations, of executing operations that required ice water running through his veins, and so as much as he wanted to have the hopeful light in his chest that any father would have that he might get his daughter back, he knew she was gone.

Seven girls, three weeks, same M.O. No, Tracy Loomis would not be coming back home. Years of dealing in death gave men like Loomis a detached certainty about it that they most often didn't want but couldn't help but have and which they knew was almost always true.

Now Steven Loomis needed to decide what he was going to do about it.

He had to decide what he was going to say to his wife when she found out what he already knew and he had to figure out how he was going to explain it to his children.

He knew, no matter what, that his family as they all knew it was shattered forever.

On his way home, Steven Loomis had tried to assume the role of concerned parent, of someone without the resources to do anything about the situation, but came to the inevitable and quick conclusion that he would not be able to just stand by.

Now he had to decide what he was going to do to find out what happened to his daughter, but most importantly he also had to figure out what if anything he was going to do to those responsible for whatever it was that happened to her.

When all was said and done, it was this last part that caused the most conflict in Steven Loomis's mind, because in spite of having convinced himself he would do nothing, he also knew that to be a lie as well.

◆

At precisely 6:30 p.m., Donald Riche stepped out of the elevator in Nancy's building, and by the time he got to her door, he was Trinity.

He had morphed seamlessly into the natural predator he was born to be. As promised, he had the DVDs and the popcorn for him and for the girls. He rang the doorbell and waited with anticipation.

Nancy answered the door after a few seconds and smiled, "Hi, Donald! I'm almost ready, I just have to finish my makeup, but come in and make yourself at home."

He walked in and went into the living room where the two girls were playing with their dolls, "Well, hello there, Mia! Who's your friend?"

Mia looked at Donald and then at her friend. She was still a bit wary of the man, but he looked nice enough and he did have some DVDs and popcorn.

She gave a tentative smile and answered, "Her name is Emily."

Trinity smiled at Emily, a beautiful Asian child with beautiful long, dark hair, "Hello, Emily, it's nice to meet you. Mia told me she liked *The Little Mermaid* and *Beauty and the Beast*. Do you like those too?"

Emily pondered for a second and responded, "Hmm, weeell, I actually like *Aladdin* better, but *Beauty and the Beast* and *The Little Mermaid* are nice too. I like the crab in *The Little Mermaid*."

What a delight this was! To Trinity, this was like a lion charming the gazelle and watching it prancing about in its own habitat without a care in the world, without the knowledge that it was in the presence of the being that would end its life.

He smiled at Emily, "Good, maybe next time if I get to watch you both again, I'll bring *Aladdin*. How would that be?"

Emily smiled, "That would be nice. Are we really going to eat popcorn when we watch the movies?"

His smiled broadened, "Yup, that's actually what we are going to do. I brought these movies for you and I brought some for myself too. So you both can play and watch your movies in Mia's aunt's room and I'll be out here, okay?"

Both girls smiled and nodded.

Nancy came out just as Trinity was giving the girls their DVDs, "Mia, did you say thank you to Donald?"

Before Mia could answer, Trinity responded, "They did and we were just deciding that they would watch their movies and play in your room and I can watch my movies out here. Would that be okay?"

Nancy looked at Mia, "You guys can play in my room, but remember not to touch any of my makeup or my jewelry. Remember what happened with my lipstick last time you played in there. I don't want that to happen again, got it?"

Mia was nodding, "Okay, Aunt Nancy, but Mr. Donald brought popcorn for us. Can we eat it in your room?"

Nancy thought about it for a second, "Alright, you guys can eat it in there, but be really careful and make sure you don't get any on my bed."

Mia answered, "We won't, will we, Emily?" Emily shook her head.

Trinity reassured Nancy, "Don't worry, Nance, I'll look in on them now and again, just to make sure they're being careful. I'm sure they will be, right girls?" Both girls nodded and smiled. Trinity was mesmerized by the natural beauty that was there, just waiting to be perfected. Even Emily's smile with a baby tooth missing was enthralling to him.

He was sure he would find plenty of beauty to do something with.

She was the first Asian girl he had considered or would work on and he was anticipating experiencing a different sensation.

Nancy took one final look at herself in the mirror before heading out. Once again, had she been a bit older or a mother herself, she might have noticed the subtle change in his focus on the girls, the change from a helpful colleague to a grown man looking a little too intently at the two little girls.

But the moment passed and Trinity went back into his façade of normalcy.

"Have fun, Nancy, and don't worry, I've got your cell phone number and I can text you if I need you."

Nancy turned around, kissed Mia and then turned to hug Trinity, "Thank you so much, Donald! I have totally been waiting to see this show, and I don't know when I would have had another chance, so really, thank you!"

Trinity played the part to perfection, not too eager, but just a friend trying to be helpful, "Don't mention it. Like I said, it's just as easy to watch movies here as it would have been at my house, and they both seem like well-behaved young ladies."

Nancy grabbed her purse and went to walk out the door, "Thank you anyway and really, I will be home right after the show…well, maybe I'll have a quick drink with the girls afterwards, but I'll still be home early, I promise."

Trinity smiled and held up his hand, "Don't worry, we have plenty of Disney to keep the girls busy."

He thought for a beat and thought best to also add, "And I'll just have them wait for you to get their pajamas on. If they fall asleep, I'll just put them on your bed until you come home."

Nancy smiled and as she was walking out of the door she turned back, "That sounds great. I'll see you later."

Trinity flashed a smile of true delight, "See you later."

As he closed the door, he turned back to look at the girls, much like a lion would look at the smallest and weakest gazelles left behind by the herd. He knew he would not be able to do anything, but he could watch and learn and enjoy.

Chapter 3

Detective Mullins walked into Bob Grady's office as he was just getting off the phone.

Grady had the pictures of all the missing girls sitting on his desk along with a stack of tips, sightings and other related materials. "Bob, we just got word of another two girls missing."

Grady looked up immediately, "And you think they might be a part of our investigation?"

Mullins nodded, "Six and seven years old, similar M.O., there one minute, gone the next."

Grady rubbed his eyes in frustration, "Damn, this is going to break out soon. Someone is going to leak it or some reporter is going to start putting two and two together. Shit, who knows, maybe it would be better if it did get out, might shake some useful information loose instead of the load of crap we've gotten so far."

Mullins responded, "You don't mean that. You know if this gets out the guy might go under or move on…"

Grady interrupted again in frustration, "I understand, but at least if that happens, little girls would stop disappearing."

Mullins stood at the door and looked down at the floor. Grady settled into the chair behind his desk. "I'm sorry, it's just that this case is really getting to me.

"We should have something, anything, by now and we don't have dick. I just don't know which way to go on this anymore. I've been on the phone with the FBI to see if we can use their profilers to develop a potential sketch of this guy, but you know how that goes."

Mullins answered, "Yeah, hit or miss and don't worry about it, Bob, I'm a big boy and I get it, I do. You're not the only one with a little girl, you know. I know mine are in college now, but they're still my little girls, always will be."

Grady motioned to the chair in front of his desk, "Thanks, here, have a seat. Let's go over what we have so far. I've been doing it over and over, but you know a fresh set of eyes can sometimes catch something that's been missed."

Mullins sat down, "Alright, let's do it. I have a conversation scheduled with the detectives handling these last cases, but I think it will be more fruitful if I can share everything we have so far with them."

Grady turned the pictures so Mullins could see them and put the stack of materials in front of him. "There's nothing really new. All seven girls were between five and six, all taken in public without a single witness.

"There's no obvious connection or anything in common between the victims other than their age and their gender. They have been taken from different areas of the city, so it's not like this guy has a marked territory.

"I don't know what else there is, Mark, but give it a once-over and tell me what you think."

Mullins looked at the pictures of the girls and sifted through the materials in front of him. He had also looked at the materials a number of times, but Grady was right, sometimes stepping away from the case and coming back to look at it with fresh eyes could be useful.

Grady was the lead investigator and was waist deep in all information related to the case every day, whereas Mullins had an opportunity to handle other matters and to step away from it, even if it was just for a day.

As he was looking through the last pages of materials and up at the map of New York on the wall with seven tacks to mark each of the locations where a little girl disappeared, something hit him square on.

He put the papers down on the desk and leaned back in the chair with his mouth open, and a slight smile starting to appear on his face.

Grady noticed it and leaned forward, "What, did you find something? Is it on the map?"

Mullins, now smiling and shaking his head, responded, "Shit, I can't believe I hadn't thought about it and that I didn't tell you."

Grady was now coming around the desk to look at the materials that he thought Mullins had found something in. A smile was beginning to form on his face as well, "What is it? Goddamnit, give, you greedy bastard!"

Mullins stood up and told Grady, "It's nothing in any of this stuff. It's about these last two missing girls. I hadn't put it together or thought about it until just now.

"These last two little girls knew each other. The two families have known each other for a while because they go to school together and are friends outside of school."

Grady grabbed him by the shoulders and also smiled, "Shit, are you kidding me? This is our first big break, now we have some parameters to narrow who we're after. Were they taken together or at different times?"

Mullins answered, looking at the map marked with the tacks, "No, they were taken from different places at different times, but within a day of each other."

Grady let go of Mullins and walked back behind his desk and sat down, "Alright, now let's just take it nice and slow. Whoever it is has to somehow be related to the two girls. There's no way it's just coincidence that these girls happened to know each other and were taken separately.

"I don't know the odds of that, but I can tell you here and now this motherfucker knew or saw both of them together before he took them. Maybe the ones before were a hunt and taking advantage of an opportunity, but he saw these two before in the same place at some point.

"Go to your meeting and see what else you can find out. Get schools, ballet classes, piano lessons, anything that connects the two girls. I'll see if I can light a fire under the FBI's ass to get that profile. Now it could really help us narrow down our possible suspects. Let's cast a wide net around everywhere these girls were together and then start squeezing."

Mullins left and Grady got on the phone immediately. This type of opportunity could break a case wide open, but it could also go away in a heartbeat. All it would take would be for two other girls, completely unrelated to these two, to go missing and they'd be back at square one.

The key was going to be how fast they could develop a list of possible suspects and weed out the ones that are obviously not involved.

If this guy got wind they had something like this, he could easily cover his tracks or throw them off in some other way. Whatever kind of monster this guy was, he certainly wasn't stupid. The fact, that he had taken the girls he had without leaving a trace of evidence proved it.

Like all criminals, Grady thought, greed or delusion or impatience had led this guy to make a mistake, one that had really renewed Grady's conviction that they would catch this son of a bitch.

♦

As much as he wanted to stay with his wife, Steven knew he had to go to the office. He had a number of pending operations that unfortunately could not be delegated, and truth be told, he had to step out of his father and husband role and into the role of intelligence and tactical operative.

He had already made up his mind to utilize every resource he had to learn more about what was going on with his daughter's and the other girls' disappearance.

His employer, Globalview Intelligence Consultants, or GIC, had already let him know that they would understand if he needed to work from home or take time off.

He, like every other senior executive, reported directly to the CEO, Art Goodman. General Art Goodman retired from the Marine Corps and founded GIC over 30 years before.

He was a savvy businessman and had developed into a strong corporate force in their industry, but above all he was a Marine and valued and respected every one of his employees, especially the ones that had served. He didn't care about the rank or the job they had performed, to him the fact that they had served was all he needed to know.

GIC's nonmilitary personnel knew him to be a strict and serious boss, but always a fair one.

Loomis knew that the General, as he was known in the industry, had a special place in his heart for him. It had been the old man himself who had spotted Steven at one of the fundraising events he had organized to help veterans.

He had mentored him personally when Loomis came into the company and had remained interested in how he developed within the company.

It was Goodman who told Loomis to take as much time as he needed. Steven knew he meant it, too, but he had to get active and keep the wheels turning. Marybeth's parents were in town and looking after her, and as much as he wanted to be there for his wife, he knew he himself had limits, and he wanted to avoid becoming another reason for his family to worry.

He walked into his office and found a new and unmarked manila folder with documents in it. The rest of his projects were neatly organized in order of priority.

Stephanie Dillon, his administrative assistant for the past seven years, had made sure things were handled until he got back. She greeted him as he walked into his office and around his desk, and although she tried to put on a brave face for him, he could tell she was worried sick.

Still she remained her cool and organized self, "Hey there. Are you okay?"

Steven answered with as much of a smile as he could muster, "I'm okay, I guess. I think you know me well enough by now."

She smiled back, "Yeah, I do. That's why I'm asking the question and not running up to give you a great big hug and to tell you 'There, there, it will all be fine.'"

This time he did smile as he finished walking into his office, "See, I told you that you knew me."

Once the awkward moment passed, Stephanie got right down to business, "The information you asked Carl to track down for you is sitting on your desk. The Kenya deal is temporarily on hold, the General knows and he's fine with it. He thinks they've been dragging their ass on purpose. Joseph Stillman is going to Rome to finish that deal..."

Steven winced at that piece of news, but Stephanie was one step ahead, "I know what you're going to say, but he offered and I think it's time he started getting his feet wet. The kid's done well and he was right next to you all the way through, so stop with the faces."

Steven put down his briefcase, sat down and turned his computer on. Stephanie kept going without pause, "The Intertel deal is still on track, there's a conference call at noon today, but they're not expecting you to dial in."

Steven looked up at her, shaking his head, "I know what you're trying to do, Steph, and really, it's not necessary. I came back to the office to clear my head a little and to get a fresh perspective on things and I'm not going to be able to do that if you and the General don't let me get back into the flow."

Stephanie was having none of it, "Listen, Steven, you've been out of the office for a week now and you've had more than enough to think about, so we've done what we would have done if you had broken your back and been out for a week.

"You'll get back into the swing of things in no time, but just let it go, don't push it. Why don't you start off by going through the stuff on your desk. I'll go get you a cup of good, strong coffee, just the way you like it, and then you can start going through the files."

He had to admit she really did have his number. He picked up the manila envelope, "Alright, fair enough. Let me take a look at this. But I will dial into the call today and I will just go over the Kenya deal. I agree they are dragging their feet on purpose, but it doesn't mean we can't still close it within the next two weeks.

"And you're right, Joe has done well and he should be getting his feet wet, but I just want to give it the once-over. Call me a worrier if you want, but you know these things can go south in a heartbeat."

Stephanie paused for a beat and then responded, "Okay, fair enough, but don't step in if you don't need to. Joe has earned it and you know it will help his career. As far as the other stuff, I know you're going to do what you're going to do no matter what I say, but I just wanted you to know that there are capable people here and we all have your back."

He looked up and locked eyes with her, "I know, Steph, I really do. Thank you. Now where's that cup of coffee I was promised."

She smiled, "Now that's more like it. Three sugars, right?"

"Do you really have to ask?"

She turned and walked out of the office, "Nope."

Steven opened the manila envelope and found 16 pages of information.

Carl Gilliam was the company's most senior and talented computer and digital intelligence executive. Steven had called him the previous week and asked that he scour the digital world for any information about all of the girls that had gone missing in New York, New Jersey or surrounding areas. He knew there would be a lot of information, but he had Carl narrow it down to girls that had gone missing within the last four weeks, were between five and eight years old, had gone missing or were taken in broad daylight, and were not within a custody dispute.

Steven read the first page. It was a note from Carl and it startled him. 'Steven, here's everything I could get without looking at some serious prison time and a hell of a fine for GIC. Two girls went missing late last week. Both in the age range, both taken in broad daylight and both taken in Manhattan. The difference with the last two is that they knew each other. You'll find some emails between the two moms about sleepovers, recitals, etc.

'I'm just a computer nerd and not a field guy, so I'll leave it up to you to sift through this and paint the picture, but something tells me this guy just made his first mistake and it's one that could really bring him down.'

Steven looked up from the pages in his hands. Two more girls, two more families that would never see their little girls again. Whoever was doing this was hunting them like prey. He knew what he was looking for and was going about it methodically. No ransom demands, no calls to the families or to police to take credit for the crimes. This guy was doing this for his own personal reasons, for his satisfaction and nothing else.

He went through the information carefully. Before the two girls that knew each other, there had been no common thread to link any of the families or any of the girls.

Carl was right, this was a mistake; the guy had made a mistake. He was sure the police were going to cast a net around both families and they were going to tighten it until they had a short list.

Now that they had gotten the profile back from the FBI, they would use it to make the list even shorter.

How the hell did Carl get this stuff? Steven had always wondered, but the truth was he didn't really want to know.

The profile Steven had in his hands right now wasn't too different from the one he had already come up with on his own. Single, white male, between his late 20s and early 40s, very unassuming, very unremarkable in his physical appearance, he had to blend in to be able to take them in broad daylight.

The FBI profilers had also come up with a couple of things he hadn't thought about, but which made perfect sense. He was most likely very meticulous in whatever his job was. He probably worked a white-collar job. These weren't crimes of opportunity, he knew what he wanted and he went out to hunt for them. They'd also come up with a theory that he was probably taking them somewhere other than the place where he lived.

According to their file, this was probably ritualistic in nature for him and his home wasn't the place for it. Steven wasn't sure about these last couple of theories, but they did make sense, as much as anything like this could make sense.

The last paragraph was hard for him to read, even though he had already come to the same conclusion. It was likely that if the girls weren't found within 24 hours of being taken, they would most likely not be found alive. The father side of him was going through the emotions of the situation again. He wiped his eyes with one hand and exhaled. Focus, he had to focus now.

The first thing he had to do was to go through all his projects, even if they were in check he needed to clear his head and bring a fresh perspective to the situation.

As much as he wanted to keep himself under control, he had to admit that he was torn. All the training in the world and all the black operations he might have been a part of could not erase the memory of his little girl's smile.

He turned his chair to his side table where there was a picture of his beautiful daughters, his wife and his baby boy. He picked it up and stared at it, and as he was looking at the picture he felt something shift within him. It was a feeling that was barely recognizable, but still familiar to him.

It was a coldness, an element of detachment from the huge grief that was welling up within him. It was something that he had learned after losing many friends on many fields over many years. You had to develop that element of detachment if you were going to move on and execute the next mission. The difference was that this wasn't an operation and it wasn't a friend or one of his men, it was his little girl, and the conflict he felt, the rage that was broiling just under the surface, was definitely something new.

Whatever level of detachment he would apply to this situation, Steven Loomis knew this was intensely personal and that was something new too.

He knew he would be able to see this from a more detached place than anyone else in his family, but now he also knew the grief and pain would be there forever. And he was beginning to realize that to do whatever he ended up doing, he was going to have to find a place for this anger the way he had found a place for his anger before.

He set the picture down, turned back around and went through the file again, this time formulating a plan for what he would do next.

Like the police, he knew that after these two last girls went missing someone was going to leak it to the press or some reporter that had already been putting things together would finally put it down on paper or on the Internet.

Once the story got out, trying to catch this guy was going to get much harder. He would cover his tracks and just move to new hunting grounds. They would catch him eventually because he would make another mistake, but it would be a while.

Steven decided he would go see Detective Grady to see where they were on this. If he had read the man correctly, it would not surprise him to see Steven showing up to ask questions about the case.

◆

Detective Grady was in the process of building a list of people he needed to talk to about the last two girls that had gone missing.

The story would pop any day now and he had to get through the best prospects before the rest of New York started speculating on what had happened to the nine little girls, and little girls like his own daughter started seeing the boogeyman under the bed every night.

He had pulled everyone in his own precinct – beat cops to senior detectives – from the other missing girl cases in their jurisdiction and had asked for help from other precincts where girls had gone missing.

Everyone now agreed that the cases were related. All the other theories about every one of the other girls had been explored, but as all the law enforcement agencies involved looked at each of the cases, a very distinct pattern began to emerge. It was the last three cases that had really sealed the deal for everyone.

As much as everyone dreaded to admit it, they had a serial kidnapper/killer loose in New York and he was targeting little girls. It just couldn't get any more nightmarish.

They also agreed that these last two gave them the best opportunity to catch this guy, so everyone agreed to help. They would keep their own investigations alive running in parallel with that of the last two girls, but they all agreed to provide resources to help with the interviewing of everyone related to their disappearance.

He also had the profile developed by the FBI to help narrow down the list. The profile was relatively helpful in that it helped to eliminate some possibilities that were almost certainly not the type, but the profile also described roughly a third of all males in New York. They would have to be careful to not rely on too many generalities and to focus in on some of the things that their own profile had in common with the FBI's.

There were three principal groups that had to be interviewed, the families of both girls, their school teachers and all other school personnel, and anyone who could be identified as having been with or somewhere near the two girls outside of school hours and away from home.

Grady had decided to take Mia Reynolds' family including all extended family on both sides that knew or had met Emily Wu, and he had asked Mark Mullins to take Emily Wu's family and extended family on both sides who knew or had met Mia Reynolds. The same scenario was being repeated with their schoolteachers, ballet or piano instructors, anything the two girls had in common, any time they spent together was being meticulously scoured for information.

Everybody had the police and FBI's profiles and would filter their people through them.

All agencies had agreed to meet at the end of the week to compare notes and eliminate as many people as it made sense to. Grady had also been coordinating with all the other lead investigators from the other precincts and the NYPD public information division just in case something did break or some reporter started asking questions.

Some of the investigators from the other precincts had already begun to mention that there were reporters sniffing around, asking questions about the missing girls.

Grady would be talking to Mia's family later today. Her mother, her father and her 12-year-old brother were coming down to the station along with any other family member that had seen or been around the girls together.

After spending 10 years or more in homicide, most detectives could sense when there was a window of opportunity, and every investigator on this case could sense this was it.

As he was organizing his notes and related materials, Bob Grady heard a slight knock at his door. He looked up to find Steven Loomis standing in his doorway.

Loomis looked tired and weary, but there was an intensity to the man that was unmistakable. It was the eyes more than anything. Grady had seen eyes like that before, eyes that had witnessed death and had peered into hell only to come out on the other side with a certain calculated coldness. The difference was that Loomis wasn't a psychopath or a sociopath. He was clearly an extremely intelligent and controlled guy with no tolerance for bullshit and the highest level of motivation anyone could have.

Grady sat back down in his chair, "Mr. Loomis, to what do I owe the pleasure?"

Loomis came into the office without being invited and sat down in the chair in front of Grady's desk. He smiled a thin, knowing smile, "I ran into Detective Mullins on the way in. He mentioned you guys might have caught a break."

Grady gave Loomis a deadpan look and took his time responding. Loomis was testing him; he was trying to find out just how much they would be willing to share with him.

If Grady had read this guy correctly, he already knew they had caught a break and knew just what that break was. "Yes, yes, we did. Well, I don't really like to think about the disappearance of two little girls as a break, but yes, two girls went missing that had a clear link between them.

"They were friends and schoolmates. Their families know each other and have attended a lot of recitals and school activities together."

Loomis was nodding, pleased that Grady was not going to try to shut him out. It was the smart play; their way of keeping him informed just enough for him not do anything on his own. "So you are working off of a hypothesis that whoever took them had to have been around both of them at some point and that narrows down the list, yes?"

It was Grady's turn to nod, "That's right. You're in the business, do you believe it is just coincidence?"

Loomis answered, "No, not in something like this. I get it. The other girls were completely unrelated to one another, they had nothing in common." He had to fight through the rage that welled up when he referred to Tracy as one of the other girls, and Grady could see it in his face.

The jaw clenching and the eyes becoming colder, Loomis went on, "So there was no pattern to follow, they all seemed like they had been taken during a hunting expedition when the opportunity presented itself, when he saw what he wanted, and with Mia Reynolds and Emily Wu, he had to have seen them together or somehow know both of them. I get it."

Grady folded his hands on his desk and leaned forward, he knew why Loomis had explained it to him.

He wanted Grady to know exactly how good his sources were, "Very good, Mr. Loomis. I'm not going to ask how you have the names of the two missing girls or how you came to formulate your scenario, because to be honest I don't want to know.

"I would just ask that you do not in any way interfere or compromise any part of this investigation. If you can do that, I can guarantee that I will be absolutely honest with you and will keep you informed as much as it is legally possible."

Grady got a sideways response, "As much as it is legally possible?"

Grady held up his hands, "Hey, I told you what you find out on your own and how you find it is none of my business, I don't want to know."

Loomis leaned back in his chair. They were on the same page. "Fair enough. Thank you for your time, detective."

As Steven got up to leave, Grady threw out another caveat, "And I will expect the same courtesy from you, Mr. Loomis. You'll let us know if you happen to run across something interesting, right?"

Steven turned around, "Sure, but I thought the NYPD wasn't too keen on civilians being a part of the investigation."

Grady crossed his arms and smiled, "The NYPD doesn't like civilians involved in a criminal case, especially one like this one, but me, I don't give a shit where the information comes from. I just want to shut this guy down."

Loomis was starting to like Detective Grady, something rare for him.

He nodded and just before turning back around to leave, he paused and without looking back said, "We have a computer we use to do geographic profiling. It uses a mathematical formula, which takes the locations where the girls were taken and develops a statistical, geographic model of where the subject is likely to live. I'll have the results of what we've come up with couriered over to you, personally."

Grady didn't say anything. As he was walking out the door, Loomis turned back to make one last comment, "And you can call me Steven."

As he was walking down the hallway, Loomis heard Grady respond from inside his office, "Yeah, well you can call me Detective Grady." Yes, Steven Loomis was definitely beginning to like Bob Grady.

Chapter 4

Felix Garcia had been a beat reporter for the *New York Chronicle* for five years now. He was assigned to cover the police blotter from three precincts in Manhattan. Born and raised in Spanish Harlem by a white mom and a Hispanic father had provided him with more of a street education than he cared for, but for which he was immensely thankful.

He smelled bullshit a mile away and could think on his feet better than any of the other young reporters at the *Chronicle*. That was why he had been assigned his own beat covering three precincts over the complaints of the Ivy League whiners stuck with covering the social pages. Not bad for a kid that had taken six years to graduate from NYU's journalism program.

He was by no means the only reporter of mixed heritage in New York, but his tall lean body, light brown skin, dark curly hair and light aqua eyes made him hard to forget. He spoke both Spanish and English fluently and had learned to seamlessly move from one culture to the other in order to fit his purposes. Unlike many of the other young journalists at the *Chronicle* who concentrated almost exclusively on their online persona, Felix had an old-school mentality that harkened back to Woodward and Bernstein.

He believed that good journalists kept their nose in the story, in developing sources and in looking for things deep under the surface, not worrying about how many 'likes' they got or how many Twitter followers they had. To Felix's way of thinking, it was the story that should win fans, not the person who wrote it.

That didn't mean that he did not have a deep understanding of social media or that he did not value what the Internet could do to bring his writing to those looking for that good story. Ironically, he had more followers on Twitter and more 'friends' on his *Chronicle* Facebook page than any of the other young reporters at the *Chronicle*.

He had traded on his family name, but not in the way of the Carnegies or the Rockefellers. He was Augusto Garcia's grandson, from Spanish Harlem, and that carried some weight when he knew he wouldn't get the information in his role as a reporter. He had more cousins, uncles, nephews and nieces than he could count, whether they were blood relatives or not was irrelevant, once a tio, always a tio and once a primo, always a primo.

Family was defined by the strength of your word and your bond. He never forgot this.

He had a reputation for being tenacious, smart, but also discreet. He had never burned a source, something that everyone that had ever given him a scoop appreciated. He was careful not to jump too quickly when he started hearing chatter or rumors about something.

Instead, he did his own homework and came up with one or two scenarios that he would work from. Once he decided on those scenarios, however, he bit down and didn't let go until he had his story.

After three years hanging around the precincts and monitoring police scanners, he thought he had a pretty good feel for when there was a real story there or when it was just bullshitting among cops.

Over the past few weeks, he had been following leads on a couple of homicides, both of which turned out to be crimes of passion, nothing to get excited over, and some burglaries where there was actually the hint of a story since one of the burglaries had been a sophisticated cat burglar right out of *Ocean's Eleven* who had made off with more than $300,000 in jewelry. He had made a mental note to follow up on that one.

Then there was the usual smattering of domestic violence cases, nothing newsworthy, and last there were the missing persons reports. Again nothing out of the ordinary, although he had noticed that in each of the precincts he covered there was a report of a little girl missing. Nothing in common with any of them other than age and they were just three among twelve others from around the five boroughs.

Still, Felix had also made a mental note to check with some of the other beat reporters about missing little girls of the same age range. Maybe there was something big there, but Felix had gotten egg on his face before for jumping to conclusions too soon. Too many options of what could have happened to them, a divorced parent simply taking their kid, getting lost, runaways, although at six he thought that unlikely, still too many possibilities to put anything on paper.

He would wait until he had something to dig into, the cat burglar story was his main focus for the time being, but this one was definitely worth filing away to follow up on later. Besides, he had accumulated enough resources within each precinct to learn if there was something worth learning.

◆

Drew Willis was wrapping up his caseload and was thrilled about going to The Hound's Tooth and having a stiff scotch.

He couldn't wait until the assistant district attorney normally assigned to this courtroom came back. Bart Logan was really starting to grate on him. The guy had a stick so far up his ass he would have trouble bending his neck to look down.

The whole week had been a series of arguments and sidebars and meetings in the judge's chambers for even the most simple of negotiations. Like Drew, Logan was just a few years out of law school and was really trying to establish a reputation as a hard-ass. What he had really achieved was to garner contempt from most of the public defenders he worked with, and not even the guys that were lighthearted and really flexible dealmakers were comfortable working with him. They just put up with his bullshit to try to get the best deal possible, if anything Logan threw on the table could really be called a deal.

As he was putting his files into his briefcase, the door to the courtroom opened and in walked Max Zeidler, a high-profile defense attorney who didn't step into a courtroom for less than $50,000. His clients were mostly Wall Street types caught on insider trading stuff, wives or husbands accused of murder with estates of billions on the line, or high-profile drug dealers. Not anything close to the street dealers, but the big fish, the guys that worked in tons.

Zeidler was in his late 50s but was in great shape and looked to be in his late 40s. He still had a full head of silver-white hair, which he slicked back. Unlike many of his contemporaries, he had not bowed to the temptations of the plastic surgery gods. His skin was wrinkled and tan and made the perfect combination with his blue, pinstriped Armani suit, his dark yellow paisley tie and his mane of silver hair.

He had first gained notoriety back in the '70s and early '80s defending the old mafia dons and doing it pretty successfully, so much so that in a couple of cases the Federal court had moved to have him disqualified over some RICO technicality or another.

Now he walked into the courtroom like he owned it, with his minions following and people getting out of his way. He actually looked like one of the dons he defended back in the day.

Drew watched the little procession with some amusement. It was even more amusing to watch Logan's reaction to Zeidler's arrival.

He stood up from the prosecution table buttoning up his suit coat with a very dignified look on his face and his hand outstretched, "Mr. Zeidler, Bart Logan, it's a pleasure to finally meet you, I've been expecting you. I assume you're here about the Pedroza case."

Zeidler stopped, looked at him, shook his hand as a mere courtesy and asked, "Where's Melanie Farris? I thought she was the one handling the case."

Logan tried to maintain his composure, but the red spreading across his face betrayed his annoyance, embarrassment was more like it. "She's been pulled into another case, so the Pedroza case has been handed to me."

Logan was trying hard as hell to remain composed, but the awkwardness of the situation was just not in his comfort zone and rather than coming off as someone with some authority, he came off as a petulant child insisting he was right.

Zeidler turned back and whispered to one of his assistants, then turned back to face Logan. "Well, Bert, you don't mind if I call you Bert, do you? Why don't we get the judge out here and get on with requesting a continuance until Melanie can get back on the case."

Bart stood his ground, Drew was impressed, "Mr. Zeidler, there is no reason for requesting a continuance, the people are ready and all the stipulations about the DNA evidence have been made. Your office confirmed it. And it's Bart, not Bert."

Zeidler was smiling. Drew knew what was coming and he was actually feeling sorry for Logan. The kid just couldn't figure out which battles he should fight.

"Alright, *Bart,* here's the deal. We have made the stipulations we have because of long and careful discussions with Melanie Farris and your boss, David Neill, you know, the DA.

"Now if we are going to have to deal with a different legal team then we will need a continuance in order to discuss the case with that new legal team, a team I am assuming you will be a part of, but not heading, no offense.

"If we are going to ask for a continuance anyway, then wouldn't it make sense to request one until the original prosecution team could handle the case again? I am sure you would still be a part of the team, but this way, things would move just so much more smoothly, don't you think?"

Drew had to sit in admiration, in one fell swoop Zeidler had let Logan down easy, without insulting him, dangled a high-profile case in front of him like a carrot in front of a horse and made him think it would end up coming off as his idea. Logan was clearly outgunned and outmatched here and he didn't even know it. He made a show of looking through the file and thinking about it, but he knew damn well what he was going to do.

Still he had to save face and get the last word in, "Based on the complexity of the case, Mr. Zeidler, the people would not be opposed to a continuance until Mr. Neill and Ms. Farris can rejoin the case. Of course that will be up to Judge Lee to decide."

Zeidler nodded and patted Logan on the shoulder. "That's a good man. Don't worry, Jerry…I mean Judge Lee…won't have a problem with it. His docket is backed up as it is."

Logan looked satisfied with himself. He turned to the judge's clerk, who was smiling at the whole exchange herself, "Heather, could you ask Judge Lee if we can meet with him in his chambers?"

Heather nodded, "Of course, Mr. Logan, I will check with him."

As she turned to go back to the judge's chambers, she caught Zeidler's eye and gave him a quick wink. While they were all waiting for her to come back, Drew, one of the last lawyers in the courtroom, was shaking his head and smiling as he finished putting his files away.

Zeidler and his entourage, most of whom were on their iPhones or Blackberries texting away, just sat and waited. He looked around the courtroom and saw Drew putting his files away and called out to him, "Willis, it is Willis, right? That was a nice outcome on the Jordan distribution and conspiracy case. I represented the co-defendant and we didn't get a much better deal. It was a nice play getting the cop to doubt the source of the container at the preliminary."

Now it was Drew's turn to try to look nonplussed and confident. He actually felt pretty good, so it wasn't all that hard, "Thank you, Max. It wasn't that hard really, the guy's report and notes were crap from the beginning. I just had to get him to admit that on the stand to the judge."

Zeidler nodded, smiling, "Sometimes that's not as easy as it looks. Good work anyway."

Drew finished packing his files and went up to shake the man's hand, "Thanks again. Hey, good luck with Pedroza."

Zeidler rolled his eyes toward Logan and made a low gesture with his hand as if to say 'We've got it in the bag,' but what he actually said in a low voice was, "If you ever think about joining a firm, a no holds-barred, balls-to-the-wall firm, you make sure you give me a call first."

Drew turned to leave, "I appreciate the offer, it is an absolute honor, but I just hung out my shingle not too long ago, you know how that is."

Zeidler smiled, "I do, do I ever. Just keep it tucked in your back pocket. You never know."

Drew turned and started to walk out of the courtroom. He had no doubt Logan had caught that whole exchange and could almost feel his eyes boring a hole in the back of his head.

Just before he reached the door, Willis heard Zeidler say to Logan, "Oh, and Bart, since this delay is caused by the people's busy schedule, you won't oppose a motion to reduce bail for Mr. Pedroza, will you?"

Bart waited a couple of seconds and looked at the clerk before stammering, "Well, ah…"

Drew had reached the door to the courtroom and made his way through it quickly lest he start laughing out loud in the courtroom and really screw up his relationship with Logan.

◆

Grady was back from talking to Mia Reynolds' family members. Nothing to really note or bear down on. Father was rock solid, mother and sisters were typical upper middle class. He had also talked to the detectives talking to the teachers for both girls and had not come up with anything promising. Both girls went to private school and had teachers with significant credentials and meticulous backgrounds that could be verified. All had checked out.

Most of them were women anyway. The ones that were males could not be more different from the profile they were working off of. They were mostly over their mid-50s, mostly of European descent and most had very mundane lives that could also be traced back almost minute by minute during their time away from school. They had families of their own with which they spent a great deal of time or clubs they belonged to or organizations they were a part of, all of them able to account for their time almost down to the minute.

They had also talked to the custodial staff. There they had actually developed a couple of possibles. Two of the yard maintenance workers had done some time and completed probation, but neither was a violent offender nor any type of sex offender.

Both were Hispanic and had agreed readily to speak with the detectives on the case. Both offenses had to do with having relations with an underage girl, usually 16 or 17, when they themselves were 20 and 21 years old. They'd been cleared immediately.

He had also had an opportunity to speak with Mark Mullins and had gotten pretty much the same story from him.

Even with the profiles they were working from, there just didn't seem to be anyone within the girls' known circle that could be their guy. Extended family was next, all the uncles, cousins, second cousins, close friends, anyone that had spent time with them or even been at the same party was being interviewed as well.

The Reynolds family was planning on coming by the station later with Mrs. Reynolds' sisters and brother. Mr. Reynolds was coming in from Phoenix where he had been for the past year, so it was mostly for emotional support that he was coming in.

Grady walked in his office and slammed the file on the desk. Damn it, they should be further along than this by now. Someone saw these girls together, liked them, targeted them and went hunting for them, and he was watching the police now. He knew they were talking to people; too many people were involved now.

The question was, was he enjoying the attention or was he panicking? Grady was assuming that this prick was probably amused by the attention, he hoped anyway. If he was panicking, he was probably hundreds of miles from New York by now and they would have to hear about some sort of similar case in Montana or Florida or some other state before they got back on his trail.

While he was looking out the window, as he was apt to do when he didn't know what his next play would be, Grady heard a small tap on the window of his office. It was one of the secretaries with two other women, "Detective, Mrs. Reynolds and Ms. Hunt are here to see you."

Grady turned around, stacked the files neatly on his desk and stood up. "Mrs. Reynolds, please come in."

Gina Reynolds walked into his office. Like every other mother, her eyes had dark circles under them and she looked like she had aged 10 years in the last week.

Gina turned and brought her sister into the office, she was holding her hand, "Detective Grady, this is my sister Nancy. She is Mia's favorite aunt and watches her from time to time. They are very close. She watched Mia the weekend before she went missing."

Nancy walked into the office, not looking much better than her older sister. She had also clearly been put through hell and her face was still streaked with makeup.

Grady motioned to the chairs in front of his desk, "Please, both of you, have a seat."

They both sat down, shoulders slumped over, faces totally defeated.

"Ms. Hunt, as you know, we are trying to figure this thing out. The fact that Mia and Emily were both taken within a day of each other makes us think that whoever did it had a chance to meet them or see them or spend time with them at some point while they were together.

"You see, when we see a direct connection like this in two cases, the best way to find out what happened is to look at everything, everyone and everywhere the two girls had in common. So, Ms. Hunt, can you think of any of your friends or colleagues, soccer coaches, anyone that knew the girls and spent time with them?"

Nancy sat with her head in her hands and thought. She shook her head, "You guys have already talked to all of my friends that knew them or had seen them together. Actually, I think a couple of my friends are still talking to some of the detectives.

"But I can tell you right now it's none of them. These are all people I've known since college. They've seen the girls together in passing maybe once or twice in the last three or four years. None of them spent any time with them or actually even really talked to them.

"My old roommate would be the one that has spent the most time with them and she is one of the ones that your officers are still talking to.

"There really is no one else. I mean, I see their dance teachers and the teachers at school when I go pick them up, but I really wouldn't be able to tell you that I've noticed anything out of the ordinary about them."

Grady was taking notes and comparing them with the list they had already compared with the entire family's possibles and they had pretty much come to the same conclusion.

Without any sort of forensic, eyewitness or hell, even circumstantial evidence, there just wasn't anything to go at anybody with.

Gina looked across the desk and with a glimmer of hope in her eye asked Grady, "So is there anything, detective? Have you gotten any information from Emily's family?"

Grady looked at her and knew he had to keep up the front, "It's still too early to tell, but nothing really promising so far. The whole department and the FBI are cooperating with other law enforcement agencies to develop as good of a case as we can, but it's still too early."

Grady had gone through this with one or another family member from the other families, so he was used to the routine and to the standard lines he had to deliver.

As he was talking to Mrs. Reynolds, he was also looking at Nancy Hunt out of the corner of his eye, and she had something on her mind.

She looked like she had something to say and was debating whether to say it or not.

Grady helped her along, "Ms. Hunt, anything you can think of, and I mean *anything*, can be helpful to us. Sometimes even things you might think have nothing to do with what we are doing end up breaking cases open, so if there is anything you need to tell us, please, now is the time for you to do it."

Nancy had her face in her hands and was shaking her head, "I've told you everything…well, almost everything."

Gina looked at her with her mouth open and her eyes wide, "What do you mean almost everything! Nancy, what the hell is the matter with you! We've been at this for over a week! You say what you have to say right now! I can't believe you!"

Nancy was crying now, "It's no big deal, Gina! I knew you'd make a huge deal out of it, but it was no big deal!

"The weekend I watched Mia and Emily, I had a friend from work watch them for a couple of hours so I could go with my girlfriends to *The Lion King*.

"He came over with DVDs and watched them for four hours and then left. It was nothing. He works at my office and I've known him for three years and he just couldn't hurt a fly. Talk to him. Ask him anything you need to, I am sure you'll see he isn't the guy you're looking for."

When she was finished, she still found her sister staring fiercely at her. Gina actually slapped her across the face, "How dare you! How dare you hold this back! She is my daughter, your niece!"

Grady came around the desk to get in between them as Nancy stood up to leave, "See, this is exactly why I didn't tell you, because I knew you would be a total bitch about it!"

She started to turn and Grady held her back by her arm. Gina went to move toward her again and this time Grady stood in front of her, "Mrs. Reynolds, Gina! I need you to leave, now. Now!"

Gina was about to protest when Grady gently led her out as he was talking to her, "She won't say anything else as long as you are in the room. She's right, it's probably nothing, but I think I'll get much further if I talk to her alone."

By this point Grady was holding her by the shoulders outside of his office and was getting her to calm down, "Now, why don't you go grab a cup of coffee while I finish talking to Ms. Hunt."

Gina didn't say anything. Tears still streaming, she walked away to get herself some coffee. Grady watched her walk away and then looked at the back of her sister's head as she sat in his office. She was young and inexperienced and to Grady she gave off the selfish and self-involved air of most young women in New York, but still she was genuinely grief-stricken and remorseful, and she was ready to talk.

Grady hadn't been just blowing smoke when he'd said it was probably nothing, but once again that sixth sense that all homicide dicks develop after spending years and years on the job was beginning to make some noise in Grady's head.

He walked back into the office, sat down in his chair and handed her a tissue, "Are you alright?"

Nancy took the tissue and wiped her eyes and nodded.

Grady went on, "Alright, Nancy, take it from the beginning and tell me about this friend of yours that watched the girls."

Nancy wiped her eyes again and went to answer, "He's just someone who works at my office, his name is Donald Riche. He is just this guy who works as a runner for the firm. Pretty friendly.

"He has always been really nice to me and to everyone else, as far as I know. He dresses neatly and pretty much keeps to himself, but it's not like he's antisocial either, you know. He's just one of those people that always seem to be there with a nice word or just willing to listen to you."

Grady was taking down notes furiously, while still trying to keep eye contact. "Alright, do you know where Donald lives?"

Nancy thought about it and answered, "Not really, to be honest with you. I just know he has a small apartment over by Houston Street. I know he rides the subway and the bus to work."

Grady kept writing, "Okay, what else do you know about him?"

Nancy thought about it and answered, "Not much, really. I mean, when he offered to watch Mia and Emily, he told me he had watched his nieces a bunch of times. He is really a nice man, you know, really gentle. Not the type that would hurt a fly."

Grady, still taking notes, went on, "Anything else? What does he look like?"

Nancy shrugged her shoulders, "You know, just regular, I guess. You know, about five nine, maybe a little taller, not really heavy, but not really skinny either. I think he's probably in his mid-30s, but looks a little younger. He has dirty blond hair and glasses. Wears a suit and tie every day and as far as I know I don't think he's ever missed a day of work since I've been there."

Grady finished writing and looked up, "So, do you think we might be able to talk to Donald if we go down to the office or if we call him to come in?"

Nancy thought for a second and answered, "Sure, I don't see why not. Some policemen have already been talking to some of the other people at my office, so I don't think he would have a problem with it."

Grady reviewed everything he had written down and looked at it against the profile.

His eyes scanned back and forth between the two pages from top to bottom and then he did it again, and he couldn't help but feel a little chill beginning to work its way up his spine. He was going to have to go out and speak to Donald Riche as soon as possible and he was taking Mark Mullins with him for sure.

In the meantime they would run his name through all the pertinent databases. Get some prints and wash those through all the other databases that made sense.

Grady wanted to have a file on this guy before they contacted him.

He wasn't sure why, but he had a very strong feeling that if they came at this guy the right way, with the right information, they might be able to get something useful if there was anything to be gotten, and something told Grady there was definitely something here.

It might be nothing major, but something to go on in any case. "Well, we'll be in touch with you and with Mr. Riche, Ms. Hunt. Don't worry, you're probably right it's nothing, but we have to follow every lead we get."

Nancy was nodding and wiping away her tears. She stood up, shook Grady's hand and left his office. On her way out, she walked past Detective Mullins who also noticed her wiping her eyes as she walked by.

He got to Grady's office, still looking back at Nancy, "What gives? Where's her sister? Why was she so upset?"

Grady was standing behind his desk with his hands on his hips. "It looks like we might have our first bona fide possible. A guy that the aunt let watch the girls the weekend before they went missing, he..."

Before he could finish, Mark Mullins interrupted, "Donald Riche."

Grady smiled, "How'd you come up with that?"

Mullins said, "Just finished talking to the Wu family. Emily told them all about Donald and watching DVDs. We're running a background on him and I have a couple of unmarked cars on the way to the office to pick him up."

Grady held up his hand, "Call them back. Call the unmarked cars back. I want to come at this guy sideways. I want him to think this is all routine, he is just one of dozens of people we are talking to.

"I will call him at his office and ask him if we can come by his house to talk to him. It will put him at ease to be in a familiar environment and it will let us know just what kind of character this guy is.

"In the meantime, run the DMV check, priors, anything on this guy. Talk to the personnel office of the brokerage firm and track down any other places of work before then.

"I want to go talk to him loaded for bear. It may be nothing, but like I said, looking at the profile we've got and the people we've been talking to, this guy comes as close to it as anyone else we have talked to. How did it go with the custodial staff?"

Mullins shook his head, "All immigrants, Russian mostly, some can barely speak English and most hold two or three jobs, so they literally do not have time in a 24-hour day to do anything like this."

Grady nodded, "Figured as much, most of the maintenance staff falls into the same category. Mark, if this guy doesn't pan out, I think we're really going to have to bite the bullet and assume it is going public in the next day or two."

He walked over to the window, hands on his hips, "Nope, if we don't get anything to hang our hat on from this guy, we're going to have to go public and ask for help."

Mullins was nodding, "What do you think about this guy Riche?"

Grady turned around, "I don't know, sounds vanilla enough, but he's one of the closest matches we have to the profiles we've developed. And honestly, I'll wait to hear back from what we come up with on all the background, but I'll be damned if he isn't starting to strike me a little funny."

Mullins looked at him, "Yeah, I was thinking the same thing. I mean 30s, a job, not bad-looking, and no one has known him to talk about a date or a girlfriend or anything other than work. All of a sudden he offers to watch two six- and seven-year-olds out of the blue on a Friday night, two six- and seven-year-olds that go missing the week after. Yeah, it sounds a little hinky to me too."

Grady was back looking out of the window with his arms crossed and biting his bottom lip, "Yup, let's get everything we can on the guy, his family, his nieces, DMV, everything, and then let's go talk to old Donald and cross him off the list or get ready to bring the hammer down."

Mullins nodded, turned around and before he left turned back toward Grady, "How much of this, if any, do you think Loomis knows?"

Grady raised his eyebrows at the question, smiled and turned around to look at Mullins, "Assume the guy knows exactly what we know and assume that he's probably got everything there is to get on this guy."

Before Mullins could answer, Captain Freeman had walked down the hallway to Grady's office.

Nick Freeman was the consummate politician. He had been in the department for more than 24 years and had never taken a wrong step in the span of that career. Grady had been wondering how long it would take Freeman to come pay him a visit. Freeman had a kind of manic energy about him, like he couldn't stand still. He was tall and thin, balding and seemed to be shaking all the time.

He got to Grady's office, looked from Mullins to Grady, and kept his voice low and conspiratorial, as if he was letting them in on something he wasn't supposed to be telling them, "So you guys heard, I take it?"

Grady rolled his eyes, "No, Captain, we haven't heard yet, what's the word?"

Freeman made a show of being exasperated and shook his head, "The Garcia kid from the *Chronicle* has been asking questions. The cat's out of the bag. I don't know if it came from inside or if he has another source, but he definitely connected the nine girls and is asking some really uncomfortable questions and they've gotten to the commissioner."

He turned to Grady, "Bob, I want you to sit down with him and see what he has. I want you to give him as much as we have without compromising anything."

Grady just stood there without an expression on his face, but behind Freeman, Mullins was cracking up without making a sound. Once he got his soliloquy out, Freeman seemed satisfied with himself, turned around and walked away without looking back.

Mullins was still laughing as he walked away. Grady leaned on the frame to his door and smiled to himself. He had to, otherwise he might cry.

Actually it wasn't that bad, the Garcia kid wasn't reckless and he'd shown a willingness to play quid pro quo. He was willing to share information when he had it, as long as it never compromised a source, and he was willing to keep things under wraps as long as it was reasonable.

Grady was actually surprised it had taken this long, especially if the Garcia kid had his nose mixed in it.

He would let Mullins gather all the info on Riche and he would sit down with Garcia. After all, he wouldn't really be lying. If he hadn't gotten anything about Riche back from Mullins, there was nothing to share with Garcia other than what he already had, and he was pretty sure the kid didn't already have Riche, so no, it shouldn't be that bad.

Chapter 5

Steven Loomis still mused over the fact that even in the first decade of the 21st century it was still a wonder to him the amount of information one could obtain if one knew where to look, and by god, no one knew where to look better than Carl, that and well-placed resources in all the pertinent agencies.

Donald Riche, 36, single, no criminal record, not even a parking ticket. He owned a van, which was registered to his name, properly registered and insured. He rented a flat just off Houston street, had been there for five years.

There wasn't a single conduct report from his employer and he hadn't missed a single day from work because of being sick. When he was 10 years old, he was removed from his home to live with relatives and never saw his birth parents again. He had gone to the University of Wisconsin and graduated with a degree in English, even though it took him more than six years. He had also taken some graduate courses in finance from NYU.

Steven was pretty sure the police had all of this already and would be looking to make their way to talk to him in person, if they weren't on the way already.

Out of everyone that Steven had looked at, this guy was definitely setting off the most bells in his head. Putting aside the profiles, he just stood out like a sore thumb, because out of everyone they had spoken to or looked at, this guy was the only one that didn't really have anything directly connecting him to any of the last two girls' circles within school or related to their extracurricular activities.

He had just happened to be available to sit for the girls the weekend before they were taken and while it was completely possible that it was just a coincidence, no one with more than half an ounce of law enforcement or investigative instinct believed in those kinds of coincidences.

Steven already had Carl scouring the digital world for any and all credit card, cell phone, email or social networking information that this guy might have generated. He hadn't come up with anything yet, but he was still running the data. Steven would just hold off for now and see what the police developed.

The electronic and digital surveillance group had been busy and had let him know all their assets were in place, so he wasn't worried about missing something important.

Instead, he needed to head home. He had already caught up here as much as he was going to catch up and was able to confirm that everything was in fact on track.

His mother-in-law had called him in a panic from somewhere in New York where Marybeth had fallen apart and told him he needed to get home. It had been a difficult call, "We were at the Center for Missing and Exploited Children and she lost it! She's hurting, Steven, you need to get home."

He was putting his files away and organizing the desktop on his computer when Art Goodman appeared at his doorway, "Getting ready to head home?"

Steven was caught off guard and a bit startled, "Huh…yeah, I am sir. Everything seems to be under control…"

The General came on in to his office, waving his hands as if to let him know he didn't have to explain, "Steven, I told you to take as much time as you needed. To be honest with you, I don't know what the hell you are doing here."

Steven latched his briefcase and looked up, "I know. I just had to clear my head, you know, had to get a fresh perspective."

Goodman nodded in understanding, "We all have our own ways of quieting the demons that come knocking and they're always different. So you take as much time as you need, and if you need anything from us, you know we have your back."

Steven smiled, picked up his briefcase and started to leave, "I know, sir, I've always known."

He shook Goodman's hand, but before he let him go, Goodman pulled Steven close to him and in a low voice said, "You know son, the hard part isn't going to be finding out what it is that happened, it's going to be deciding what it is you are planning to do about it."

Steven looked at the old grizzled eyes that still held a spark and experience only gained by holding men as they died and ordering others to their death. Goodman was just under six feet tall and had a full head of silver hair and a lean, hard physique earned through decades of physical training and discipline. There was nothing physically remarkable about him, yet he was incredibly intimidating when he wanted to be. Steven had more than once seen the man take absolute control of a room full of senior executives, A-type, alpha male personalities. He did it naturally, never raising his voice, always saying something that mattered. Always with that intense, penetrating stare that made it seem like he could see through you.

He was about to make a comment about the justice system and how he was planning on letting that work, but this was the General and he knew just how much it would sound like bullshit, so instead he just nodded and went on his way.

The call from his mother-in-law had shaken him. Going through that juxtaposition, talking to his mother-in-law and then running into the General had in a way crystallized what Steven had already been struggling with himself: The pain of losing his daughter left an emptiness he knew he would never fill, but years of training, of responding to any and all situations had also made him realize that his days as just a father, a grieving father, were over.

He would grieve, he would be there for his wife and his children, he wouldn't let them down, but it wouldn't be all of him, either. The part of him that died with Tracy would always be missing. It wasn't something they would notice, but it was something he'd know.

He had already made the decision that he was going to be a part of bringing this to an end. He didn't know how or when, but he knew that to not do it would leave him with almost as big a hole as Tracy had left and it would be one he couldn't live with.

◆

Donald Riche had pretty much kept to himself the whole week. He had tried to remain under the radar as much as he could, which wasn't much more than usual. He knew there was some sort of activity in the office and that the police were talking to Nancy.

He also knew that eventually they would come talk to him and he had been preparing for it.

There really wasn't that much to tell. In the world they lived their lives in, he was a well-groomed professional who had been nothing but helpful to anyone they asked.

He had an impeccable record at work and had never gotten so much as a traffic ticket. He would be just as shocked and surprised as everyone else about the disappearances. Did they have any suspects? Of course he would do anything he could to help. Nancy was his friend! He had been waiting for them for some days now and was prepared for them.

Now, sitting at his desk and filing his work away, Nancy walked up to his cubicle, "Hmm, Donald, you know my niece Mia is missing."

Donald looked up with as sympathetic a look as he could put on, "Yes, I heard, Nance. I'm so sorry. Is there anything I can do?"

Nancy half-smiled, "Thank you, no, but I did want to tell you that the police are talking to anyone that saw or was with the girls at all before they were taken, and since you took care of them that Friday…"

Donald stood up and held her hands, "Of course, Nancy, I understand. They're just doing their job. Don't worry, I'll be fine."

Nancy began crying again, "I'm so sorry, Donald. You were just trying to help and look at what you're having to put up with."

Donald put his arms around her and she allowed herself to be hugged, "Thank you, thank you for being so understanding. I'm sure it's just going to be real quick, you know, just so they can scratch you off their list."

Riche patted her back consoling her. He was smiling and was also sure it would be nothing more than a standard interview asked of dozens of other people just like him.

Donald Riche had been meticulous about almost everything he had done and was sure he was beyond the reach of those looking for him. In this he was about to find out just how wrong he could be.

He walked into his apartment later that evening and set a few bags of groceries down on the counter. He looked around. The décor was minimalist and tasteful. Not a single ornament or lamp or rug was out of place and none was superfluous. To anyone walking in, it would look like a staged apartment used to show prospective tenants.

He walked into his bedroom where more of the same awaited. His closet was organized by garment, color and size. Even the colors were organized by shades going from dark to light. His shoes were all meticulously polished and organized in a shoe rack.

He hung his coat on the coat rack and smoothed out the wrinkles and removed the two remnants of lint that were visible on it.

As he walked into the kitchen he corrected a spatula that was leaning a bit too far over out of its container. The kitchen, like everything else, was immaculate. It had a small pantry in the corner and every one of the handles and pieces of hardware were as shiny as when he'd bought them.

Just as he was leaving the kitchen, he heard the doorbell ring. He was startled but didn't panic. He walked over to the door and looked out of the peephole. Just outside the door were two men who were clearly policemen.

Donald waited by the door for a few seconds and opened it, although to keep up appearances he kept the chain to the door engaged.

He cracked the door open, "Yes, can I help you?"

Grady responded, "Mr. Riche, it's Detective Grady and Detective Mullins from the NYPD. We called you earlier and asked if we could come by to chat."

Donald did remember them and had in fact been expecting them. Actually he had been expecting just one officer, so seeing the second officer was in fact a bit of a surprise. Still, he was not worried in the least.

As he disengaged the chain to the door, "Of course, of course. Just let me take the chain off the door." He then opened the door and waved the officers in, "Please come in. Excuse the mess, I wasn't sure when you would be coming by."

Grady and Mullins came into the flat and looked around. If there was a mess to be excused, neither officer could spot it. Like all police officers coming into an unfamiliar situation, their training took over and they instantly began to make mental notes about the guy's place.

The first thing that struck both policemen was that there wasn't a stitch out of place. Grady and Mullins had at one point or another each had their own place and knew although they tried to keep things presentable there would always be a pot or a plate or a glass or something out of place. Sometimes it might be a pillow and blanket on the couch from a buddy crashing over, sometimes it was empty pizza boxes. It could be anything, but most of the time it was something.

The thing both officers noticed at almost the exact same time is that there was nothing, *nothing*, out of place here. It was almost as if the guy didn't really live here.

Riche closed the door behind them and motioned to the living room, "Please come in, sit down. Can I get you any water, something else to drink?"

Mullins and Grady declined politely. They were still scanning the walls without being too obvious.

While paying attention to the fact that there was nothing out of place, both officers also noticed that there was not a single picture of a human being anywhere around the apartment. No pictures, no paintings, nothing that showed any connection to anyone. In and of itself, that might have been ticked off as a curiosity, but coupled with everything else, the reasons they were here and what both had to admit was something physically quirky about Donald Riche, it was definitely something to file away for later discussion.

By now the detectives had Riche's criminal, school and work history. They knew he had no family he kept in contact with. They knew he had never been in trouble with the law, that he owned a van registered in New York, and that he rented an industrial place close to the Brooklyn Bridge for which he was charged monthly out of his checking account.

They had his transcripts from Wisconsin and NYU and had any and all performance reviews he had ever gotten. It was interesting that although in every review he had gotten glowing comments, every supervisor or teacher had made some sort of mention of the fact that while Donald was respectful and polite and that he had absolutely performed every one of his duties exactly as he had been asked to, there seemed to be a detachment from Donald toward his classmates, coworkers, supervisors, anyone he had to deal with.

In every case, there was nothing anyone could put their finger on, it was just a sense that he was not willing to let anyone in past a certain point.

Yes, prior to coming to visit Mr. Riche, detectives Grady and Mullins had put together what was starting to look like a really interesting file on the guy.

Detectives from other precincts were tracking down anyone else that might know him or might have any information about him. They would speak with university teachers, supervisors, coworkers, but Mullins and Grady would be willing to bet that they would get the same type of story.

And now that they were standing in front of the man, Mullins and Grady stole a sideways glance at each other and could understand what they had read. There was nothing remarkable about the guy, he looked nice enough, he was clean cut and professional, not a wrinkle on his clothes, but there was something that made it seem like he was playing a role, like he had the conversation and the exchange already planned out.

The three men walked into the living room. Donald sat on the love seat and the two detectives sat on the sofa. Grady opened his briefcase and pulled out a file. He laid it on the coffee table, opened it and brought out the pictures of the missing girls. Donald looked at all of them and lingered on the pictures of Emily and Mia and his face softened.

Grady picked up on it, "Do you recognize any of these girls, Mr. Riche?"

Donald looked up at him, "Of course, you guys know I watched Mia and Emily for Nancy. I am just sick about all of this. I don't know how to console Nancy and I just don't know how to go about helping."

Mullins picked it up from there, "Do you recognize any of these other girls."

Riche looked at him, puzzled, "No, I've never seen any of them."

Mullins went on, "I think the best place to start is how you came about watching the girls for Nancy Hunt, how you came to meet them."

Donald went into the story about the girls in the office going to *The Lion King* and Nancy being disappointed and how he had wanted to help her out. Mullins wrote down some notes.

Grady interjected, "So you didn't have any plans of your own and you wanted to help Nancy?"

Donald answered, "That's pretty much how it went."

Mullins asked, "Had you watched Mia and Emily before?"

Donald shook his head, "No, in fact that was the first time I met Mia, at the office with Nancy."

"And what about Emily?"

Donald responded without hesitating, "I didn't meet her until I got to Nancy's house."

Without having to compare notes, the two detectives could tell this guy had his story straight and that he was well within his comfort zone, which is exactly where they wanted him, comfortable. Now, also without having to coordinate, they knew it was time to start throwing this guy a couple of curve balls.

Grady started it, his tone changed a bit and his body language also shifted. He moved closer to Riche, "So you own a van?"

Riche was a bit puzzled, "Yes, yes I do."

"What kind of van is it?"

Riche answered, "It's a 2002 Ford."

Grady pressed on, "What do you use the van for?"

Riche was a bit taken aback, "What do you mean what do I use it for? I use it for transportation."

Grady smiled, "I would imagine that, but you know, when someone owns a van, they usually have things they need to transport."

Riche now had a questioning look on his face and the veneer of control was starting to crack, "I don't have anything to transport. I just bought the van because it made it easier to move from college and things like that."

Mullins interjected seamlessly, taking on the 'good cop' role so subtly and smoothly, Riche never saw it, "I totally understand. I used to have one of those old VW buses. I went everywhere in it. It sure was convenient."

Donald took the lifeline, "Exactly, so you know."

Mullins nodded, "Sure I do, I brought home my clothes, my furniture, you know, all my college stuff. What do you use yours for?"

Donald continued, "Well, the same things, you know, clothes, furniture, that kind of thing."

Grady watched the exchange with a detective's eyes. He noticed how Riche got flustered at the question, how his pupils dilated and his palms left wet marks on the table.

He had to be careful, though. Any subject being interrogated by the police was apt to get nervous, and if this guy was a promising lead, they had to tread on eggshells.

Grady softened up a bit, "So you just use it to haul your stuff around, is that it?"

Donald nodded, "Exactly. Just whatever I need it for."

Mullins and Grady were taking notes and, as was often the case with persons of interest, it is something they say on their own that makes them even more interesting.

It was no different with Donald Riche, "Sometimes I go up the coast and look for antiques. There really are some hidden treasures up there."

Without looking up from their pads, Mullins and Grady paused for just a beat and glanced sideways at each other.

Without deciding which one was going to take the opening, Grady stepped up, "Do you deal in antiques, Donald, you don't mind if I call you Donald?"

Donald thought about it and realized they probably already knew the answer to that, "No, I don't. I go looking mostly for myself."

Mullins and Grady then did look up from their pads and looked around the apartment. They looked at each other and then at Donald.

Now it was Mullins that asked the question, "Donald, man, I got to tell you that coming in here, I don't know what the name of this type of decoration is, but what I do know is that I don't see any antiques anywhere in here."

Donald looked around. He hadn't thought about that when he said it. He looked at the walls, at the furniture all around and at the furniture they were sitting on. And then a palpable change came over him.

Grady and Mullins saw it immediately. The ready smile, that open demeanor, the helpful and sensitive eyes were all gone. His body language also changed.

He moved farther from the detectives, he sat up straight and he looked at them with a cold and determined look, "Detectives, I don't like the way this conversation is going. I invited you into my home. I told you both on the phone that I would like to help you any way that I could, and what I think I'm getting is a bunch of questions that don't have to do with the girls or trying to get them back and I don't like how this is going."

Grady was kicking himself; he might have come at him too quick. He should have eased into it a bit. Mullins had also been a bit surprised at how quickly Grady had tried to throw Riche off, but here it was.

Mullins had to figure out a way to bring his guard down again, if it could be done. "Mr. Riche, there's no reason to get upset, we're just trying to think of anything that might help us. You can understand that, right?"

Mullins was trying to make him a partner in the search, someone that they were looking to for help. If they were right about this guy, it would definitely appeal to his ego.

Riche had flipped, though. He now understood he wasn't just one of dozens of other people they were interviewing, they had put him on a short list of possible suspects.

Once he made that determination, he stopped the façade and knew he had to do whatever he needed to do in order to protect himself, to protect his work really. "Gentlemen, I appreciate what you are trying to do and as I told both of you, I am more than willing to help in any way that I can. I met the girls Friday just over one week ago at Nancy Hunt's house.

"I felt I was doing Nancy a favor because she really wanted to go to the theater with the rest of the girls. I showed up at her apartment at the time she asked me to with DVDs for the girls. They watched movies in Nancy's room and I watched movies out in the living room. Nancy came home at around eleven thirty, the girls were asleep on her bed and that was it.

"I really don't have anything else to say to you gentlemen that I think would be useful to your investigation, so if there's nothing else, I really have some things I need to get working on." Mullins and Grady closed their notebooks.

While Mullins was getting ready to take his leave, Grady wasn't quite ready to just get up and leave, "Mr. Riche, I understand what you are saying, but I want you to understand something also. Nine little girls are missing. Nine families are going crazy trying to figure out what happened to them. Mia and Emily were taken within a day of each other. They were the only two girls taken who knew each other, which means that whoever took them had to have seen them together or spent time with them together.

"You see, we don't believe in coincidences like that. And maybe it is just really bad luck that it was you, but as you have quite eloquently explained to us, you both saw and spent time with both girls the week before they went missing. So yeah, we're going to ask you and anyone else who might have also been with them *whatever* we need to ask in order to eliminate them as a suspect or to figure out anything that might help us. We're going to ask it, whether it makes you uncomfortable or not."

Mullins could see this going sideways quickly and tried to pull it back, knowing it was probably too late. "Mr. Riche, we're asking these types of questions of everyone that was with the girls. It's nothing against you personally."

Riche didn't break eye contact with Grady and his look was decidedly different than that with which he had welcomed them.

His eyes were hooded and cold now and he was in full defense mode, "Of course, I'm sure all the people you've talked to own vans and are single males and babysat the girls the Friday before the week they were taken."

He stood up and stretched out his hand, "Well, detectives, as I said, there really isn't anything else to say. If you have anything else to ask,

I will give you the name of my attorney and you can deal with him directly."

Grady and Mullins both stood up and shook his hand. Riche escorted them to the door, opened it and waited for them to leave.

On his way out, Grady stopped midway out the door, "We'll be waiting for your lawyer's information."

Just before continuing to leave the apartment, Grady paused again, "Mr. Riche, you rent a warehouse in an industrial area near the Brooklyn Bridge, right? Probably to keep all those antiques and all..."

Riche kept his expression neutral, "Good evening, gentlemen, you'll hear from my attorney."

He closed the door behind them and then turned to lean his back against it. He put his head in his hands and tried to pull himself together. He had made a mistake and he knew it. He shouldn't have taken Mia and Emily; they were too easy to relate to each other.

No matter, too late to take it back. The only thing he was really worried about was the fact that he might not get to finish his work the way he wanted to. Not the thought of prison, the death penalty or any other possible punishments, it was just the work that concerned him.

He would have to hire a lawyer and not say a thing and, who knew, it may all just blow over. They had absolutely nothing other than the fact that he had met the girls. No physical evidence, nothing.

As he thought about all this, Trinity started to feel more confident and he actually began to feel something new, a new sense of pride that he had completed the work he had in the midst of forces that were stacked up against him.

He did his work by himself, and all the forces against him had many men and resources to pit against him. He was equal to the task; he had been equal to the task all along. Now it was time to find the best lawyer he could find.

Mullins and Grady walked to the elevator without talking and without looking at each other.

As soon as the elevator doors closed, Mullins started, "Bob, I know what…"

Grady turned to face him, shaking his head with a sardonic smile on his face. "He did it. The son of a bitch did it."

Mullins was already shaking his head, "C'mon, you can't make those kinds…"

Grady pushed the stop button on the elevator and looked at Mullins square in the eye, "Goddamnit, Mark, I know the protocol and I know what we have, which isn't shit, but you know that motherfucker took those girls. Nobody else we have interviewed, none of the 36 possibles have even come close.

"Did you see how he got when we asked about the van? Did you get a look at his apartment? We've both been doing this long enough, and even though I will never admit to this conversation outside of this elevator, you and I know this is our guy. Now we just have to build something to take to the DA."

He pulled the stop button. On the way down, Mullins said to Grady, "We have to figure out how to get a search warrant for that van and for that warehouse."

Grady hung his head and nodded, "I know, and any judge will laugh us out of his chambers with what we have so far." They stood next to each other without saying anything for a few seconds.

It was Mullins who broke the silence, "You know, I was just thinking this might be a piece of news we could share with Steven Loomis."

Grady looked at him, and Mullins went on, "I mean, he does have resources and he's not bound by any of those probable cause, search warrant tie-ups we're bound by. He's a citizen."

Grady was smiling, "And you're the one that wanted to hold out on him."

Mullins chuckled as they got to the ground floor and walked out of the elevator. "Well, you do this shit long enough and you take whatever you can, whatever way you can get it."

As they exited the building, Grady stopped and faced Mullins. "Seriously, we share what we have, including Riche as part of the investigation, and we let him take it from there. It can't look like we're getting this guy to do our dirty work for us."

Mullins nodded, "I got it. Do you really think Loomis would just go barreling in? No, he'll take it nice and slow and will be really meticulous about it."

Grady continued walking, "Yeah, now we just need to coordinate with the rest of the task force and start spinning a story the Garcia kid can put down on paper."

They walked without talking for a couple of blocks then Mullins said, "I like that kid. He's no bullshit and he doesn't go for the tabloid angle."

Grady agreed, "Yup, so let's work something up with the public information office and get it ready."

Chapter 6

Loomis met Grady at a coffee shop on 5th avenue. Grady was already sitting in a booth digging into a plate of eggs, bacon and hash browns.

Loomis sat down and the waitress came over, "Do you know what you want?"

Loomis answered, "I'll just have a coffee."

As soon as she left, Steven turned to Grady and quipped, "Do you always have breakfast like this?"

Without looking up or slowing down, Grady answered around a mouthful of hash browns, "No, I'm cutting back. You know, trying that 'more healthy' lifestyle and all that crap. Hey, listen, I am assuming that you know who we've been talking to."

The waitress came back with the coffee. Loomis waited until she left before he answered, "Yes, well, I'm not sure I have everyone, but I do have the ones that seem to be of interest."

Grady looked up, "You got a guy named Donald Riche?" Loomis grinned, "Yes, he is one of the ones on our list. Why?"

Still eating, Grady went on, "So, Mark Mullins and I went to talk to the guy."

Loomis waited, Grady just ate. Loomis leaned back; he knew the game.

Grady wasn't just going to give him a rundown of their interview, he was going to wait until Loomis asked, "And how did that go?"

Now Grady did stop eating. "What do you know about Riche?"

Loomis thought about it. He had gone through the file several times, "Single, mid-30s, runner for a brokerage firm, no priors, not even a traffic ticket. He owns a van, rents a garage or storage space near the Brooklyn Bridge, and has never been married. Of all the people that we know of, he is one of four that come close to fitting the composite profile."

Grady kept his eyes on Loomis. This was one of those moments where a look between two professionals communicated things that sometimes words were just not adequate for.

Grady started talking, and eating, "So we talked to the guy, perfectly normal. Had us over to his place and was willing to answer whatever we asked, until we got to talking about the van. He got nervous and defensive, and before we could even ask him about the warehouse he rents and why he rents it, he lawyered up."

Grady looked up and stared directly into Loomis's eyes. In that look he told Loomis that working within his world this was as far as he could take it with this guy for right now. Both men knew Grady could not come out and ask Steven for anything.

He had promised to keep him in the loop and he was doing exactly that, but he had also asked Steven to reciprocate and the look from Grady now told Loomis he intended to hold him to it.

Loomis listened and got the message, "You think it's him, don't you?"

Grady just looked at him, Loomis kept on, "You think it's him and you have nothing to get a warrant for his apartment or for the van or for the warehouse."

Grady went back to eating, "Detective Mullins and I are going to do whatever we can to take something to the DA and to a judge, but honestly, we're going to get laughed out of the building. There isn't a shred of physical evidence. The guy is squeaky clean, and you're right, no history.

"I know you've been in front of fanatics and terrorists, but I don't know if you've ever been in the presence of evil, in the presence of someone who has something different behind their eyes. But Loomis, off the record, I mean I'll deny I ever said it kind of off the record, that's this guy, that's how he felt.

"I may be wrong, but I would rather be wrong and scratch this guy off the list than to waste a lot of time running in circles. I will tell you this, though, even if he isn't the guy in this case, there's something there, something...creepy, about the guy."

Steven Loomis listened carefully. He understood exactly what Grady was saying, he had a strong gut feeling about this guy, and New York homicide detectives took that almost as seriously as physical evidence or an eyewitness.

The problem was that they could never move on their gut feelings, and Grady had just shared with him that it would take a significant amount of time for him and his task force to develop enough to dig deeper into this guy because he was limited by what his job allowed him to do, *his job* allowed him to do.

Steven looked intensely at Grady, who was in the middle of taking a bite of hash browns, and nodded almost imperceptibly.

He finished his cup of coffee, put it down on the table and went to say goodbye, "Thanks for the update. I've actually got to get going. I have to get to the office. I've been out for a while and there's just a lot of stuff I have to catch up on."

As he was getting ready to leave he grinned at Grady, "You should really try to mix in some fiber into the 'healthy lifestyle crap' thing."

Grady went on eating his breakfast and looked up as Loomis was leaving. "Don't mention it. And I did try that bran crap. It tasted like shit. A man has his limits."

He kept his eyes on Loomis as he walked out of the restaurant. Yeah, the guy would use whatever resources he had to get as much as he could.

Grady kept eating his breakfast and kept thinking that the man definitely looked different. The look that Grady had seen in all parents, the look of desperation and helplessness, was not there. The grief was there, but it wasn't there like it was for most parents who lost their children.

In Steven Loomis, Grady saw an intense and thoughtful look driven by the grief and by what felt like an intense and quiet anger just under it. It wasn't something that was draining from him, it was something that was driving him and could potentially make him a wild card. Still, Grady knew he could count on him to get him more information on Riche, and in the end, the upside outweighed the downside.

Loomis had been reading through everything Carl had gotten on Donald Riche. His childhood, foster system, went to college and got a degree, never in trouble with the law, no meaningful relationships to speak of. He had worked at his current brokerage firm for three years, but he had worked a variety of jobs since he graduated from college.

One interesting thing Carl had been able to find was that Riche used his credit card to buy dry ice, machining equipment and supplies, and medical equipment and supplies for some time now.

What the hell could he want all of that for? Of all the people the police had on their short list, this guy matched the composite profile better than anybody.

Even without all of this, his conversation with Grady had told him everything he needed to know. This was the guy, though nothing Grady said could be construed by anybody as anything other than a casual conversation with the lead detective on the case sharing some information with one of the parents.

But Steven wasn't just one of the parents and Grady wasn't just trying to keep him in the loop. He was letting him know that under the rules the police had to follow and with what they had, it would be almost impossible to get anything of value on Riche anytime soon and he was letting Steven know where to use whatever resources he had.

Steven had gone to the field division earlier that day and requisitioned two groups. Everyone knew not to ask any questions. He had tasked one group with surveillance. Two teams of two operatives would rotate and would watch the guy 24/7. In a case like this, the subject was usually a lone operator, someone that had no financial motives and who took his time to enjoy what he was doing. He was also meticulous, so he wouldn't leave things behind or engage in phone conversations.

The second group was tasked with looking into the warehouse the guy was renting and going through his apartment. It wasn't going to be too hard to find out what the guy was up to without leaving a single trace that they had been at either place. Steven knew the trick would be how to get the information to Grady in such a way that it didn't screw up the case against the guy, if there was a case there at all.

Will Talley and Ben Stewart were the best surveillance team the company had, and when they found out what this was about, they were the first to volunteer. The team that would rotate with them would be made up of whoever was available at that particular time.

All of them were experienced operators, ex-military, police and some international guys, including former MI6, SVR and Mossad agents.

Talley and Stewart had been on nighttime duty with the guy for two days now and had gotten absolutely nothing. The guy came home from work, went into his apartment and stayed there for the duration. The day shift guys hadn't fared much better. He went to work, sometimes brought his lunch and sometimes went out with coworkers.

This guy was about as vanilla as they come, but still, there was something off about him. Like everything he did was a role in a movie and he had the starring role. It was nothing that anyone around him would notice, but these guys were professionals and they picked up on even the slightest deviations from what 'normal' should be.

Travis Pruitt and Victor Demers were also the best the company had at getting into and out of places without leaving a trace that they had been there at all.

Some of the stories about the places Travis had been able to get into and out of were still being debated. Stories of getting into vaults, elevators and Fort Knox-type security locations had been circulating around the company for some years. Most people thought it was just exaggeration, but the fact was that every one of the stories was true.

Pruitt and Demers had also been watching the guy to find out what exactly they were dealing with. Was it just the guy's apartment and the warehouse he rented or were there other locations they needed to breach? The surveillance guys also briefed them on the guy's routine, which was as predictable as they could possibly hope for.

In the end it was just his apartment and the warehouse. They had both agreed that they would hit the apartment first, which would be the easiest, and the surveillance team was already covering the warehouse.

Breaking into the apartment was truly like a walk in the park for Demers and Pruitt. They weren't sure exactly what they were looking for, but they were clear on the situation and were looking for anything that they could use to confirm what almost everyone already thought, that if this wasn't the guy they were looking for, he was definitely in the ballpark.

Like the two NYPD detectives before them, the first thing they noticed when they walked into Donald Riche's apartment was just how incredibly clean it was. There was not a single object out of place, all of the decorations, the kitchen utensils, the furniture, everything was meticulously placed and organized.

They worked their way through the apartment, thoroughly examining any and all places where Riche could have hidden anything. They also used scanners and sensors to test the walls for potential hidden compartments.

They found nothing and left the same way they'd come. The warehouse was going to be the next place they hit.

They noticed the mail that had been arranged on a desk and took a picture. Before leaving, Demers went through it. As he was going through a number of utility bills, he came across a bill that caught his attention. It was from a pharmaceutical supply company and the name on the account was not Riche's.

◆

As expected, once the story broke all of New York was speculating on what could be going on. Along with that speculation came the same type of fear that New Yorkers could not help but associate with 9/11.

The police, the FBI, all other agencies really, didn't have anything to go on. No one was safe. It was palpable. Mothers held their children closer if they went out with them at night at all.

Every news outlet had their own theory, their own sources and their own experts commenting about what could be happening to the girls in New York.

The NYPD was in overdrive and the task force had just gotten a big boost from the mayor, but none of it did anything to appease the public, which like in almost every case like this, did its own to create even more panic. It was fear feeding on fear, something not unique to New York, but the city had an extra element of hubris to how information was first disseminated and then grew.

By the time the sixth week the girls had been missing came around, there was no one in New York that didn't know about the case. Everyone had a name for the case, 'The Boogeyman' or 'The Vanishings' and on and on. It was as though naming them made it easier to talk about.

The news led with it every evening. All kinds of crackpots were in chat rooms across the Internet either postulating on what was happening or taking responsibility for the disappearances. Twitter feeds and Facebook pages were dedicated to the case.

Only in New York could comparisons range from Jack the Ripper to organ black markets to Russian adoption rings to alien abductions. And like in almost every other high-profile serial disappearance or serial murder case, there was the usual number of psychic detectives offering their services, for a fee of course.

None of it went unnoticed, especially by one Donald Riche.

Robert Grady was sitting at his desk, which was now completely buried in papers and empty styrofoam coffee cups. Mullins came in without knocking.

Grady looked up, "Well?"

Mullins shook his head, "Nothing. Our most promising individuals all lawyered up, just like Riche. We have absolutely no probable cause that we could take to a judge to get a search warrant for their houses or for Riche's warehouse.

"Riche's lawyer already called to let us know he knows we don't have shit and to make sure we don't try to come up with some bullshit story to get a warrant. I don't know where we go from here."

Grady thought about it for a second, "We stay on them. Sooner or later that son of a bitch is going to get the urge and, lawyer or not, he's going to slip up."

Mullins responded, "You mean Riche?"

Grady stood up and, as it was usual for him when he was thinking, walked over to the window, "Yeah, Riche, goddamned Riche. I'm telling you he's our guy. We're just going to have to wait him out or hope that we get some information by some other means." Grady gave Mullins a knowing look when he said that.

Mullins responded, "You mean Loomis, don't you? You mean let's see what we get from Steven Loomis."

Grady once again said, "I just said we would wait him out until we get some information by some other means, whatever those means are I don't care. Do you?"

Mullins shook his head emphatically, "Shit no, I told you before and I'll tell you again, I'll take it however we can get it."

Grady smiled, "Which is why we always talk about information by some other means and not Steven Loomis, right?"

Mullins grinned back, "Steven who?"

Grady walked back to his desk and sat down, "Exactly. By the way, you know how you said all the persons of interest lawyered up, well it turns out that the assistant at the dance school has a sex-related offense in his past and…"

Mullins interrupted, "He didn't register."

Grady continued, "He didn't register, so you know that now means…"

Mullins interrupted again, "We have something to pressure him with to get him to let us have a look-see in his apartment and car and locker and whatever else."

Grady said, "That's right. If his lawyer knows what he is doing, which he does, we should have a consent to search this afternoon. But you know his file, he doesn't fit the profile.

"The sex-related offense had to do with banging a 17-year-old when he was 24, so I personally don't think you're going to find anything, but who knows, stranger things have happened. Here, take the rest of this to put in his file. Call the lawyer up, I'm sure he's expecting it by now." Before leaving, Mullins sat down in front of Grady's desk.

Grady looked up and smiled, the man just looked beat to hell and like he had to vent, "What's going on, Mark?"

Signaling behind him with his thumb, Mullins let it out, "Have you heard some of the shit that's been going around? Vampires? What the fuck is that all about?! Satanic rituals?! I mean, I've been around Robert and I know the kind of crazy shit cases like these generate, but this is crazy even by those standards.

"Did you know there's even a story out there that it's a cop taking all the girls and that all of a sudden he's going to find them all alive and be the big hero. I mean, can you believe that shit?"

Grady was smiling at his detective, not unkindly, "Yeah, I know, but we knew when it broke it was going to blow up, right? Remember after 9/11 all those wackos with conspiracy stories about how it was the president that ordered the attack and all that other crap with the computer coming up with the plane and the two buildings if you put something down in a word processor?

"There's always going to be crazies that come out of the woodwork when something like this hits."

Mark Mullins was shaking his head, "I know it, like I told you, I've been here before, you know that, it's just this one's gotten to the point of being ridiculous. Maybe it has to do with the fact that it's little girls that's making it get more under my skin. Anyway, sorry, I just had to let some steam off."

With that he got up to leave. Grady told him, "Don't even think about it, we all have to let some off from time to time. Call the lawyer, I'll let you know if I hear anything on my end."

As Mullins was leaving, one of the desk cops stuck his head in Grady's office, "Detective, there's a Felix Garcia here who says he wants to talk to you. I asked him if he had an appointment and he said he didn't, so I told him you were busy, and he said for me to tell you he was here because you'd want to talk to him."

Grady mumbled to himself "Damn kid is persistent..."

The desk cop said, "Excuse me, sir?"

Grady made a gesture to let Garcia come on back. Felix walked into Grady's office with a smile on his face, "Did I tell you this was going to turn in another O.J. or what?"

Grady chuckled, "Yeah, yeah, what can I do for you? Oh, and nice work on the piece you wrote."

Garcia said, "Thanks. The reason I wanted to talk to you is because there is word out there that there is some progress on the case."

Grady leaned forward, "Oh really? And what are the sources of this new revelation?"

Garcia smiled, he was expecting some brinkmanship, "You know I can't tell you that. What I can tell you is that I know that most of the list the interagency task force had yielded nothing useful. I can tell you that all the teachers, dance instructors, gymnastics coaches have been interrogated and you've gotten nothing so far."

One thing you had to admit was that Garcia was 1) connected and 2) did his homework.

He continued, "But word is that there may be three or four possibles from outside the girls' school and extracurricular activities. Now I know you can't tell me who they are, but maybe you could let me know how you developed those names."

Grady, still leaning forward and completely deadpan, said, "By doing outstanding detective work, Mr. Garcia."

Felix smiled, "So that's how it's going to be. I'll get it sooner or later, I just thought maybe we could speak off the record on this."

Grady, still looking at him, said, "Good luck."

Garcia had expected Grady to say no, but he hadn't expected it so abruptly. That told him they definitely had some strong potential suspects and didn't want to screw the case up at all by revealing any information. He was playing it very close to the vest. Garcia couldn't blame him, that's how he would have done it.

Chapter 7

Steven Loomis was sitting in his office with only his desk light on. It was winter and it was past seven, so the office was just illuminated by an amber glow.

He was waiting for the teams tasked with surveillance and intelligence. Although both teams had been tasked with keeping an eye on Riche, they had also run brief stakeouts on the other persons of interest. Besides, Riche's routine had not deviated one iota since they started the surveillance.

Intelligence had not gone as far as to enter the other suspects' apartments. From what they got from surveillance, they could tell there wasn't much there, and some of them had families whose schedules would take a while to pin down.

They had all agreed that any information would only be transferred face-to-face, no email, no phone, no cellular, even encrypted communications equipment. That hadn't come from the General, but Loomis knew that's how he wanted it. Will Talley and Ben Stewart were the first to show up.

Loomis had been staring out at the city. He turned around when he heard them come in and smiled, "Long time, gentlemen. Please sit down. How's Jeanie, Ben?"

Stewart chuckled, "Still a pain in the ass."

He turned to Talley, "How about you, still single?"

Talley put his hands behind his head and leaned back, "Of course, who am I to deprive all those lovely women of the Talley magic?" They all laughed.

Loomis went on, "It really has been a while."

Stewart nodded, "Since the op in Panama. I got to tell you, Steven, I miss those days."

Loomis smiled, "Yeah, and back in those days, you couldn't wait for a quiet corporate gig." As Loomis was finishing that last comment, Victor Demers and Travis Pruitt walked in.

Demers was the first to speak, "Sorry we're late for the party." They both came into the office and sat down. Demers and Pruitt carried themselves very differently than Ben Stewart and Will Talley. They had very dry personalities and were all business. Each was north of 6 feet, well over 200 pounds and in supreme physical shape. Their size and countenance made them poor surveillance operatives; they had a hard time disappearing into a crowd. Anyone with any sort of basic operational experience would be able to spot them a mile away. What they lacked in surveillance capabilities, however, they more than made up in tactical, infiltration and exfiltration skills.

Demers was the first to speak. "We went into his apartment, we did it from top to bottom, and we could find nothing. This guy is meticulous about everything he does. Even the ornaments and knickknacks seemed to be arranged in patterns. There was not a speck of dust on any of the surfaces, not the bathroom, not the kitchen, nowhere. We grabbed some DNA samples for comparison if we need them later. He also had a bill from a medical supply company. What a runner for a Wall Street firm wants with medical equipment, only he knows.

"Sorry, Steven, if this guy is doing anything, he is doing it somewhere else. And that bill is giving me a bad vibe."

Travis Pruitt was the next to speak, "We're planning to take a look at the warehouse tonight if everything works out.

"We still haven't located the van and neither have the police. It would make things much simpler. We're pretty confident it's at the warehouse. Only place it could be."

Steven ran a hand through his hair in frustration, but there really wasn't anything else to be done until they got a look at the warehouse. "Thanks guys. I really appreciate it."

They all stood up and patted Steven on the shoulder or shook his hand as they left. He sat down back at his desk and stared out the window again. He had been thinking about Tracy a lot the last couple of days, all the vacations and the bedtime stories, all of it.

He had missed her more in the last couple of days than since she'd vanished. For some reason, all throughout this nightmare he had thought of her as one of his children. Now, tonight, he was thinking of her as his Tracy, with her sparkling eyes and ready laugh.

In the solitude of his office, under an amber glow Steven Loomis put his head in his hands and began to sob like he had not done until now. He didn't care if he felt weak and he didn't care that it would muddle his thinking. Right now he was just a daddy who would never see his little girl again.

Once he allowed all his emotions to pour out, once he suffered what he knew he would suffer sooner or later, he stopped.

He wiped the tears from his face and began a completely different train of thought. Who would do something like this? What kind of mind did it take to see a defenseless little girl of six and take her to do who knew what to her, actually to nine little girls?

Steven Loomis had seen some of the worst the human race had to offer. He had seen the horrible things humans could do to each other, but throughout his career everything he had seen, everything he had experienced, and seen people do for each other and to each other had to do with a cause.

This was different, this *felt* different. Whatever this was about, it had nothing to do with a jihad or a crusade. It had nothing to do with anything that Steven could conceive as a motive. Not greed, not jealousy, not insanity, there was thought and consideration in how the man had taken the girls. There was intellect running through the underbelly of all of it, of that he was sure. Whose intellect and motivations was what he was truly looking for. He'd known he would not find his daughter alive for some time. Now what he wanted was answers to his questions.

◆

Demers and Pruitt got to the industrial complex just before midnight. They were carrying their standard kit but could easily see they wouldn't need most of what was inside of it. The complex was like dozens of others with an outside chain-link fence gate that rolled open, a small guard shack with an overweight guard in a rent-a-cop uniform, and eight warehouses side to side on each side of the alley beyond the gate.

The idea was to check in with the guard and then go to your warehouse. The first and really the only hang-up was going to be the guard. The dog barking on the other side of the gate, probably a mastiff of some sort, was not going to be a problem. They had brought prime filet laced with tranquilizer for just such an occasion.

The problem was going to be getting to the guard without raising any alarms. That in and of itself was precisely what they were good at;

the problem was going to be rendering the guard unconscious. They considered a number of options, but a small dart with a quick-acting sleeping agent was going to be the most effective and least damaging to the guy, who after all was just doing his job.

They'd staked the place out for a couple of days and had decided tonight would be the night. After sitting in their sedan from a vantage point where they could see the complex for a couple of hours, they felt they had enough information to make it to the warehouse completely undetected. They had spotted all of the cameras that were in the complex, which weren't many, and had the equipment necessary to neutralize them. The easiest thing would be to cut the power once the guard was out, but security cameras were often on a separate circuit for precisely that reason and some security systems had an automatic silent alarm when the power was cut.

No, they would deal with them one by one. The whole thing shouldn't take any more than an hour, if that. They had both dealt with situations like this before and were competent operators, but still, neutralizing human assets was not their specialty.

The dog was barking incessantly at anything that moved, which was actually to their advantage since the guard, accustomed to the dog barking, didn't look away from his small TV. Demers and Pruitt decided to make their move. They carefully walked down the hill from which they had been observing everything, both dressed in black assault suits minus the armor. Once on the ground, they split up. Pruitt moved toward the gate hugging the wall and got close enough to the gate to hear the television the guard was watching. He threw the meat laced with tranquilizer over the fence, and at the same time Demers, who had found an excellent vantage point to shoot, fired the dart.

The guard had just begun to notice the red dot on his shoulder when he felt a sting on his upper chest. He was able to stand up and utter "What the f…" before going down. It took the dog a few minutes longer, but finally he too was down. Demers and Pruitt then went to the electrical grid by the guard shack to see if everything was on one network or if there was a trip alarm. They weren't too surprised by what they found; it was a straightforward electrical system. Only the alarm was on a separate grid and they could bypass that with no problem.

These warehouses close to the shore were dilapidated and often used by the mob for whatever they needed to use them. Sophisticated security systems just weren't conducive to engaging in transactions or storing swag in the warehouse if they needed to, and the owners knew it. If they didn't have to spend 30 grand for cameras and motion detectors, why would they? The type of security system the mob used was far more immediate and far more brutal, and it did not involve the police. All of which worked in their favor.

They knew the warehouse they were interested in wasn't rented or controlled by the mob and judging by the condition the warehouses were in, there would be no readily visible damage that anyone would notice. Once inside the complex they headed to warehouse 11, Riche's warehouse. There were chemical odors emanating from inside, but that was not unusual. Between the river, some of the hazardous materials kept in some of the other warehouses and the diesel fumes from five barrels lined against the wall, it was impossible to discern one specific odor. The warehouse had a side door and a bay door that rolled up to let a truck or other equipment in.

After making sure there was no one else there, Pruitt made short work of the side door and walked into the place with Demers close behind. They put on their night vision goggles. The low-light devices allowed them to see clearly, although everything appeared through various shades of green. There were several barrels with hazardous material signs on them in the first room they walked into. They could also now see where the van had been this whole time, and they could see that the warehouse was divided into separate spaces and that, once again, everything was spotless.

There was a long plastic curtain like the kind used in beef freezers and slaughterhouses. It was about a quarter of an inch thick and a grayish white. It went almost the entire width of the warehouse but stopped just short of the wall.

The space Demers and Pruitt were in looked like a machine shop. There was a table saw, a lathe, a band saw, all spotless, but arranged awkwardly. They moved on to the space beyond the plastic curtain and were absolutely shocked to find something that looked like an operating table. It clearly wasn't one but had been dressed up to look like one. On a bench that stuck out from the wall were all sorts of surgical instruments, scalpels, forceps and devices neither operative had ever seen.

All of them appeared to be either already sterilized or being sterilized in a machine used to do just that. There were also other nonsurgical cutting tools hanging from the wall, perfectly organized. Some of the tools were missing, but an outline in marker let them know they were probably in the sterilizing machine.

The two operatives had been all over the world, each had years of experience in the field and in some of the most dangerous and difficult situations anyone could be faced with, and yet neither one had felt the unease they felt now. This was a bizarre space, and the smell of cleaner, sterilizer and alcohol made it even eerier.

As they looked down the bench, they could see an industrial sharpener and beyond it two industrial-sized, top-loading freezers sitting side by side. They walked in the direction of the freezers and just as they got past the space the van was occupying, they came upon a scene that would stay with both of them for the rest of their lives.

Upon first inspection it looked like a typical little girl's room. There was a four-poster bed with decorative swirls. Around the room were shelves full of dolls of all shapes and sizes, most of them were

Barbie-type dolls, some were complete, but most were in some state of disassembly or taken apart, some had the eyes cut out, some had arms or legs missing. There were four sets of handcuffs, one attached to each of the posts.

Demers and Pruitt were standing completely still and in complete shock trying to take in what was in front of them.

On the other side of the bed were two refrigerators standing side by side along the wall that ended at the corner of the wall the top-loading freezers were up against.

As both men stood without a clue as to what all of this meant, they both seemed to get just what was in front of them at the same time.

Demers asked Pruitt to turn on the overhead light, "Vic, you know we can't…"

Demers didn't let him finish, "Goddamnit, Travis, turn on the light, I don't give a shit who sees it! You know what's in here. Jesus Christ, I don't want to look at what I know is there, but we have to."

Pruitt headed to the light switch, "I know, Vic. I've never even come close to this type of shit." Both took their night vision gear off before the lights turned on.

He made it to the light switch and turned it on. After their eyes adjusted, they picked up on a few things they had missed: a tall garbage can that appeared to have linens in it, a chain hanging from the ceiling, and vials of various drugs that they recognized as paralytics and sedatives. There was an IV stand next to the bed and a stainless steel table next to that, beyond that were the two upright refrigerators. Demers and Pruitt decided they would look at the industrial freezers first.

As Demers got to the first one, he could see there was a padlock on it. He pulled out bolt cutters and cut off the lock.

Somewhere in the dark recesses of their minds, the two operatives knew what it was that they were going to find in the freezers, but no amount of imagination could prepare them for what they saw once they opened the lid. Inside of the first freezer, looking up was the head of Tracy Loomis. It had been cut with incredible precision and her eyelids and eyes were missing. Next to her were the heads of two other little girls of roughly the same age, one without a scalp. Underneath the heads there were various body parts, arms, legs, a small torso, all neatly stacked.

Nothing in the freezer had been just tossed in. It had all been neatly stacked; every part had a place for it. Judging by the number of body parts and the depth of the freezer, they guessed there must be about four bodies in it. All Pruitt could manage to whisper was, "Holy God…" before Demers just let the lid slam shut. Both of them felt lightheaded and had to take several deep breaths to quell the nausea that was hitting them.

Once both men had composed themselves, they checked the other freezer, which was stacked in the same way as its twin, although not as full. Once they closed the second freezer they went to the two upright refrigerators, feeling more steeled for what they might find, but once again, whatever they had expected to find in the two refrigerators did not come close to matching what they actually found.

Pruitt opened the first refrigerator this time and once he did, he thought he had found a life-sized doll. A little girl stood there, dressed in a frilly blue dress. She had curly blond hair and her open eyes were a light blue. Except there was something wrong with the way her hair sat on her head. It was as if it had been placed there, but not quite straight enough.

Demers came from behind Pruitt to take a look and from behind him said, "Oh, my God, look at her neck." Pruitt directed his attention to the girl's neck and what he saw actually made him dizzy and he swayed on his feet. Had Demers not been behind him he might have actually fallen straight back.

The head on the girl didn't belong to the rest of the body. There were stitch marks around the neck and upon closer inspection they could see that the skin tone of the face did not match the skin tone on her arms. As they continued to examine the girl, they also noticed that the wrists had similar stitching and that the skin tone on the hands also had a different hue to them. The stitching on the other hand was not completed, it was about three-quarters of the way around, and through the open wound Demers could see a shiny object. He bent down to get a closer look and realized that it was a polished, stainless steel rod.

All of a sudden everything in this pit from hell made sense.

The son of a bitch was assembling this girl. He was taking whatever parts he wanted from the other girls and putting this one together, and Demers would bet anything that they would find the exact same thing in the other refrigerator. He couldn't keep these bodies frozen because he needed them to be more pliable, but he knew a standard refrigerator at above freezing temperatures would not slow down the decomposition enough, which is what he probably used the chemicals and the dry ice for.

Pruitt closed the refrigerator door and put his hand on Demers' shoulder, "C'mon we found what we needed to find. Let's get out of here. I don't want to stay in here one more second."

They both stood without saying a word for a few seconds. Demers finally broke the silence, "We can't. The police have nothing on this guy, and if any of this evidence is tainted in any way it could jeopardize the trial. They can't come in without probable cause, but the owner of the place can open it if there's some emergency."

Pruitt looked at him, puzzled, "What are you saying? You want to set fire to the place?"

Demers was already on his way to the barrels they saw when they first came in, "No, but I'm sure some sort of chemical spill coming from inside the warehouse is going to catch someone's attention. They'll have to open it for safety reasons."

Pruitt was nodding now, "I got you. Let's tip a couple of these over and make sure they run under the bay door into the alley."

Demers was already prying the lid from one of the barrels, "Exactly."

Pruitt paused for a moment, "What about the van? We haven't even looked in it."

Demers stopped what he was doing and looked at Pruitt with a perplexed look on his face, "Are you serious? Do you really have any doubt about what is most likely in the van? No, we've got what we need. Once they open the place, there will be more than enough probable cause to look in the van. We're done here."

Pruitt nodded and without another word began to pry the top from the barrel next to the one Demers had already gotten open. One of them was almost certainly formaldehyde, the other one was clearly some sort of caustic agent. Both had a pungent and strong chemical smell.

They both spilled the barrels making sure that the chemicals ran under the bay door and into the alley. They made their way out of the warehouse and were satisfied that once the guard came to he would immediately smell the chemicals and probably associate it to whatever had happened to him. Whether he did or not, he would almost certainly call the fire or police department to report the chemical spill, which was clearly coming from warehouse 11.

After storing their gear and once they were back in their vehicle, Demers and Pruitt sat in silence for what seemed like hours, each processing what they had seen in their own way. Both were seasoned operators and thought they had seen everything there was to see about what human beings could do to each other, and both had their notions of evil completely redefined tonight.

After taking a moment for themselves, Demers thought about the inevitable question, the one they both had been thinking about and dreading the most. What were they going to say to Steven? What were they going to say to their boss, their friend? How do you tell a father that you saw his little girl's severed head in a freezer? A little girl they both knew. They knew they couldn't avoid him, and they also knew they had to tell him something before the police found out and told him in their own way. They also knew that he was waiting for them, for their report.

As Victor Demers had these thoughts swirling in his head, he could feel tears welling up. He wasn't a father, but he could imagine the devastation, the immense loss not only for Steven but also for the families of all the little girls. It was that thought and the sheer outpouring of adrenaline that had the hardened operative on the verge of tears. He didn't need to turn to see that Travis was having a similar reaction.

Demers finally broke the silence and said, "You know he's waiting to hear from us. Jesus, Trav, I just don't know what the hell to tell him."

Travis had already composed himself and knew the answer to that question, "We just tell him that he's the guy. We keep it professional, but we warn him that it's not going to be pretty. Steven already knows that, he knows his little girl is gone, and that is what will hurt him the most in the end. What this fucker did with her body doesn't have to be a part of his pain."

Demers was on board immediately. He had been thinking along those lines already, so hearing Travis articulating the thought was a relief. After sitting in their car for a minute or two without saying a word, Demers turned the key to the ignition of the black Lincoln and started driving back into the heart of the city.

Neither man said a word the entire drive. There just weren't any words that could be said that would make any sense.

Demers, realizing if they were going to handle this as professionals they had to get back in operational mode, said, "Did you notice how fucking clean the place was? Not a spot anywhere. And the son of a bitch was smart enough to pick an industrial warehouse where he could drain whatever chemicals he was using and mix the blood in with them without raising any red flags."

Pruitt was nodding, "Yup, I was thinking the same thing. I just can't imagine how you detach yourself to be able to do something like that. I mean, we do what we have to for the job, but even then there are things that are hard to swallow, you know? Things that leave a mark for good.

"Just seeing what we saw left a mark that will never go away, so I can't imagine how you actually do it, how anybody could do it."

Demers responded, "People like that...they're different, you know? I mean different in a way we can't understand, and I would be willing to bet my life savings that this guy was this way from the day he took his first breath. Someone doing something like that...they didn't learn to think the way they do, there is something different in their brain.

"This guy never saw the world we do. He lives in some fucked up version of the world we live in and he sees that as normal. It's the only way he could do something like that, it has to be, otherwise, Trav, everything I know...everything I thought I knew...about the human race has been a complete farce."

Travis Pruitt actually felt some relief listening to Demers. He had a sardonic grin on his face, "If that guy wasn't born with a brain wired differently, then you better move over and make some room for me in that world of yours. I get you, Vic, and yeah, the guy was born a predator.

"I'm not a shrink, but if one saw what we just did and didn't immediately know the guy was some sort of freak, he should have his license pulled." Both men knew they were being redundant, but it helped to talk about it as an op.

Chapter 8

Steven Loomis left the office late. He had been reading all of the research he had found and had been completely engrossed by it. He was amazed at how much information there was available on cases similar to this one. There was information on the investigations, on the various law enforcement organizations, on the victims and what he cared about the most, the perpetrators.

There were thousands, if not tens of thousands, of reports about the people that were ultimately found to be guilty of the crimes. Aside from the thousands of police reports, opinion pieces and sensationalistic journalists, he found that the forensic psychiatric community was the best source of the type of information he was looking for.

Most of what he found was standard reports done by psychiatrists at the institutions where the prisoners were being kept. After some time, they all seemed to meld together and take on the same tone. There were countless references to the Hare Scale. As Steven understood it, it was a scale developed in order to assess whether the individual was a psychopath or not. Over time, the scale had appeared to become the standard used by forensic psychiatrists, prison parole boards, and researchers in the field of criminal behavior and corrections. It had been revised, and the revised version was still the go-to resource on the subject of psychopathy.

There were a small but distinguished number of scientists that were doing work that was far from the norm in forensic or criminal psychiatry. These individuals were exploring the hypothesis that there were instances where no scale or norm developed until now could define or otherwise explain their behavior. Their contention was that there were individuals whose physiology, mental and cognitive processes, and even genetic makeup were so far from that of established human norms that they belonged to another species.

One researcher based in New York, Doctor Tyrone Leonard, Professor of forensic psychiatry at Queens College, had established a hypothesis based on evolution. His research appeared to point to the new species as what he considered an expected step in the evolutionary ladder. He was the only one of the researchers Steven was able to find who had actually come up with a name for the new species. He had named them *Homo sapiens predaer,* or *Homo predator*. A lot of what he had read was over his head, but one thing Steven did understand was that Leonard was very clear in positing that this new species had taken *Homo sapiens'* place at the top of the food chain.

There was another researcher that Steven had found also in New York, a professor at Columbia who had developed a scale, similar to the Hare Scale, with one major difference, his scale used 'evil' as a unit of measurement. Individuals would fall on any one of 25 levels of his scale depending on the way they committed their murders, how many people they killed and various others criteria. Where this guy's work, his scale, seemed to intersect with what Leonard was doing was on the last three levels.

Steven would pack all of this to take home and read in more detail, but as he understood it, the highest three levels of the scale defined behavior that was beyond that of a human being; they defined the crimes and behaviors of individuals beyond any established definition, scale or norm for psychopaths, sociopaths, schizophrenics and so on.

There were many others out there, but these were the ones whose research seemed most solid and who appeared to have invested a great deal of their careers in supporting their findings. It had been these scientists who had captured his attention, the ones that had actually provided a semblance of an answer to the questions he had and, truth be told, the ones whose findings and hypotheses coincided with a lot of what his own thinking had been.

He looked up at the clock and found that it was past midnight – no sense in waiting for Pruitt and Demers. Who knew how long it might take them to get a look in the warehouse, and he was exhausted.

He grabbed his things and turned off the lights and made his way to the street to hail a cab. One thing about staying at the office this late was that there was never a shortage of cabs. Steven caught a cab within five minutes of hitting the sidewalk. After being on the road for just over 10 minutes, his cell phone went off. It was Victor Demers, "Hey Vic, what did you find?"

On the other end of the phone, Victor Demers simply said, "Steve, we need to get together." Steven felt a pit in his stomach. He thought he was ready for it but now realized the part of him that was a father would never die, "I just left the office. I'll just have the driver turn around."

After a brief pause, Demers said, "Steve, we need to meet somewhere else. Just pick a place."

Now Loomis knew they found something, something they didn't want to talk about at the office and something that they didn't feel comfortable talking about on encrypted cellular phones, "Alright, there's a greasy spoon café about two blocks west of the office and a block…"

Demers interrupted him, "Harry's All Night Café, yeah, I know where it is. It's as good a place as any at this hour. We'll see you in a few."

◆

The guard at the warehouse was finally waking up. He felt groggy and couldn't remember what happened, it was like he just blacked out. Then he remembered the dot and the stinging sensation on his chest. The dart was still stuck there. He pulled it out and examined it. It was like nothing he had seen before. All of a sudden he realized he didn't hear Jake barking anywhere.

He got his flashlight and exited the booth, thinking his dog was dead. He finally found Jake just a ways down the middle alley close to one of the bay doors, near him was a half-eaten piece of steak. He had been poisoned and was dead. Before he could really grasp the thought the guard, Melvin Jackson, heard Jake whine a little and then lift his head.

Melvin forgot about the dart and everything else for that second, "Hey there, boy, what happened to us, huh?"

As he was petting the dog, he could see the dog, like himself, was coming to. Now Jackson, still a little out of it, could smell a pungent smell and immediately went back to the guard shack to turn on the floodlights and to rewind the tape on the cameras. He immediately saw that the cameras had been off and that the main breaker had been turned off. Holding a flashlight, he went over to the breaker and flipped it on.

He went back to the shack and turned on the lights and could see a big spill coming out from under a bay door. He couldn't tell what it was, but it had a strong chemical smell to it. It was running down the middle of the alley, as all bay doors sloped toward the middle and then down toward a drain at the end of the complex. The strong smell was burning his nose and he had no idea whether the stuff was flammable or explosive, he could just tell it was still coming out from under the bay door. He didn't know if it was a leak or if it had something to do with him and his dog getting knocked out with a dart and a steak laced with something.

Jake was on all fours now, even if a little unsteady. "C'mon, boy, let's get back to the shack and call the police and the fire department and everybody else so we can do our job and get the hell out of here."

Melvin did just that, he went to the shack, dialed 911 and walked up the hill in front of the complex a little ways to wait for the cavalry. In all his years, he had never been caught up in something like this and he wanted no part of it. He'd just taken the job to supplement his social security, not to get himself and his dog knocked out by God knows what and to wake up to that nasty-smelling chemical sludge, no sir.

He could already hear the sirens coming in the distance and it was the sweetest sound Melvin Jackson had heard in as long as he could remember.

◆

By the time Steven's cab had turned around and gotten to the café, Demers and Pruitt were already there. He was under no delusions of what they were there to tell him, but he wanted to know the whys and the hows of something like this.

He had already gotten used to that steady ache and tightness he felt in his chest and knew it would evolve and change, but never be completely gone. That Demers and Pruitt wanted to meet outside the office told Steven a couple of things. Neither man wanted this to be traced back to them in any way and they both wanted to be there and in a public place, because they considered it to be a more predictable and manageable place than the office, a place without as much video and audio surveillance as the office had. Whatever they had to tell Steven, both men felt it would have an impact on him. They both knew his background and the types of operations he had been a part of, so the fact that they felt that whatever they had to share with him was something he might not be ready for was making Steven Loomis the most anxious.

The coffee shop was right out of a painting, the lights glowing through the windows providing the only light, more of a glow, at street level in the neighborhood. As he walked, in booths that hadn't been changed since the Korean War lined the outside walls and windows, letting the people sitting in each get lost looking into the New York night when they were sitting alone and providing those that were accompanied with a sense of privacy. The long counter in front of the kitchen followed the L shape of the coffee shop and was also lined with metal stools with red cushions matching the booths. A cash register sat at each end to allow patrons to leave through either of the two coffee shop doors. An old-fashioned case sat in the middle of the counter slowly rotating with what was left of that day's selection of pies.

Late-night diners ranged from people that were clearly regulars, eating their usual and reading the paper, to young students getting in some late-night studying to people getting off work and doing the crossword puzzle. A waitress, who looked like she had been there since the place opened, was going through the night's receipts.

She looked up as Steven came in and motioned with her head, "Your friends are sitting in the corner booth."

After 30 years of working at places like this, she knew that men dressed like these men, coming to a place like this at one o'clock in the morning, weren't coming in for the meatloaf special. She went back to her receipts. She knew if they needed something they would ask for it.

Steven looked over in the direction of the booth, saw Pruitt and Demers, and headed over. Both men had coffee and untouched pie in front of them, which meant they had found something, enough to stay there for a bit. He looked in the direction of the waitress who had kept one eye on him and one on her receipts just in case he did want something when he sat down. He gestured for some coffee and mouthed the word 'black' as he did so. She nodded, put her receipts book in her apron and picked up the pot. She would need to brew a new one. Even for this place, what was in there now was more a dark sludge than coffee.

There was no sense in going through any small talk at all. All of them knew what they were there to do and the best thing to do was to just get to it.

Steven knew it had to be hard for his friends, so he got the conversation rolling, "Alright guys, what do we have?"

They had both already agreed to be as matter-of-fact and professional as possible, and that is exactly how Demers responded, "He's the guy, Steven. He's the guy that took all of them."

Steven Loomis looked at both men and understood that whatever they had seen had a profound effect on both of them. Like any other human being, Steven had pondered on what they might find if this was the guy and he had come up with some pretty hard scenarios, but these weren't beat cops, they were men that had seen and experienced some of the worst things anyone could experience and they looked haunted. Steven looked down. He wasn't surprised. He had been pretty sure this was their guy, but hearing it confirmed still hit him hard.

He looked from Pruitt to Demers and back again, waiting for them to give him more details, "C'mon, guys, do we really have to do this?"

There was a brief and uncomfortable silence before Victor Demers went to speak, but he was interrupted by Travis Pruitt, "Look, Steven, the son of a bitch took nine little girls who will not be going home, ever. I think you know that whatever we saw, whatever he did with their bodies won't change that. I can't imagine what you are feeling or going through right now, and I know about your background, hell, all of our backgrounds, but I sure as shit would think you want to remember Tracy as you knew her.

"I know how this is going to come across, but as your friend I am telling you to just let it go. He's done, off the street. Let it go and get back to Marybeth and your other children."

Steven Loomis knew Travis Pruitt as well as anyone could know him. Like most operatives, he had a Special Forces background and was a consummate professional. He wasn't the warm and fuzzy type, none of them really were, but Pruitt was especially detached. He knew that Travis was well aware of his background. He also knew his family well, had been to their house, and hearing him say all of this told Steven Loomis everything he needed to know about what the two men had seen. In their chosen profession, a lot of the most important things that needed to be communicated went unsaid, a lot of blood spilled over a lot of mud gave them an additional sense, a sense that picked up on what the rest of the world often missed. In this exchange Travis Pruitt had said to Steven Loomis that what they had seen, which included Tracy, was so horrible that Steven would be better off not knowing any more. The exchange also told Steven that even though the two men *knew* Steven had to find closure his own way and would probably see what they saw in the end, it felt wrong not trying to get him to drop it.

The two men had put their careers on the line and their personal time on the line to do what they did, and it wasn't lost on Steven, "I can't tell you how much I appreciate it, guys. I'll take it from here."

And with that, Steven Loomis let Pruitt and Demers move on. He could see how hard it had been on them and was once again reminded that once you were a part of their brotherhood, you were a part of it for life.

Demers said, "Don't give it a second thought, you'd have put yourself on the line for either one of us in the same situation. Steve, I don't know what you're going to decide to do about this from this point forward, and I don't want to know right now. You know whatever it is, we've got your back. The General, us, everyone at the company, you know that."

Steven looked down to compose himself for a second, "I know guys, I really do, and I won't forget. Thank you." With that, they shook hands and Pruitt and Demers stood up and left.

Steven sat back down in the booth just as Esther Jones was coming back with his coffee. It smelled good and strong. She set it down in front of him and asked if he wanted sugar and milk. He shook his head slightly but didn't look up. Over 30 years Esther had seen looks like that many times and had always pondered what was behind the eyes. So many stories, either heard or imagined, had taught her that this particular look meant her customer was not there, he was somewhere else feeling God knows what. This guy was not her run-of-the-mill customer. He was dressed in an expensive suit and overcoat, probably in his mid-40s or early 50s, but built like a brick. Whatever he had just gone through with the other two guys left him a bit shell-shocked and Esther knew to just let him be.

For his part, Steven was processing what he had been told. There was nothing surprising about anything he heard, except the way Pruitt had broken his professional approach, even though he knew once he made his decision Steven was going to do what he was going to do. It was as if he wanted to get whatever had spooked him off his chest and to warn his friend about what he would probably end up seeing, all without having to be obvious about it.

Steven knew that in situations like these, humans, all humans, were always likely to imagine the worst and even controlling his emotions he was no different. A thousand horrible images flooded his mind. He didn't fight it, he just let it come as he knew it would sooner or later and then processed it accordingly. Now that he knew what happened to the girls, he remembered what the General had said and wondered what it was he was going to do about it. He had an idea, but he hadn't made up his mind.

Now he was going to have to completely compartmentalize his life. By now, the police, the fire department, or both, were opening Riche's warehouse, and he needed to get home before his family learned anything. Once he spoke with his mother-in-law and made sure the kids were okay, he would have to figure out where Marybeth was, really was, emotionally. This story would dominate the news for the next few weeks, if not months, and he knew no matter how hard he tried he would never be able to shield her from it for long, and he wasn't optimistic about how she would react. He needed to put a plan in place to put Tracy to rest, and to get his kids through it with as little disruption to their lives as possible. He had already made the decision that once Tracy was taken care of, Bethany and Chris would go back to their grandmother's house along with their mother. Right now, that was the only way Steven could think of keeping his family out of what was sure to be a media frenzy.

As he sat in the booth with his coffee in front of him he was going through a checklist of what he would have to do when it came to the family coming to New York from various cities across the country, dealing with funeral arrangements, and a thousand other things. The reality was that he was doing everything in his power to avoid the inevitable, deciding what to do about Riche. He knew what he was planning on doing tonight, but beyond that it was a haze for Steven, and that was not a feeling he was comfortable or familiar with. He had a few hours before daylight and then it would be all over the news, so if he was going to do what he had in mind, he had to get moving. He put a twenty on the table, put the sugar dispenser on it and walked out of the diner.

◆

The entire warehouse complex had been cordoned off, and there were more vehicles from all the pertinent agencies than could be counted. NYPD, the FBI, the medical examiner's office, the fire department and hazardous materials teams had all been dispatched. The news vans and helicopters would not be far behind. Grady had been the first detective to speak to the first officers on the scene. Actually, the first on the scene had been the New York Fire Department with two black and whites just behind them. Melvin had called in the hazardous material spill and the assault on him and his dog. When the fire department got there, they could tell immediately by the smell that they had a caustic and hazardous agent coming from warehouse 11. The police took a statement from Melvin and took possession of the dart he had been shot with. Before the hazmat team arrived, both the police and the fire department had made the decision to break into the warehouse to ensure there was nothing still spilling the sludge and to determine whether the entire block would need to be evacuated.

Once they were in the warehouse, the horror that had made up Donald Riche's existence became known to the world. All four uniformed NYPD officers and the firemen present were being debriefed and counseled by the time Grady got there. Mullins had gotten there 15 minutes after Grady, and by that time there were at least 10 black and whites, two engines, the hazmat team and a helicopter at the scene. Grady had waited for Mullins to go back inside. Once the detective squad and the crime scene investigations team had been deployed, access to the warehouse was completely cut off to everyone who was not absolutely necessary.

Grady had done a quick walk-through and ordered everybody not essential to the immediate processing of the scene out of the warehouse. They still didn't know what chemicals they were dealing with, whether they were flammable or caustic. He had waited for the hazmat team to green light the CSI and FBI lab guys to go back in. The people from the coroner's office would go in next. Grady could tell who had been in the warehouse and who hadn't just by looking at their expressions. Those that had gotten sick had been discreet about it when they could be, but the haunted look in their eyes wasn't something they could get rid of. Grady himself had a hard time reconciling what he had seen with any semblance of reality or even humanity.

After an entire career in the NYPD, he thought he was pretty much impermeable to anything, and he was, he just had never imagined he would ever be exposed to anything like this. He doubted there was one soul right here right now, no matter how long they'd been at the job, that could have seen anything like this in their worst nightmares.

A SWAT team had already been dispatched to Donald Riche's apartment and he had been taken into custody without any incident. He was back at the precinct and not saying a word. He had been allowed to call his lawyer. Mark Mullins had been there to make sure everything had gone by the book and that no one got a little too zealous doing their job when it came to handling Riche, something that tended to happen from time to time with child murderers and rapists.

The last thing they wanted was for some technicality or another to put a kink in the case, although from what Grady had seen in the warehouse and what he'd been told by the crime scene investigations team, there was a mountain of biological material all over the place and Grady was willing to bet that most of it was Riche's. Still the best thing that could happen is that Riche would confess once faced with the evidence.

He had asked for Riche to be allowed to talk to his attorney but not to be interrogated yet. As Grady was thinking that the DA's office would also want to send someone down for the questioning, Mark Mullins finally arrived at the scene.

Grady threw away the styrofoam cup with cold coffee he had been holding and met Mullins before he got all the way to the warehouse, "How did it go?"

Mullins, holding his own cup of fresher coffee, answered, "By the book. No resistance, no trouble, nothing. Riche answered the door, the SWAT point man knocked and he answered before they'd needed to bust down the door. They took him into custody and that was that."

He took a sip of his coffee and went on, "He was brought to the station and again everything went by the book. By the time he got there, everyone knew and everyone was waiting to see him. I was there to greet him and make sure nobody got cute or heroic."

Grady asked, "How did he respond when you greeted him? What did he look like?"

Mullins took another sip, shook his head and answered the question. "I have to tell you, Bob, it was creepy as hell. He saw me and recognized me and just said, 'Good evening, Detective Mullins.' Just that, nothing else, but it wasn't what he said that made the whole thing creepy, it was his expression.

"He was completely calm, he wasn't asking questions about the reason he was being arrested or saying anything about being innocent, nothing. His expression and the way he acted were almost like he was relieved. We booked him, fingerprinted him and I took him to a holding room.

"I asked him if he wanted something to drink and he asked for coffee. Before I could leave the room, he just said, 'Detective, I will need to speak with my attorney, please.' So I let him call his lawyer and that was that. His lawyer got there right before I headed over here, so I decided to wait for a few minutes. He went into the interview room and came back out about 10 minutes later, right before I was going to leave. He was white as a ghost and just let me know they were going to be a while.

"He looked haunted, Bob, like he was going back in because he had to, but what he really wanted to do was just to get the hell away. Maybe it was me just reading too much into all of this, but the whole thing was surreal and creepy as hell."

Grady took it all in, he hung his head and then looked up at Mullins, "I don't think it was you just reading too much into it. Go ahead and take a look at the scene. The CSI team and the medical examiner's team are in there now. Everyone else is being kept clear of the scene, but they know you are coming."

Mullins said, "Alright, I'll head over there."

He started on his way and Grady grabbed his arm before he could get on his way, "Mark, this one is bad. I know we talked about it and how bad it felt, but this is like nothing we ever thought about and it *will* give you nightmares. I haven't gone to sleep and I'm already having them. The first guys on the scene are all being counseled and I think we'll be looking at some posttraumatic claims before long. I'll understand if you don't want to take a look now. We'll have all the pictures and evidence we need to hang a case on the guy from here and from his apartment, so I'll understand if you want to steer clear for now."

Mullins looked at Grady and saw something in his friend's eyes he had never seen before, fear. Robert Grady, a grizzled and seasoned homicide detective in New York, someone who made his way up the ranks by being a beat cop, in the vice squad, organized crime detail and many others and had seen the worst humankind had to offer, had fear in his eyes. Whatever he had seen had scared Robert Grady and that more than anything else gave Mark Mullins pause, but he was a cop and this was also his case, and as much as he might want to avoid seeing something that was going to give him nightmares, he couldn't shirk what he felt was part of his responsibility.

He looked Grady in the eye, squeezed his shoulder and went on his way. Mullins arrived at the crime scene, which was surrounded by uniformed officers and hazardous materials guys and a multitude of vans and trucks. He went straight into the scene and the first thing that hit him was the smell. There was a strong chemical smell, but mixed with it there was a smell Mullins was very familiar with, the smell of decomposition. Even with as many chemicals as there were in the warehouse, Mullins could still distinguish the smell of death.

Before he had a chance to actually see any of the bodies, Mullins found himself in the middle of what looked to have come straight out of a nightmare. The warehouse was clearly set up as a workshop of some sort. As he was trying to make some sort of sense out of what he was seeing, Mullins caught a glimpse of one of the open upright refrigerators and watched as one of the guys from the CSI team had to leave the warehouse because he couldn't take it anymore. It was just a fleeting glance, but it was enough to make Mullins understand why Grady had looked so haunted. There was a little girl in there, obviously dead, but there was something else wrong with the picture. He couldn't see exactly what, but he now knew he wouldn't be looking into all of the freezers.

Mark Mullins was also a grizzled and experienced homicide detective with the NYPD and he had also seen horrible things, but he knew his limits and he knew he had never imagined anything like what he was seeing. He knew if he were to go farther in he might just want to hang it up, and he wasn't ready for that. He took a look at the tools sitting on the bench, the power tools on the floor, the freezers and the little girl in the upright refrigerator, and put together the picture. That alone was hard for him to process and from what he could see, what Grady said made more sense to him. There was enough here now, and there would be even more after it was all processed and the coroner's office was done with the autopsies, to make a case against Donald Riche.

Mark Mullins would hold true to his convictions and do everything he needed to do to carry out his job as well as he could, but looking at every body part in those freezers and refrigerators was not necessary for him to feel like he could do his job. If he did it now it would be more out of curiosity than out of necessity, and he just couldn't live with that idea, the idea that he didn't have to look but did anyway.

He took his handkerchief out of his pocket, put it up to his nose, and headed back to meet up with Grady. The two men looked each other in the eye without saying a word. They didn't need to. Mullins could already tell what Grady was thinking about, Steven Loomis.

Mullins asked anyway, "Tracy Loomis?"

Grady nodded slightly and answered, "I made the ID earlier. I don't know how we are going to want to handle that."

Mullins said, "He seems like a pretty solid guy. I just don't see him as a wild card."

Grady looked long and hard at Mullins before saying anything, "I know he's not, but you know we are going to have to level with him, and you were in there, you saw. How in the world can we even begin to imagine how a father is going to react to something like this happening to his six-year-old girl?"

Mullins nodded and then realized something, "How did they get into the warehouse, I mean who called it in and why?"

Grady answered, "The night watchman said he was knocked out by some sort of dart he pulled out of his chest. When he came to, his dog was still out with a half-eaten steak laced with tranquilizer lying beside him, and a strong chemical smell was coming from one of the warehouses.

"When he went to check which one it was coming from, he saw chemicals pouring out from warehouse 11. He called the chemicals in to hazardous materials and the police to give them the dart he says he pulled out of his chest. The first uniformed officers on the scene looked at the dart, had a conversation with the guard and started to think he might have made that part up, and that what really happened was that he fell asleep at the switch and the 'accident' happened while he was sleeping. The cameras were bypassed and the main power breaker switched off. The CSI guys have the dart and the half-eaten steak and are going to run tests to see what it was that was in them."

Mullins looked at Grady. The two men knew what had happened and were trying to figure out how to reconcile all of it with what had been found.

Grady was the first to speak, "You know it was him, Loomis. I talked to one of the SWAT guys, a former sergeant in Special Forces, about the dart and it is definitely something used in tactical operations, but he explained it was the type of thing used more in private security or mercenary operations than in law enforcement.

"Everyone is so focused on the scene that the guard's story is getting drowned out. After he saw what he saw in the warehouse, he was taken to the hospital. I don't think he remembers or cares about the dart right now, but that's going to change when things slow down and people look at this more carefully."

Mullins was smoking a rare cigarette, something he did almost exclusively when he was drinking, and thinking about what Grady had just shared with him, he said, "He knew we had nothing on Riche or any of the others and had to find a way to give us a cause to go into the warehouse. He knew we would have to wait a while to get a warrant, if we could get one at all, and knew Riche might be gone by the time we did. Is that what you're thinking?"

Grady answered, "Yup. To be honest, I'm more worried about how he's going to react to this than about anyone finding out how those chemicals spilled."

Just as he was finishing the sentence, Grady got a call on his cell phone. It was one of the uniformed officers stationed outside the perimeter who had a guy asking for Detective Grady. Grady didn't have to ask who it was, he just told the cop he would be up there in a couple of minutes. Mullins heard his side of the conversation and also knew who it was. He thought it would be best for Grady to meet Steven Loomis by himself, not to try to escape from it but because from this point forward the less people that knew about this and how deep it went, the better it would be for everyone. Besides, there was plenty for him to do and heading back to the station to see how Riche's interview had gone was first on the list.

Chapter 9

rady made his way to the cordoned-off area where the uniformed officers were stationed. He could see news vans already parking and correspondents setting up for their reports. Every single officer or investigator at the scene had already been warned to not say a word to any of the media. Grady, coordinating with the public information office, would make a preliminary statement and the commissioner would hold a formal press conference the next day.

Steven Loomis was waiting for him. He looked tired, but under control. He had probably been briefed by whoever had pulled off this operation. Grady knew that the conversation would be difficult. Both men knew what could or could not be said. Grady knew why Loomis was here and he didn't know if he would be able to give him what he wanted.

Grady started the conversation, "So I take it you heard."

Loomis understood that Grady knew he had been behind the chemical spill in the warehouse and that he knew none of this would have happened this quick without it. In other words, Grady knew he owed Loomis. Still, he couldn't go past a certain line, no matter what the scoreboard was.

Loomis waited a few seconds to answer, "You know I have and you know why I'm here."

Grady hung his head and looked back up to Loomis, "Yeah, I think I do. Thing is, I don't know if I can help you get what it is you came looking for."

Loomis looked at Grady intensely and said, "I'm not asking for much and I know you could find a way to do the right thing. I put my job and the jobs of other people on the line to make this happen and you know it."

Grady responded, "So you're saying that if you don't get what you're looking for you're going to leak this?"

Loomis smiled a thin, sad smile, "No, Robert, I think you know that's not how I work. But if you can't grant me this one favor then you obviously don't work the way I thought you did."

Now it was Grady's turn to be sardonic. He looked out over the river for a minute before turning back to address Loomis. "Supposing I was able to get you in. Are you sure you want to see what's there? I know your background and you know mine, so I think we both know we can dispense with the bullshit. This is bad and I mean really bad.

"I would think the memory you would want of your little girl is one with her beautiful face doing something fun with you and your family. What is it that you are looking for? Closure? Because I can tell you, brother, that there is no closure there, just pain and things that will change you forever."

Loomis appreciated what Robert Grady was trying to do but knew he was doing it because he felt he had to, to get off his chest what he had to get off his chest. In the end he also knew Grady would let him through.

"No, Robert, I got closure a long time ago. I am here because if I don't know I will always wonder, and I don't want to just leave it to my imagination or to however the DA and the media choose to spin the case."

Grady looked at him for a long time. He could understand what the man was saying, for some avoiding the unknown was a better coping mechanism, for men like Loomis it was better to make things tangible, process them and move on. Grady imagined Steven Loomis had quite a bit of experience doing just that, you couldn't be in the types of operations the guy had been in and not have the ability to compartmentalize and move on. Grady told the uniformed officer, a kid barely out of the academy, to let Loomis by.

After walking a few yards he said, "Wait here."

He knew there were people from a lot of precincts and a lot of agencies. He walked up to someone he knew from the coroner's office, someone who knew not to ask questions, spoke to him for a few seconds and took the man's windbreaker. He made his way back to Steven Loomis and handed him the windbreaker. Steven took off his pea coat and put on the windbreaker.

Grady simply turned around and said, "Follow me."

The two of them walked past the various technicians, police officers and firemen without getting a second look.

They got to the edge of the warehouse's bay door and before actually walking in Grady walked over to the CSI van and grabbed a gas mask for each of them. "There's some nasty shit here, put this on."

As he handed him the mask, he looked at Loomis and hung on to it for just a half a second. The look was Grady's last attempt to convince Loomis to not do this. The look he got back, which was completely emotionless, did more to make him nervous than anything else Loomis had done or said until now. He turned around and went into the warehouse and began to let Loomis know what they'd found so far in a monotone and professional way, as detached as he could be. He figured that the more professional he was, the more he could assess Loomis's reaction and keep the overall situation low-key.

It wasn't just Loomis he was worried about, he was also thinking about some of the other technicians and officers wondering who this guy was. There were enough people from different precincts that he doubted anyone would pay attention to anything other than what they were dealing with.

Still he had to play the part, "The call came in as a hazardous material spill coming from this warehouse; it came from the night watchman. Two black and whites and the fire department responded first and got into the warehouse to find all this. By now we have DA investigators taking their pictures and talking to the cops and firemen first on the scene. Homeland Security also sent someone from the FBI to look into the terrorist angle, especially because of the chemicals."

As they were walking, and even with the gas mask, Steven could smell the chemicals and the underlying smell of human decay. It was faint, but it was there. He was a trained tactical operator and he had been trained to not miss anything, so he took everything in and stored it in his mind. He saw the tools, the warehouse turned into a workshop with its various areas; he took note of the neatness of the place. Other than the spilled chemicals, every tool, every object was neatly placed and cleaned to perfection. He saw the sterilizing machine and understood how the tools could remain in such pristine condition. One thing Loomis was sure of was that this took a lot of planning, expense and careful consideration in how things were placed. There was an order to how the warehouse was divided. He didn't know what that was, but everything was here for a reason.

As they kept walking, Grady kept debriefing Loomis, "We hadn't been able to find the van because he had it parked here. We've gone through it and it was exactly what we thought it was, a trap and a mobile workshop for him. We found dozens of dolls and other toys little girls might like divided off from the rest of the van where he had portable coolers, vials of drugs and a set of tools similar to what you see on the bench over there.

"There are basically four sections that seemed to be organized in some sort of fashion, we're still doing a workup as you can see."

Loomis took in every detail. The tools were cutting tools and surgical instruments, scalpels, forceps, a variety of surgical scissors and what Steven recognized as orthopedic surgical drills. There was a tray with other hardware he couldn't make out. To his left he could see two side-by-side top-loading industrial freezers, and as they came through the plastic curtains that separated each area, he saw the first thing that hit him and hit him hard, it was a staged little girl's room with a white four-poster bed dominating the space. His eyes were immediately drawn to each of the four posts. There was a set of handcuffs attached to each of the posts. As he looked around, he saw a small vanity and shelves and shelves of dolls, Barbie-type dolls, some complete but most of them in various stages of being disassembled or being put together. There were doll limbs scattered all over the shelves. Based on everything else in the warehouse, it was the strangest and most surreal scene Loomis had ever seen, and it didn't take him long to put together what had gone on in this pit from hell.

He had seen similar places in other parts of the world, but they had been used for other reasons on other people, not on little girls. He didn't betray any emotion, however.

Grady walked over to the industrial freezers, "This is where he kept the remains of his victims." Grady hurried along, went on to walk toward the upright refrigerators and continued debriefing Steven.

For his part, Steven had stopped at the top-loading freezers and stood there staring at them. Before Grady noticed Loomis was not right behind him, Steven had started to open the lid of the first industrial freezer. As Grady turned around and noticed where Loomis was standing, he hurried back toward him and could only get

"Steven…" out before Loomis had opened the lid to the freezer and looked inside.

So far, all the scene processing had involved cataloging where things were, taking pictures, collecting any and all objects that could hold any DNA, and processing the van, along with taking a preliminary inventory of all the power tools that could not be moved right now.

All of the forensic evidence related to the actual victims had not been moved yet, however, so when Steven Loomis opened the first freezer the first thing he saw was his daughter's severed head, eyelids and eyes missing. He held the lid open for just a half a second and then let it slam shut. He had seen what he needed to see. It was as if the air had been let out of the room and he felt faint for just a beat. The image was far beyond what he had ever imagined or thought about. He thought he had prepared for anything, but now faced with the reality of his loss and with the horror that his daughter must have endured, something went off inside Steven Loomis.

He never betrayed any emotion and was once again composed by the time Grady made it over to warn him. His eyes were cold and distant, but still processing everything around him. He didn't need for the investigation to be completed to understand what had happened to his daughter in this hell. Grady looked at him and became immediately concerned by what he saw from Steven Loomis, which was absolutely nothing. No screaming, no crying, nothing. All Grady could manage was, "Loomis, are you okay?"

Steven looked at the freezer for a few seconds more and then at Grady, "Yes, I'm fine. I just felt a little faint for a moment."

There was an uncomfortable silence between the two men. Grady didn't know what to say. What could he say to someone who had just witnessed what Loomis had? He finally said, "I'm sorry, Steven, I am really sorry for your loss."

Loomis looked back at him, "Thank you. And thank all your guys for all the work. I know how hard this must be on them. So a chemical spill is what tipped you off?"

Grady looked at him, a bit puzzled, as if to say 'you know damn well it was.' Instead he just nodded and said, "Yeah, night watchman called it in. He also talked about some sort of dart sticking out of his chest."

This was Grady's way of letting Steven know about the only thing they had that no one could really account for or even relate to everything else, that and the steak with tranquilizer for the dog.

Loomis didn't flinch, "Oh, what's that all about?"

Grady responded, "Probably nothing, the watchman forgot about it once the warehouse was opened. He figured whoever did this had probably done that to him and his dog. He thinks he was lucky."

He was sure Loomis was catching his drift, but as Grady was relating the story his tone let Steven know that he knew that Steven and his people were responsible.

He continued, "With everything else we have to process, it's something that's likely to fall through the cracks."

Once again Grady let Steven know without saying anything that this would remain between the two of them. He didn't think it was necessary to bring Mark Mullins into the mix. Steven looked at Robert Grady for a few seconds, nodded slightly and nothing else was said about the chemical spill again. Grady was still concerned. Steven Loomis's demeanor had not changed one iota since he lifted the lid to that freezer. Grady had seen reactions like these before from some of his officers, reactions that spoke to a quiet rage, an internal mechanism that triggered something in the individual. Usually, however, the reactions Grady saw were almost catatonic. This was different. It was complete control. It was a look and a demeanor that spoke of purpose.

To Robert Grady, Steven Loomis had been pondering how to proceed, and lifting that freezer lid and seeing what he saw provided him with the answers he was looking for. Little did Grady know just how right he was about that.

Steven Loomis himself wasn't completely aware of exactly what he had gone through. He just knew that in the middle of the horror he was seeing and experiencing and the grief and sadness he was feeling, he had found a certain answer, an understanding he now knew he had been looking for. He now felt something had fallen into place. His training and experience allowed him to separate emotion from action.

 Grady knew Loomis wasn't going to be going off on some sort of rampage and he came across as being very much in control, without emotion and with a purpose, all of which made Grady very nervous, more nervous than had Loomis lost it.

He felt he had to say something to Loomis, if for nothing else than to just check off that box in his own mind, "Steven, I can't imagine what this must feel like, I really can't, but he's done, he's off the streets, and now we really do need to play it by the book. None of us want any technicality or screw-up at the lab to delay this in any way.

"The eyes of New York are going to be on all of these departments and everyone will need to be on their A game. It's over. We got him and he will not hurt anyone again."

Steven looked at Grady with an almost curious expression, like a parent listening to the logic of a child and just going along with it. Still, he didn't lose his composure and didn't want to give Grady something else to think or worry about. He himself still needed to come to terms with what it was he was feeling, how this would all affect his family and what if anything he was planning on doing about all of it.

Something was beginning to take form in his mind. It was nothing new, nothing he hadn't pondered about over the years, but it was something that the scene he found himself in had begun to crystallize in his mind.

He looked at Grady again and stuck his hand out, "Thank you, detective, thank you for all the work and for everything else. Now I just need to go take care of my family. Like you said, this is going to be all over the news, and Marybeth is not doing well. I'm assuming you have him in custody by now?"

Grady nodded, "Yeah, he is being held at the station. He is with his lawyer right now."

Loomis nodded, gave one last squeeze to Grady's hand and walked away. Grady was left standing there looking at Loomis walk away, and as any good detective would have, he felt a pang of unease. He couldn't pinpoint what it was, but he had learned to listen to his gut instincts long ago.

◆

Steven Loomis was deep in thought as he headed home. He had been thinking about what to say to his family. Christopher was too young, but Bethany was old enough to understand and he knew how cruel kids could be sometimes.

Marybeth had been in a world of her own for weeks now, going in and out of bouts of deep depression and manic energy. She and Steven had not really communicated with each other since this all started, and now he had to go home and not only confirm what they were almost certain of, but he had to give her the details of what had happened to Tracy, as much as he thought she could handle, anyway.

With everything happening in the past weeks, Christmas had come and gone almost unnoticed by both of them. It had been only his in-laws that had made one even possible for his kids. New Year's had also come and gone like any other day.

This was going to be everywhere for a while and Steven knew Marybeth was going to fall apart. He had to convince her to go to her parents' house and he was going to need his mother-in-law to help him convince her.

The bigger question was what he was going to do. He had already accepted his daughter's death and had begun the mourning process that he knew would come. He thought he was ready for anything, but clearly what he had seen tonight was nowhere in the realm of what he had considered.

In his former life he had seen carnage, had seen children blown apart, sometimes by weapons deployed by his own country. He knew the horror and psychological trauma that seeing a child in that condition could do to a parent, so it wasn't the graphic nature of what he had seen that had landed a blow straight into his psyche. It was that there was just no reasoning behind it, no reasoning he could understand.

In all of the experiences he had in the service, as horrific as they might have been, he had been able to discern a line of thought, of rational thought that had led to the moment. Greed, religious fanatics, political dissidents, there was always an undercurrent he could recognize, but not here. All he had found at the warehouse was foreign to him; it had no purpose, no notion of a cause as misguided as that cause might have been. Even in genocide there was a belief, a shared belief, as completely misguided and wrong as it was, that what was being done was being done for the greater good of a people. Individuals had taken advantage of that belief for the sake of power or money or devotion, and he knew there was an element of insanity in every one of those individuals, but once again this was different to him.

In all his experiences, Steven Loomis had never been able to truly believe or actually feel the presence of evil, pure evil, not until tonight. What he had felt and seen tonight didn't fit into anything that he had learned through a lifetime of war, violence and tragedy. To Steven, whatever had compelled Riche was outside the parameters of what he had drawn for humanity, and those were some wide parameters. Ironically, it was precisely his experiences that had made sure his view of humanity was very pliable and broad in what could be defined as human behavior and motivation. No matter how he turned it, no matter how he tried to relate it to the things he had seen before, Loomis just couldn't wrap his mind around the fact that a human being had done this and had done it on purpose, with dedication and care.

There had been instances before where he had questioned the sanity of some of the enemies he had encountered, where he had pondered whether there might be something out there, something that just didn't fit into what he had been taught was within the realm of humanity. He had certainly considered that possibility before. He had wondered what the purpose or mission was for people like Dennis Rader, the BTK Killer, or Ted Bundy or Jeffrey Dahmer, and now he had his answer.

They weren't people at all. They didn't fit into the realm of human parameters. He could not bring himself to accept that he belonged to the same species of animal that could engage in this kind of cruelty, this kind of predatory behavior.

Now what he had started researching, what he had read about, a different species beyond what could be defined as a psychopath, became real for him. It wasn't just that he understood it, it was that he *felt* it. There were those that researched things like this, people who tried to explain the why of things, but all the explaining in the world meant nothing until you felt it inside. He likened it to being told about the power of the sea, about the immense vastness, all told by men that had more salt water in their veins than blood. As a young Navy officer he listened and understood and tried to learn, but it wasn't until he saw, until he felt 50-foot swells in the Atlantic tossing an aircraft carrier around like a toy, that he truly understood that power and the fear that it brought with it.

He had come face-to-face with evil tonight, not the kind you hear or read about or the kind people write books about, but the kind that grips your heart and turns everything you thought you knew about the world around you upside down. There was enough introspection left in him to know that he was going to do something about it. Maybe he didn't have all the answers and maybe he wasn't trying to come up with any, he just knew that right now, in this case, with the animal that had taken and butchered his daughter he was going to do something.

He thought he knew what he had to do, but everything was still too fresh, and he knew better than to make decisions without considering everything. Like all good spec ops officers, he understood that in any situation there were tactical considerations, but always in pursuit of a strategy, of a bigger endgame.

Tonight, in the drive between that hell hole and his house, he had come up with the outline of a tactical plan.

The car finally got back to the house. Steven paid the driver and got out. He had been so engrossed in his own thinking throughout the drive home that he had not yet figured out what he was going to say to Marybeth. Maybe that was better; maybe if he just went with his instinct, it would be better than something that sounded made up and insincere.

As he walked in the door, he knew immediately he would not have the chance to bring it up himself, the television was on and Marybeth and her mother were sitting in the living room watching it.

After he took off his coat and before he could come into the living room, Marybeth met him in the hallway, "Is it true? They know what happened?"

Steven put his keys down on the table and paused for a couple of seconds before answering, "Yes, honey, they know what happened and they know who did it. Well, they think they know who did it."

Marybeth, her face streaked with tears, was once again close to the breaking point and as her mother was coming to try to help, she finally let go, "What does that mean? What do you mean they think they know who did it? Do they or don't they?! How can you not know about something like that! Can't you do something, can't you ask someone?!"

Her mother tried to hold her, but Marybeth shrugged her off and kept on, "What happened to her, Steven? You tell me what happened to her! She was my baby, damn it, and she was alone, and it was my fault! Please, please let me know what happened to her!"

Steven stepped forward and put his arms around her without saying anything. Marybeth struggled at first and tried to break free, but eventually she just broke down into deep sobs and allowed her husband to comfort her.

"Shh, it's okay, honey, she is at peace now, they all are. Just let it come, baby, let it out."

She could not stop sobbing and crying out, "She was alone, Steven! She was alone when she died, I wasn't there for her, and he took her and I wasn't there for her!"

Steven just held on, "You were there for her, you were always there for her. Now you just have to let her go, be at peace."

Lucy, Marybeth's mother, put her hands on her daughter's shoulders, she was also crying but was keeping it under control for the sake of her daughter. "That's right, honey, you are a wonderful mother and your other children need you."

Marybeth looked into Steven's eyes with disbelief and for the first time, resentment, "What's the matter with you?! Our daughter is dead! She is gone and all you have to say is that I have to let her go! He took her from us, took her from me, don't you see that? Don't you care? How can you just stand there and tell me to let her go?!"

Her mother put her arms around her from behind and tried to soothe her, "Beth, you need to calm down. You have two other children that need you. They are going to look to you to figure out how to deal with this, especially Bethany.

"Now, let's go in the bedroom and take your medicine, honey, you need it right now." Marybeth let go of Steven and walked away from both him and her mother.

As she walked away, she turned back just long enough to respond to her mother, "What kind of a mother am I going to be for them? I couldn't take care of my little girl, how am I going to take care of my other two children?"

With that she walked into the bedroom and slammed the door.

Steven stood in the middle of the hallway, head hung, his own tears welling up in the corners of his eyes. His mother-in-law walked over to him and also hugged him as she let go and started crying herself, "Steven, I am so sorry, so, so sorry."

Steven hugged her back and talked softly to her as they held each other, "Lucy, she won't make it through this. It is going to be everywhere. You already saw it on TV and they haven't even finished processing the scene.

"This is ugly, Lucy, the loss of Tracy and all the other little girls is horrible enough, but it is much uglier than that and it will break Beth. She is already on the brink and if she keeps hearing what everyone has to say, what the experts have to say, and you know that there will be pictures and blogs on the Internet, she won't make it. Do you think they can go back with you and Tom?"

She pulled back and wiped the tears from his face, "Of course, dear, of course. I have already been talking about it to her and I think she understands. Bethany's school is aware of the situation. They completely understand and will do whatever they need to when she comes back."

Steven looked up into her eyes and felt a sense of relief, a sense that his family was covered. He had always taken pride in believing that he was the one to provide that security, that cover, but now he knew he wouldn't be able to care for his wife the way she needed to be cared for, not right now.

Marybeth Loomis was going to need a lot of help and time to get over this, and as guilty as it made him feel, as powerless as he felt, he knew he couldn't provide that help, not yet.

He smiled at his mother-in-law, "Thank you, Lucy, I honestly don't know how we would have made it without your help, without the whole family's help."

She knew he himself had no immediate family and took his face in her hands, "Of course, that's what families do for each other, and this is your family, all of us, don't you forget that."

He clung on tighter and let the tears flow, he let himself be comforted, something that he hadn't done until now.

"Steven, I have always thought of you as a son and I know you are hurting too. It's okay to let go, to allow yourself to grieve and feel the loss. It's going to be hard to get past this if you keep it all in."

They held each other in silence for a few more seconds and then Steven composed himself and gently pulled away, "I know, Lucy, trust me, I know. I'm trying to figure out how to get past this myself. I just know I can't be there for Beth and the kids the way they need me to be there for them right now.

"I need to figure out arrangements for Tracy and I really need to have you and everyone else in the family be there for Beth and the kids. I am planning on it being something small, just family and just the family that can make the trip easily. This doesn't need to be, can't be, too elaborate. Once that is done then I think they need to go with you as soon as possible."

Lucy answered, "Of course, do you need help with the arrangements?"

Steven shook his head, "No, I've got that covered. Everyone at the office has really stepped up for me, especially our CEO."

Before letting him walk away, Lucy grabbed Steven's arm one last time, "I mean it, Steven, if you don't let it out, let it all out, it will eat at you for the rest of your life." Steven gave her a sad smile, nodded and walked away.

Chapter 10

teven left early the next morning because he knew he was going to have a busy day. He had actually reached out to Doctor Tyrone Leonard the previous day and, surprisingly enough, he had agreed to meet with Steven at his office on campus. That had been before news of Riche and the girls had hit the wires.

A young graduate assistant showed Steven to Leonard's office. The door was open and Dr. Tyrone Leonard was on the phone. He waved for Steven to come in and motioned him to have a seat in one of the chairs in the office, the only one without a stack of books on it. His first impression of Leonard was that the man was whip-smart. He was short in stature, probably no more than 5'5'' or 5'6''and a build leaning toward stocky with deep ebony skin and hair that was now completely white. What caused the biggest impression were his eyes, however, which were a honey color and spoke of years and years of education and experience, both in his profession and in his life, but they also held a brightness, a sense of joy that was hard to miss.

He was finishing his phone conversation as Steven took a seat, "I'll be happy to do the interview, but I'm afraid we'll have to do it here on campus…that's correct, I simply can't take the time to come in and do it at your studio…okay, I will talk to you then…you're welcome. Goodbye."

He turned to face Steven and welcomed him with an outstretched hand, "Mr. Loomis? Tyrone Leonard."

Steven shook his hand, "That's right, Doctor, I'm sorry to interrupt. We can reschedule the meeting if you'd like."

Leonard smiled broadly and waved with his hands, "Oh, don't worry about that. I don't know if you've heard, but there was a break in the case of the girls' disappearance that has been on the news lately."

His demeanor changed a bit and took on a sad, but pensive look, "They found their remains in a warehouse. They have a man they think is responsible in custody."

Then just like that, he brightened up again and continued, "So, you can imagine that given my work and my field of expertise, there are a lot of journalists wanting to do an interview, always looking for an angle, I suppose."

As Leonard was speaking, Steven debated with himself whether to tell him about Tracy. He decided against it. If he told the man his daughter had been one of Riche's victims, it might taint his opinion or worse yet, it might make him so uncomfortable that he just refused to talk to him.

Steven was sure that the man would put it together before the day was over in any case, "I understand and I really appreciate you agreeing to meet with me."

Leonard nodded, "Always happy to speak with someone with genuine interest in our work. I think you'll find that to be true of almost every scientist. Now, how can I help you?"

Steven hadn't really come prepared with questions for the man, but he knew what he was looking for, so that seemed like the best place to start, "Well, Professor, I have been reading a lot of your research, what I could find anyways, and I think I understand what your conclusions are. I just don't quite understand how you got there."

Leonard, smile still on his face, leaned back in his chair and asked, "Okay, and what is it that you think I have concluded."

Steven leaned forward, "As I understand it, you have come to the conclusion that there is another type of human, that evolution has changed some humans so far that they are now a part of a different species."

Leonard shook his head slightly, "Well, Mr. Loomis, you have part of it right, but you have one big part that is wrong." Steven waited for him to go on.

"You are correct in that my conclusions have come about as a result of the study of evolution and natural selection, but you are wrong in your understanding that what I found is a different type of human. What I have found is a different subspecies of human altogether. For practical purposes, a different species from humans. Scientifically we are defined as *Homo sapiens*, are we agreed on that?" Steven nodded. "Okay, that means we are a part of the *Homo* genus and our species is *sapiens*, hence *Homo sapiens*. Technically, however, it is *Homo sapiens sapiens*, the subspecies for modern man. The oldest evidence of what we now consider human was found recently, in 2003, and they date back 160,000 years. That fossil defined something that has come to be known as *Homo sapiens idaltu*. So the genus is *Homo*, the species is *sapiens* and the subspecies is *Idaltu*. Are you following me?"

Steven was fascinated, "Absolutely. I had never heard of what you are talking about."

Leonard's smile widened, "You are not unique. Most people haven't. The reason that finding was so significant is because as you and I both know, most of science believed that we evolved from Neanderthals, which based on this finding is obviously not the case." Steven now looked lost. "Forgive me, I'm used to speaking with scientists. The reason it is clear we did *not* evolve from Neanderthals as previously believed is because this fossil, the Idaltu fossil, predates Neanderthals by 85,000 years. That means, obviously, that they existed before the Neanderthal. So, all of this means that we have had to revisit the whole evolutionary process."

Steven's look let Leonard know that he did not get how any of this related to what he had asked.

Leonard recognized it and chuckled, "As always, I digress. As you can tell, I am very invested in this science and sometimes I don't know when I am going off course. Back to my work. I had been doing research for more than 30 years on how humans have evolved and specifically on the possibility that we share the planet with another species within the *Homo* genus, a species distinct from *Homo sapiens sapiens*. So, we are not talking about a different type of human, but a different species from modern humans, still in the *Homo* genus.

"Until now, science has only recognized *sapiens sapiens* as the only species and subspecies existing within the *Homo* genus, and what I am proposing is that now there are *two* subspecies under the *Homo* genus, *Homo sapiens sapiens* and what I have called *Homo sapiens predaer,* or *Homo predator*. For purposes of our discussion, we'll simplify and just make it *Homo sapiens* and *Homo predaer*.

"Now you can see why the 2003 discovery was so important, that finding meant that at one point there *was* a different subspecies under the *Homo* genus walking the earth. They were clearly *Homo sapiens*, or human, but different from what we understand as human today. If ones were alive today, I venture to say we would most likely not call them human, we'd define them as a different species, as it should be. It's the same with *Homo sapiens predaer*. We've come to define them as a different species."

Steven now understood better, but still had a few doubts, "I think I get what you're saying, Professor, but what is still confusing me a bit is the whole *Homo sapiens* thing. If they're *Homo sapiens,* doesn't that mean they are in fact human, which would mean they're the same species as us, wouldn't it?"

Leonard smiled more broadly. He had clearly been asked this question or one very similar to it. "No worries, it's something I get asked a lot. So rather than speaking in terms of human, let's talk about it in terms of canines, shall we?"

Steven nodded. Leonard explained, "Okay, well, the wolf's binomial name, scientific name if you will, is *Canis lupus.* I think when I talk to you about a wolf, you would most likely agree with me that while it is within the canine family, it is quite different from a family dog, would you not?" Steven nodded, "Of course. I think anybody would." Leonard continued, "That's right and it wouldn't just be you. Society as a whole views family dogs quite differently than they do wolves. I venture to guess that if someone shot a wolf that came onto their property, they'd be completely exonerated, they'd be shooting something that could harm them or their family. I also venture to guess that if the same thing happened with a family dog, the individual would be prosecuted for their actions." Steven nodded again, "I'm with you so far."

Leonard leaned back, ready to bring it all together, "And yet the wolf and the family dog are both *Canis lupus,* but the family dog is actually *Canis lupus familiaris,* the family dog. So both are in the same species family, but the family dog is a different subspecies from *Canis lupus.*"

Steven paused for a second and then nodded. It made sense to him and Leonard noticed the look of someone for whom a light bulb had just gone off.

He chuckled, "Now you see why this science has been my life." Steven nodded, "I do, I really do. How were these 'humans' they found in 2003 different?" Leonard explained, "They were much larger than modern humans, their musculature and the size of their brain cavity was larger. Before you ask, I will tell you. No, this was not a form of Neanderthal or other human predecessor.

"The skull did not have the broad frontal extrusion or 'bump' of the brow and their brain case was round, not football-shaped as was the case with human predecessors. These were in fact a subspecies of human, the same way *Homo sapiens sapiens* and *Homo sapiens predaer* are subspecies of human.

"The term subspecies is a bit misunderstood. Most people see it as being less evolved or enlightened, but in reality a subspecies simply means it is a more specific or narrow definition of a particular species. The term 'specialized' is derived from the word 'species.' That's why, when I'm speaking with laymen, I simply use *Homo sapiens* when I am referring to us, modern humans, and *Homo predaer* or *Homo predator* when I refer to the other species under the *Homo* genus."

Steven now interjected, "I can see why you'd want to simplify. So the finding in 2003 meant that your theory about a different subspecies from *sapiens* within the *Homo* genus now had more credibility."

Leonard raised his hand, index finger in the air, "Bingo! That's exactly right. As you can imagine, our work has found some very vigorous resistance and just plain disdain all along the way. This changed things. Don't get me wrong, there are still some very zealous detractors and skeptics of our work, and there will always be. I've come to make peace with that, but it is most definitely not the way it was before.

"Anyway, over the past 10 years, and especially over the last three years, we have been able to confirm a lot of our initial hypotheses about the new species. We have better technology and there are far more scientists conducting studies, which means we have a constant influx of new information.

"Since 2003, we have also had a significant increase in our funding. We now have much more reliable numbers as far as population, and we are designing some tests to further confirm our initial definition process."

Steven now wanted to get down to the real reason he was here, "So if I understand you, Professor, you are now *certain* that this species exists, you are not trying to establish whether it does or not. Now you are simply refining how you define them and how many there are."

Leonard nodded, "That's correct, Mr. Loomis, we are certain, or as certain as one can be when it comes to breakthrough science, that is. We *know* they exist. We have established what defines the species and how it is different from humans. We are now trying to examine if there are more fundamental differences, differences at the genetic, chromosome and molecular level, and we are trying to get a read on what percentage of the population could potentially be members of the new species."

That perked Steven's interest, "And how many do you suspect have the potential of being a member of this new species?"

Leonard paused for a beat, "Well, our numbers indicate that the number can be as high as one percent of the total U.S. population. We haven't even begun to think beyond our borders."

Now it was Steven who leaned back in his chair; that meant that about three million people in the U.S. could potentially be members of the new species. A chill came up his back. Three million potential predators, creatures that looked and behaved exactly like humans, but who did it for the purposes of catching their prey.

Leonard could see the wheels spinning in Steven's head. His wasn't an unusual response when numbers were brought up.

Still, Leonard wanted to make sure Steven understood the numbers, "Now those are broad estimates, mind you. And remember that we are talking about three million people that are *potential* members of the species. There are many factors involved, but I think it would be safe to assume there are at least one million individuals who are likely members of the new species."

The number still had an impact on Steven, "One million potential murderers is still a huge number."

Leonard shook his head, "Yes, Mr. Loomis, one million *potential* murderers. Not everyone who is a member of the species has necessarily murdered anyone, although I must admit it is exceedingly rare for us to find a bona fide *Homo predaer* who has not killed yet."

Steven had one more question for Leonard, "So, based on what I've read from you and other researchers, what defines this new species is the level of brutality, the motivations for their crimes and how sophisticated their planning was, is that correct?"

Leonard answered, "That's part of it. We have many elements we look at, but you hit on two of the most important ones.

"We also look at early childhood indicators, environmental influences in the home and beyond, as you said, their level of organization and planning. Then there are, of course, the physiological and cognitive differences, as well as self-defined and measured differences in sensory ability.

"Like I said, there are many elements to defining a *Homo predator*. Also, remember what I said, even if someone is a *Homo predator*, it doesn't mean they've acted on their impulses or desires.

"At the end of the day, however, we almost always begin with well-planned, brutal and sadistic crimes. That's what almost always brings someone to our attention initially, which is why I told you that you had hit two of the most important elements."

His response brought up another question for Steven. "I don't get it, Professor. I will be the first to admit that I am not an expert on evolutionary science, but how is it that when a new species or subspecies emerges, they emerge along what we as humans would consider the most *devolved* of behaviors. I mean, given what I know of human evolution, the Greeks, the Romans, the Mayans and all the other advanced cultures across history, they have all seen this predatory behavior as brutal and something to be punished and deterred.

"And it's not killing I'm talking about. Every one of those cultures and then some have always utilized murder and war as a means to an end. Revenge, religion, and power have all driven humans to kill one another throughout time. But they are *motives*, motives that can be understood. I am talking about killing for sport, for what seems to be the simple joy of killing human beings. Even gladiators killed each other for glory and to perpetuate their name. How is it that these new *evolved* humans all exist within the realm of that type of senseless brutality and sadism?"

A wide smile spread on Leonard's face, Jesus, the guy was engaging, "Very good, Mr. Loomis, very good. Also something our detractors and skeptics bring up. The fact is that there are other scientists also exploring the idea of a new species, but from a very different angle from ours."

Steven waited. He wanted Leonard to go on and the scientist complied, "I think the best way to explain it to you would be like this. We can agree that within the realm of humanity there is a continuum of behavior, a continuum where there are incredibly good, almost saintly people or even deities on one end and incredibly cruel and evil people on the other end, right? We are all familiar with the idea of God and the devil. That must be the most basic example of the continuum we are talking about. "

Loomis nodded. Leonard went on, "Okay, I think we can also agree that most of us actually fall somewhere in the middle. That is, some of us lean more to one side than the other, but for all intents and purposes, we all reside somewhere in the middle, most of us in a continual struggle to lean toward the good."

Steven nodded again. He thought he could see where Leonard was going, "And you think that this new species also has that same spread."

Leonard nodded, "That's the idea. As is the case with humans, *Homo predaer* that exist at the fringes, on either end, are the ones that stand out the most, the ones that draw our attention and thus the first to be found or defined.

"My interest, my education, my work and my career have always dealt with deviant human behavior. From very early on, I decided to concentrate on establishing the reasons that humans, psychopaths, sociopaths and others with mental deficiencies, do the things they do and to try to understand it at the very edges of established norms, where new science is found.

"It was only natural that if there was something beyond *my* end of the human spectrum, the bad end for lack of a better word, I would be likely to run into it.

"So, to finally answer your question, we call them evolved from a survival of the species and natural selection standpoint, not from the standpoint of altruism.

"The fact of the matter, Mr. Loomis, is that there is now a species higher on the food chain than humans, there is a new apex predator sharing the planet with us."

Leonard said this last part with a thin smile on his face, but there was something else there too, worry, serious worry.

Steven, now getting up, had one last question, "You said there are other scientists studying the new species, but not at your end of the spectrum. Do you know any of them?"

Leonard thought for a second, "I know a few of them from conferences I have attended around the world. There are some incredibly interesting studies going on in Germany and Holland. The best one here in the states is Dr. Jim Scoma out at the University of

California at Irvine. He is a character, but a brilliant scientist. His work has delved more into the opposite end of the spectrum from mine."

Now at the door, Steven, surprised by that, stopped and asked with a bit of sarcasm, "You mean people like saints, like Jesus or John Paul II or Mother Theresa?"

Leonard, now standing himself, chuckled, "That's a bit further down the spectrum from where he is looking, but in essence, yes, he is more dedicated to individuals who also fall outside of human norms in many of the same ways, from a physiological or a sensory ability standpoint for instance, who lead normal lives, but who do extraordinary things, not just once, but on an ongoing basis. He has more of an uphill battle than those of us on the other end of the spectrum, believe it or not."

Steven looked puzzled, "Oh? How's that?"

Leonard's smile widened again, "You see, we're more likely to accept that acts of predation or hunting behavior can in fact define another species, something not human. But when it comes to acts of extraordinary kindness or altruism, we want to believe that they are the actions of our species.

"We want the good and are more willing to accept the bad is the result of evolution. When I say we are willing to accept the result of evolution, I mean it in a hypothetical sense, of course. The fact is that both areas of research, Dr. Scoma's and mine, have found very vigorous detractors and naysayers, not the least of which has been the religious establishment."

Steven could understand it. It was human nature.

Leonard turned, sifted through some papers on his desk, found a pen and wrote down a number. "Here, this is Dr. Scoma's number. I'm sure he would have no problem chatting with you about his work."

Steven took the paper and shook Leonard's hand, "Thank you for your time, Dr. Leonard, I appreciate it."

Leonard nodded, "It was a pleasure, Mr. Loomis. I'm always up for talking about my work. I hope I have answered your questions and given you what you were looking for."

Steven looked at the man directly and held his eyes for just a beat, "You have, Professor, you have, again, thank you." He turned and walked down the hall he had come from. He made it to the street and caught a cab almost immediately.

◆

Harvey Lynch had gotten exactly six hours of intermittent sleep in the last three days. Even with every one of his clerks and paralegals handling calls and preparing for their case, he still could not separate his role as an attorney from his capacity to understand what he had heard his client tell him as a human being. He had spent a total of 12 hours speaking with Donald Riche and for the first time in his career was truly at a loss as to how to best proceed. He knew he would have to represent him at the arraignment and enter a plea, but he still didn't know exactly what that plea was going to be. In all of the time he had spent with him, and no matter how many times he explained that he would have to enter a plea, he had not gotten a straight response from Riche. What he had gotten had been some of the most horrific mental images he could have ever imagined and a look into the mind of a true monster.

Donald Riche had laid everything out for Lynch; he knew he was his attorney and the duty that entailed. He knew if Lynch wanted to drop him as a client he would now need to formally petition the court to do so, and based on Lynch's reaction, Donald Riche knew Lynch was not going to drop him as a client, regardless of how much he might want to.

Now, with the arraignment looming, Lynch was determined to get Riche to understand that he would have to stand in front of a judge and answer whether he was guilty of the charges being brought against him or not.

Riche was being held at the central holding facility, which is where Lynch was headed for his third interview with Riche. After the first two, Lynch had developed a thicker skin for the things Riche was telling him, what he could still not get over was the way Riche looked when he was talking about what he'd done.

From the beginning he had acknowledged everything he had done, how he had done it and why he had done it. He had explained to Lynch that since he was a young boy he knew his destiny was to correct what nature had gotten wrong, he knew that a power greater than him had placed him on the earth to right what man and the world had ruined over the ages. He didn't consider himself as one of 'them,' something that also included Lynch, he existed in a body that wasn't his and he knew the reason for that. He had to fit into what the world considered normal in order for him to carry out his mandate.

He had explained how he had tried to correct women when they were older but had found out they were too far gone, that in order for his craft to reach the sublime level it was meant to he, had to get the girls when they were pure of body and soul, before they were corrupted by the world around them and their imperfect parents.

It wasn't all of this or the gruesome details that still got to Harvey, those things had given him nightmares every time he closed his eyes for the past two days, but it had gotten easier to listen to over time. It was the joy, the sheer delight that Riche's eyes reflected when he talked about it.

Harvey Lynch had seen some of the preliminary photographs from the scene and read some of the coroner's reports and had a hard time reconciling that carnage with the almost giddy mood that Riche got in when Lynch laid the pictures out on the table and started to explain what the prosecution and the police had by way of evidence. He had looked at the photographs not with regret or sadness, but with *pride*.

Today, he would have to get Riche to let him know what he was planning on pleading or how he wanted to proceed with the case. Harvey had already explained that it was customary to plead not guilty at the arraignment in order to let all of the evidence be processed, regardless of what he would want to do later on in the process. Basically Harvey was just going to ask Riche to plead not guilty to give him the time he needed to mount a defense.

After listening to Harvey, Donald looked at him with almost pity in his eyes, "Harvey, Harvey, of course I am going to say I am not guilty. What would you have me plead guilty to?"

Lynch looked at him, not able to believe what he was hearing, "Donald, what are you talking about?! There are nine dead little girls and there is a mountain of evidence showing you did it! You told me you did it and it is illegal, do you understand that?! Everything you are being accused of is a horrible crime in New York, it is a horrible crime anywhere in the world!"

Donald continued with the condescending tone, "Of course it is, in *your* world, do *you* understand that? There is more out there and you and everyone in your world will never understand the grander picture, the mandate. You kill each other without purpose and for that there should be a punishment, but mine is a purpose beyond anything your world will understand.

"I don't know this for a fact, but something beyond me tells me there are others, there are others who have their own mandates, their own destiny. I would like to think I was the only one destined to correct the things man has screwed up, but I am not worthy of being the only emissary of destiny. I am not the first one, you know I'm not, and I won't be the last and you know that too.

"Don't worry, Harvey, when we get up in front of that judge, I will tell him and the world I am not guilty because there is nothing to be guilty about."

Harvey breathed a sigh of relief, "Okay, but in this hearing you will only say 'Not guilty,' do you understand? We will have plenty of time to let the world know about everything you want them to know as the case goes on, but at the arraignment you just say 'Not guilty,' you got that? Just that." Trinity leaned back in his chair and crossed his legs and with a comfortable smile simply said, "Yes, I will say just that. You're right, there will be enough time to tell the world, to explain the beauty of what I was doing, of what needs to be done."

Harvey packed the photos, his notes and his pocket recorder, something he had begun using in his conversations with Riche, more than anything to protect himself and to have some sort of record of what had transpired between them. As his attorney he would never release the tape, but as a human being he would have it and put it in a safe place, should anything happen to him. Someone, some doctor somewhere would surely make use of this, trying to understand what it was that this man, this creature was actually made of, what made him tick.

"Good. Now, Donald, you understand you still shouldn't talk to anyone, right? No one at all."

Donald, still relaxed and content, said, "Yes, Harvey, I understand, all in good time, all in good time."

Harvey finished packing his things and left the interviewing room. At least he knew they could get through the arraignment without much trouble. After that, he was still trying to figure out how to come at it.

It was obvious the guy was guilty, he confessed to everything and there was a mountain of forensic evidence that could convict him, even if he was able to somehow prove he was in an entirely different continent when the girls went missing. So the "who" was not in contention, neither was the "how." There was also a mountain of evidence making it very clear how he had done it. The big question was why, and from what Lynch had heard over the last few days, it was clear that this man was sick. He was a schizophrenic or a psychopath or a sociopath or something much worse, that would be something that the experts would have to determine. Lynch knew if this went to trial it was going to be all about some sort of fucked up childhood and how it affected Riche as an adult. The whole guilty by reason of insanity went out the window when Riche had explained in detail how he lured his victims, how and why he rented the warehouse in the industrial park and how he had been careful, almost meticulous about not leaving any evidence. No, Donald Riche was definitely not going to go down the 'Not Guilty By Reason of Insanity' route. Even if he had the best medical and psychiatric experts money could buy, the political fallout from anything but a conviction with the maximum sentence allowable by law was not something anyone involved in the case, from the mayor to the commissioner to the DA, were willing to bet their reelections on. At this point, Lynch was angling for some sort of plea that would put Riche away for life without the possibility of parole by having him plead guilty to some of the cases and pleading guilty to lesser-included offenses for the rest.

Lynch had been around the block, however, and he knew that the political value of a televised trial with all the world watching was worth millions if not billions to too many people up for reelection, so the likelihood that they would be willing to give up their day in court and the opportunity to grandstand and come in as the knight in shining armor rescuing New York from this monster was slim indeed.

Harvey Lynch was a smart and competent, if somewhat uptight attorney and one of the things that made him smart and competent was knowing that there was no way in hell his small law office would be able to shoulder the weight this case carried with it. He had already put out half a dozen calls to high-profile litigators that might be willing to partner with him when this thing went to trial. So far, only three had been willing to talk and only after negotiating extremely favorable financial terms for themselves. Lynch didn't care, after hearing what he had heard from his client, all he wanted was to have this thing over with as soon as possible so he could begin the counseling and recovery process he knew he would need after this.

Chapter 11

Felix Garcia headed straight down to the precinct. It had been a few days now since the arrest and he had kept his reporting low-key and to the point, all in the hope that Grady would give him 20 minutes where he wouldn't hold anything back. He understood that the first couple of days after the arrest had been a madhouse of forensic evidence, public information, coordination of involved agencies and all the rest, but now he felt there was enough of a lull in the action that Grady could give him 20 minutes of his time.

He headed down to the precinct not willing to take no for an answer. He would wait hours if he had to, but he had held up his bargain with Grady and now wanted some reciprocity. He walked in and as usual said hello to the watch sergeant and asked for Grady, and as usual he was told Detective Grady was busy, but if he wanted to leave a note or a message, the watch sergeant would be more than happy to relay it to him.

Felix finally lost his patience, "C'mon, Sarge, you know me and you know Grady and I have a working relationship, so how about you let him know I'm here and that I just need twenty minutes of his time."

The watch sergeant, an old hand at dealing with reporters, said, "I know, I know, trust me, Felix I know, but you've seen what it's like around here, we've got guys that haven't been home in two days, Grady being one of them. If I let you through, you know he'll have my ass."

Felix answered, "I get it and I don't want to be a nuisance, but he and I came to an understanding and I've held up my end of that understanding. If I can't get just a few minutes with him, I'm going to have to go with whatever sources I can dig up, right or wrong.

"You know all the bullshit that's being floated out there about the NYPD not doing their job and about how this guy should have been stopped much sooner."

Garcia knew he was pushing the right buttons because an expression of indignation came over the sergeant's face, "What the fuck did they want us to do, go knocking doors down? And if we had, we'd have some fucking liberal group crying about civil rights and all that other bullshit."

Felix was nodding, "Exactly and I just want to get things right, my paper wants to make sure everyone knows everything that could have been done was done. That's what I want to talk to Detective Grady about and it won't take more than 20 minutes of his time."

Watch Sergeant Simms thought about it for a beat and said, "Just wait right here."

He went to an office in the back, picked up a phone and dialed. After what seemed to be an animated conversation, he came back. "Alright, you have 10 minutes and not a second more."

Garcia picked up his briefcase and made his way to Bob Grady's office. He knocked on the door and came in at the same time, "Hello, detective."

Grady looked up from his desk, "What's up, Garcia? As you can see, we're a little busy around here, so make it quick."

Garcia sat down without being invited, "You and I had a conversation, and if I remember correctly, we had a tacit understanding that I'd keep my pieces low-key and to the point and you'd share more with me when you got something."

Grady stopped shuffling papers and looked up incredulous, "Are you fucking serious? Look around, Felix, this place is a madhouse, I can't remember the last time I got more than three hours of consecutive sleep. I've been dealing with the task force, the media, the DA and some of your colleagues from the tabloid rags, and you expect me to come find you with every piece of new information?"

Garcia answered, "No, I don't, but I do expect that you send me an email or call in response to mine even if it just to tell me you can't get together now. I just need five minutes of your time; you know there is a whole bunch of information out on this already. I know most of it is bullshit, but there is enough there for me to put together a story. I just wanted to see if there's anything out there that's just blatantly wrong or made up. I still want to keep my pieces low-key and factual. I'm staying away from the sensationalistic angle all together. There's plenty of that out there already. I just thought you might help me keep it that way."

Grady looked at him for a few seconds and let a hint of a smile creep across his face, "Alright, alright, you made your point. What is it you're looking for?"

Garcia pulled out his computer and began, "Can you tie Riche to all the disappearances in New York?"

Grady answered him, "Yes, at this point we have enough forensic evidence to tie him to all the disappearances of the girls that went missing that fit the profile."

Felix went on, "Any indication whether there may be more victims out there?"

Grady, now looking down at his paperwork, said "We haven't had a chance to interview Riche. He lawyered up when we went to his house, and we haven't been able to interview him without his attorney. No way to know. If I were a betting man, though, I'd bet there are a lot more victims."

Garcia was typing into his computer and Grady looked up from what he was doing, "You know you can't print that, right? That's just my opinion."

Felix smiled, "Aw, c'mon, you know I know better than that, besides you'd have to be pretty slow to think these nine were his first or would have been his last. Don't worry, I won't print that. We'll just go with the standard 'At this point it is unknown whether Riche can be tied to other missing girls cases around the country' or something to that effect."

Grady knew he liked the kid for a reason. He wasn't pushy and had the common sense that could only be acquired from the world he came from, he was also a good strategic reporter, opting to go for the exclusives and the more serious and real side of a story rather than the knee-jerk reaction of someone who just wanted to sell papers by writing about blood.

"Anything else, Felix? As you can see, I got a shitload of paperwork to deal with, not to mention the goddamned Mayor's office calling every 20 minutes to find out what is going on."

Felix had thought about it for a while, and he was at conflict with himself because he couldn't get past that it might just be morbid curiosity rather than journalistic acumen that prompted him to ask the next question.

In the end he had to compromise a bit of both, "Is there any chance that I could look at some of the crime scene photographs?"

Grady looked up and looked at him intensely, without blinking.

He liked the kid and wanted to help him, but what he was asking for might derail what to Grady seemed to be a promising career, "Listen, Felix, in this line of work, you better than anybody know that the things we see, the things we deal with, are a reflection of what humanity has to offer. We in the force ask all the time how some of the things that we see can ever come to pass. If you are religious, it is enough to make you question your faith. I imagine that given the things you cover, you also ask those questions from time to time and that's part of the game, that's part of what we signed on for, and so we develop leather skin and look at it as part of the world we chose for ourselves.

"This is different. You know how long I've been at this and you know the things I've seen and the people I've had to deal with. And none of it, and I mean *none* of it, in more than 20 years prepared me for this. We have first responders that are being treated for posttraumatic stress disorder, we have three beat cops that resigned the day after we found the warehouse.

"You're a good reporter and I know you want to get as much of the actual facts as you can, but son, this is one that will change you forever. So you have to decide whether you are willing to cover the stories you need to cover with an objective eye, with the cold and fact-based way of a reporter, or whether you want to bring your soul into this.

"I'll show you the pictures. You've been square with me and I will be square with you, but I just thought that I had to warn you that once you ring a bell it can't be unrung."

Felix Garcia sat in complete silence. Of all the responses he could have anticipated Grady giving him, this was not in the realm of possibility. He was willing to share, but Felix could see Grady had genuine concern about doing it. Concern for *him*. As a human being, he was definitely leaning to not looking at the pictures. As a reporter, though, he couldn't let something like this pass him by, "Duly noted, detective, but you know I have to see them. I have to have some perspective when I write what I write, and there is so much speculation and bullshit out there that I need to ground my work in what actually happened, as hard as that might be to look at."

Grady looked at him for a couple more seconds and slid a legal-sized envelope across the desk to Garcia. He didn't say a word. Felix took the envelope and began sifting through the photographs and as he did so he started to question his judgment. The color drained completely from his face. He knew what he was looking at didn't add any journalistic value to anything he might write, and he now knew that whatever he might have imagined in his head did not come close to what he was looking at.

Grady was right, he wasn't a greenhorn whose biggest shock had been a bad car accident. Felix Garcia had been around a bit and had seen some of the most brutal crimes one human could commit against another, but this, this was different. This was far beyond what the human imagination, even one that had been exposed to the worst in man, could come up with.

He finished looking at the pictures and all he could manage was, "Jesus Christ…"

Grady took the envelope back from him and looked at him again. The kid was young and still learning, and Grady was willing to bet that this had been one of the most profound lessons that Felix Garcia had gotten in his young career.

◆

Tracy Loomis's service had been a small private affair. Even the media respected the service, staying at least a few hundred yards from the family and guests. Relatives that were able to make it to New York on short notice had been present as well as some of the families with which the Loomis family had had a relationship through the girls. Marybeth had gone through the whole process in a near-catatonic state, and Steven knew he needed to get her out of New York as soon as possible. As promised, his in-laws had made arrangements for her and the kids to go back with them for as long as it was necessary.

The day after the service, as everyone was packing and getting ready to leave, his mother-in-law caught him staring out the living room window in contemplation. "Steven, we are almost ready to head out."

He turned around and smiled at her, "Thank you, Lucy, thank you so much. In all of this chaos, the one thing that I have been able to count on has been you and Tom, and I can't tell you what that means to me. Take care of Marybeth, she needs it more than anyone right now, and slowly try to get the kids to understand what happened."

Lucy grabbed both of his hands, "You know we will, you don't have to worry about them, they will be well taken care of. What about you, Steven, what are you going to do?"

Steven looked out over the city before answering, "I'm going to try to get back to work, to get my mind occupied with something else and to try to figure out how to move forward from here."

Lucy squeezed his hands and let go, "Well, if you ever need to just disconnect, to deal with this on your own terms, you know our home will always be open to you. Your family will be waiting there, when you're ready."

Steven put his hands on her shoulders and squeezed, "I know it. Thank you and Tom for everything."

Lucy turned and left the living room and Steven went on looking over the city. He didn't want to seem as if he too was falling apart. He wanted to seem as though he was going to try to get back to his normal routine, go through the grieving process that was sure to come and eventually join his family. The reality, however, was much different. In the past three days, Steven Loomis had gone through a deep introspection trying to find what felt right to him. From the beginning he knew he would have to do something about this and had been trying to decide exactly what that would be. He had thought about coordinating with the DA and NYPD and making the resources of his company available to them, but the political angle had shot that idea out of the water almost immediately. He had considered forming a group of the parents of the victims, but as he thought about it more and more, that would not address what he felt needed to be addressed the most. It had not been until 2 o'clock the previous morning that he had come to a final decision as to what he would do. It wasn't a decision made out of anger or desperation, it was a decision he had carefully considered and one that he knew would be the only one to bring him peace, perhaps not immediately, but eventually.

As he watched his family packing to leave and said goodbye to his children and wife, Steven Loomis felt the most at peace since this whole ordeal had started. Beth was still in a haze, something he knew would be the case for some time. He didn't want to push her, so he just simply let her know he was there and would be there when she was ready.

After seeing his wife and children off to the airport, Steven headed over to the office. Everyone was gone for the day, except for the odd office where the lights were still on, lights that Steven could see in various floors. He greeted the guard and headed for the elevator. He headed to the only elevator that went to the top floor, Art Goodman's office. Loomis knew he would still be there; he was always the last one to leave. Steven walked from the elevator to his office. All the hallways were dark and the only light illuminating his way was coming from underneath the General's door.

Steven knocked on the door and Goodman responded from his desk, "Come in."

Steven walked in and directly to the front of his desk, "Listen, sir, I just wanted to say thank you for everything you and the company have done for us. I just don't know how I could ever say thank you enough."

The General looked at Steven for a second, opened a drawer in his desk and pulled out a humidor with Cuban cigars.

He turned the box toward Steven, "Montecristo? They're the real thing, you know, not that Dominican crap."

Steven smiled and said, "Sounds tempting, but no, thank you."

Goodman bit off the tip of the cigar and lit it. Being the CEO had its perks, but being the General was the ultimate perk.

After a couple of initial puffs, he looked at Steven and said, "You know, Steven, a long time ago I made an oath, an oath to honor and defend my country and our way of life, and it's an oath I have carried with me my entire life. Part of that oath also included taking care of all the people that were a part of my team. That held true in war and it holds true here.

"You are a good man, Steven, a good executive and a great father and husband. I wasn't helping you out, neither were any of the others, not really, they were just being true to themselves, just as you would have been."

Steven stood, just listening. The General was coming to a point and Steven knew it, but as always he was coming to the point at his own pace.

Goodman once again reached under his desk and brought out a bottle, "Single malt Scotch, 21 years old. It's the only thing I drink, this and my damn cigars are my only vices, but I suppose a man could do worse."

He didn't bother to offer Steven a glass this time, he just poured himself a drink, neat.

Steven said, "Yes, sir, I guess you are right, a man could do much worse than a couple of cigars and some Scotch."

Now the General, looking intently at Steven, took a sip of his drink and finally said what he really wanted to say, "Now what do you say we dispense with the bullshit and get to the real reason you are here."

Steven went to answer, but Goodman stopped him, "Remember it's me, Steven. I don't care how awful you might think whatever you have to tell me is, what I won't abide by is bullshit. So, once again, what do you say we get down to what it is you have to say?"

Steven hung his head and looked back up with a wry grin on his face. The old man hadn't lost a step, "Sir, I'm going to be talking to Brian Case at Tactical Assets about something sensitive and I just wanted you to hear it from me before you heard it from anybody else. With everything that's happened, I just..."

The General interrupted him again, "Listen, son, every man, and I mean every man, has a moment in their lives when they need to look deep into their heart to make a decision, they might not want to make it, but they know they have to. People like us needed to make those kinds of decisions more than others. Our work, our life, demanded it. Leading men into war is a big responsibility and one that stays with you for the rest of your life."

He paused and took a couple of puffs from his cigar in contemplation and Steven remained standing, not knowing exactly what the General was getting at. "Sir, I don't think I get what..."

Goodman put up his hand, "You had a decision to make, one that you know you would need to live with forever. I've told you that from the beginning. Now I don't need to know what that decision is, how or why you made it, but I told you before I am behind you and this company is, too, and that's always going to be the case.

"Now if you need to go to Tactical Assets and talk to Brian Case about our inventory so you can catch up after being gone for some time, I understand."

Steven and the General locked eyes for what seemed an eternity.

Steven simply nodded slightly, "Yes, sir." He turned around to leave the General's office. The old man knew that whatever else Steven had done or thought about, he had developed a plan. Maybe he hadn't worked it out all the way to the end, but the General knew that as a SEAL Steven had been trained to assess and address tactical objectives first, and that's exactly what he was sure he had done.

Right before he walked through the door, Goodman said one last thing, "By the way, Steven, talk to Case about some of the new hardware we just got in."

Steven stopped, didn't look back and went on his way. As usual, the General said almost everything he needed to say to Steven without actually saying anything. Steven went to the elevators and went from the top of the building to the very bottom of the building, the reinforced basement that had been converted to store all of the hardware the company used. Access was granted through a fingerprint scan and putting in a code on a keypad.

Brian Case was sitting at his desk behind the bulletproof glass partition that kept the weapons, surveillance equipment and electronics, anything that might be needed for any operation around the world.

Steven approached the gate to grant access to the actual warehouse and without saying anything Brian Case pressed a button to let him in. The General had made a call. Steven walked in knowing exactly where he needed to go.

He stopped by Brian's desk. "Hey, Brian, did we ever get the CheyTac M200s we were waiting for?"

Without looking up, Brian pushed a thin, paper manual toward Steven, "The General said you might be coming by to bone up for some upcoming deal or something. Here's the manual for it, the ammo is in the rack above it, as well as all the attachments, suppressor, scope, you know, just so you know everything you need to know for your presentation."

Steven took the manual and said, "Thanks, Brian."

He went to walk away and before he could round the first corner down the aisle to find what he was looking for, he heard Brian call out to him, "Hey, Steve, I'm really sorry about Tracy, I really am, we all are. At least they caught the animal that did this, right?"

Steven stopped for a brief moment, "Yes, they did and thank you, Brian, I really appreciate it, thank everyone else for me too, will you?"

He rounded the corner and went to the locker with the CheyTac M200 in it. Above it were all the modifications available for it, a custom-made suppressor, telescopic sight and the ammo. He opened the locker with a master key, picked up the weapon, the scope and the box of ammunition along with a carrying case.

There was much debate as to what the best sniper rifle in the world was, but for Steven's money there was no better rifle for his purposes than the CheyTac, light, accurate up to 2100 yards. The Canadian Timberwolf C14 was a close second, but it was only accurate up to 1500 yards. Steven could always tell someone had never actually used a sniper rifle in the field when the first thing out of their mouth was about the Barrett A107 .50 caliber. The thing was a cannon, bulky and not designed for human targets but to penetrate hardware, it was overkill if what you needed was something easy to carry and accurate. The ballistics and kinetic impact from the Barrett literally flipped human targets through the air when it hit. Perhaps appropriate for the shock and awe element needed in the Middle East, but overkill for New York City.

Steven packed all the gear in the carrying bag and walked out of the basement. As he was waiting for the elevator, Brian finally looked up from his newspaper and called out to Steven before the elevator arrived, "Hey, Loomis!" Steven turned around. "Good luck." Steven nodded and gave Brian a brief, sad smile just as the elevator was opening.

◆

The Manhattan criminal court building was a large and regal structure. So many infamous trials had gone on there, so many criminals from so many high-profile cases, that it almost gave the old building a personality of its own. Once one walked inside, there was a cacophony of sounds, lawyers explaining things to their clients, defendants professing their innocence, lawyers negotiating. There were shoe shiners, one of the last places they could be found, offering their services at the entrance.

That's what the courthouse was like on any given day. Today, however, the place was complete pandemonium. Today was the day that Donald Riche would be arraigned.

Drew Willis had been in the courthouse when other high-profile cases had invaded the courthouse, but he had never seen anything like this. There were cameras everywhere, in the courtroom where Riche would be arraigned and around almost every corner of the hallways in the courthouse and stationed at every exit door.

Drew was sitting on a bench on the third floor going over his files when he heard a commotion over by the elevators. The elevator door opened and out walked Donald Riche, flanked on four sides by armed guards, wearing an orange jumpsuit and shackled at his wrists and ankles. A throng of reporters was following the procession and shouting questions that were for the most part unintelligible. They headed into the courtroom while most of the reporters remained outside.

Willis was sure the courtroom was packed. Inside along with the other defendants were reporters from every major network, the families of the victims, with the exception of the Loomis family, and the attorneys handling the various cases. David Neill, the DA, was there to represent the people of New York along with Michael

Gordon, a senior ADA, and to his surprise, Bart Logan was also a part of the prosecution team. The defense team, Harvey Lynch along with another attorney Drew didn't know and what was probably a legal assistant, was flanking Donald Riche.

Drew was surprised at what Riche looked like because he looked just like the guy next door. Medium height, medium weight, stylish glasses, nicely cut hair, as far from a monster as you could get.

Wanting to get the cameras out of the courtroom as soon as possible, Donald Riche's case was the first on the docket. Drew came into the courtroom to find it was standing room only and he was only allowed in because he himself had a case on the docket. When he walked in he was surprised by the level of noise in the courtroom, cameras whirring and people chattering, that is until the bailiff announced the judge's arrival on the bench.

Even after the announcement, the noise level went down only gradually. Finally, once the courtroom was quiet, the court clerk called the first case, "Your honor, the first case is the People vs. Donald Riche, case number NY-1593245."

Judge Harlan Robinson, a seasoned superior court judge with a booming voice and a cold, all-business manner, called the court to order, "Very well. Who represents the people?"

Neill stood up, "David Neill, District Attorney, representing the people, your honor."

Judge Robinson grinned and looked up from the file, "Well, Mr. Neill. It is always good to see you in the courtroom, even if it's once every six months or so."

A low chuckle rippled through the crowd, Neill blushed but said nothing.

Robinson turned his attention to the defense table, "And for the defense?"

Lynch stood up, "Harvey Lynch, your honor. I will be representing Mr. Riche throughout these proceedings."

Robinson flipped through the pages of the file in front of him and addressed the defendant, "Mr. Riche, are you aware of the charges being brought against you?"

Donald Riche, in a most serene voice, said, "Yes, I am."

Robinson continued, "And are you aware that you need to enter a plea at this time?"

Before Riche could answer, Lynch jumped in, "Your honor, we would request a continuance in order to allow the defense to have Mr. Riche examined by a psychiatrist in order to determine whether a plea of not guilty by reason of insanity is warranted."

Lynch knew that in order to pursue an insanity defense, it had to be established at the arraignment. He knew very well Riche would never be found insane, but still needed to establish the possibility of pursuing a 'not guilty by reason of insanity' plea.

David Neill immediately stood, "Your honor, the people would object to a continuance. Mr. Lynch has not engaged in any conversation with our office advising us that he was planning on pursuing an insanity defense. Mr. Lynch knows the standard for an insanity defense, and as we know, Mr. Riche clearly took measures to cover his crimes."

Lynch responded, "Your honor, there has been no legal finding that Mr. Riche committed any crime, and we object to the district attorney coming to a conclusion without a single issue litigated yet."

Willis was impressed that old Harvey wasn't intimidated by the cameras or by Neill. He was actually making a good argument for a continuance.

Judge Robinson considered both sides' arguments and finally turned to Lynch, "Mr. Lynch, as far as you can tell, do you feel your client at this point is capable of assisting in his own defense?"

Lynch was caught off guard, but he couldn't lie, "Yes, your honor, at this time I believe Mr. Riche can assist in his own defense."

Robinson continued, "Then I am going to deny the continuance. Mr. Riche will enter a plea today. You are of course entitled to have him examined by your experts and psychiatrists. The court is perfectly willing to allow Mr. Riche to withdraw his plea and enter an insanity plea if there is enough credible evidence that it is warranted."

Neill interjected, "Your honor, the people would also like to have Mr. Riche examined by our own psychiatrists. We will coordinate with Mr. Lynch in order to not cause any further delays."

Judge Robinson now addressed Riche, "Having understood all the charges against you, Mr. Riche, what is your plea, guilty or not guilty?"

Once again, almost casually, Riche responded, "Not guilty, your honor."

The judge continued, "Very well, a plea of not guilty will be entered on your behalf. I am going to set the preliminary hearing two weeks from now, for January 30th. I am assuming that both sides will have had a chance to have their experts examine Mr. Riche, and even if that is not the case, both sides understand the hearing is just to determine if there is enough credible evidence to bind Mr. Riche over for trial."

Drew was surprised. He knew that the judge had explained the purpose of the preliminary hearing for the benefit of the cameras and the reporters. Even old Harlan had been caught up in the hype. He usually wanted to move through the docket as fast as possible, obviously not today.

Once the proceedings for the Riche case were over, both the defense and the prosecution teams packed up and stood from the table.

Drew knew that Riche would be taken down through the parking lot beneath the courthouse, where all high-profile and particularly violent offenders were transported. Because of the high profile of the case, Riche would probably be transported in a cruiser or an unmarked car with a motorcycle escort from the courthouse to a holding cell at the city jail.

With the Riche case disposed of, the courtroom vacated almost immediately leaving only bailiffs, defendants and attorneys in the courtroom along with the court staff. Melanie Farris was now sitting at the prosecution table ready to deal with the rest of the day's cases. Drew headed to the front to talk to her. He was thrilled she was back, but wondered why Neill had left her out of the prosecution team. Almost as soon as he formed the thought, he answered his own question. Neill wanted the spotlight on himself and himself only. Having Michael Gordon, a senior assistant district attorney, but one that handled mostly white-collar crimes and had very little criminal trial experience, would allow Neill to say he had senior ADAs on his team but would keep the attention on himself. Bart Logan was there for decoration and to do all the research on whatever citations came up during the proceedings.

As soon as Drew got to the prosecution table and got a look at Melanie he could tell she was not at all pleased about the situation, which meant he had a long day ahead of him.

Steven Loomis was in a vacant office in a building about two blocks away from the courthouse. He had scouted the area and found that there were a number of offices for lease within one or two blocks of the courthouse. He had seen three possibilities and asked to see them to make sure there was a direct line of sight and a window that could be opened. All three had line of sight, but only one had a window that opened. The previous two days Steven had walked the streets around the courthouse, looking for potential problems. He assessed the level of pedestrian traffic that could block the line of sight into the basement parking lot of the courthouse. He had considered various options, but the reality was that once Riche was taken into custody, there would be only one way to get to him without endangering anybody else.

He had watched through the scope as guards walked prisoners into the van to take them back to the central jail. Security had tightened severely after September 11, but even with that being the case, Loomis had been surprised at the ease with which he had been able to put together his mission.

He noticed that there were two guards on either side of the back doors, two guards stationed by the elevator where the prisoners came out, and two more stationed at the passenger and the driver side doors. Each prisoner would make his way from the elevator to the van shackled at the feet. The routine had remained consistent in the two days Steven had scoped it out. They had to walk approximately 10 feet between the elevator and the back of the van, which meant about 15 seconds to take the shot. The other thing that would make it difficult would be making sure no photographers happened to be crossing right in front of the ramp of the parking lot when Riche came down. The ramp in and out of the basement let out on a side street, which meant less pedestrians, but he'd still have to be careful since the media would always be trying to get a better picture.

Because the parking lot was underground and the van was always parked in the middle of the parking lot where the elevators were, Steven had an opening of about 18 inches to get the shot through. During his time in the service, Steven had gone through extensive firearms training and had acquired more experience on the job. He had a ribbon as a marksman and had progressed to the expert level, but he was not a professional sniper. That was the reason he had chosen the M200. The technology employed to design the weapon was the latest in long-range target acquisition and could almost aim and fire itself.

Throughout his surveillance Steven had determined that the wind would not be above five miles an hour at the spot he would be firing from. The wind tended to get diffused by the high-rises, so a truly gusty day was relatively rare. He set his rifle on a desk in the office about three feet away from the window, to avoid anyone seeing the long barrel of the gun sticking out the window. Given that he'd decided to use subsonic rounds, the suppressor would muffle most of the sound. The sounds of the city, horns, traffic and the bustle of pedestrians, would also help make sure the sound of the rifle would most likely be lost in the mix. He was now in full operational mode, with a singular goal in mind and every one of his senses dedicated to accomplishing that goal.

Over the past two days, he had slowly transitioned from Steven Loomis, senior executive with a global security firm to Lt. Commander Steven Loomis, US Navy, DEVGRU SEAL team.

Donald Riche was walking toward the elevator with something akin to giddiness. He was fascinated by the entire process that he was being forced to endure, all in the name of his mandate. His happiness stemmed from his ability to adapt to everything that was being put in front of him in spite of the fact that what he wanted most was to shout out to the world and let every one of its inhabitants know about what he had done, what he had been destined and tasked to do. Most of all, he wanted to tell them how different he was from all of them, how superior he was. He wanted them to know that he could hear, see, smell and feel things they could not, that he'd always been able to. He knew they wouldn't believe and they would laugh, but it was true, he knew it to be true. He would have his opportunity to do it, to make sure that he was heard around the world, something he had not imagined in his wildest dreams.

Seeing all the cameras in the courtroom, he came to realize that everything that would be said, everything that would be talked about and argued, and whatever he explained and showed would be broadcast around the world. Every single person around the world who had a television or a radio, read a newspaper or surfed the Internet would know about what he had done, what he had accomplished. He didn't mind the chains on his ankles or on his wrists. He knew it was also part of the game, part of what they needed to feel safe and to perpetuate the game their life was.

In reality Riche was being handled the same as any high-profile violent defendant. The tactical unit moving him around had been trained to handle families and others in court, the media in the hallways and around the courthouse when the defendant wasn't in a courtroom. Only the most experienced officers, officers who wouldn't be distracted, who wouldn't be swayed by the media attention, were put on Donald Riche's detail.

Once they were in the service elevator, all members of the team relaxed a notch. They knew there would be no press, no cameras, no one other than officers between the elevator doors and the van that would transport him back to the central jail for holding.

Chapter 12

Robert Grady had wanted to be at the arraignment hearing. As the lead investigator on the case, he felt he *had* to be there. He had been to the arraignment of every serious felon he had ever collared. In this instance he had wanted to be there, but given the evidence and the facts as they were known so far, he knew the judge would never set bail anywhere near what Donald Riche could make.

In fact, the judge had deemed the case to be a no-bail case given the circumstances, the nature of the crime and the attention the entire world was paying to this case. Harlan Robinson was a fair judge, but he was also a smart one, and he knew if he set bail at whatever amount and the defendant was somehow able to come up with the money, with a case like this, his career would essentially be over. Appellate and federal court would instantly be erased from his future, having a child abductor and murderer free on bond would be all the opposition would need to derail any of his ambitions. That, along with the pictures he had been presented with, had been enough for Judge Robinson to make this a no-bail case.

Grady had arrived at the courthouse shortly after the actual hearing had taken place, but given everything that was moving around the case, he also turned his level of concentration down a notch. He knew Riche would be taken down into the parking lot through the service elevator, the way all felons of his type were, so he decided to use the stairs to make it down to the parking lot to see Riche being transported to central for holding. He'd been told he missed the hearing near the entrance, before heading up the stairs. It was just one floor down, so he knew he would be able to get down into the lot before Riche and the tactical team made it to the bottom.

Grady in fact did arrive before the elevator doors opened. He positioned himself next to the elevator doors where there was a small group of officers waiting. As soon as the elevator arrived, the tactical team handed the prisoner off to the guards that would escort him to the van. There were two sets of guards, one to receive him off the elevator and one to guide him into the van. It seemed like an overly redundant and overly cautious protocol, but it had worked for years and it let everyone know that the NYPD was on the ball.

The elevator arrived and Riche and the officers got out. After they got out, the officers guarding Riche took positions to keep any curious pedestrian or media away, even though they knew neither would be allowed down into the basement. They all knew that cameras were positioned outside to get a picture of the van coming out of the parking lot and that some photographer might just risk trying to get a better shot. They'd be ready if it happened. The tactical unit was no bullshit and took their job seriously.

Steven Loomis knew the time that had been set for the hearing, the DA's office had called his family as they had called every other family to let them know the time and date of the hearing, but by then Steven had already decided on his mission. With his family gone and out of sight, he was able to concentrate on what he determined to be the right course of action.

He didn't know how long the hearing would be or how many cases would come before Riche's, but he was patient, very patient. There was no way to be a covert operative without having nerves of steel and a heavy dose of patience. The key to any significant operation was timing, knowing exactly when to move and when to stay put. As he sat and waited, he noticed that the police were keeping the ramp clear, just as he'd expected.

He saw the elevator arrive at the basement. He knew it because he saw the guards tighten up, something they hadn't done with anybody else. He began to control his breathing, making it even and deep, he put his eye to the eyepiece on the scope, determined the distance and angle and made the necessary adjustments on the scope. The M200, a 27-pound weapon with the latest technology, responded instantly, accurately. There was no anger, no sense of revenge, just the mission and his training.

Steven waited and paced his breathing; it was only a matter of seconds now. All he had to do was make sure that he had been handed off the same way as all of the other felons he had scoped out before, that there weren't any variations from the norm. If Steven saw any variation from the norm, he would hold off. There was no way he was going to take the risk of someone being out of place or out of order. Things could definitely get bad when you improvised like that in a mission like this.

Grady stood back and looked at the man responsible for the horror that he had witnessed not so many nights before. Perhaps it would have been easier for him to accept, to reconcile with what he had seen, if what came out of the elevator was some sort of monster, but what he actually saw was the same meek and quiet guy that he and Mullins had interviewed. Someone he might have had a beer with under different circumstances. The reality, or what passed for reality, for Grady at the moment was that the man he saw coming out of the elevator had kidnapped, raped, tortured and mutilated nine little girls and had done it with meticulous care. The reality was that in all the years he had been on the force he had never felt like he had come face-to-face with pure evil, with something that didn't fit or could not fit into the parameters Grady had set for even the most depraved, violent and deranged human minds.

This was a case that would forever change Robert Grady and he knew it. Being here, seeing Riche being passed along just like any other man was the first step for Grady to begin the process of moving on. He would have to testify, but he was more able to do that as a part of his job, with his own human emotions in check. Seeing Riche as a criminal, a monstrous and depraved criminal to be sure, but a criminal nonetheless, was part of how Grady planned to begin to deal with the nightmares that were coming every night now.

Steven, now fully in operational mode, was breathing rhythmically, timing his breaths based on what he saw through the scope. Keeping his heartbeat in check and in rhythm with his breathing. He calculated distance, wind and the drop of the bullet in his head and decided how much he would lead his target. He utilized the mil dots on the scope to determine the timing of the shot. When he saw what he expected, he exhaled, held his breath for a half a second and timed the shot between heartbeats.

As Riche was being transferred from one set of guards to the next, Grady heard a distant crack. To anyone on the street who might have heard it through the sounds of the city and the traffic, it might have sounded like a backfire or a firecracker, but to Grady and most of the guards around Riche, most of whom had spent time in the service, it could only be one thing. The sound had a metallic, muffled quality about it, which helped to hide it in the noise of the city, but it was still unmistakable.

To Grady the next three seconds seemed to take an eternity. Within a half a second of hearing the shot, his instincts took over and he began to simultaneously hit the floor, go for his gun and look for the source of the shot. Within that same half a second, everyone around him either dropped or went for cover, all going for their side arms as they did so. As he was going down, Grady had Riche in his line of sight out of the garage and he watched as Riche began to turn his head in the direction of the sound, but within that same half a second Grady saw his head come completely apart, sending blood splatter and brain matter onto everyone and everything within four feet. As his body dropped straight down, the guards behind and in front of him went down to one knee and drew and trained their weapons out in the direction the shot came from. There was only one direction from where the shot could have come, but there was no way to tell from how far or what angle it came from. After Riche was hit and everyone realized there were no other shots or people hit, they went into emergency mode with everyone taking on prearranged duties immediately.

Still within the span of those first three seconds, Grady took stock of his own body and was the first one to speak up, "Is anyone else hit?!"

No one answered, but given that everyone down there was a trained tactical officer, they realized almost immediately that there had been no other shots and that there would most likely not be any more. There was no need to check on Riche and whether he was alive or dead, his head had literally been shot in half. It had been an incredible shot given the space the line of sight allowed from the street into the loading area. The unit commander got on the radio immediately letting everyone know there had been shots fired, that the prisoner was hit and almost certainly dead and that no one had seen nor could otherwise tell what building the shot had come from.

The courthouse went into immediate lockdown and SWAT teams surrounded the building keeping everyone, including the press, away from all entrances and exits. Whoever was in the building would remain there and whoever was on their way in would be kept out until it was determined that it was safe.

Robert Grady got up and walked over to the body of Donald Riche. He holstered his weapon and made his way to the commander of the tactical unit, Charlie Burns, who was also standing over the body. "Jesus Christ, Bob, can you believe this shit? Had to be ex-military, had to be, there's no way a civilian, even a SWAT sniper, could have gotten that shot through at that angle, no way. Judging by the lag between the sound of the shot and when he was hit, I'm going to say it was about five hundred yards, maybe more because the motherfucker had to be up high, but not too high, angle wouldn't have been right."

Grady listened as Burns continued to talk in a manic, nervous way that was obviously fueled by the adrenaline of the moment. Charlie was talking more to himself than to Grady and Grady knew to let him just vent it out. The SWAT units were already around the building and all exits and entrances were secured. Paramedics and a team from the medical examiner were down in the loading bay dealing with the body and the tissue that could be recoverable. It had been three minutes from the time the shot was fired to this point, but those first three seconds would be burned into Detective Bob Grady's memory forever.

With everything going on around him, with everyone scrambling to do what they thought to be the right thing, Grady was beginning to get a sinking feeling in his stomach. There was absolutely nothing to indicate who had done this, and given the news coverage that had been given to the case, there were at least 1,000 possible suspects who had the skills, the hardware and the opportunity to do it, but there was only one that Grady could think of with the motivation to do it and the skills to do it like this. It wasn't some wacko flying into the garage shooting up the place or someone wanting to get their name in the headlines, although most of these guys would think that's exactly who it was. Grady knew better. He knew this had been carefully and professionally planned, that every detail of how it had gone down had been anticipated and accounted for. Grady knew this because 25 years of police and military experience had served him well; he had spoken to the man that had done this just a couple of days ago. And while he would take a while to admit it to himself, Robert Grady had known that this was exactly what that man was going to do back then.

Steven Loomis had followed the shot all the way in, the way he had been trained to and the way he had always done it. Once he knew he had hit the mark, he allowed himself to inhale once again. He was still in operational mode, functioning on autopilot. There was no joy or sense of revenge, there was just the sense of satisfaction, of having completed the mission successfully without anyone getting hurt. He was well aware of what he had done, and more than ever, he had the clarity of his motive front and center in his mind. He had planned for every contingency and had understood the consequences of his actions from the moment he had made his decision. Over the years, Steven Loomis had struggled with the morality or righteousness of some of the most important operations he had been involved in, and in every instance he had to weigh his own personal views against his operational order and what his country considered to be of vital interest. In every instance, he had understood that doing what his country deemed necessary was what he had signed up for, what he had sworn to be governed by. In some instances, his own personal views happened to coincide with what his country needed him to do, and in every one of those instances he had experienced a clarity of purpose, an unflinching conviction that what he had done was right, not by his standards or by his country's standards but by human standards. He had never felt that clarity of vision, that unflinching certainty, more than he did at this moment. His tactical skills were as sharp as they had been while he was in the service and he immediately went about closing this end of the operation. He still knew that this was the easy part; the hard part was still to come. The only weapon he would have to use from now on was his brain.

He packed his rifle and his scope, looked at the map that showed what the likely reach of the net would be by now and plotted his route out of the building. He'd been wearing coveralls with a maintenance company logo on them. He'd been just one more anonymous maintenance worker that came and went without anyone taking any real notice. He took the coveralls off and packed them in the same pack his rile was in. He was wearing a grey pinstriped suit and a purple paisley tie, his hair was neatly combed and he had a briefcase in one hand and his pack on his back.

He walked to the stairs where he had already scouted out a place behind an intersection of pipes and valves where he could place the pack. After dropping off the pack in the stairwell, he went back to the hallway to use the elevator, as using the stairs would be conspicuous and something an amateur would most likely resort to.

Loomis walked to the elevator, pressed the down button, and when the elevator arrived he stepped in. When he stepped into the lobby, he could hear the sirens. He could see the black and whites racing, the uniformed officers setting up a perimeter, and confused and scared pedestrians running from the courts building. As he suspected, they were doing that a full block away from where he stepped out onto the street. He turned to his right, went to the corner and hailed a cab. He would be heading to his office next. He had to talk to the General and he had other arrangements to make. He had to get some files he was going to need from his office and he had to make arrangements to join his family at his in-laws' house.

◆

Grady was still in shock. He hadn't even registered that he had brain matter and blood on himself. He was leaning against the transport van, trying to get his bearings, smoking a cigarette, something he didn't do often, and drinking a Sprite. He watched all the activity around him. Although the crime scene investigation team was scouring the area for any potential evidence, Grady knew that the only evidence was either still lodged in Riche's body or spread all over the wall or on the people that had been within 10 feet of him. There would be nothing else to be found on him, and if Grady was right about his suspicion, even the ballistics would be of little use as he imagined it was most likely an advanced military bullet not accessible to just anyone on the street.

It was hard to figure out what to do next, but after giving the scene commander his statement and having been given the go-ahead, he decided the best place for him would be back at his office. He had a feeling that's where he would need to be. By now the entire city of New York knew about the incident and there were a million stories about how it had happened, and the media already had people on the scene and were lining up their in-studio analysts and experts. All had their own thoughts about what happened, all of it speculation and all of them promising 'to keep you informed as more details came in.' Twitter feeds exploded with the incident and there were second-by-second updates. There had not been any cameras rolling when the shot happened, as most crews were still setting up to get the van coming out of the garage. But there was more news footage and phone-shot video of the aftermath than anyone could possibly watch, even if they had hours to do it.

Grady got in an unmarked car and weaved his way past the barricades, showing his badge to get around. As he was leaving, he noticed that the tactical unit and the SWAT team were already expanding their net and were setting up a perimeter that was going to encompass two full city blocks. Grady knew, however, that the shooter was long gone and if his instincts were right he knew where he would be heading.

Steven Loomis headed straight to the General's office. He knew the story would have reached him by now. Goodman had three screens in his office, all tuned to various news outlets, so even though the details would be sketchy he would know what had happened by now and he would know exactly who had done it.

Steven walked past the offices and cubicles that lined the hallway to the General's office. Although he could see nobody was looking or turning their heads, he knew that they would also know something by now and that some of them would also know or strongly suspect his involvement. They were all involved in the security and intelligence industry after all.

Steven got to the General's office and knocked on the door. From the other side came a simple, gruff "Come in."

Steven walked into the office. He didn't know exactly what it was that he wanted to say to the old man, but he figured he would just approach it as an operational report. "I think you've probably heard about the situation at the courthouse."

Goodman's bright blue eyes were looking intensely at Steven, but he said nothing and just gave him a slight nod.

Steven continued, "Sir, I know you don't abide by bullshit and I'm not here to give you any. I used the company's tactical assets to complete my task. Whatever happens, I will always remember what you've done for me. If I decide to eventually take responsibility for this, I will let everyone know it was without the knowledge or approval of anyone in the company.

"I want to thank you for all your years of counsel and the lessons you've imparted. It has been an honor and a true privilege to work with you and with the rest of the team. I am very sorry if my actions bring unwanted scrutiny and attention to the company. I think under the circumstances I have no real alternative but to resign my position."

With that Steven handed the General a sealed envelope, which he did not open. The General looked at the envelope and then at Steven. He put the envelope down on his desk without saying anything, stood up and walked to the cabinet where he kept his Scotch and his cigars. He pulled out two cigars and poured two stiff Scotches and went back to his desk holding a glass out to Steven.

Steven went to speak, "Sir, thank you, but I don't think I should…"

The General waved him off, "Nonsense, I think this is precisely when you should."

He walked over and put the cigar and the drink in front of Steven and went back behind his desk. They lit their cigars and drank their Scotch in silence with the television screens turned to a low volume in the background, one of them giving minute-by-minute updates of the situation downtown.

Finally the General broke the silence, "Max Zeidler."

Steven hadn't heard what he had said, "Excuse me?"

Goodman puffed on his cigar, "He's represented a few people here on some pretty dicey situations and he is the best there is. He's on retainer to help us with whatever we need."

Steven froze, he couldn't believe what he was hearing, "Sir, I can't allow the company to pay for my…"

The older man interrupted, waving his hands, "Steven, before all of this I told you all of us had to make hard decisions, life and death decisions. We made them on the battlefield and we have to make them in what we do. When your little girl went missing and you found out who had done it, a decision had to be made – you would either let the law handle it or you would handle it.

"I think I've told you that more than once, whatever else you had to think about, it would always come back to that deciding question: Do I let it go or do I do something?"

Steven stood listening, sipping on his Scotch and smoking his cigar. The old man had been right. This is precisely when a Scotch and a cigar could soothe the nerves.

"I've known you for years, Steven. I know what kind of father and husband you are and what kind of man you are, and believe it or not this is precisely what I thought you would decide." The two sat in silence for a few seconds.

"I also told you we *always* take care of our own, out in the field and here at home. For what it's worth, I think you made the right decision. Some things that need to be done can only be done by those that have the skills and the motivation to do them, and this needed to be done.

"I don't know what comes next for you, what you are planning on doing, but whatever that is, people will understand. Now I'm going to put this letter in my safe and we'll see what the future brings.

"In the meantime, you'll take a short leave of absence and go join your family; that is where you need to be. We'll backstop you here if the need for it arises."

That let Steven know that the old man had thought he might do something like this and had already established a plan for whatever contingency came up, the police, FBI, anything.

Steven had put down the drink and the cigar and had only one more thing he needed to talk about with the General, "Sir, Marybeth and the kids are at her parents' house, I was thinking of tapping into my 401(k) to…"

Again he was interrupted, "Don't worry about that. If the time comes, we will take care of Beth and the kids through some of our international operations. They will be fine."

At that point Steven finally let loose of all of his emotions, of the stress and tension that he had been operating under for the last couple of days. He put his head in his hands and began to cry softly, partly because the adrenaline was wearing off and everything was starting to come crashing down at once and partly out of immense grief. The realization of what he had done, of its consequences and of the effect it would have on his family, was placing its full weight on his shoulders and he finally let go. He was also enormously grateful to have worked for this man, a man for whom the human side of what they did was just as important as everything else.

Goodman stood from behind his desk, walked over to him and simply put his hand on his back. They stayed like that for some minutes and then the silence was broken, "Steven, take care of whatever you have to take care of. Go to your family and if you need to, call Zeidler. He'll know what do."

Steven nodded, wiped his face, stood up and took the General's hand, "Sir, I can't begin to thank you and..."

Goodman waved him off with a small smile, "Enough of that crap, just remember to call Zeidler if the time comes. He's on retainer and he's the best."

Steven went to his office and picked up all the research he'd printed out and all of the files Carl Gilliam had put together for him and put them in his briefcase. As he was thinking of what he would need, he remembered and came back to pick up the number that Leonard had given him, Dr. Jim Scoma's number.

Robert Grady got to the precinct and went immediately to his office. He closed the door behind him, went to his desk and pulled out a bottle of Maker's Mark from the bottom drawer of his desk. He emptied the bit of cold coffee from the paper cup sitting on his desk and poured himself a healthy shot, something he hadn't done in some time. He leaned back and turned to face the window. He went back to his desk, picked up the phone and made the call he knew he had to make.

After he picked up Scoma's number, Steven Loomis was going through the little notes Steph always left on his desk at the end of the day with the little details that all of the files of his deals were most likely missing. There were quite a few. As he was looking through the notes, he came across a sealed envelope from the General's office. He read the note inside and once he was finished burned it and put the ashes in the trash. Just as he'd thought, the General had already developed a plan. He looked around his office and was getting ready to leave when his phone rang. Everyone in the office knew about his situation, so he knew it wouldn't be anyone from GIC, and every one of his clients was being handled so he knew it wouldn't be any of them. It had to be the General or someone in his family.

He came around the desk and picked up the phone, "Hello?" He recognized the voice on the other end of the phone immediately.

"You really didn't trust us to take care of it? You think we are incompetent, I guess."

Steven sat down, "Hello, Detective Grady. I'm surprised to hear from you."

Grady wasn't going to let it go, "Seriously, this is how you want to handle this?"

Loomis didn't have a plan formulated for whatever would come next, but now, having this conversation with Grady, he realized he would have to have a conversation with the man eventually. He was incredibly thankful that he'd opened the note from Goodman before the phone rang.

He still needed to be careful with what he said, however, because whatever else Grady might be, he was not stupid, "Detective Grady, I don't know what it is you are referring to, but if this has something to do with the shooting at the courthouse, you need to know I was in a meeting, a videoconference as a matter of fact, at the time the shooting occurred."

Grady paused. Had he made a big mistake? Like with Riche, had he made his move too soon, made too many assumptions? Then it hit him. Of course Loomis would have thought to have an ironclad alibi, something that was solid. He probably had at least a dozen people who would swear that he had been in that conference room at the time of the shooting. Now what, did he push the point with Loomis or did he take more time and regroup?

Maybe he'd settle for something in the middle, "I see. Well, my mistake, I thought I would call you, you would own up to shooting the man that murdered your daughter, which we both know you did, and then we would figure out what to do next. I forgot about the resources at your disposal and that you would have an airtight alibi before you ever thought of actually shooting him."

Loomis felt a pang of guilt. Maybe he was right, maybe he should just own up to it now. That was the problem, though, *maybe* that was the thing to do.

He needed time to figure out what he was going to do next, what the right thing to do was, and that meant that *now* was not the time. "Detective Grady, I know it's been a difficult case and that you and your team have invested a lot in it, but I'm not your man. I can see why you would think that it was me, but I've been straight with you throughout this whole thing, and like I just explained, I was in a meeting at the time."

Grady listened. Loomis almost had him going again. Almost. Robert Grady had honed his instincts over a lot of years, working cases in vice, organized crimes and homicide, and whatever else he knew to be true, he knew that this man had shot Donald Riche just an hour earlier.

"Well, my mistake then. I *am* sorry about your daughter, Loomis. You take care."

On his end of the phone, Steven hung his head and said his goodbye, again with a pang of guilt, "I appreciate it, detective. I'm sure we'll see each other again."

Grady couldn't resist, "Yup, I think you can count on that."

They both hung up. Loomis finished packing his things and finally left his office. He had the bag with the things he would need from home ready and packed in a small duffle bag he'd left in the GIC lobby behind the front desk. He picked up the duffle bag, went down to the street, caught a cab to the airport, and got on his way to his in-laws' house.

As a police officer Robert Grady had always enjoyed the clarity of what was right and what was wrong. It was true that in 25 years on the force there had been times when that line had been blurred, but in the end he had always been able to come back to the compass that had guided him through his career. This was different. He had been conflicted from the beginning, from the moment that he allowed Loomis to become a part of the investigation. He had known that in reality it was the most prudent thing to do, that the man's experience, resources and most of all his motivation would make him more of a hindrance to the investigation had he tried to shut him out, but deep down inside Robert Grady had known that this scenario was in one way or another a very real possibility. He had known that because he himself was a father, because Loomis's entire career and training was geared toward assessing situations and coming up with an operational objective to be met.

Grady could rationalize all he wanted and try to make himself believe that he thought Loomis just wanted closure, just to know what happened to his daughter so he could move on. He could try to do it, but now he knew he would never succeed.

What bothered Robert Grady the most about all of it, however, wasn't that he had known this was going to happen and hadn't done anything about it, actually had facilitated it to an extent. No, what bothered Robert Grady the most was that he was actually glad it had happened. It was something he would have never believed of himself. Throughout his career, he had run into the worst humanity had to offer and as much as he had wanted an angry father or husband or brother to exact revenge, to punish those that had hurt their families, he believed in the justice system, believed in his job and in the job of all of those that were charged with bringing the bad guys to justice. He had never felt sympathy for those that wanted to play police, judge and executioner, and yet here he was, sitting in his office, glad that the son of a bitch had his brain blown out, that he was no longer drawing air.

As he was sitting in his office lost in contemplation, he heard a knock at his door. He turned to see Mark Mullins on the other side of the glass and he waved him in.

Mullins came in and was clearly excited, "Hey, Bob, were you there when…"

He caught himself in mid-sentence when he saw Grady and saw that his suit was covered in blood spatter.

He looked at the cup in his hand and the bottle on the desk and let himself plop down on the chair on the other side of the desk, "Mind if I get myself one of those?"

Grady pushed the bottle toward him. Mullins downed the coffee he had left in his mug and poured himself a stiff drink.

"I guess you were pretty close, huh?"

Grady smiled sideways, "About as close as I could get without getting shot myself…"

Mullins took a sip of his drink, "Any idea about who did it?"

Grady drained his cup. If he hadn't put it together yet on his own, maybe it would be better to leave Mullins out of it. "Nope, you've heard the news, they sent half of the NYPD looking for the guy and they came up with nothing." Both men sat without saying anything for a couple of minutes.

Finally Mullins broke the silence, "You know it had to be a pro, right? I mean, it definitely wasn't some wacko with a gun taking pot shots. I've been at that building and I've loaded plenty of perps at the loading dock. To put a shot in there from any distance, you'd have to have had some training. Do you think it might have been an inside job? Plenty of people out there who wanted the guy dead."

Grady listened to his friend and just looked at him.

He was quiet for two beats after Mullins was finished speaking and then he spoke himself, "Well, you are definitely right about one thing, whoever did it had some training and not just some training, he had to be a sniper or a marksman.

"He also had to know enough about police procedures and how Riche would be transported. He also had to know the speed with which the department would respond and how far the immediate response net would reach, because he would have had to had set up the shot far enough away that he would be beyond the immediate perimeter.

Mullins was listening and nodding. Everything Grady was saying made perfect sense. "You're right, that's a pretty specific set of skills, the thing now is going to be looking into who had enough of a reason to…"

It was then that it also hit Mark Mullins, "Oh, my god…Loomis?" Grady just looked at him.

Mullins went on, "He couldn't have, Bob! He's not a nut or some sort of wacked-out vigilante, I mean, is he?"

Grady gave Mullins a knowing look, "I just spoke with Loomis, caught him at his office. He says he was in a meeting, a videoconference, at the time the shooting went down. That means that not only were there other people in the same room who will swear up and down that he was in that meeting, but there is a video feed with a time stamp that can be checked to corroborate his story."

Mullins stared at Grady as he was processing what he had just heard. Like Grady, once he made the connection, there was no doubt as to who had done this. There were simply too many coincidences, not based only on the facts as everyone knew them: that Loomis's daughter had been one of the victims, that Loomis had been a Navy SEAL commander for 10 years, and that the shot that had killed Riche could only be made by a few people, most likely with sniper training.

Those things alone made Loomis a prime suspect. Mullins also knew what Grady knew, that he had been in on part of the investigation, that he had been the catalyst for the police to go into Riche's warehouse, that he had seen his daughter in that freezer. Those were all things that, for Mullins, made Loomis not the prime suspect but the only suspect. Hearing what he had just heard from Grady went directly against what he thought was certain and like Grady he was going through a moment of doubt. His own moment of thinking that maybe, just maybe, it really hadn't been Loomis. But like Grady, he was also not a green detective with just a couple of years under his belt. He was a seasoned homicide detective with years of experience in investigation.

Grady just watched Mullins go through the same process he'd gone through when he had spoken to Loomis. He watched him go through his own moment of doubt and also watched as he had come back to what he knew to be the truth.

Mullins shook his head, "I don't care if Jesus himself comes down from heaven and swears on a bible that Loomis was in that meeting, it was him. You know it and I know it."

Grady didn't say anything; he simply took a sip from his cup and nodded.

Mullins went on, "Shit, we let him into this, we let him see his daughter! Goddamnit!"

Grady leaned forward and looked at Mullins. He could see he was really taking this hard, "Listen, first of all we don't have any evidence that it was him. I mean, I think we both know it was him, but the man has a pretty rock-solid alibi and he's denied doing it.

"Until there is some concrete evidence, there is absolutely nothing that ties Loomis to the shooting…nothing except for us and what we know."

Mullins looked intensely at Grady without saying anything. Both men were thinking the same thing, 'Are we going to say anything?' In the end that was really the question, wasn't it? Grady was right, there was absolutely no physical evidence and both men knew that there would be none, that if it had been Loomis, not a hair would be found anywhere near the shooter's position. And even finding the shooter's position was going to be difficult to do if not impossible.

Finally Grady broke the silence, "You know we are going to have to say something…actually, *I'm* going to say something. It was my call to let him into the investigation."

Mullins looked truly insulted, "You're shitting me, right? We both made the call. There's no way I'm letting you take the rap for this, no way!"

Grady shot back, "Mark, listen, the only reason for us to say something is to bring Loomis in and only one of us needs to say something to make that happen. There's no reason for both of us to ruin our careers. C'mon, it doesn't make sense, man. Listen, if it had to be both of us to say something to make a case against him, I could understand, but it doesn't have to be like that."

Mullins just stared at Grady. He knew he had a point, but he still felt like shit and there was nothing Robert Grady would be able to say to change that.

Mullins shook his head, "I can't believe this, you know if we hadn't let him in he would have done it on his own, and he would have gotten in the way. It was just a no-win deal all along."

Grady nodded and said, "Yeah, that's about right, he would have put himself right in the middle of it. But we both know we only got into the warehouse because of him, and sooner or later Riche's defense lawyers would have looked into that."

Mullins nodded. Both officers could see that their careers were most likely over and that it was going to be because they let a good man take the embodiment of evil off the face of the earth. Both men knew that in the end they would do the right thing and would provide whatever information they had to in order to make this case.

Grady was the next to speak, "Well, let's see how the investigation goes. For all we know, he's telling the truth, it may not have anything to do with Loomis."

Mullins nodded, "I guess that's probably the best for now. Damn, just never saw this coming, Loomis or not. I honestly never saw this coming."

Grady got up and walked to the window, and lied, "Neither did I, Mark, neither did I. Let's think about what we want to do next. You know that even if we do share everything we know, even if we flat out say it was Loomis, we wouldn't get very far once he presents his alibi, the video, all of it. And let's not forget who it is we're talking about him taking out, a fucking monster."

Mullins got up and walked to the window next to Grady, "Yeah, I thought about it myself. It would be a hell of a hard case to make, even if we did give up what we know about Loomis and his involvement. The investigation, the trial, everything, it would be a lot of resources to bring him up on charges, that's if the DA and the grand jury were willing to look past his alibi and all the evidence that he was in that meeting."

Grady turned to look at Mullins, "Well, that's why I said let's think about what we do next."

Chapter 13

Steven Loomis made it to his in-laws' without incident. On the way there he thought about his family and about what the General had said. There were things he needed to take care of, things he had thought about but which now were not just potential plans but realities.

His family had been expecting him and when he got there it had been his children that had greeted him first. Christopher was too young to know what the situation was, he was just happy to see his daddy and ran to him as soon as he saw him. After picking up his son and giving him a big hug and a kiss, Steven saw his daughter Bethany. Even though she was only nine, she knew what had happened to her sister and what her family was going through. Bethany had always been the more introspective and thoughtful of his children. She had been mature beyond her years from an early age and had tested through the roof on every standardized test she had ever taken. Her parents had refused to have her skip a grade twice because they'd been worried about her growing up too fast. Now looking at her, Steven knew that she might not know exactly what had happened to her sister, but she knew, she felt, how deep it went and could see what it was doing to her family. In these past weeks Steven could see his daughter had grown up far beyond her short years and it broke his heart.

She didn't run up to her dad, she simply walked over to him and gave him a long hug, "I missed you, Dad. I miss Tracy and I miss all of us being together."

Steven held her close and took a couple of seconds before responding to her, so she wouldn't hear his voice cracking, but he failed miserably, "I know, baby, I know. I miss all of that too. But we're here now," Steven now held her at arm's length, "and you know what, we're going to start making things better, okay? I'll need your help to do that, though. I need you to try and go back to doing the stuff you've always done, talk to your friends, do all that stuff you do on the Internet looking up interesting things from different countries, that stuff."

Bethany, tears streaming down her face, said, "I'll try, Dad. I've been trying, it's just hard. It's going to take a long time to just go back to how things were. I'll be okay, though. Mom needs your help more than I do."

Steven kissed the top of her head. Yes, regardless of what his or his wife's wishes were, his daughter had grown much older than her nine years, "I know, sweetie, that's why I'm here, to try to help her. Will you help me with her too?"

Bethany wiped the tears from her eyes, smiled a small, pained smile and nodded. Steven gave her one last squeeze and let her go.

After greeting his kids outside, he walked through his in-laws' front door and as he was putting his bags down his father-in-law, Tom Delaney, came out of the kitchen, wiping his hands on a towel. "Hey there. How was your trip?"

Steven walked over to where he was standing and shook the man's hand, "Uneventful, thankfully."

They both went into the kitchen where Steven could see Tom had been making himself a sandwich.

"Where are Lucy and Beth?"

Tom finished making his sandwich and offered half to Steven, who only now realized he was starving. He took the half Tom was offering and began to wolf it down.

"Easy there, you're going to give yourself heartburn. I loaded it with Dijon mustard. They went into town to get some stuff for dinner. Neither one of them was up for making anything nor were they willing to trust my cooking skills."

Both men sat down at the kitchen table. Tom brought a couple of bottles of cold beer and handed one to Steven.

Steven took two long pulls from the beer, "God, that tastes good."

Tom nodded, "You must be exhausted. I can't imagine that you've gotten a good night's sleep while this has been going on."

Steven confirmed that for him, "You're right, I haven't gotten more than two or three hours of consecutive sleep since this all started."

Tom nodded and both men drank from their beer. They both sat at the table in quiet thought as they finished their beer. Over the years Steven and Tom had enjoyed many such moments. Neither man was the type to have to keep talking when they were alone with each other, something that was rare and which Steven appreciated immensely. Tom Delaney had been the most solid role model Steven had to look to until he met Art Goodman, the General. When Steven had met Marybeth Delaney during his time at the Naval Academy, he had known he would marry her after their first date. A mutual friend had introduced them. Steven had dated some in high school, nothing serious or long-term. He had been focused on sports and on his studies and figured he would think about getting married after he was finished with school, maybe once he was an officer. All of that had gone out the window when he met Beth. They had spent the entire night that first date talking, about life, about their dreams, their pasts, everything. They had started at a restaurant and when the place closed they had gone to an apartment that belonged to a friend of hers near the Academy. They had not realized how long they had been talking until they saw the first rays of sun coming through the window. Steven had driven her home and had walked her to the door. Tom Delaney had been waiting for his daughter and he was not pleased. When she went to open the door, he beat her to it and pulled it open himself. The first thing Steven had thought right then was 'Why didn't Beth tell me Charles Bronson is her dad?' Steven had also learned at that moment that one could project power and intimidation without being boisterous or trying to be tough.

Unlike the Hollywood legend, however, Tom Delaney was the father of the girl he was bringing home at the break of dawn. Beth had been just as startled when her dad pulled open the door. The first thing that came to her mind was to simply introduce the two, 'Hi, Daddy….uh, this is Steven Loomis.' Tom had given his daughter a look that said 'Why can't I stay mad at you' and had stretched out his hand. Truth had been that Tom respected the fact that the kid had walked his daughter to the door and stood there to make sure she made it home alright, 'Tom Delaney. Pleased to meet you, Mr. Loomis.' If Steven hadn't been intimidated by Tom's Charles Bronson looks, he would have been by the man's grip. It was like a vise.

"How is Beth doing?"

Tom looked at him and shook his head slightly, "She's still very frail. She blames herself for it."

Steven hung his head, "I don't know what I can do to let her know it wasn't her fault."

Tom went back to looking out the window at his grandchildren, "Nothing you can do or say that's going to do that. She has to work it out on her own and you have to let her. I keep saying the same thing to her mother, but she gets upset every time I do. Says she needs us now."

Steven, now also looking out at his children, nodded, "She's her mom, Tom, and she's watching her little girl suffering. Of course she's going to want to be there, to do something, anything, to make it better."

Tom turned to look at him, "I know that, Steven, she's my daughter too, but sometimes the best thing you can do is to let the people you love find the strength and courage to accept things and to move on from them on their own. It's the only way they will truly get better and move on.

"If you really love her as much as I believe you do, you'll let Beth work through this without trying to prop her up, without trying to do the suffering for her, because as much as you want to, that's something you'll never be able to do. What Beth needs now is to know that you'll be there when she's ready, when she needs the help."

Steven had always thought that his father-in-law was one of the smartest people he knew. It wasn't that the man was Princeton educated or that he'd made partner at his law firm at 29 that made him believe that, it was that Tom never, not ever, said anything without thinking.

He had never given Steven bad advice, not even when he had to take the side opposite of his daughter, and it was no different now. He was right, of course, but the hardest part for Steven was not being able to do anything for Beth and even harder was going to be just standing by, waiting for her to find her footing. That's the part that would really test him.

"How are *you* doing?"

Steven turned to face him, "I'm alright. You know, I'm going through it in bits and pieces I guess. It's like I have little periods when I feel like I don't have to be a husband, a dad to Chris and Bethany, an ex-SEAL, when I can just be a human being. It's those times when it hits me the hardest, when I let it pour out. It's the only way I know how to do it Tom, the only way."

Steven did just that at that moment, he just let it pour out and sobbed softly, his head in his hands. Tom nodded and his face and eyes softened. He walked around the table, stood behind Steven and massaged his shoulders gently, "I know, son, I know. Let it come, it has to at some point. I know you and the kind of man you have been to my daughter and my grandchildren and the kind of officer you were when you were active. This isn't an op. You're allowed to just grieve. We're here for you and for Beth and for the kids, so just deal with it as it comes."

They remained like that for some time, Steven allowing all of the pent-up anger, sadness, helplessness to just come pouring out. That and all of the tension and focus from the last couple of days made it that much more intense. This was the first time he'd had the time and was with someone that he trusted completely and felt comfortable being this vulnerable in front of. The only other people he felt that way about were his mother-in-law, the General and, of course, his wife. Right now it was his father-in-law, right here, right now, that was there for him, like he'd been there many times before after tough ops, nightmares, things he couldn't talk to his wife about. Today, as he mourned the loss of his own daughter, Tom Delaney went from being his father-in law to just being his father, and for that he was immensely thankful.

♦

Drew Willis had just finished the third 14-hour day in a row. With the Riche shooting, the court had been a mess for the 48 hours right after the shooting. The disruption caused cases in almost all of the criminal courts to get backed up.

Trying to get around the investigative teams and the media covering the case had been a real pain in the ass for the past four days. On the upside, however, Drew had gotten some deals for his clients that he might not have gotten had any of the regular ADAs been in the courtroom. Both Farris and Logan were both MIA, probably dealing with whatever the implications of the shooting were for David Neill and the DA's office.

Most of the seasoned criminal defense attorneys had seen the opening the second they saw the green, young attorneys with the big stacks of files. So, even though the last three days had been a marathon, he'd done well for his clients. He was finishing up his day, long after his other associate and all the paralegals were gone, and packing the things he wanted to take home with him when his cell phone rang. He chuckled and hung his head, "Really?"

He didn't recognize the number and debated not picking up the phone, but at this time it could only be one of his big clients, the clients that had him on retainer.

He decided to answer, "Hello?"

He was surprised by the voice on the other end of the phone, "Hey, kid. I bet you're still at the office, aren't you?"

Drew looked at the ceiling and chuckled, "Max Zeidler, the man himself. Yeah, still at the office, on my way out actually? You?"

Max chuckled himself, "You got me. Still at the office, but hey, I'm here because I'm avoiding my in-laws. They're in town. As far as they know I'm in the middle of the biggest case of my career and stuck at the office. I have to say, though, I think my humble abode is a bit more comfortable than that old barber shop you do business in."

Drew laughed, the guy was charismatic even over the phone, but he was tired and wanted to head home, "To what do I owe the pleasure?"

Max, in the middle of chewing on whatever it was he was eating, answered, "Have you thought about coming on board with us?"

Drew actually had given it some thought, some serious thought.

The long hours, dealing mostly with small-time criminals were definitely taking their toll, "Actually, Max, I have. I really have and I have to tell you, it's tempting, but at the same time I'm thinking 'Been there, done that.' I can't go back to being the lowly associate anymore. I may be working long hours for less pay, but I make my own rules, I'm not a slave to billing hours. You know what I'm saying, I don't need to explain it to you."

On his end Max smiled a sideways smile, "Yeah, that I do, that I do. I think you misunderstand. I wouldn't bring you in as a lowly associate. I have plenty of Ivy League pricks doing that already. You wouldn't come in as a partner, of course, but you'd definitely be a senior associate, and in this firm the only place for you to go from there is partner. I think we'll start you at what all senior associates make."

Max told him the figure. His monthly take-home pay would be roughly what three months from the firm would yield him, provided of course they were good months.

Zeidler went on, "You'd also participate in our profit sharing plan, of course, which can increase your salary by another 25 or 30 percent." That meant another $100K to $120K per year.

Drew sat down on the couch in his office, he certainly hadn't expected Zeidler to call him, especially at this hour and especially to make him this offer. "I'm not going to lie to you, Max, that does make a difference, a big one actually. I'll tell you what, let me talk to my other associate here and to my paralegals and we can talk in a couple of days."

Max, always on the make, asked, "Any of them any good? If they are, bring them with you, we're always looking for good talent."

Drew smiled, "There's a couple of paralegals I would like to bring with me, but my associate and the rest of the paralegals and assistants would stay here and handle our current clients. If they want to grow it, it's on them."

Max responded, "Leaving yourself an out, are you?"

Drew, picking up his bags and starting to shut the lights off, answered the question, "Nope, if things don't work out with you, I can always just hang my shingle again. I did it before and I don't mind doing it again, if I have to, that is. I've built up a decent client list and I think a pretty good reputation as a criminal defense attorney."

Max, also grabbing his coat and getting ready to leave, let Drew get off the phone, "We wouldn't be having this conversation if you didn't. I'll wait to hear back from you. Get home and get some sleep, kid. You sound like you need it."

Drew turned off the last light and left his office, "I'll call you in a couple of days. Bye, Max."

◆

Steven was taking an early morning walk. Beautiful wooded paths surrounded his in-laws' house. It was just a couple of degrees above freezing, as winter mornings in Vermont tended to be, but the sky was clear and Steven enjoyed the cold. After years in deserts across the Middle East, where the daytime temperature could hit 115 degrees in the shade, and humid, muggy jungles in Africa and South America, he enjoyed the change of seasons here and in New York, and winter was his favorite season.

The cold helped clear his head, helped him get focused again. The past couple of days had cleared his head and recharged him enough for him to figure out his next move. That first evening, after Beth and her mother had come home from shopping in town, they'd eaten dinner in an awkward silence at first, nobody wanting to say anything, maybe they'd all been lost in their own thoughts. It had been Bethany, his daughter, who had broken that awkward silence when she talked about something she had researched on the Internet about The Great Wall of China being a lot longer than what people had thought. As she explained that it had been satellite imagery that led experts to reconsider the length of the wall, she'd given her father a look that said 'I told you I'd do what I could to help.' Steven had smiled at her and nodded in recognition of the unsaid message and asked her about it. He loved her more in that moment than he'd ever remembered loving her before. Then her grandfather joined the conversation talking about why it had been built and her grandmother told her about her and Tom's two trips to China.

It had been enough; they talked about other interesting things Bethany had researched. Beth prompted her to talk about her research on the God Particle, a particle that scientists had been trying to find for years. Bethany lit up, she had been researching all about it before everything had happened and was only too happy to explain what it was and why it was so important that the scientists find it. She had never taken a course in physics, something she was unlikely to do until she got to middle school or high school, but she had done some reading and research on her own. Steven remembered walking into her bedroom and being surprised at finding books by prominent scientists. They weren't textbooks or anything too advanced, more like books for the layman interested in the subject. Still, Steven doubted the authors of the books considered a 9-year-old girl their target audience.

After dessert, when both kids had gotten up from the table, Beth surprised Steven by bringing up the shooting at the courthouse, "Do you know any details about what happened at the courthouse today?"

Steven was taken by surprise. He hadn't given much thought to what he would say to his family about what he had done…a big, if understandable, oversight.

He'd taken a sip of his wine and turned to answer, "No, honey, I don't know any more than what they've been broadcasting since it happened. I was in a meeting when it happened."

Beth had simply nodded.

Lucy had jumped in then, "Well, good riddance, God forgive me for saying it, but I am glad that monster is dead."

Tom had also made a comment, "From what I've been hearing they have no idea who might have done it. There is a lot of speculation, as usual, from so-called experts, but none of the agencies involved have made any statement about anything other than to confirm the guy is dead. The NYPD has not said anything about it."

Steven had just listened, nodding at the proper moments. It was a difficult situation and he simply did not want to utter a single word without any further thought. After a few more minutes of that conversation, with nothing of substance being said, and once Lucy had shooed everyone out of the dining room and she and Tom had started cleaning up, he and Beth had a chance to talk. They'd gone outside with a cup of coffee splashed with some Amaretto and watched the last of the sunset together.

At first Beth had simply leaned on him and put her head on his chest, something that made him feel much better. He'd put his arm around her and just held her and waited for her to talk, if she wanted to. And she did. They both did. They talked about everything, about what each of them had gone and was still going through. It was the best conversation they'd had since Tracy had gone missing. There was far more to be said, but that first night had been a good first step back.

As Steven walked through the wooded trails, he also thought about two very telling exchanges he'd had over the last couple of days, one with his wife and one with his father-in-law. The first had been with Beth and it had caught him completely by surprise.

They were driving back from town where they'd gone to pick up some groceries and some DVDs for the kids. They'd been making the 30-minute drive back in silence, both lost in their own thoughts, holding hands in simple reassurance, when Beth had turned to talk to him, "I know you know more about what happened at the courthouse."

His first instinct was to deny it, but she hadn't let him, "I know you're going to deny it and I understand if you don't want to talk about it, God knows I don't know if I'd want to hear it anyway, but I wanted you to know that I'm here if you want to talk."

Steven hadn't said anything at first, he wanted to give some more thought to what he was ultimately going to say to his wife, but he also knew he couldn't hide from her, he had never been able to. Even when he was a SEAL and had come back from difficult operations, she had always been able to tell when there was something there, something in him that he'd eventually need to let out.

He had never discussed the details of his operations, but he had talked about his own feelings, what was going on with him as a human being, and that's what he'd done this time. "Beth, I don't want to lie to you, you know that, but honey, I don't know what my next move is going to be. You're right, I do know more about what happened, but I don't know what I'm going to do with what I know about. I don't know the best way to move forward yet."

Beth had listened and when he was finished she'd given him a small, warm smile, "I know, Steven, I understand how you work, remember? We've been together for more than half our lives and that counts for something, you know? I know you've never kept anything from me, just like I know that ultimately, there's nothing I'd be able to keep from you.

"Oh, I know there are a lot of things about the things you did, that you had to do, that you can't tell me about and I understand that. I signed on to be a Navy wife and I know what comes with that, but I'm talking about you as a human being, as a father and husband. I know that when it came to those things, you always shared whatever you had going on inside of you."

Steven had nodded. He hadn't known what it was that he was ultimately going to tell her, but he did know that whatever it was he would start with that, with his feelings and that's what he'd done, "You're right, I've always shared what I had going inside, deep inside. I'm sad, Beth, I'm going through this, or trying to anyway, as a father would, but I'm also angry and, honestly, confused. Not because I don't know what I'm feeling or what is going on, but because I just don't know how to handle what needs to come next.

"In the service and even at GIC, I never made a move, never, without having the endgame, the final outcome, figured out. This is different, I never had time to figure that endgame out, that final outcome. I did what I did because I saw the necessity to address something that needed to be done and I wasn't sure somebody else would be able to do, but where I go from there, I don't know."

And there it was, he hadn't told her what he had done, but he had told her enough that she *understood* what he had done. He'd done it because he'd known it was something that was inevitable, but he'd also done it because he understood that whatever he did next would depend on where his wife was, really was, and he wouldn't know that until he shared with her what he had just shared with her.

Beth looked at him for what seemed like an eternity, obviously processing what he'd just told her and trying to figure out how to respond. She wasn't a trained operative, she was just a grief-stricken mother and a wife, so her response had simply been a reflection of her feelings as both, "Well, you're one of the best men that I know, you and my father. We made a vow a long time ago and it's one that we've always been able to keep, and we've done it because of trust, ultimate trust, in each other.

"I guess what I am saying, Steven, is that I trust you; I trust that you did what you did because it was necessary, because it *had* to be done. I know how much your family, the kids, me, my parents, I know how much all of us mean to you, so I know that whatever it is that you did you didn't just do out of anger or rage, that you thought about us."

Steven's face was streaked with tears. Listening to his wife, her own voice breaking, let him know that she would be there; whatever else was true, that would always be the case. She had also let him know she understood that whatever it was he'd done, he'd done because it was necessary and not out of a fit of rage or anger or a need for revenge.

"Again, you're right. As always, you're right. That's exactly true, it had to be done, but do you now understand what I mean when I say to you that I don't know, I'm not sure, where to go from here?"

She nodded, "I do. I do because I've also been thinking about where this goes from here."

Surprised, he turned to face her and got another small, understanding smile, "I've known you for more than half of your life, sweetheart. I told you, I may be grieving but I'm not stupid, and I think I've known since the moment it happened, since I first heard it on the news. I knew you'd tell me in your own way, sooner or later, when you felt I was ready for it or when you thought you had no choice, but I knew we would have this conversation eventually.

"Do you think I didn't think about doing the same thing? I wanted him dead, with every fiber of my being I wanted him dead, and I wanted to do it with my own two hands.

"I'm sorry I can't go through this with you, because you know that if I could, if there was a way for us to stand together and go through it together, that's exactly what I would do, I would try to own this along with you."

Steven, face now dry, started to protest and again she'd beat him to it, "I know you are trying to protect us, all of us, from what you've done, the way you have over the years. But this isn't something you *can* protect us from. We're a part of it, like it or not. It's not your fault, it's just how things worked out.

"I think besides taking my little girl, that's the worst thing that monster did, he pulled us, all of us, into a nightmare. And that, Steven, is never going to be something you can protect us from, because we are already here. I think that the best thing I can do for you, the only thing actually, is to let you know that I love you, that your family loves you and always will, and that we will always be with you, no matter what."

She'd paused for a second and squeezed his hand to let him know that what she was about to say came from her very heart, "I can also let you know that whatever you decide to do, I have faith that it will be worth whatever we all have to go through. I know you will make sure of that, that whatever is coming will all be worth it in the end."

Steven had pulled her hand up to his lips and kissed it, looked her in the eyes and nodded, and with that he knew that his wife was in the right place, that whatever he decided, she wasn't going to fall apart. It was ironic to him that all those years of tough situations, of doing things far from home, things he couldn't talk about, of killing people and then having to go through it himself and then going through it with Beth, had prepared her for precisely for what she was having to go through now. Things like this were what kept Steven's belief in something higher, some intelligence or order that brought things together, that allowed things to line up, like this.

It had been a huge relief, a weight off his shoulders, and more than anything he had realized it was the biggest piece of the puzzle that had been missing for him. That conversation with her, and the conversation with his father-in-law, had been what he'd needed in order to put together a plan and make a decision.

He was coming down a trail and watching more of the sun come shining up through the trees as he recalled the conversation he'd had with Tom Delaney just the previous evening.

They'd been playing chess, something both men had enjoyed doing together throughout the years. They were in Tom's study, the sounds of some Disney movie or another coming through the open door. Both men had a cup of steaming coffee with a hint of brandy next to them. Steven had always held an edge over his father-in-law when it came to chess. He had done quite a bit of study of the game and had played at the expert level during his years at the Academy. Tom was no slouch, he himself held a high rating in the game, but the edge had always gone to Steven. That night, however, playing with the white pieces, Tom had Steven on the ropes and had the whole night.

Steven had been pondering his next move when Tom interrupted him, "You know that Beth and the kids will always be taken care of, right Steven? You know we'll always take care of them."

Steven looked up from the board with a look of genuine puzzlement, "Excuse me?"

Tom looked him right in the eye when he responded, "I'm not sure how you are involved in what happened in New York, I'm not sure I want to know, but I wanted you to know that your wife and your children will always be taken care of."

As had been the case with his wife, when Steven went to respond his father-in-law had raised his hand to stop him, "I'm not saying any of this to place blame, Steven. I told you before, I know what kind of man you are, and that meant that I know you would never do anything without thinking, just out of some sense of vengeance or vigilante justice.

"I also want you to recognize that at least when it comes to your family, we know you were involved somehow. Hell, even Lucy made a comment about it in passing. I think you've always known that and I think you've always known that the time would come when you would have to talk to us about it, to Beth at least.

"I don't know when or how it is you are planning to talk to her, but I wanted you to know that Lucy and I will always take care of her and the kids, no matter what happens, no matter what you need to do."

Steven had just looked down at the table and allowed Tom to get what he needed to off his chest. He knew that his father-in-law did not know that he and Beth had already had a conversation, Beth would have let him know, but now he came to understand that the two of them, father and daughter, *had* spoken about it.

He looked back up across the table and responded, "I do, Tom. Whatever else is true, I've always known that much."

Steven understood that his father-in-law didn't mean financially. The Loomis family was certainly not wealthy by New York standards, but they were on the edge of being considered just that, even by those lofty measures. They had always been careful with their money. Neither he nor Beth had any student loans and even early on they had always done well with each house they had bought and sold. They had invested their money, whatever little there was early on – nobody got rich on a Navy salary – always with Tom's advice.

By the time he left the service with a full military pension, their money had grown substantially. Once he came on board at GIC, his entire pension had gone straight into their investment portfolio and, in spite of the ups and downs in the market, had grown to just over three million dollars over the 20 years since they'd begun investing.

After paying the mortgage on their condo in SoHo, there was still more than two million dollars in their portfolio. All of that did not include a separate account, which Steven had opened after his second year at GIC. Beth had known he had opened the account. He'd told her that it was a 'just in case' account, something to have as a failsafe. Beth hadn't asked 'just in case of what exactly' or 'a failsafe for what' but he knew she understood. That account, composed of his bonuses and GIC stock, was now also worth more than three million dollars and it would keep growing as long as it remained untouched.

He'd been paid well at GIC, making in the low six figures at the beginning and getting up to over two million dollars last year. The children also had money put in trusts for them, trusts that had been established by their grandparents but which Steven and Beth had contributed into over the last five years. He now thought, with deep sadness, that Tracy's money would be split and put into her siblings' accounts.

Whatever worry Steven had about his family's welfare, it had never been about money and Tom knew that, so when he said Beth and the kids would be taken care he meant emotionally, he meant that both Bethany and Christopher would be watched over, educated, protected not only by their mother, but also by their grandparents.

Tom gave him a brief smile and nodded, "Good. Now, whatever else you need to do, whatever you decide needs to be done, you'll decide with a clear head and the comfort of knowing that your family will be okay." He paused for a second, looked down at the chessboard and then back up and directly into Steven's eyes, "No matter what comes next, I know you will make the right decision."

The man knew the life. He'd been there when Steven had come back from different difficult operations and had helped his daughter when Steven couldn't do it. Steven returned the smile and put an end to the conversation, "Thank you, Tom, for everything. Not just for now, for this, but for everything you've done for us, both you and Lucy. For everything you've done for me, personally."

Tom just smiled again, gave him a quick nod and looked back down at the table, "Now, you better pay attention to what you're doing because you're about to lose your queen."

Steven went back to considering his next move; a plan was forming for him now. Fifteen minutes later the game was over, Tom having won it decidedly. It hadn't been his next move in the chess game that Steven had gone back to considering.

He'd walked a good three miles, coming down and around a small pond in the middle of the woods he'd been walking in, remembering both conversations and thinking about how much he'd needed to have both of them in order to decide anything. He was standing looking across the pond when something hit him square in the face, something he hadn't thought about, but which should have been clear from the beginning. Now that he could think with some clarity, with some real perspective, it became clear immediately and it was something urgent enough that he pulled out his cell phone to make a call that he should have made days ago. He dialed the number for Robert Grady's cell phone number.

Grady was sitting in his office putting together a file on the Riche shooting. What he was really doing was trying to think about what his next move should be. He was only a few years away from retirement and he would try to keep his pension if he could, but he knew he would not compromise the case in any way and would completely own up to whatever his role had been in this mess if necessary.

The investigation following the shooting had led nowhere, as he knew it would. Every agency involved had already contacted individuals of interest, including Loomis who had spoken to an NYPD detective on the phone and told her exactly what he had told Grady. The NYPD had tried to contact those at the 'meeting,' but all had been out of the country at the time, unreachable for the next few days. They'd been provided with a time-stamped video feed of that meeting, however, which had satisfied the investigators for now.

As he was starting the new file, his cell phone rang. Whoever it was would have to wait. He picked it up just to see who was calling and immediately went to answer it, "Hello, Mr. Loomis."

On the other end of the line, Steven responded with no emotion, "Hello, Detective Grady. I don't want to take up too much of your time, but it occurred to me that if you believe that I did the shooting, you and Mark Mullins might do something stupid and share our discussions and what happened at the warehouse with those involved in the investigation."

Grady, looking out the window and smiling, responded, "I never thought *you'd* do something as stupid as this."

Loomis was curious, "Something as stupid as what? Call you to make sure that you kept to our previous understanding?"

Grady, now standing, responded, "No, call to plead your case to save your skin."

Now it was Loomis's turn to smile, "To save *my* skin? Detective, I have already spoken to two detectives from the NYPD and you know damn well they've already contacted the company and verified everything I told them. You also know there is not a single shred of evidence to support this theory of yours and that the only way that I would come back into consideration would be if you and Mullins let the team investigating this know about our conversations and the warehouse, which, by the way, there is also no evidence I was involved with in any way. I went there because I was monitoring police scanners and wanted to confirm it was my daughter, period.

"If you and Mullins talk, I *might* come back into consideration, but you and Mullins will *certainly* face repercussions and we both know that too.

"This case has a political angle, detective. You and I know that if no arrests are made, your superiors will most certainly be looking for someone to place some blame on, anybody, in order to deflect bad press, and if you and Mark speak, it will be you they look to."

Grady, now sitting behind his desk, had in fact thought about all of it. He and Mullins had spoken a few times about it and come to the exact same conclusion.

Still he wasn't going to admit that to Loomis, "So I take it you're calling me out of concern for us, Mullins and myself, is that it?"

Loomis answered him immediately, "Believe it or not, Robert, I appreciated, still appreciate, how you and Mullins handled the case and our discussions. So yes, I would certainly not want you and Mullins to end what are certainly brilliant careers by talking about something that you did to help me out."

Grady bristled, "Hey, let's get something straight. I did what I did because I wanted to catch this guy. I wanted to catch him and *prosecute* him. Don't forget that."

Steven hung his head, "I know that, detective, I didn't mean to imply otherwise, but let's be real. You and I both know that you also did what you did because you are a dad and because you could understand what my family and I were going through.

"Look, I don't want to argue this point anymore. You know I have been straight with you and you know about my record in the military and at GIC. If I had something to do with the shooting, don't you think that I would *eventually* own up to whatever it is that I did?"

Grady perked up at the emphasis on the word *eventually*. He didn't say anything because he thought Loomis had more to say, and he was right.

Loomis continued, "I guess what I'm trying to say is that you followed your instincts about me, about my background and what I would do when my daughter went missing, so trust those instincts, they haven't let you down before and they won't let you down now. I think you already know that, too, because otherwise you would have said something immediately after the shooting happened, after you and I had our conversation.

"You didn't because, again, you followed your instincts and if you get nothing else out of this call, understand just that, that I'm calling to let you know that you should continue to do that, trust your instincts and not do something stupid."

There it was, like most of the conversations between the two men, everything of substance, the actual point, went left unsaid, but was completely clear to both men. Loomis was letting Grady know that when the time was right, he would take ownership of his role in the shooting, regardless of the consequences to himself. Now, talking to him and hearing him say all of this, Grady could better appreciate what Loomis had been dealing with. He made the decision to take out his daughter's killer, but he probably hadn't thought about it further than that right away. Hell, with everything that the man had gone through, Grady had been surprised he'd been as effective as he had been in planning what he had done. He probably hadn't told his family that he'd be doing what he did, and once he pulled the trigger his first instinct had been to go to them and make sure they'd be alright once it all came down. Grady knew all of this because that's exactly how he had imagined he might play it if he found himself in the same circumstances.

As had been true throughout the case, Grady would, in fact, follow his instincts, "Alright, Steven, I'm not sure what it is that you have planned, but you're right about one thing. It'd be a long shot that they'd bring you up on charges, even if Mark and I tell them everything we know about or suspect.

"I am also absolutely buried in cases that took a back seat while all of this went on, so Mark and I both agreed that we'd give it some thought and decide once things settled down."

On his end Loomis also got the unspoken message 'We decided to wait to see what you were planning on doing,' but he simply responded to what Grady actually said, "I think that was a good idea. I can imagine how busy the two of you are, and the last thing you need is to go chasing ghosts, especially when you know that eventually they will probably come to you. Goodbye, Robert, I'm sure we'll speak again."

This time Grady wasn't snide when he said his goodbye, "See you later, Loomis. Good luck to you."

After they hung up, Grady pulled out his Maker's Mark and poured himself a drink, even though he'd just finished his breakfast coffee. He was sure that they'd speak again, he just didn't know how long it would be before they did, but he definitely felt better about the wait. He picked up the phone, called Mark Mullins and let him off the hook as well. Their careers would not come to a sudden end after all.

Steven hung up on his end and let out a big breath. He had no intention of allowing Grady or Mullins to end their careers in order to bring him in. If he had read Grady correctly over the course of the case, which he felt he had, the man had gotten the message and would hold tight. Grady was an excellent detective and Steven knew one couldn't become that without the ability to assess a situation and decide when it was prudent to just stay put. It was something that he himself had been trained to do and to which he'd adhered his entire life. Until now. Until this.

He was making his way back up to the house, up a trail on the opposite side of the mostly frozen pond. The sun was now in full morning glory, lighting up what was looking like a clear, gorgeous day. There were now more morning joggers and people walking their dogs, all of them nodding wordlessly as they ran or walked past him. His plan was now on more firm footing. He had made certain his family was covered and had also made sure that those that had helped him along the way, the General, Grady and Mullins, all of them, were also taken care of. Now he just needed to figure out his next tactical move. He knew what his overall objective was, he just didn't know how to best accomplish it.

Things had become much clearer once he'd had the conversations he needed to have, so he reasoned that the answers would continue to become clearer as he proceeded to have some of the other conversations that he planned on having. By the time he got back to the house, now permeated with the smells of breakfast and the sounds of two children trying to get back to their lives, he had made the decisions he felt he could with the information he had.

When he walked through the door he found his wife, his children, his in-laws, all engaged in conversation, with Beth looking fresh and engaged and his children doing children things on a cold winter morning.

Steven let a smile spread across his face, what felt like the first real smile since this all began, and allowed himself to simply be a husband and a dad. He went straight to Beth and hugged her and kissed her cheek and allowed his children to run up to him and to hug him. He picked up Chris to spin him around. Steven Loomis allowed himself to just be a husband and a dad that beautiful morning, because he wasn't sure when the next time would be that he'd be able to be those things or if he'd even be able to do those things once he did what he needed to do.

Chapter 14

rew was sitting in the middle of his new office. He was looking around, chuckling softly as he did so. It would indeed be a humorous sight if anyone were to come into his office as he stood there in contemplation. All the files from his office were contained in eight cardboard file boxes, which now sat on the massive mahogany desk in his office. He saw the wall-length file cabinets and calculated that his files would take up approximately one tenth of the cabinet's capacity. His office was decorated in a muted and modern style that juxtaposed a law office feel and minimalist Scandinavian furnishings. He had to smile. Max had wanted to make sure the décor reflected power and influence, something the entire law offices did in spades, but that it reflected the personality of its new occupant as well.

The law offices of Corliss, Zeidler and Kirk occupied three whole floors of the building and those were huge, city-block-sized floors. Drew imagined that there were probably a total of 140 or 150 attorneys in the firm along with 8 or 10 junior partners and partners.

They took on almost all types of cases from maritime law to international copyright and patent cases to the area that Zeidler headed, criminal law and appeals from all over the country. A criminal case coming into the firm had to meet certain criteria. It had to be either extremely lucrative or high-profile, preferably both. Zeidler had clawed his way to the top and he never forgot where he came from, so the firm did its fair share of pro bono cases, especially high-profile pro bono cases.

Drew had spoken to his staff shortly after speaking to Zeidler. He had also spoken to his only associate explaining that he would now hold down the fort. Drew would continue to share the expenses and would continue to refer cases he was not able to handle. He wanted to make sure that he had an out if things didn't work out with Zeidler, even though he'd told Max that wasn't the case.

He had debated whether to take the offer or keep trying to grow his small practice and it had been a short debate. His office had been doing well, they were profitable and Willis had scored some serious credibility points over the past couple of years, getting some very favorable results on a number of difficult cases. Even so, he wanted more. It wasn't about the money; it was about getting cases he could really sink his teeth into.

He seemed to have a knack for criminal law. His courtroom presence and his litigation skills were impeccable and he knew it. He had proved it more than once during some of the most serious cases he'd taken. He was able to take a seasoned vice detective and cut him to ribbons on cross-examination before the detective knew it was happening. He would lull him into complacency by asking questions that were well within the officer's comfort zone. The detective would be confident, sure of his answers and thinking about lunch or an after-work drink. Willis would then slowly begin to trip him up with contradictions to previous testimony or to notes in the file or to testimony from other witnesses, and before the detective could regroup and qualify his answers it would be over. He'd done it more than once and had developed a reputation for being a 'sneaky little bastard' among the law enforcement officers he went up against.

Now he wanted to utilize those skills on more difficult cases, on cases where the stakes were high and his opposition was the best at what they did, and he knew that would not happen for some time if he remained a sole practitioner with a small firm. Cases like that did not just come in off the street.

Drew Willis was settling into his new office and imagining what it would be like to lead the defense on a high-profile case, not knowing that within less than 48 hours he would be presented with the highest-profile case of all.

◆

Now back in New York, Steven Loomis had a clear and defined idea of what he wanted to accomplish. On his way in from his in-laws' he had gone over the path that had brought him here, to this point. He'd recalled how he had known that he'd use whatever resources were at his disposal to look for Tracy when she'd gone missing. He remembered trying to come up with answers for what had happened to her, how he'd looked to science and forensic psychiatry, and the moment when everything he'd read about and researched had become a grim and shocking reality. After witnessing what he'd witnessed at the warehouse, two things became clear for Steven, Donald Riche was not a human being and nothing he'd seen in that warehouse, nothing he'd felt, spoke of a human mind, even a sick and depraved human mind. The scene spoke of something else, of something with high intelligence, focus and drive, of a predator that fed on human fear and suffering.

Loomis had been exposed to countless atrocities across many countries and had felt the despair and horror that war could bring, the sense of helplessness that death and loss brought to the loved ones of those lost. What he'd felt at that warehouse was nothing like that; it wasn't like those scenes of destruction had been. No, what he'd felt at that warehouse was like he and the others there with him had uncovered the den of an unspeakable predator, of a force beyond what any of them had ever encountered. He saw and felt everything himself, but he also saw that the others there with him had also felt it and they had been overwhelmed by it.

By the time he'd left the warehouse, he understood what Tyrone Leonard had been talking about when he explained to him just how different the species he'd researched and named were from the human species, he understood why the man had been so certain about what he'd found.

That was the first thing he'd concluded. His next conclusion had been that Riche would never be punished for what he'd done. The justice system had been established and evolved over time with the idea that those that came before it were humans, humans that had committed horrible and senseless crimes, but humans nevertheless. Incarceration, however long, was meant to punish, to let those who committed crimes know how reprehensible their acts had been. Likewise, the death penalty was meant to show not only the perpetrator of the crime, but all those that were aware of it, that some crimes were unforgivable and that the only justice that was appropriate was to take the offender's life. All of it was meant to rehabilitate or to punish or to deter others, but it was all designed with the expectation that it would be humans committing the crimes, humans receiving the punishment and humans being deterred from committing crimes.

Riche would not have ever believed that any punishment handed down to him was really a punishment at all. He would have believed that he was above it all, that all of it, the trial, the charges, the punishment, whether it was lifelong imprisonment or death, was meant to punish simple criminals, not him.

Steven had also known that Riche would continue to be what he was, a predator, no matter where he went. Even among others that had committed similar crimes, rapists and murderers, he would eventually grow to understand them, to understand how he might be able to use them to fulfill his own purposes. He'd also do it to those charged with looking over him, psychologists, officers, anyone in his circle of influence. It may have taken a long time, years perhaps, but he would have victimized, he would have preyed. He would do this because that is what his nature would call upon him to do. He would be no more able to keep himself from doing this than a tiger might be able to keep itself from preying on whatever prey it found itself surrounded by when it got hungry.

So Steven had decided almost immediately that whatever else happened, he would have to eliminate the threat, eliminate the predator that had taken his daughter from him. He had stopped to consider his decision, to make sure that he was not making it because of the pain and rage that he felt or because he wanted revenge. He knew that to make a decision based on such emotions would be a mistake, so he called upon years and years of training and experience to guide his thoughts and actions. He had enough introspection left in him to know that there would be no way to completely divorce his emotions from his actions, but he wanted to make sure it wasn't emotions driving his decisions.

Those were the decisions that had brought him here, to where he was today. Now, with some time to reflect on everything that had happened, he had defined his ultimate objective: to let the world know about what he'd seen, what he'd experienced, about the science of the new species that had replaced humans at the top of the food chain. He had to make the world aware that every day, at school or at work or even under their own roof, there was a chance, a remote chance to be sure, but a chance nonetheless, that they were being hunted by something far more terrifying than any human, psychopath, sociopath or not, could ever be. He knew that was his ultimate goal, but he still did not know how it was that he would accomplish that.

He had an idea, but he wanted to make sure that it was the right thing to do, because once he did it there would be no turning back. He was on his way to speak to Leonard again and planned on speaking with Jim Scoma, the researcher out in California. He thought that, as had been the case before, his conversations with those that had researched the new species, people that were guided by science and did not have any moral or emotional agenda to drive their conclusions, would bring more clarity to the situation and would help guide his decisions.

He had called Leonard and asked to meet with him again, and after a short pause Leonard had agreed to meet with him. That pause had let Steven know that Leonard had put together who he was and why he'd wanted to learn more about his work. Steven wasn't sure whether Leonard had put everything together and knew he'd had something to do with the shooting at the courthouse, but he knew the man was smart. Once Leonard knew that Steven was the father of one of the victims, it would not have been too difficult for him to imagine that he might have had something to do with Riche's shooting, especially after their conversation. Even if the only thing that Leonard had figured out was that Steven was the father of one of the victims, he owed the man a visit.

The same graduate student that had brought him to Leonard's door before was there to greet him. Leonard's office door was open and when Steven knocked lightly on it he'd been in the middle of sorting out what looked to be test booklets.

He looked up from the small table and smiled, "Mr. Loomis, I have to say that I was surprised by your call. Please, come in."

He moved the tests to another table and motioned for Steven to take a seat at the small table he was sitting at. There was no hesitation or fear in his demeanor, which told Steven that maybe he'd just figured out that he was the father of one of the victims and nothing more.

Steven shook the man's hand and sat down across from him, "Professor, I wanted to speak with you again because I feel that I wasn't completely forthright with you when we spoke before, and that's not how I normally do things. I hope you can understand my reasons for holding back on sharing some information. It has been a difficult time for my family and me."

Leonard held Steven's eyes with a soft, understanding smile on his face, "I understand completely. I was terribly sorry to hear about your loss. I can't begin to imagine how hard it must have been on you, how hard it probably still is. If it makes you feel any better, I was actually thankful that you did not share your circumstances with me, because I think if you had, I probably would not have agreed to meet with you or, even if I had agreed, perhaps I wouldn't have shared all of the information that I shared with you, and then I would have felt bad about it. So, you see, I think it was the right thing to do at the time."

Leonard was trying to put Steven at ease about their earlier encounter, something Steven appreciated immensely because it made the conversation he was looking to have with the scientist a bit easier.

Leonard, a bit more focused now, asked Steven the obvious, "How can I be of assistance?"

Steven had thought about the conversation and the questions that he needed answers for, but he also knew that he had to come at it correctly, patiently, because given what had happened at the courthouse Leonard might be more guarded about what he shared, in spite of the curious, open look now dominating his expression.

"Thank you for your kind words, professor, I appreciate the sentiment, and again I am sorry for withholding the full circumstances of my situation. I wanted to see you again because I have some questions that we didn't address in our previous conversations."

Leonard nodded thoughtfully, still focused in on Steven, "Okay, and what might those questions be?"

Steven now leaned closer, "Well, I have to be honest, what you shared with me last time is incredible. I can't imagine that discovering a new species, a species that as you said is above humans on the food chain, is something that happens every day. It seems like something that would be a huge event for humanity, something that would be on the news or in headlines in magazines and newspapers.

"I would think that you would be beseeched by interview requests on all kinds of talk shows or newscasts. And yet, there hasn't been anything like that. Everything I found about it was online on blogs and obscure theses from students across the country."

As he was speaking, Leonard was nodding with a much broader smile on his face and a sparkle in his eye. Clearly this was something that he himself had thought about or been asked about time and time again. He chuckled as Steven was finishing, "You are absolutely right, there has been no big story or big transcendental pronouncement about what we've found, but I can assure you it has not been for a lack of trying.

"We announced our findings in all of the proper peer-reviewed journals and published all of our work, including the raw data by the way, on my own blog online and on the university's blog. We even put out a press release through the PR Newswire. I don't need to tell you how much interest all of it generated, the fact that you are asking about it now should be answer enough."

Steven leaned back and nodded, "That's what I mean. It just seems incredible that none of this, none of your work or the work of the other scientists I read about, has been discovered by the world.

"I can't believe that the world would not want to know about this, about the threat that it poses to everyone who comes across one of these things."

Leonard responded, "It's not that they don't want to know, it's that they don't realize the significance of it as it relates to their everyday lives. To most people, these are abstract theories, stuff of science and academia, and not related to their world, the 'real' world.

"Listen, this year scientists at CERN finally discovered the Higgs boson or what some call the 'God Particle.' It is something scientists had been trying to find for decades and it has the potential to completely change the fundamental laws of physics, in essence it has the potential to change the fundamental understanding of reality as we know it. There were a few headlines about it in some of the more intellectual publications and there have been scores of presentations by scientists all over the world.

"How many people do you think even know about it? I would venture to guess that it's not more than roughly 10 percent of the population, and that is probably too high. And of those that have heard about it, however it is they heard about it, how many do you think understand the implications of it? Probably less than one percent.

"I'll give you another example, Japanese scientists announced that they were able to grow eggs, *human eggs*, from embryonic stem cells. Even more astounding, they announced that they believed they could grow human eggs from *any* other human cell. Theoretically that would mean that they could take DNA left by Brad Pitt on a drinking glass and grow eggs genetically similar to Brad Pitt without him ever being aware that it had happened. That has very significant, real-world implications and yet very few people have ever even heard of the discovery, let alone understand the implications of it. We won't even begin to discuss the discoveries in the fields of genetic engineering, computing, programming, microbiology or nanotechnology, to name just a few.

"No, Mr. Loomis, the world is interested in mindless voyeurism, in watching a group of mindless youth consuming vast amounts of alcohol while they share a house on the New Jersey coast. They care more about what label a candidate is wearing or who they are sleeping with than they do about the substance of that candidate's policies."

Loomis took it all in and nodded. What Leonard said seemed incredible. These were major, history-changing discoveries that were going completely unnoticed by the world at large. Still, he knew the man was telling the truth. He himself had been completely unaware of Leonard's and the other scientists' work. Until it had touched him personally, until he'd paid for the ignorance with the confusion and helplessness he'd felt after his daughter went missing.

Leonard went on, "I was disheartened and angered by it when I was young and naïve, and I vowed that my discoveries would be so monumental that the world would not be able to ignore them. Now I know better."

Loomis had another question, "Why go on then, professor? Why continue to do the work and the research if you know that the fruits of your work are being ignored, that the world is bound to suffer because of their ignorance? It seems like it would be incredibly frustrating to do what you do."

Leonard, looking a bit forlorn and sad, responded, "Because, Mr. Loomis, that's what scientists do. We do the work and we come up with our findings and hypotheses in the hope that someday, when humanity is ready, it *will* all make a difference in people's lives.

"Throughout history, every time mankind has evolved, taken a step forward, you can always trace it back to science. It is a scientist's job to do the research and find the truth. It is humanity's job to take the science and do something with it. Doctors, explorers, aeronautical engineers, they are the doers, the ones who bring the science to the masses and the ones that make it matter in a concrete way.

"I have to be honest and say that we also do it for the love of science, of discovery, because when we run up against walls, when the answers seem to elude us, it is only that love that drives us.

"Einstein put out his theories of relativity and special relativity knowing that most people of his time would dismiss his work as nonsense, as the imaginations of a young theorist looking to shake the foundations of his field. He also knew that many of his hypotheses would not be validated until he was long gone. It was his internal curiosity, his desire for the truth of reality, that drove him, and I suspect it is that same curiosity that drives most scientists."

Steven listened intently. Leonard could tell that he was trying to process everything that he had just shared with him.

He got up from the table they were sitting at, walked over to the shelf, picked out a book, and gave it to Steven as he came back to sit down at the table, "Here, this is a book written by Dr. Samuel Grossman. He is a professor of forensic psychiatry at Columbia University. He has also done significant research on the same topic.

"I believe I told you about him when we last met. His approach involves more of an abstract approach than an evolutionary one. He has actually developed a scale to measure the level of deviance of those he studies. He has come to establish the concept of 'evil' as an empirical measurement that he uses on his scale."

Steven was a bit confused, "I remember the name, but I would be lying if I said I remembered his work. I read so much that it's hard to keep it straight now. What do you mean he uses 'evil' as an empirical measurement?"

Leonard explained, "I mean exactly that. The different levels on his scale determine how 'evil' someone's actions are. So, for example, the lower levels on the scale represent a very low level of 'evil.'

Usually, it is people in the throes of a fit of rage or who display a gross disregard for safety that end up on the lower levels of his scale. Where our work intersects is at the highest levels on his scale. Those levels represent planned, sadistic and cruel murders, the type of behavior that also draws out attention.

"The book I just gave you outlines his work in detail. Although his approach is different from ours, the basic conclusions are the same. The three highest levels on his scale define behavior that is not within human norms, that does not fit within any recognized standard for deviant human behavior.

"He also has a show on public television that features most of the levels of his scale, but not the three highest levels. I imagine the types of crimes that define those highest levels are too much for a television audience.

"Anyway, there are a lot of us exploring this science, some of us take an evolutionary and philosophical approach, while others concentrate more on the physiological and genetic elements, but all of us are working from similar, if not the same, hypotheses."

Steven was absorbing everything that Leonard was sharing with him. It was precisely the type of information that he had been looking for.

He had one last question for Leonard, "Thank you, professor, again you have been more than generous with your time. I have one last question for you. You told me before that there were physical differences that you had been able to establish during your research. I read some of your papers and you explained in them that the differences were in some areas of the brain, are there other physical differences that you have been able to identify?"

Leonard's smile brightened up again, "You mean are there differences you can readily see, differences that don't require a microscope to find, is that it?"

Steven now let a small smile appear on his face, "Yes, I suppose that's what I am talking about."

Leonard paused for a couple of beats, trying to think about the type of work Steven was asking about. "Well, there is a researcher out of the University of Nebraska, Dr. Allen Schultz. He and I were introduced about three years ago by one of my assistants. He has been doing work on involuntary physical triggers. He is one of the foremost experts on interrogation techniques and on lie detection. He has been nicknamed The Human Lie Detector by some of his students.

"Anyway, he has identified 44 involuntary indicators when someone is trying to be deceitful. Things like involuntary movement of the eyes, minute shakes of the head or tightening of the facial muscles. He has studied thousands of subjects, using the most sensitive measuring equipment to register every minute change in intonation, pitch, modulation, everything, and he has discarded every element that could potentially be controlled or suppressed by his subjects. That's where the 44 indicators come from. Every one of them is something that he has over time determined cannot be controlled by even the most skilled liar.

"He has worked with professional interrogators, former CIA agents, military intelligence specialists, every type of professional whose work demands that they know how to deceive and how to control their responses, and not even those professionals can suppress the indicators he has identified. So when one of my assistants found out about his work, she thought we might be able to collaborate.

"We met and agreed to work together, testing both of our hypotheses through several sets of controlled interviews. We utilized 22 of our most promising subjects, individuals we were certain were *Homo predaer,* and we set up all of Dr. Schultz's measurement equipment. Every one of our subjects was either able to suppress the indicators or the indicators were simply not present. None of our subjects were told what the indicators were, so the most likely explanation is that they simply did not have the same physiology as the subjects that Schultz had researched.

"He was completely astounded by our findings and decided to explore them along with us. Remember, he had developed these indicators after interviewing and measuring *thousands* of people over many, many years. He had been certain that his indicators would revolutionize the science of lie detection, and now he had to reconsider those findings."

Steven nodded in understanding; that was precisely the type of thing he was looking for, something that could be identified without looking through a microscope, something that had real-life weight to it. He understood the scientific aspect of Leonard's work, but he was looking for something that regular people, everyday individuals, could relate to, understand and perhaps even internalize. It was also a perfect example of how the world was simply not equipped to deal with *Homo predaer*. Human lie detectors would be useless on them.

He got ready to wrap up their conversation, "Thank you, professor, you have been incredibly kind with your time. I don't want to take up any more of your day."

Both men stood up from the small table. As they were shaking hands to say goodbye, Loomis felt the academic's hand tighten as he proceeded to almost floor him, "Goodbye, Mr. Loomis, I hope that I have given you the answers you were looking for, but I also hope that my work is not responsible for the path that you have chosen to pursue."

Steven held the man's eyes and he noticed the intensity in the man's voice and in his eyes. He knew, had known before they'd even began their conversation. Whatever it was that Leonard believed or was speculating about, he had not spoken to the police or to any of the investigators assigned to the case. Now as he was saying goodbye to

Steven, Leonard wanted him to know he had figured out he had something to do with what happened to Riche.

Leonard let go of Loomis's hand and before opening the door and before Steven had a chance to explain or say anything in response, he concluded their conversation, "Mr. Loomis, you seem like an intelligent and considered individual, and I know from what I've read about you that you have a beautiful family and a thriving career. I hope that the choices that you have made were not made in haste or in the pursuit of something as banal as revenge. You don't strike me as that type of person, but tragedy can bring out unbecoming qualities in people."

Now Steven did respond, "You're right, tragedy tests us in ways that we would never imagine, and you are right, I do have a beautiful family and that's something that I would never put at risk. Rest assured that I have not made any decision without understanding its implications or how those implications might affect my future and my family.

"I have run operations in almost every continent, professor, and I have seen violence and some of the worst that humans inflict on one another. Revenge and senseless violence were trained out of me long ago, if they were ever there in the first place.

"Your work has informed my decisions, but it has not driven them. I am not made to be guided simply by others' work, even someone as accomplished as yourself. It's just not in my DNA, so don't worry about our conversations, this one or the one we had before. Again, thank you for your time and for your concern."

Leonard's face was transformed by that engaging smile that just seemed to materialize on his face without any effort whatsoever and he went back to the same affable personality with which he'd first greeted Steven. "It's my pleasure, Mr. Loomis. Like I told you before, I am always happy to talk about my work. Good luck to you." And with that their conversation was concluded.

As Steven had expected, his conversation with Leonard had provided clarity and understanding and with that a better sense of what he had to do.

Chapter 15

Steven hailed a cab and headed back to his condo. He had reached out to Jim Scoma, the scientist in California that Leonard had referred him to, and had scheduled a call with him for later that afternoon. Once he got to his condo, Steven settled in, emptied his bags and made himself something to eat. They were simple tasks, but it felt good to be back at home and to get back to even a semblance of normality. He sat down at the small kitchen table with his laptop and as he ate his sandwich he read about the research that Leonard and Schultz had done.

Like everything else that he had found, this was fascinating and at the same time absolutely chilling. He imagined the chaos, pain and damage that these individuals could cause. Technology had allowed humanity to make discoveries that had seemed impossible just a decade earlier and those discoveries had benefited countless numbers of people, but technology also provided a glimpse into worlds that had before simply gone unnoticed, maybe unimagined.

This was such a glimpse, a glimpse of a world where humans were prey and the predators hunting them were among them, blending perfectly, using their weaknesses, their vulnerability to ensnare them.

This wasn't a world of zombies, or aliens or other fantastic monsters that human imagination had given birth to since the time that men had gathered around fires to tell their stories and tales of conquest. These monsters were much, much more dangerous, far more frightening than anything ever imagined or invented. These monsters went unseen and unnoticed; they used their appearance like a tiger might use its stripes to blend into the jungle around them. Steven thought about all of this and could not help but to think about his own daughter, about Riche and how he had probably hunted her and the other children, how none of them recognized him as the monster that he was, and it was that thought that gave him the most regret.

These thoughts were inevitable and he knew it, whatever else he was, whatever else he might become, he was still a grieving father.

His conversation with Leonard had done exactly what he thought it might. It had clarified why it was so important that he let the world know about the new species, about the science and about the danger that it presented to humanity.

People lived their lives, day in and day out, with a vague awareness of the dangers that might await them around any corner. At cocktail parties people lamented senseless violence and the decline of humanity, but they all lived with a sort of self-woven security blanket, a comfort that if they did not drift into an undefined underworld and if they took normal precautions and were vigilant then nothing untoward was going to happen to them, nothing was going to rip up their lives. Security alarms, neighborhood watch programs, guns and even law enforcement were the embodiments of how society dealt with the dangers it envisioned.

These predators were nothing like the dangers they imagined, however. They didn't wait for their prey in dark alleys and abandoned, drug-infested buildings. They were not driven by greed or jealousy or drug-induced paranoia. These beings *thrived* in the places that seemed to offer humans the most safety, places like churches and schools and even their own homes. These predators relied on the 'security' these places offered; they relied on that false sense of security and order to ensnare their prey when they least expected it. His daughter hadn't been taken from a dark alley or a deserted park covered by darkness. She wasn't taken by a deranged lunatic where nobody could see it was happening, she was taken from her mother, in broad daylight with dozens, probably hundreds of people around and she was taken without a single cry for help being uttered. Steven had read the case file and that had been the case with every one of the girls. All of them had been taken from places where they should have been safe, all of them taken without warning and without a single trace of what had happened to them.

Riche had looked like a harmless, decent and educated individual. He had functioned among people with ease and had established a complete persona, an identity that had accomplished exactly what he'd hoped, to lull his victims into a feeling of safety or confidence, to allow him to go unnoticed and unchallenged.

Steven had also read the file on Riche and what hadn't been in the file the media had already reported on. His early childhood had been troubled, although not extremely. His mother had left him when he was nine, but she'd never abused him. After that he'd lived with relatives, all of them had been decent families that had provided a sense of stability and care, if not love. They'd been supportive of him in everything he'd undertaken. Everything in the file let Steven and every other expert that had read it know that Riche had not been made by his environment, he had simply been born that way. Upon reaching adulthood he had understood that in order to engage in his brutal crimes, he would have to blend in, he would have to hone his hunting skills, and he would have to build a life that presented him to the world as a harmless and gentle soul.

As Riche had grown older, Steven imagined, he had refined his techniques, his predatory instincts to a point where he had become an almost perfect predator. There had been no evidence that there were more victims out there, but Steven and every expert studying the case believed that these last nine had almost certainly not been his only victims. Some people, Steven included, believed that there were more victims. A few of the experts and profilers had theorized that he had most likely been perfecting his techniques before he took the girls, and that meant he had most likely taken and murdered many more victims before he'd begun working on the last nine girls.

Stven finished his lunch and closed his computer, wondering how many others like Riche might be out there, but he stopped himself before he could get very far. He knew it might cause him to lose his focus and his objective might once again become unclear.

He went into his study and dialed the number for Jim Scoma. His research had let him know that Dr. James Scoma was genius-smart, but most definitely an eccentric. He had graduated from high school at the age of 15 and had obtained his first PhD in organic chemistry at the age of 19. He held three other PhDs, including one in philosophy, one in psychology and one in mathematics, and as if that wasn't enough, the man had a medical degree with a specialty in forensic psychiatry. He had published no fewer than a 103 papers on a variety of topics including the expected extinction of the bees, global warming and the correlation between chaos theory and the evolution of social media. He had done revolutionary work on parallel systems programming and how it related to biological systems and evolution.

For the past 10 years, Scoma had been conducting research on genetic mutations and on evolutionary theory projections as it related to human cognition and sensory abilities. Most of what the man had written was way over Steven's head, but what he had been able to understand was that Scoma believed that evolution had not stopped at *Homo sapiens*, it had continued to march on, at first with small, unnoticeable mutations within the human species, but eventually establishing a separate and distinct species from humans, perhaps more than one.

Leonard had been right. His work did not concentrate on the fringes of aberrant human behavior, but rather on other areas of the spectrum Leonard had explained to Loomis.

Steven dialed the number and Scoma picked up the phone on the third ring.

After saying their hellos and engaging in the requisite small talk, Steven got down to business, "Dr. Scoma, I have spoken with Dr. Leonard and I think I have a pretty good understanding of his work and his findings. I was hoping to also understand the work you are doing, how it's similar to his work and how it might be different."

On his end, Scoma smiled, sat behind his desk, put his feet up and proceeded to answer, "Sure, no problem. I have to warn you, though, once I get rolling I tend to get excited and just ramble on. If it starts happening, just stop me and ask me to rewind."

Steven responded, "Fair enough, I'll be sure to do that."

Scoma went on, "Okay, so, you know about Leonard's *Homo sapiens predator* and how he got there. He employed some of the same theories on evolution that we have, but given his area of focus, it was clear that whatever evolutionary step he was going to run into would be at the 'bad' end of the scale, for lack of a better world.

"We have simply not concentrated on the behaviors on his end of the scale, but rather on behaviors and abilities present in other individuals, behaviors and abilities that were clearly beyond what we, science, had established as human norms. We focused on abilities such as a hyperdeveloped sense of smell, auditory sensitivity far beyond what we had defined as humanly possible, same thing with eyesight and with every other one of the human senses. Synesthesia was a natural field for us.

Steven interrupted, "What's synesthesia?"

Scoma answered without slowing down, "It is when the neural pathways in the brain that control each of our senses become entangled or overlap. People see sounds or they taste what they see, not figuratively, mind you, but literally. We are starting to find more and more people who have more than two senses that are interacting – seeing *and* tasting sound, that kind of thing. It was something virtually unknown previously, but it is definitely becoming more common."

Steven interrupted again, "So it's an indication of evolution?"

Scoma went on, "Well, there's a lot more to it, but essentially, yes. It lets us know that this adaptation is becoming more common, which is not surprising given the amount of stimuli our brains have to deal with today. We also paid particular attention to every one of our subjects' cognitive processes as they relate to morality. Before you ask what we mean by that, I'll tell you. It is what people might commonly call their internal 'moral compass.' We were looking for clarity, for a defined and clear point of view as it related to their view of the world.

"It was fascinating stuff. We looked at philosophers, artists, clergy, anyone who adhered to a very clear idea of what they believed humanity should be.

"Don't get me wrong, we were always of the opinion that humans, well, most of us anyway, naturally develop a sense of right and wrong. That basic construct is what guides parents when they are raising their children. It is something we found to be true in various cultures around the world, not just here in the US.

"When we did research among natives in New Guinea, the Indonesian islands, even in the remotest Amazon villages and corners of Africa, parents always instill in their offspring a clear idea of what they believe to be right and what is wrong. So killing an innocent person for no reason is something that is 'bad' regardless of where it happens and protecting and nurturing your family is always good. That didn't mean their idea of a reason meshed with ours. A man in Papua, New Guinea might kill his wife for speaking to another man without an elder present. That would clearly be appalling to us, but it is a *reason* nonetheless, a reason they've been taught is enough to warrant killing."

Scoma was going too fast for Steven. He was indeed captivated by the science he was researching and was talking more to himself than he was to Steven.

If he was going to get the information he needed, he had to focus the man and ask the questions he had, "Whoa, hang on there, professor, let me process what you are saying."

Scoma chuckled on his end of the phone, "I told you I might get rolling. I apologize, it's just that with Tyrone's breakthroughs and some of the stuff we have come up with on our own, it is an exciting time for our field, a very exciting time indeed."

Steven could hear that excitement in the man's voice, but he needed to get down to business, "I think I understand what you are saying. There is a universal, moral code that seems to govern how most people act, the decisions they make, and it's that moral code that guides us as parents to instill it in our children."

Scoma went on, "Exactly! So you get it! Here is the fascinating thing, however. We also studied instances where children had been deprived of social education, of even the most basic of human social norms. These were what could be termed 'feral' children. Incredibly difficult to find, had to go to Africa and South Asia to find them.

"When we conducted our research, we discovered that even in those extreme instances, there is an inherent or inborn framework, a 'moral compass' that humans appear to be born with.

"We tested the theory further by using babies that had not yet begun to speak or even crawl. We partnered with Yale's Center for Infant Cognition to design the tests. We showed these babies two puppet shows with two puppets. In one of them, one of the puppets steals something from the other and runs away while the other one cries. In the other show, one of the puppets helps the other to get something out of a box. When children were asked to select one of the puppets, they almost always chose the 'good' puppet, the one that helped the other to get the object out of a box.

"So all of this tells us that humans are genetically wired to be 'good,' to be kind and caring, and to help those that need help. This is not limited to our work; it is something that has been established time and again by scientists all over the world. We are naturally an altruistic species, if you will.

"I am telling you about it because that was the premise, the bedrock of our research. I don't think I need to tell you that as we get older, as we are affected by our environment and by whatever education our elders provide, or fail to provide for that matter, this clarity of purpose, this internal compass, is blurred. It becomes distorted by religion or political beliefs or social pressures. In other words, we grow up.

"The people we studied, the ones that make up the body of our work, are those who never lose that clarity, people who keep a clear and well-defined sense of absolute right and wrong and adhere to that throughout their lives, in spite of their education or social pressures or religious influences, most often at a cost to themselves."

Scoma stopped to take a breath, long enough for Steven to interject, "I get what you are saying, it was mentioned in the research paper you published last year. I guess what I am wondering is how exactly do you find those people? I mean, when I spoke to Dr.

Leonard, I jokingly mentioned Mother Theresa and Pope John Paul II, but I was joking.

"Now, as I hear you talking about it, I see that maybe it wasn't such a joke. Still, I can't imagine that there are many people out there like them."

Scoma responded, "You are absolutely right! They are absolutely one of a kind. But to answer your question, no, those were not the kinds of individuals we were looking for, because as good as they were, they had very intense and direct exposure to organized religion. True, they are some of the clearest manifestation of the dogma of their religion, but we were looking for people that were not affected or guided by religious norms.

"No, our work considered people like Leonardo da Vinci, Newton, Edison, Copernicus, Einstein, people that were not guided by religion but by a natural desire to better understand nature and mankind.

"Every one of those men were most likely geniuses far beyond what we could possibly imagine. Can you yourself imagine what the world would be like if they had chosen to use their intellect in a selfish or evil way? Can you imagine what someone like Einstein could have done if he had chosen to lend his genius to Hitler? They could have shaken the very core of human history and completely derailed forward progress.

"Anyway, I'm getting away from our work again, sorry about that. Those were the guiding principles for our work, but not the only ones. We also wanted to research people that seemed to have abilities beyond those that we had previously established were the norms for human beings, even exceptional human beings. Like I said, hyper-developed senses, ability to regulate core body temperature at will, ability to sense a change in barometric pressure or the UHF waves that earthquakes emit.

"We utilize super computers to scour the Internet for mentions of such instances and then we search for those involved in them." He chuckled, "We even look in the tabloids! Most of it is crap, of course, but every once in a while…"

Steven now looked at the phone in his hand, he was willing to listen to Scoma, but what the man was saying seemed out of a comic book and not part of scientific research, "Come on, professor, please don't take this the wrong way, but I find some of what you are saying hard to believe. I read some of it in the paper you wrote and I guess that's why I wanted to speak with you, because I do think some of it sounds like science fiction more than science."

On his end, Scoma smiled, clearly this was not the first time he'd heard the same thing from others. "Mr. Loomis, you are not the first to say so and I can almost guarantee you that you will not be the last. I understand how it sounds, but the fact is that we found not one or a few of these people, but hundreds.

"You have undoubtedly heard of the mother who lifts a car to save her trapped child. That story is often told to illustrate the human capacity of a mother when her child's life is at stake.

"Well, what most people don't hear is the fact that there have been countless experiments that have tried to replicate such a feat and they have all failed. We have documented hundreds of cases where a mother was presented with that life or death situation and was sadly unable to rescue her child. So those that have been able to lift a massive weight or been able to bend a car door mangled in a crash, a car door that would not yield to the 'Jaws of Life,' were not simply moms in a panic. They had the physical ability to do so, an ability that perhaps before that moment they'd never needed to utilize but which had always been present before and was present thereafter.

"Interestingly, almost every one of the women we spoke with was able to later duplicate their superhuman feat without the panic and adrenaline that an unexpected situation might create.

"We then went to the Himalayas where some Tibetan monks practice Tummo. Tummo is a form of intense meditation where the monks utilize their mind to raise their core body temperature. Now I have to tell you, when we first started to research this I would have not believed that what I saw was possible. When these monks engage in Tummo, they wear nothing but a loincloth. We are talking about them doing this in below-freezing temperatures and biting wind.

"Anyway, in addition to wearing nothing, they take sheets and submerge them in water that is just above freezing and then they wrap their bodies with those sheets. When they do it, they take care not to have the sheets actually touch their skin. They make a sort of cocoon around their bodies. Any normal human being would most likely go into hypothermic shock within minutes and die shortly thereafter. The monks sit in meditation, no shaking, no shivering, nothing.

"What really blew my lid, however, was the fact that after a short time the sheets were actually steaming; they weren't just dry, they were actually hot to the touch. I won't go into everything we did as far as trying to duplicate that ability in a laboratory setting and the genetic measurements we took, but what I will tell you is that they have, over time, developed genetic mutations, mutations they are born with, that allow their bodies to regulate temperature and to project the heat. We think it is a combination of blood pressure, metabolic rate and muscle regeneration.

"I don't know how much you know about human physiology, but I will tell you that it is not humanly possible to project heat generated by the body. You can transfer heat, you see. If you lie next to someone, they can absolutely draw heat from you, but for a human to actually send that kind of heat to another being or an object without touching it is not possible. Our bodies are simply not meant to do it, but here are these monks doing it in the Himalayas.

"We also looked at people that were able to hear sounds that human beings cannot possibly hear, not even blind humans who have a much more acutely developed sense of hearing."

Steven was still skeptical, "I've seen television programs where they show people with 'superhuman' abilities, people with incredible strength or people who can perform amazing 'superhuman' feats. Is that what we're talking about here? Because honestly it seems like so much Hollywood crap."

Scoma answered, "Yes and no. Yes, we are talking about people with abilities that simply go beyond what we have determined are possible for humans, even exceptional humans. But no, we're not looking for 'one offs' or what some mislabel 'freaks of nature.' Perhaps it's such an individual that may call out attention, but we're looking for mutations and abilities that have become the norm for a group of people. We're looking for things that are genetic, inherited by those that are a part of that group. History and nature are filled with 'one offs' and we wanted true evolutionary mutation.

"So, for instance, we tested children near the Himalayan village where we found the monks doing Tummo. To be honest, we didn't really have to test them. I cannot explain to you, Mr. Loomis, what it was like to stand shivering in freezing temperatures in spite of several pairs of long underwear, gloves, a hat and the best jacket that The North Face can make while a group of children played throwing snowballs wearing nothing but a sweater and a light coat. And they were flushed and sweating when they were done! To them it was like playing in warm 70-degree weather. Whatever it was that triggered it, there is now a definite genetic mutation among their people and they are obviously being born with this ability."

"It was the same when we looked at Sherpas. We wanted to know what allowed them to live as high up as they did and to function as if they were at sea level. We weren't able to get our equipment up to where they were, so we couldn't take the measurements we wanted. So we examined their bodies. We looked everywhere and came up empty until we looked at the underside of their lips. There we discovered a network of capillaries far beyond those of normal humans and we had our answer."

Steven was trying to digest everything the man was saying as fast as he could, but he was having a hard time.

He could see why Leonard had said Scoma was a character, but he had to focus and get the answers he needed. "If I understand correctly what you are saying, these people, your subjects in all of these studies, are doing things that are simply impossible for humans to do. You have tried to duplicate these things with ordinary people and were unable to. I guess that my biggest question is, how does all of this relate to the work that Dr. Leonard and some of the others are doing?"

Scoma was quiet for a couple of seconds. Given how much and how fast the man had talked before, this told Steven that he was considering how to best answer the question. After what had happened at Leonard's office, with him figuring out what he had done, he thought that Scoma also knew who he was and what had happened to his daughter. Maybe he had also figured what he had done, still, the scientist answered him, although at a much slower and deliberate pace, "Well, I'm trying to come up with a soft or easy way to say this, but I can't come up with one. Tyrone's, Dr. Leonard's, work has also identified individuals with many of these abilities, which is where our work intersects. Where it is completely different from what we do is what we were talking about at the beginning, the 'moral compass.'

"His work, as you know, is focused on individuals who are guided by a different compass, one that does not in any way fit within what science has established as being even remotely human. If we were talking about the Pope and Mother Theresa in our work, his work has brought to light individuals who function at the other end of that spectrum."

Steven understood exactly what the man was saying, it meshed with what Leonard had already told him and what he'd figured out on his own.

He asked, "What I can't understand is, why would nature, evolution, create beings that are guided by what I can't help but think is an evil compass? I am not a religious man and I can't really abide by the idea that Satan or some other evil entity is sending his armies onto earth."

Scoma answered his question, "And you would do well to keep the whole religious thing out of it, because it has nothing to do with religion or even 'evil' as you and I have come to understand it.

"You see, these creatures, *Homo predaer*, seem evil to you because you are looking at the situation and judging it through a human lens. Their behavior is what our society has determined is evil, but it is not evil to *them*, it is simply nature.

"Nature, Mr. Loomis, is not bound by moral norms nor by social judgments, it is governed by adaptation, individual and group adaptation. Survival of the fittest, if you will. That phrase is outdated and not truly reflective of what actually brings about evolution. Humans have usurped that phrase. We've applied it to sports, to business, to whatever suits our purposes, but in its purest form it is an exquisite and brilliant system. Organisms, from the most complex to the simplest one-celled organism, go through a life cycle: they are born, they consume, grow and die, and the cycle begins again. Some are prey, some are predators, and sometimes when the environment changes the predator becomes the prey. No more and no less. It has nothing to do with strength or weakness, it has to do with adaptation. Those that are able to adapt are more likely to survive than those that cannot. We are also learning about how symbiosis and how symbiotic relationships bring about evolution.

"This new species is exactly that, a species within the same genus as another species, *Homo sapiens*, but with the ability, the inborn ability, to use their skills and their environment to their advantage, to ensure their survival and their place in nature's ecosystem, the ecosystem that they share with us and with other species.

"If you take all the social and religious judgment out of it, you see that what Tyrone found was simply one of the next steps in the evolutionary process. What I am now researching may be the step after that or perhaps another species different from both *Homo sapiens* and *Homo predaer*. Tyrone's, Dr. Leonard's, work has culminated in the definition of the new species. He has been doing it much longer than I have and he understood what he was looking for and likely to find early on. He didn't decide to define his new species until he had enough empirical data to back up his claim.

"I haven't been doing my research nearly as long as he has, because it was not until recently that I realized what it was we're finding. You're not the only one to be skeptical, Mr. Loomis; believe it or not, scientists are some of the biggest skeptics when it comes to revolutionary findings. We're constantly trying to figure out how to fit our findings into what has previously been established as the norm. It isn't until we come upon something over and over that simply will not fit into those norms that we begin to posit that we may be onto something that has simply not been found before. I am confident I am not far behind, now that I know what it is I am looking for and what is potentially out there.

"Look, I have a hard time talking about this because, yes, I am a scientist, but I am a human being first, a father and a husband, and to be honest with you, thinking about Dr. Leonard's work and the species he found in anything other than a scientific light scares the crap out of me.

"I've seen what these beings are capable of doing, what they are basically *designed* to do, and I can tell you, Steven, I can call you

Steven can't I, that we are in no way prepared to deal with this. Before Tyrone and some of the others' work, science insisted on trying to fit them into the human model, just like I did. We came up with new and improved definitions and mental conditions to try to explain away what is clearly not human behavior.

"Have you ever taken a good look at what defines a psychopath? It is defined in a number of different journals, but it's pretty similar wherever you look. What people don't see, however, is that those definitions are always changing. They're always changing because they have to encompass more and more behaviors that were perhaps not included before."

Steven said, "You're right, every time I found a scale or a test was being used I noticed that whoever was doing the testing or using the scale seemed to retrofit their subject into the scale or definition."

Scoma exclaimed, "Exactly! So you've noticed what I'm talking about. Well, that comes about because of what I said before; scientists are the biggest skeptics when it comes to new science. Some scientists are simply unable to fathom that the idea of what has been established as a norm could be incomplete or, God forbid, wrong! So, they take whatever the behavior or action and try to shoehorn it into what has been established as the norm.

"That's why Tyrone's work is so important and remarkable. He was willing to take the leap, to say 'This just doesn't fit what we've decided defines a psychopath' rather than to stretch existing norms or definitions even further.

"I've gone and rambled again, I'm sorry, I do that when I get excited…and when I'm nervous, and talking about this makes me both."

Steven had what he needed. Out of everything that Scoma had shared with him, it had been the change in his demeanor, in the way he talked and his tone that had caused the biggest impact on Steven.

The man wasn't lying, he sounded both scared and nervous when he talked about the new species. Remembering what he'd seen at that warehouse, Steven could not blame the man, not one bit. The other thing that had had a big impact was what Scoma had said about humans not being ready or prepared to deal with these new beings. It was precisely what Steven had speculated about when Tracy had gone missing and what he'd decided once she had been found. He had killed Riche for that very reason, because he knew that the system as it existed was in no way equipped to deal with him. Even back then, Steven had realized that perhaps this hell, the hell his and the other families had gone through, could serve to bring attention to the new science, to the existence of these things.

He asked Scoma one last question, "I understand how your work and Dr. Leonard's intersects much better now. What brought you two together in the first place? I mean, from what I've read your work together didn't begin until five or six years ago."

Scoma was quiet on his end of the line. Steven waited and wondered if he had hit on a sensitive topic. Steven was about to just end the call when Scoma finally answered, "Uh…well…uh, we wrote a paper together about seven years ago. It was a paper on how prey will employ grouping or pack behavior to defend against predators. Schools of fish, flocks of birds, a herd of water buffalo, that kind of thing. I had been doing some computer modeling on that behavior and he reached out to me. He was at that time in the process of writing a paper on his potential new species and how *Homo sapiens* still held an advantage because of what we came to term the group defense.

"He'd been positing that since humans are inherently social creatures, whatever advantage the new species held would be evened out. We ended up postponing publishing the paper until 2009."

Steven looked at the phone in his hand with a puzzled expression. Scoma's answer was slow and hesitant; completely different than every other answer he'd given Steven until now. His voice lost all the vibrancy it had held before. The man sounded almost apologetic.

Steven decided to end the call, "Professor, you have been very kind with your time. I appreciate all the information."

After a brief pause, Scoma was back to his excited and fast-talking demeanor, "Don't mention it, I don't really get to talk about my work with, you know, regular people. What I mean to say is that I don't really get a chance to talk about my work with people that are not scientists, that's what I meant to say. Anyway, if you have any other questions or if I can be of any more assistance, just shoot me a call or an email, and hey…say hi to Tyrone for me."

With that Steven concluded the call, "Will do. Thanks again."

After his conversation with Scoma, Steven hung up the phone, made a pot of coffee and poured himself a cup, enhanced by a small shot of brandy. He sat down in the living room, where he had spread out all of the files with the research he had done, the files on Riche and his own notes on everything. He looked out the window, something he did when considering a particularly difficult decision. He also thought about Scoma's strange behavior. He had mentioned a paper he wrote with Leonard years before. Steven thought he had seen the paper, the only one with both of them as authors, but he had read so much written by so many that he just could not remember it. Something was just beyond his reach, like a memory too faint to remember well, but which still had enough to cause uneasiness, like peering over the side of a 1,000-foot building. He'd felt that faint sense of vertigo many times over the years during SEAL ops and it had never let him down. But what the hell could it be about a paper? He figured maybe Scoma had his own issues with what Leonard was working on, issues he wasn't comfortable sharing with Steven. Maybe they'd had a falling out while writing it. Whatever it was, he decided to put it aside and concentrate on what was in front of him.

His objective was clear, but the path to get there still avoided him. He now knew that no matter how much he tried to bring attention to the science, the world would for the most part ignore it. Even if he invested his own money to hire the best PR firm, Leonard's findings would eventually be forgotten, if they were even noticed in the first place. No, simply shouting from the rooftops would never do the trick. What he needed was to make it impossible for the world to ignore the science, impossible to pretend it wasn't there. He needed to make it a part of water cooler conversations, fodder for every talk show and news magazine; he needed to shine the brightest light there was on it, popular culture. Once it became that, a part of pop culture, there would be no turning back.

He also had to make sure that it wasn't looked upon as a stunt, as a desperate attempt at getting attention. He needed the weight of the law to validate its existence, or at least to validate it as a reasoned possibility.

Steven had been considering all of this along with the other objective that he'd been circling around, taking responsibility for what he had done. From the beginning he had known that at some point, when the time was right, he'd have to own up to what he had done. He had avoided it in order to think, in order to take his time and come up with a plan to follow.

Now, as he sipped his coffee and kept trying to marry his two objectives, the answer appeared simply and without fanfare. He was struck by its obviousness and by its logic. He had been overthinking all of it, not surprising given what he'd been through. As he finished his coffee, Steven thought about how he would begin to execute his plan, now prepared to go with what was the most simple and logical next step.

Steven Loomis began to figure out a way to turn himself in and to tell the world the absolute truth, the reason that he had decided to kill Donald Riche. Once he turned himself in, there would be no question as to who or how it had been done. No, the question that the world would have is *why* it had been done. That would be the most difficult obstacle to overcome, because the world would, without doubt, think the answer to that question was obvious. He'd done it out of revenge, out of overwhelming grief and rage, and trying to convince anyone that it had been because of anything other than that would be an uphill battle. It was something he knew he would not be able to do alone.

As smart and experienced as he was, he knew that to do what he intended to do he would need someone to advocate not only for him, but for his ultimate objective as well. Now he needed to review the law, because the opponent he was about to face used statutes and legal precedents as a weapon. Such was the knowledge required when you planned to take on the United States legal system and to redefine what the world knew as human. Now that he knew what his path would be, he needed to have one last conversation. He picked up the files, took his cup to the sink, picked up his coat and called a car to take him to GIC headquarters and the General's office.

Chapter 16

After calling in all the favors and pressing every one of his sources, Felix Garcia had hit a dead end when it came to law enforcement's interest in Steven Loomis. He'd found out that Loomis was in a meeting at the time of the shooting and that GIC had provided a time-stamped video of the meeting to investigators. The police had not been able to interview the other people that had been at the meeting, but the video was enough proof that Loomis had been at the meeting to send them looking in a different direction.

Garcia was stumped. He really had a feeling that it had to be Loomis who had shot Riche at the courthouse. Now he was going to have to run down some of the other leads he had about another shooter. He had developed a list of possibles, people that had been even remotely connected to the victims or to the investigation and who had some military training. He had run them down, but he knew he wasn't going to find anything.

He had witnessed as the media circus following Riche's arrest had turned into a media frenzy after the shooting. Newspapers, television, radio, Internet, every single form of media was following the case with reports from their 'man on the scene' every single day. The coverage made the white Bronco chase and OJ Simpson's arrest and trial seem like a blurb on the five o'clock news.

If he was to be honest, he was actually a bit intimidated. As a reporter assigned the police precinct beat, he was used to competition and to the constant pressure of finding something that nobody else had. That's the kind of information that won Pulitzers and got the attention of the networks. That's what got you a seat at the big boys' table.

With more than five hundred journalists from all over the world, getting something that nobody else had was going to be next to impossible. Still, he wasn't completely discouraged. He might not have a team of researchers, producers and investigators to hunt down leads for him, but he had something nobody else had, experience on the streets, New York streets. He had sources everywhere, from prostitutes to drug pushers to highly placed police administrators and they all trusted him and, he hoped, liked him. He'd never burned a source and he'd always told the story straight, without the cheesy, yellow, sensationalistic spin that most rags resorted to nowadays.

He wasn't looking for 'Likes' on his Facebook page or hashtags about his stories on Twitter. He was a serious journalist and he was willing to wait for something worth writing. He had a feeling that no matter what happened, he was going to have more than enough to write about before everything was said and done.

◆

Felix Garcia was not the only one deeply concerned with the Riche case and the courthouse shooting. There was another individual perhaps even more interested than Garcia. He had been following the Riche case with the utmost interest and attention even before Riche had been caught. He wasn't part of the media or an investigator. He was something else entirely.

He had been immediately interested when he had come across reports of the missing girls and became even more focused when Riche and what he was suspected of doing had been broadcast. He was particularly interested in the reports about the warehouse and what had been found there. He had scoured the Internet for any detail that may not have been reported by the media, joining in online chats about the case and visiting any blog or website that purported to have 'exclusive' details about the case, particularly about the warehouse. He had also tapped many of his sources for more information and he had been following every single Twitter feed related to the case and every single newscast that promised new information.

He had been disappointed when Riche was shot at the courthouse, because that meant there would be no trial, no testimony from the man himself about what he'd been accused of doing. That, more than everything else, was what had disappointed him the most, not hearing about the details, the planning and execution of what Riche had done. He wanted to hear the man's voice, analyze his demeanor and his intellect. Of course there was no guarantee that Riche would have spoken if there had been a trial, but if he had been right, if his analysis of Riche had been correct, he was sure the man would have talked, indeed he would have been most eager to explain exactly what he had done and why, and that was the part the disappointed him the most. He would never get to hear that now.

Like Garcia, this individual was particularly well informed. He also had contacts in the right places to find out the information he was looking for, but he had to be careful not to show too much interest, not to seem too eager for more details. He could always claim professional interest if anyone were to ever question his intense interest in the case. As a neuropsychologist and criminal-profiling consultant, it would only make sense that he'd be especially interested in the Riche case. Only he and he alone knew that his interest in the case had nothing to do with his profession, that his interest in the case was intensely personal.

Dr. Nigel Barlow had not given up hope yet. His sources had informed him that the investigation to find Riche's killer continued. He would keep his ear to the ground. He knew that sooner or later there would be more information about the case and that when that happened he might be able to learn what he needed to learn, what he was really interested in. Barlow's interest in the case was not driven by professional curiosity or even sick voyeuristic interests. His interest in the case was more akin to the interest that a hungry wolf might feel when it caught the smell of prey in the air.

Barlow had just finished up a session with one of his oldest and most important projects. His visitor grabbed his coat from a rack and walked over to the wet bar that was on the far wall of the office they were in and put the glass he'd been drinking 50-year-old Scotch from in the sink. Barlow walked to the door to let him out. The man stopped before leaving, "So, Nigel, any chance we'll be able to get together for golf anytime soon?" Nigel shook his head smiling, "I will absolutely try to make that happen, but I am in the middle of a project, and you of all people know what a hectic time that can be."

His visitor grinned, "Ah, I understand. I absolutely do. Still, let me know if you're able to get away and I will send the chopper to bring you up to Westchester. You have got to see the redone 17th and 18th holes at the club. They are amazing."

Barlow smiled, "Splendid! I shall contact if you if I am at all able to take a few hours off. In the meantime, don't forget what we talked about and what we decided."

The man put his coat on while nodding and walking toward the elevator, "I got it, I won't forget. Good night, Nigel."

Barlow raised his hand, "Good night, Senator."

◆

Steven got to the GIC building just after five, when administrative staff had gone home for the most part or were in the process of packing up for the day. He didn't stop on his floor. He didn't want to run into Stephanie or anybody else. He wanted to talk to the General and to get the show on the road. Now that he had a concrete plan, he wanted to move forward with it.

He got to the old man's floor, went to his office, and knocked lightly on the door, which was open as usual.

The General looked up from a file on his desk and Steven could see the genuine pleasure on the man's face. "Steven! It's good to see you! Come in, come in, have a seat. Just move that crap from the chair and put it on the table."

Steven put a stack of files on the table on the other side of the office and sat down across from his boss. "Thank you, sir. It looks like you've been busy."

Goodman made a shooing motion with his hands, "That? They're just files on some of the deals we've closed in the past couple of years. I like to look at them from time to time. There's a lot you can learn from looking back at how the business landscape has changed from then to now. You look great, rested. I knew spending time with your family, away from all this shit, would do the trick."

Steven nodded, "That it did. I do feel better, clearer. You were right, being with my family gave me some perspective and allowed me to focus on figuring out what my next move should be. Actually, that's what I came to talk to you about."

The General leaned back in his chair and folded his hands on his lap, "Okay. I didn't think you came to talk about old files. What's on your mind?"

Steven shifted in his chair. One thing was thinking about what he needed to do, but it was quite another to actually articulate the words, to say it, especially to this man. "Well, sir, I think we both know what happened at the courthouse. I wanted to speak with you about it in a more meaningful way afterwards, but I honestly wasn't sure what my intentions, my ultimate intentions, were.

"I want you to know, no, I need you to know, that I didn't do what I did because of some desire for vigilante justice. I didn't make the decision out of anger. Don't get me wrong, when I saw the warehouse and what he'd done to my daughter, I was enraged, I wanted him dead, but you need to know that in spite of that, I really believed that I would let the court system handle it. It's ironic, my anger and rage actually ensured that I wouldn't make a decision until I had a chance to cool down and think about things. It's the way I was trained and I don't need to tell you that it sticks with you for life."

He paused to assess the man's reaction to what he was saying. The old man just sat there, with a focused and curious expression, but he didn't say anything.

Steven continued, "I made the decision to shoot Riche because I felt that our system, our justice system, just wasn't prepared for someone like Riche. Wherever he got sent, for however long he got sent there, he would never believe or think of it as punishment. Even if he got the death penalty, he would still not see it as a punishment. He would have seen it as something that we needed to do in order to be safe from him, in order to contain him and what he represented. He would have seen it as our weakness.

"I did a lot of research about this, sir, and what I have found is absolutely incredible, fascinating but also terrifying. There are a number of researchers who have dedicated their careers to studying people like Riche. These scientists have been exploring the idea that there are individuals out there who do not fit within the parameters we have set for human behavior, even sick human behavior.

"There are reams of information, but I only printed out the most pertinent data to show you. Basically, these scientists have concluded that there is another species on the planet that shares a common genus with us, but it is completely different. They interviewed thousands of people and categorized them using established scales for psychopathic and sociopathic behavior. They ruled out every mental disorder and they developed scales of their own.

"The most accomplished researcher when it comes to this field is a professor at Queens College, here in New York. Dr. Tyrone Leonard has defined this new species as *Homo sapiens predaer* or *Homo predator*. They look human and they act human, but they act the way they do as a part of pursuing their prey. They are born predators with the best camouflage known to man and with the intelligence and cunning to use it.

"After reading all of the research and speaking with Leonard, I realized that's exactly what Riche was, a born predator with the drive and the intelligence to take nine little girls in broad daylight without leaving a trace. You've been hearing the news, most people believe that his last nine victims were definitely not his only victims. Authorities in some of the places he'd been have begun to put together lists of missing persons that they now believe fell prey to Riche.

"Art, I know how this must sound to you. I know it sounds crazy, but what I saw in that warehouse, the care and thought that he put into it, is like nothing I've ever come across, and you know what I've come across."

The General was nodding. Steven didn't usually address him by his first name, only doing it in very intense and critical situations.

He looked at Steven, not in judgment or with skepticism, but with something closer to impatience. "Why would I think it sounds crazy? I've seen the pictures and I've heard the details. Hell, even before this, before Riche, I've pondered many times how it is that someone can do some of the things we've seen, and I know I'm not the only one. For decades people have speculated about what makes someone like Ted Bundy or Dennis Rader tick. People make offhand remarks here and there about how these things are monsters, not possibly human. They say those things and get a chill up their spine, but they never stop to think, really think, about what creates these monsters.

"So now that this tragedy touched you and your family, you decided to go through the looking glass and find out what these things really are. You found what you were looking for and you made a decision that needed to be made based on the best information you could get. Why would I think any of that is crazy?"

Steven's shoulders relaxed and he was surprised to find out just how tense he had been when he first walked into that office. He realized that the General was his first audience, the first person to hear his ideas and his reasons for doing what he'd done, and if he hadn't believed Steven or just thought he was crazy, Steven's hopes that the world might believe him would be very slim.

He got the files from his briefcase and slid them across the old man's desk, "Here's all the research I've done. There are some of my notes from my own conversations with the experts in there as well."

The General took the files, put his reading glasses on and skimmed through them. "Christ, I need a new pair of reading glasses. I swear I think I'm going blind."

After a couple of minutes of leafing through the material, he looked up over his glasses and asked Steven the hardest question, "So, now what? I know you also didn't come here just to give me these files. What are you planning to do next?"

Steven shifted in his chair again. This was exactly the reason he had come here, to let his boss in on what his plan was. The old man hadn't shown even the slightest surprise or incredulity at what Steven had shared with him so far, but then again he hadn't told him everything yet.

"You're right, that's not why I came here. I came here because you have been more than generous with my family and me and I wanted you to be the first one to know. I also hoped that you might have some advice for me, that you might let me know if you think I'm crazy."

The General went back to just sitting with his hands on his desk and looking straight at Steven, "Well, you're right about one thing, I will absolutely tell you if I think you're crazy. You know that I don't like to be bullshitted and I don't like to bullshit others, so I'm all ears."

Steven went on, "I've known even from the beginning, from the time I made the decision to shoot Riche, that I would eventually turn myself in. Maybe I should have done it right away, but honestly I didn't really know if that would be the smart thing to do. I was operating on adrenaline and training and I felt hazy, like I used to feel when we ran ops with no sleep for days.

"Anyway, I wanted to make sure that I hadn't done it out of anger and revenge. I wanted to understand the reason I did it and I wanted to make sure that it would be worth it, that everything I knew my family had and would be going through would have a higher purpose."

Steven paused and leaned forward in his chair, "When I talked with Leonard, the scientist I told you about, I was amazed that nobody knew about his work, none of what I'd read was anywhere to be found in the public consciousness. It seemed like the world would or should know about it by now, like there would be headlines everywhere, but there weren't. To find out about his work, about the science of it, you have to do a lot of research in a lot of obscure places and I couldn't understand why.

"After talking to him, I realized that I really shouldn't have been surprised by the lack of interest. He told me about other scientific discoveries, stuff that's been found recently too, not years and years ago. Amazing stuff, General, growing human eggs from embryonic stem cells, discovering the God particle, things that will literally change humanity and I hadn't heard about any of it. We keep an ear to the ground because of what we do, so I think we're better informed about news events than most and I hadn't heard about any of it. Once I understood that, it made sense that nobody would have heard about the discoveries he has made.

"I guess what I'm trying to say is that I think the best thing I can do now is to bring attention to them, to the science and what it means, I mean *really* means, day to day, how they can destroy a life in the blink of an eye."

Steven paused again to get a sense of where the old man was. He went from looking directly at Steven to looking out the window of his office, obviously thinking about what he'd just heard. Steven knew the man and knew he wouldn't say anything unless he was certain about what he was saying, and he'd just heard his best and most senior executive tell him that he believed there is another species on the planet higher on the food chain than human beings. It was understandable that he'd take his time before responding.

When he finally looked back at Steven, his demeanor had changed. He was not simply listening to him saying what he had to say, but ready to take an active role in whatever Steven was planning.

"You started this conversation by telling me that you knew you'd be turning yourself in, and now you're telling me that you intend to bring attention to this science, so I am assuming that you're about to tell me how it is you are going to do both. I think I have an idea of what you're planning to do, so let's hear it."

Steven couldn't help but smile, the man knew him too well, "You're right, that's exactly what I'm planning on doing. To be honest with you, I made things way more complicated than they needed to be. I was overthinking everything."

The General nodded, "Happens sometimes, especially when you're operating on adrenaline and coffee."

Steven went on, "Once I had a chance to take a step back and think about everything, it was almost ridiculously obvious. If I turn myself in, the question of who shot Riche and how he was shot would obviously be answered.

"I read the statute for murder and when you think about it, most people charged with murder defend themselves by arguing that they didn't do it, that it wasn't them who killed anyone. When it is obvious it was them that killed, they argue that it was an accident, that they didn't mean to kill anyone. In my case, none of that is in question. I did it and I intended on doing it, planned it in fact. When I turn myself in, it will be clear who did it and how I did it."

The General was nodding in understanding, "So the only thing in question will be why you did it. I'm certainly not a lawyer and I don't understand how these things work, but I would think that in that case, when it's clear that you did it, how you did it and that you intended to do it, the only way to mount a defense would be to argue insanity or some other condition that drove you to do what you did."

Steven shook his head emphatically, "That's what you'd think, but that's where this science, what I found, makes all the difference."

The General now had an expression of genuine puzzlement on his face, "I don't think I follow you, son. I'm not sure where you're going with this."

Steven leaned forward in his chair, clearly energized with what he had to share with the man, "The charge of murder, the way it is written, says that in order to be convicted of murder the prosecution has to prove that whoever is being charged killed another human being and that they did it with malice and premeditation.

"We just went over the fact that who did it and how won't be in question and neither will the issue of premeditation. I planned to do it and I intend on saying precisely that, that I intended on doing it."

Steven paused to see if the old man was getting what he was trying to say. At first he still looked completely lost, but Steven could see the gears turning.

He was working through the problem, and Steven could see he almost had it, but it kept eluding him. "I don't see it, I don't see how you'd defend yourself without arguing some sort of temporary insanity."

Steven leaned closer and proceeded to work him through it, "Okay so the law says that to be convicted a human being had to have killed another human being with malice and premeditation, right? And we just went over the fact that who did it and how are not in question, nor is whether it was premeditated. That leaves one single element that is in question."

The General looked at Steven, still with that quizzical look on his face, and then it hit like a ton of bricks. His eyes flew wide open and he slapped the table with the palm of his hand, "He wasn't human! You're planning on arguing that you can't be convicted because the son of a bitch wasn't human! I'll be goddamned!"

Steven let him take it all in before saying anything.

He was shaking his head in amazement when all of a sudden he thought of something, "Is that even allowed, Steven? I mean, are you allowed to bring into question whether someone was a member of the human species?"

Steven answered the question, now hearing it asked he was struck by how farfetched it truly sounded, but he'd known he would be asked that question sooner or later. "I don't know for sure, but from a legal standpoint I don't see why not. I have found science, solid, credible science, that supports the idea that there is a separate species from humans on the face of the earth. The man I shot was almost certainly a part of that species, so I think it's a valid argument. Whether a judge or more likely a jury buys it is quite another story.

"And the reality is that it won't matter whether I can prove he was one of these things, as long as I can prove that he could have been, I'd be in good shape. In this country, you don't have to prove that you're innocent, you just have to bring doubt about your guilt. At least that's how it's supposed to work."

The General, now back behind his desk, replied, "I know, but has anybody ever made that argument in court? Doesn't the law basically assume the fact that if someone is killed, they were human?"

Steven, now back to pacing, answered, "No, to answer your question, nobody has made the argument before, but I don't know if a similar set of circumstances has ever come up. When I was thinking about this, I wondered the same thing. I wondered if anyone had ever had the same set of circumstances and I couldn't find anything, but what I did find was scores of cases where a judge or a family makes the determination that someone is no longer human and they pull the plug on them."

The old man looked lost, "I don't get it. What does that have to do with what you are arguing?"

Steven sat across from him, "Think about it. There is a human, let's say, that because of an aneurysm or some other brain injury they are brain dead. Let's say that they remain that way for years and after all that time their family makes the decision to pull the plug. They would go to court and make an argument to allow them to pull the plug on their family member. After listening to the doctors and their opinion, the court would grant the request. The family would then pull all life-sustaining measures and the person would eventually die.

"So, in that case, the court would make the decision to end the life of what we know was a human being, but legally their life can be ended because of that legal determination, but it is still homicide."

The General was still not getting it, "I understand, Steven, but that's different. In that case, the person would be brain dead. They would just be a collection of organs and they would not be the person their family knew and loved."

Steven exclaimed, "Exactly! In that case, the court would make the determination that the individual was no longer human. Whatever it was that made them human was contained in their brain. It wasn't the fact that they had arms and legs and a head, it was something else and that something else was gone.

"Look, I'm not saying it's the same thing or anything like what I am proposing, I'm just pointing out that the law does make such determinations. My argument is simply that Riche's behavior, his atrocities, the care he took, everything indicates that he was something not human.

"I have found the science that points to the fact that he was something other than human or at the very least that he *could have been* something other than human.

"Trust me, I know this isn't going to be easy, and to be honest I don't even know if I'll be able to find a lawyer that will help me with it, but I'm going to try."

The General was nodding, he might not have understood everything that Steven was trying to explain to him, but he knew that Steven was headed into the eye of a storm and he knew he was going to need help doing it. "Remember the card I gave you, Max Zeidler, give him a call. If anybody can make this fly, it'll be him."

Steven nodded, "I was planning on heading to his office from here. I just wanted to make sure you heard it from me first, and I wanted to make sure that you knew it wasn't some sort of stunt, that you knew I thought this through."

The old man got up as Steven was getting ready to leave. "You don't have to worry about that. In all the time that I've known you, I've never known you to make rash decisions. I hope this all works out the way you want, son. It's going to be a heavy price to pay, no matter how it goes."

Steven shook his hand, "I know, sir, I know how much you've done for me and I will never forget it. I know one thing, whatever ends up happening, this science, this threat will be known to the world. Whatever happens to me, once it's out, I will have accomplished my goal."

The General now took on a concerned tone and look, "Wait a minute, are you saying you don't care what happens to you? That you're willing to give yourself up to get this science out there?"

Steven stopped and turned around, "No, don't get me wrong, that's not what I mean at all. I'm going to defend myself with everything at my disposal. I'm nobody's hero, sir, and I'm definitely nobody's martyr."

The General smiled and held Steven's arm as he shook his hand, "Good man. Now, call Zeidler. I'll give him a call to give him the heads up. The bastard charges us enough."

Steven returned the gesture, "Thank you, sir. I appreciate it."

He left his boss's office and went to make a call he knew he had to make before he got on his way.

♦

Grady was going over case files that he'd been unable to get to with everything else going on when his cell phone rang. His first inclination was to just let it go to voicemail, but he decided instead to look and see who was calling him.

When he saw who it was, he picked up immediately, "Hello, Mr. Loomis. I'm not going to ask how you got my cell phone number."

On his end, Loomis smiled, "I suspect you probably know why I am calling."

Not knowing who was listening and knowing that Loomis could have the phone line tapped, Grady was careful in how he replied, "Well, I think I may have an idea, but I don't want to assume anything. You know what happens to people who assume."

Loomis smiled on the other end, "Well, I wanted to call you to let you know that your idea is correct. I will be talking to my people shortly and we will all be coming in to have a cup of coffee with you and Detective Mullins."

Grady could see that Loomis was also being very cautious with what he said over the phone.

Loomis went on, "We should be there in about an hour and we can talk about how things have gone."

Grady was still trying to absorb the statement. Steven Loomis was calling him to tell him that he was going to turn himself in. He was going to contact an attorney and then head into the station, and if Grady was reading him right, he was planning on giving a full statement.

Of course Grady couldn't be sure of what Loomis was going to say, so he kept his optimism in check. "Great. We will have a fresh pot of coffee ready and waiting. I will let Captain Freeman know…"

Loomis interrupted him, "Detective Grady, if you wouldn't mind, I would like to chat with you and Detective Mullins. If you need to tell your captain, so be it, but I would like to speak with you and Detective Mullins only, please."

Grady winced. He knew he had to tell Freeman and he knew he would want to be in on the interrogation, no matter what. "Mr. Loomis, I don't know if that will be possible. Captain Freeman is going to want to be part of the conversation."

Loomis replied calmly, "I understand that, but if you want to have a full conversation, you will explain to the captain that it will only happen with you and Detective Mullins in the room. He can watch the tape later, but my only request is that it be you and Mullins in the room.

"I really think you will probably want this conversation to be as complete and specific as it can be, and I would hate for my people to have to keep interrupting because there is someone in the room that shouldn't be there."

Loomis could not have made it plainer: 'You want a full confession? You will make sure Freeman is not in the room.' Grady was sure Freeman was going to scream bloody murder, but he also knew there was no better way to save resources and manpower than to get a full confession from the person that had committed the crime. He would go to the chief if he had to in order to make it happen.

"I think we can arrange for that to happen."

Loomis answered, "I knew you could, detective, I wouldn't have asked otherwise. I will see you in an hour."

Grady hung up his cell phone and immediately dialed his office phone to call Mark Mullins, "Mark, can you please come in here? Yeah, I mean right now…just got off the phone with our guy."

Mullins held the receiver with a puzzled look for two seconds and then it dawned on him, "Shit! I'll be right there!"

Mullins practically flew to Grady's office and came in, shut the door and sat down on the chair in front of the desk.

"So, what did he say?"

Grady was leaning back on his chair, still trying to settle fully into the situation. "He was very careful about what he said, I was too. He basically said he needed to talk to his people and that once he did that he wanted to come here and have a chat with you and me only. He was very clear that he wouldn't talk if there was somebody else in the room."

Mullins was smiling. He was already anticipating Grady telling Freeman he couldn't be in on the biggest investigation going. He knew he would make a stink about it, but he also knew Freeman would concede in the face of losing a full confession. "Man, Freeman is going to blow a gasket."

Grady was also smiling sideways, "I know and I don't care. This is the best and most efficient way to resolve the case of the Riche shooting, and I know the chief will back us up to get that confession."

Mullins answered, "Not to mention it lets us off the hook, officially I mean."

Grady was nodding, "I agree, unless Loomis decides to come clean all the way himself. He doesn't strike me as someone who would do that, based on the conversation I had with him before this call. He knows it's our ass if he spills everything he knows."

Mullins replied, "Yeah, he doesn't strike me as that kind of guy, either. If he just comes in and owns up to the shooting, it means we don't ever have to say anything about what happened."

Grady put his hands behind his head and leaned back, "That it does, that it does."

Chapter 17

After hanging up, Loomis picked up his coat and briefcase and headed down to the street to hail a cab to the offices of the lawyer he'd been referred to and to begin his journey in earnest.

At Max Zeidler's office, a sense of controlled chaos was the norm, but today that controlled chaos was multiplied tenfold. Every intern, assistant, paralegal and young associate was busy looking up citations, case law, appellate decisions, and anything else that had to do with insanity and temporary insanity defenses. The criteria for a temporary insanity defense in New York were very tight. Bottom line was that for it to be used successfully, the defendant must have been in such a state of mind that he or she did not believe that what they were doing was wrong or criminal and nothing about their behavior could point to them being aware of any wrongdoing. It was very clear that for such a defense to work the defense attorney had to unequivocally prove that his client was factually and completely insane during the commission of the crime. What made it more difficult than a defense of not guilty by reason of insanity was the temporary element. Basically, the jury would need to be convinced that the insanity was temporary and only present during the time of the commission of the crime and that once that passed, the defendant returned to a normal state of mind.

Nobody in the office knew how many cases had actually used the defense successfully, which is why everyone was knee deep in reference materials and Lexus/Nexus citations and anything that could be found online. Still, nobody had any doubt that if anyone could pull it off it would be Max Zeidler. The man had become a legend winning cases like this, and if he was taking a case in which he was thinking about using the defense, he probably already had his opening argument for the trial ready.

In fact, Zeidler was in his office reading up on the last two cases in New York to have successfully used a temporary insanity defense. The last one had been in 1982 and it had involved a man who had a stroke and had temporary psychosis as a result of it. He killed his wife with a butcher knife because he believed her to be a masked intruder coming into his home to kill him. He had called the police, had walked them to the body, and had very lucidly explained how he had taken the knife and defended himself from the monster that had invaded his home. It was not until an hour later, when he began to understand what he had done, that the man had absolutely fallen apart and had to be restrained and put on suicide watch.

That case had everything going for it, a psychological or physiological trauma that had affected the defendant's cognitive abilities profoundly and a man that had been married to his wife for 38 years, had never even gotten a traffic ticket and had never shown even a hint of violence toward anyone, let alone his wife. It had everything going for it and it took the jury just under two hours to come back with a not-guilty verdict, and it took that long because they needed to take a break to eat something. Zeidler believed that he had just such a case in this one. If he was right about what was about to walk into his office, it had everything he would need for just such a defense.

Drew was in his office trying to get a handle on some cases he had brought with him and a few others he had gotten since coming on board with Zeidler.

Zeidler walked in and sat across the desk from him with that cat-that-ate-the-canary smile on his face, "Are you ready to put everything aside and get into the case that will make your career?"

Drew put down the file he was holding and smiled, "I can't wait to hear this. If this is going to be the case that will make my career, I am assuming you're going to be in on it too."

Zeidler chuckled, "You bet your ass I am. Are you kidding? A case like this comes along once in a lifetime, well, in my case a few times, but still, it's going to put your name in the headlines."

Drew leaned back in his chair, "Alright, already, I give, what is it?"

Zeidler got up from his chair and walked over to the window, "Global Intelligence Consultants is one of our largest corporate clients. We bill them well over ten million a year, handle everything from patent law to international jurisdictional issues, congressional hearings, and every once in a while we also handle some high-level criminal stuff for them. Nothing spectacular, forged passports, illegal entry into various countries, that kind of thing.

"It's usually federal cases and most of the time there are people involved at very high levels of government, so the cases usually don't see the light of day.

"Anyway, their CEO, Art Goodman, known by everyone and God as the General, just called me. He told me that he was sending someone my way who had something to do with the shooting at the courthouse. At first I thought that maybe it had been one of his operatives that had killed Riche, that maybe someone had given an order and it had gotten done. It's happened before, but not this time."

Drew also stood up and walked around his desk, "Wait a minute, are you telling me that people get killed by operatives from this company under the orders of some unknown government entity?"

Max turned around, "Oh, come on, Drew, are you serious? Do you really think it's that unlikely that when a known drug lord or a particularly unsavory Middle Eastern moneyman becomes too much of a problem, the General gets a call and the problem disappears? Think about it, people disappear without a trace every day in this country.

"Anyway, that's not what this is. I remembered that GIC had come up with the whole Riche thing when it first broke, and then I remembered why. One of the victims was the daughter of a senior executive at GIC, a Steven Loomis."

Drew, now standing next to Zeidler also looking out the window, said, "I remember the name. He's the ex-SEAL the police looked at after the shooting at the courthouse. He was the only family member of one of the victims that had the background to do something like that."

Zeidler nodded, "That's right, but they eliminated him as a suspect pretty quickly. CNN reported that he'd been in a meeting at the time of the shooting when they were reporting about who could have shot Riche. The General didn't say whether it would be him coming in, but he said that we are to provide the person coming with every available resource, whatever the cost. That's someone with a personal stake in this talking. He's never called me directly and he's never said anything like that before.

"My bet is that Loomis is coming in to figure out a way to turn himself in. I have every one of my interns and clerks looking up every possible angle on a temporary insanity defense. If it is Loomis, we're looking at an almost ideal setup for making the argument that he was temporarily insane.

"I don't have to tell you how difficult it is to win a case with that defense, but this is an ideal set of circumstances – a monster as the victim, an all-American ex-military hero for a defendant, the whole world outraged about what Riche did, I mean, it doesn't get any better than that."

Drew shook his head slightly. It was amusing and also a bit disturbing to listen to Zeidler refer to a horrible murder case and a devastating loss as an ideal set of circumstances, but Drew had to admit that he was right. It was the best setup for a temporary insanity defense that he could think of.

Still, it was human beings that they were talking about, a man's daughter and now his life, and Drew hadn't been in the game long enough to develop the thick, cynical skin that Zeidler had.

Drew stood up and followed Zeidler into the hallway where he gave instructions to two of the associates doing research, "I want you guys to find out who the best expert is for temporary insanity cases. Call Dr. Newberry and ask him, he'll know."

Drew followed Max into his office and as both men were about to sit, his phone rang.

Zeidler put it on speaker. "Mr. Zeidler, there is a gentleman here to see you."

Zeidler couldn't imagine who it could be right now, "Does he have an appointment? Could Louis receive him?"

The receptionist came back on, "He says he doesn't have an appointment, but that you would be expecting him. He says someone named 'The General' sent him to talk to you."

Zeidler almost jumped out of his chair to pick up the phone. He hadn't expected Loomis so soon.

"Bring him back to my office right away! And Missy, I do not want anyone, and I mean anyone, bothering us, no calls, no buzz-ins, nothing, is that understood?"

Missy responded in her most even tone, "It is, sir."

Missy brought the man to the door and then turned and left. The man knocked lightly on the door where Zeidler met him, hand outstretched, "Welcome, welcome, please come in, Mr. ...?"

Steven shook the man's hand and went into the office, "Loomis, Steven Loomis. It's nice to meet you, Mr. Zeidler. Your reputation precedes you. The General has nothing but the utmost confidence in you and your firm."

Max smiled as he led Steven to the other chair in front of his desk, "Well, we've handled some pretty serious cases for him and for your firm. The respect is mutual, by the way, the old man has more juice than any 10 players in this city, and he knows exactly how and when to use it."

Max spread his hands to encompass the scene before them, "Case in point."

Loomis was looking around the office when he turned to Drew, who was standing next to the other chair by Zeidler's desk, "And this is…?"

Zeidler was caught off guard for a moment, "I am so sorry! This is Drew Willis, he just joined our firm and will be co-counsel in our matter."

The two men shook hands. Drew felt the sheer power in the guy's arm through the handshake. He looked at the well-built and impeccably dressed man and at the cold and focused eyes. Drew guessed the guy to be about 6'1" and about 195 pounds. For his part, Loomis took a liking to the kid almost immediately. Although clearly younger than both other men in the room, he carried himself with a lot of confidence, not cocky or obnoxious, just a quiet inner peace and strength. Drew projected that confidence through bright and curious eyes and through the ability to make the people around him feel at ease without sounding like a used car salesman.

Once the three men were seated, Max spoke up first, "Can I get you anything before we start, water, Scotch?"

Loomis folded his hands on his lap and replied, "No thank you, I would just like to get going with this if you don't mind."

Max nodded, "Not at all. Please let us know, how can we help you?"

Steven looked down at his folded hands and paused for two seconds, he took a deep breath in and proceeded to explain his situation, "By now I think you have probably heard about the shooting at the courthouse and about the case that the shooting was associated with, the case involving Donald Riche."

Max and Drew both nodded, but kept quiet.

"Well, one of his victims was my daughter Tracy." Steven paused at this point. He closed his eyes and Drew could tell he was still hurting.

He opened his eyes and continued, "He took her from Central Park when she was with her mother and her brother and sister."

Loomis stopped again and looked at Max, "I think I will take you up on that water now."

Max stood up and went to a small refrigerator in the corner of the room where he retrieved a bottle of water.

He handed it to Loomis, "Take your time, I know it must be incredibly difficult. If you need to stop at any time, let us know."

Steven took two long pulls from the bottle and put the cap back on it. "I'm good. It's just that this is the first time I have actually articulated any of this and I'm a bit surprised, I didn't expect it to affect me like this."

Drew gently put his hand on his shoulder. It was a simple gesture, unrehearsed and done completely without thought, "Hey, Mr. Loomis, I can't imagine having gone through what you've been through, so don't feel bad for being human, just take your time."

Normally Steven would have been put off by the contact, but he could see that it was nothing more than what the kid thought would be a humane gesture toward someone who was obviously hurting.

He turned to look at Drew and gave him a small nod, "Thank you, I'm okay."

He took two more long pulls from his water bottle and went on, "Anyway, I found out that she hadn't been the only one, and early on I knew she probably wasn't coming back. After a week, I was sure of it.

"As you know, I am in the intelligence and security business and have some resources, which I utilized to find out what was going on with the investigation. I could see that the police and other law enforcement organizations were doing everything they could but still were having no luck. Eventually, as you know, Riche was found out and arrested."

Drew chimed in, "They found his warehouse, right? Where he did everything."

Steven nodded, "Yes, that's right. I found out about it through my own sources and I decided to go see what they found. I got there before the whole world got the story, so I was able to get close. I was able to see my daughter. Well, her remains anyway..."

Steven ran a hand through his hair and with every fiber of his being fought the urge to break down crying in front of these men. Max was taking copious notes and Drew just looked at Steven, not able to comprehend the kind of horror this man must have faced that night.

Even so, he had some questions, "Steven, is it okay if I call you Steven?" Loomis nodded.

"Maybe you got there before everybody arrived, but there had to be some security around the scene, even a couple of uniformed officers from the first-responder black and whites."

That comment confirmed Steven's first impression of Drew, the kid was sharp.

He saw the loose end in the story and pounced on it, "Very good, Mr. Willis, I'm impressed, but I will tell you that a worried, irate father looking for closure can work wonders, especially when he's dealing with young patrolmen."

Drew listened to him and nodded, but wasn't convinced. He knew Loomis wasn't lying about anything he was telling them, but he also wasn't being entirely forthcoming, and given what Drew thought Loomis was about to share with them, he wondered who he was trying to protect, because it obviously wasn't himself.

Steven went on, "In any case, when I saw what I saw, I made a decision. The shooting at the courthouse was that decision. It was me, I shot Donald Riche."

Both Drew and Max were completely transfixed by the story. They both knew what was coming, but it was still a shock to hear this man just come out and with a completely straight face admit that he had shot another man in the head. Like most all other criminal defense attorneys with any significant experience, both Max and Drew had represented people accused of murder. In most of those cases, for Drew in every case, their clients had vehemently denied having committed the crime, even when faced with mountains of evidence proving that they had in fact done it. In almost every case, the defendants had been lifelong criminals or people who were too greedy or who had just flat out lost their minds. Now both lawyers were looking at representing a man who was none of those things, a man who was clearly educated and who was very rational and deliberate about what he had done. A man who did not look conflicted in the least.

Max Zeidler was the first one to break the silence, "Well, Mr. Loomis, we'll be happy to represent you. I assured the General we would take care of you and we are already preparing to do just that."

Steven was somewhat taken aback, he hadn't really finished telling them his story. It actually seemed as though Zeidler didn't really care what the rest of the story was, as though he knew what he needed to know.

Drew Willis was in fact waiting for just that, the rest of the story, but he didn't know how exactly how to go about interrupting Max, who seemed to be all done with the discussion and itching to get going with the defense.

"Alright, so the first thing to do will be to figure out a timeline and to find out what the DA has. We'll put our best investigators on this. Drew, our people are already working on a temporary insanity defense and we'll need to have that pretty well sewn up…"

At this point, Steven composed himself and was compelled to say something, "Wait, wait, wait a minute. Mr. Zeidler it is my intention to turn myself in to the police when I finish speaking with you. It was my impression that you and your firm would assist me in doing so."

Zeidler was completely dumbfounded and truly at a loss for words.

Drew took the opportunity to interject, "Mr. Loomis, Steven, have you really thought about what you are doing? I mean, once you talk to the police and the DA, there is really nothing for us to contest, nothing for us to use at trial. The whole point of retaining an attorney is to defend you, someone who will advocate for you."

Steven looked at both men and calmly explained, "Mr. Willis, it is absolutely my intent to defend myself. I have no intention of turning myself in and pleading guilty on the spot. That would be completely useless."

Hearing this, Max relaxed a bit, "Okay, no problem, we can help you talk to the police and to turn yourself in, but we have to do it in such a way that it will still give us something to argue, something to defend you with."

Steven looked at him and nodded, "Agreed. I was only planning to make a statement taking responsibility for the shooting. I was not planning on explaining myself or on trying the case at the police station. I have you gentlemen to do that for me."

Max was actually smiling now and Drew could see that he was already anticipating a sensational trial with a dream defendant and perfect circumstances. Drew had to admit, if this wasn't the ideal set of circumstances to present a defense of temporary insanity, then there were no circumstances to do so.

Max responded, "That's good, I think it will work to our advantage because it will take the guesswork out of figuring out what they have or how they intend to proceed. Do you already know what it is you'd like to say?"

Loomis responded very calmly and very deliberately, "Absolutely, I intend to speak with the detectives that handled my daughter's case. I believe they already suspect my involvement in the case. In any case, I am planning to say exactly what I said to you guys, that I am responsible for the shooting incident at the courthouse. I am also going to tell them that I doctored the tape that they reviewed of the meeting I was supposed to be at when the shooting occurred. "

Drew listened intently and tried to read the man's true intentions, tried to figure out if this was some kind of sick game, but there was absolutely nothing about Steven or what he was saying that didn't ring right. The man planned to just go in and tell the police what he had done.

If he was going to represent him, however, he had to explain to him what he would be facing. "Steven, you do realize that the police won't just let you come in and say 'I did it' and have that be it, right? I mean, you know they will try to get as much information as they can so they can tighten up their case. They will want to know the why and the how and if there was someone else involved and…"

At this point, Steven gave him a small grin and held up his hand, "Mr. Willis, Drew, may I call you Drew?" Willis nodded.

"Drew, I spent 20 years in the Navy, this first 10 years doing military investigation and the last 10 as an officer with the Navy SEALs. I am now a senior executive with a global security and intelligence firm. I can assure you that I am more than aware of every interrogation technique the police will try to utilize, and I can also assure you that I have no desire to engage with them.

"I want to make my statement and then rely on you gentlemen for the rest. Whatever I have to say about my motive or how I came to make the decision I will reserve for my discussions with you. For now all I want to do is to get this off my chest and let the people who are trying to figure out who did it get a rest."

Max stood up now and started walking a short oval pattern inside his office as he spoke, "I think that will work. We will be there and once you have said what you want to say, we will step in and terminate the conversation. You do know you will be placed under arrest, correct?"

Steven just nodded. Max went on, "There will be a bail hearing set in the next couple of days. I'm not sure on this one, but I would imagine they will ask for no bail and the judge might just grant it. If they do set bail, I am pretty confident it will be set at about $1 million, at least."

Steven responded, "Well, that's just like no bail for me. I don't have a million dollars lying around to post bail, and I do not want to use my family's money or put up my assets to obtain a bond. I did this, I don't want to risk my family's financial stability in any way."

Max looked at him with that cat-that-ate-the-canary smile, "Well, I have good news for you on that end, Mr. Loomis. The General has deposited well over that amount into an escrow account to be used exactly for that, and he is willing to deposit additional monies into it should it be needed."

It was Steven's turn to be speechless for a couple of beats. Once he stopped and thought about it, he had to admit he wasn't surprised.

That was just like the General, still he just couldn't let the man pay for his decisions. "I appreciate that, Mr. Zeidler, but I can't accept that. My company and Mr. Goodman, the General, in particular, have already been way too kind to me and I don't want to take advantage of that."

Max was nodding and saying nothing. When Steven finished, he spoke again, "He said you would say exactly that and he said, and these are his exact words, 'Don't pay any attention. Sometimes he doesn't get that there are times for all of us when we need someone to cover our ass.' So you see, it is his intention to put up the bail no matter what. You know Art, you know he always gets what he wants, so just go with it. Besides, he'll get every cent back, unless you are planning on running, that is."

Steven answered, "Yeah, the old man does seem to get his way more often than not. And no, I am not planning on running. That's the last thing I would do." Max sat back down behind his desk, "Good, then it's settled. We will go with you to the police station, you can make your statement, we will call the meeting to an end, they will arrest you, and we will start working on getting you out on bail as soon as possible. Is that acceptable?"

Steven gave him a small smile and answered, "That sounds like a plan, gentlemen."

Max got up again, pushed a button on the phone to give instructions, "Missy, please tell Marcus and Laura they are working for Drew as of right now."

Missy came over the speakerphone, "Very good, Mr. Zeidler."

Max went on, "And Missy, can you make sure we have a car outside in 10 minutes? Thank you."

Steven took advantage of the time to make what would probably be the hardest call he would have to make in this whole process. He didn't want to make the call on a cell phone that wasn't encrypted and he'd left his work phone at the office. "Gentlemen, is there a phone that I can use to make a call? A secure phone if you have one."

Max smiled, "Yes, there is one, Mr. Loomis. As you can imagine, we handle a lot of very touchy situations."

Steven nodded, "Of course, you have the General as your client after all."

Zeidler motioned for Steven to follow him, "Come this way."

They walked down a hallway to a big conference room, "Here you are, Mr. Loomis, you'll have all the privacy you need."

Steven went in to the conference room and before closing the door, turned to address Zeidler, "Thank you, and listen, we're about to go to battle together, so please, it's Steven."

Zeidler smiled, "Fair enough, Steven, and it's Max from now on."

He should have made this call first, but with everything moving so fast, he just hadn't found the right moment to do so. Loomis finally closed the door and started to call his wife.

◆

Beth had been almost constantly busy since Steven had left. She found that keeping herself and the kids occupied went a long way to soothing her nerves. She was still having nightmares, but they were much less frequent now and she continued to see an excellent therapist. All in all, things were going as well as she could hope. Her one worry right now was Steven. She knew he was struggling with Tracy's death and everything that had come along with it. She knew that he was getting ready to do something extremely difficult and she wished, as she had many, many times over their marriage, that she could make things easier on him. She had learned over the time they had been married that the best thing she could do for him, to make things easier on him, was to be strong, to let him know that she and the kids would be fine. She had hoped she had let him know precisely that on their last conversation, but there was just no way to know whether he had taken what she had said to heart.

She was lost in her thoughts about Steven and all the rest of it as she worked her pruning shears over her mother's immense bed of beautiful roses of almost every hue, something she'd enjoyed doing every time she visited her parents, when her mother called out for her. Steven was on the phone.

She rushed in, took her pruning gloves off and took the phone from her mother, "Thanks, Mom. Hey you, I've been thinking about you."

Steven smiled on his end, "Glad to know I wasn't the only one. How are you, how are the kids?

Beth sat down at the dining room table, "We've been busy, but you know Bethany, you've only been gone a day and she already wants her daddy."

Steven hung his head, he missed his family and he knew what he was about to undertake would keep him away from them for some time, if not forever. "I miss you guys too. Listen, Beth, I am calling you because I am about to turn myself in for what happened at the courthouse and I didn't want you hearing about it on the television."

He paused, waiting for her reply. She was quiet for a moment, but then she replied in a surprisingly even tone, "Well, I knew the time would come when you would take responsibility one way or another. I know what kind of man you are, you know that, and I knew even before our conversation that you would do exactly what you are about to do."

Steven was relieved, but only for a moment, because he still had to tell her the most important and difficult part of what he was planning. There was simply no way to get around it or to make it any easier, so he proceeded to explain everything, what he had found in his research, his conversations with Leonard and Scoma, his objective and how he planned on accomplishing it. Now Beth took some time to process everything he was saying. She had known that he hadn't killed Riche out of anger or a desire for revenge. She knew him too well and had been with him during some of the most difficult missions he'd been a part of in the Navy for her to think that. She'd wondered a few times what *had* driven her husband to do what he did, and now she knew. It was still shocking to hear it, however, and to hear everything else he had told her.

When she had thought about him turning himself in, she had also wondered what would happen afterwards, how would he defend his actions? What could he possibly present as a defense, and now she knew that too. She'd thought about all of these things and pondered a hundred possibilities, but in everything she had pondered, she had never once imagined this would be what he would present as a defense, and it was that part that now concerned her the most.

"Steven, are you sure you want to do that? I mean, I understand what you're telling me, what you want to accomplish, but don't you think that making that argument is going to make people think that you've lost it, that you're absolutely crazy? And what about your lawyers, do they know what you're planning on doing, how you're planning on defending yourself?"

They were valid questions and he knew it. He had the answers to some, but not everything she was asking. "I know how it sounds, babe, trust me, but think about it. If I wasn't planning on presenting this argument, what other possible defense would I have? Once I turn myself in, there would be no doubt as to who did it and how and, honestly, most people would also assume the why.

"Everybody would assume that I killed him out of revenge, out of anger and rage. Hell, I think they're still going to think that regardless of what I argue. I've already talked to the lawyers, but I haven't told them everything yet and they're assuming that I'm going to be presenting some sort of temporary insanity defense."

Beth, now more engaged and clear in what they were discussing, made his next point for him, "Well, that makes all the sense in the world. Like you said, what else would you argue as a defense? Have you thought about the fact that maybe they're not willing to move forward with the defense you are planning on presenting? It's going to be their reputations and their firm's reputation on the line."

Steven had, in fact, thought about precisely that, "I have thought about it and I'd be lying if I told you I knew how they're going to react. The General referred me to the firm that's going to be handling this for me. They have handled some pretty difficult cases for GIC, and the guy that'll be leading the defense is Max Zeidler. He's known as a pretty aggressive and creative litigator. He's handled some pretty high-profile cases involving mobsters, judges, senators, that sort of thing. If anyone should be willing and able to present this defense, it would be him.

"The other lawyer on the team is a young guy, but he's pretty sharp and has the same kind of maverick air about him that Max does. Once this breaks, it's going to be huge, bigger than either one of us could imagine. You've seen the coverage on Riche and the shooting, it's been ridiculous, and this is only going to make it even more of a media event, but that's precisely what I need, the reason I am doing this.

"Once I present my theory, there is no turning back, it will be out there, the science, Leonard and the others' work, the world will not have a choice but to take notice of this.

"You and I know the damage that one of these creatures can inflict on a family, any family, and even though everybody gets scared and talks about being alert and aware when something like this happens, they have no idea of what the threat really is, of the danger that exists out there, every day."

Beth had listened intently to everything he was saying. It all made sense, but she was still worried for him, terrified if she were to be honest. "Everyone knows that there are people out there that are monsters, Steven. Riche is not the first to do something like this by any stretch, you know that.

"Do you think this will make a difference in how aware people are, in how they take precautions and educate their children on the dangers they face every day? We did that, we educated our girls and explained about bad people and how dangerous they are, and what good did that do?"

Steven could sense she was starting to break down. He needed to bring her back to their conversation, if nothing else to get her thinking about something other than what had happened to their daughter, "Yes, Beth, we did talk to our girls and other parents talked to their children as well. People take precautions every day because they are aware that there are in fact people out there, criminals that take advantage of them or victimize them in some other way.

"This is different, Beth, these individuals aren't criminals, not in the sense we know them. This is their *nature*, what they are *born* to do. It is the way evolution works, honey, they are not human, they look human and act human, but they are something else.

"Criminals, the people we warn our children about, are human beings, they are made criminals by their upbringing or they become criminals because of greed or trauma or drugs or some mental deficiency. These are the things the world knows about and what they educate their children to be cautious of, what we've prepared ourselves for.

"But they are human beings in the end, no more capable of carrying out their crimes than another human would be able to. They are bound by the same limitations that we're bound by, the same physical abilities, the same intellect, the same physiology. It's a level playing field. If we're cautious and aware, then we are on the same playing field as them, as the criminals.

"These things are different, Beth, they are *physically* different, they are able to do things that humans are not able to do, and they are able to use that to hunt, to do what their nature calls on them to do."

Beth had to interject. She had heard what he had explained before about the science and about what he would be arguing, but now it became more concrete, more real, and she simply could not believe what he was saying. "What do you mean they have abilities we don't have? What do you mean it's not a level playing field? What you're saying isn't possible, Steven. It sounds like science fiction, like some bad novel!"

Now it was his turn to lose his cool, "Haven't you been listening to what I've explained to you, Beth? To what I found in my research? Don't you think I thought the same thing, that I was even more skeptical than you are? You know my training and you know where I've been and the things I've done. Do you think I'd be willing to take this risk, to put you and the kids through this, if I wasn't sure about what I'm doing?"

Beth, tears now streaming down her face, answered in the most even tone she could manage, knowing that he'd hear her tears anyway, "I do know, Steven. I told you that I trusted you and that I would stand by you no matter what and I will, always. It's just that this is so hard to put my head around; it's so hard because it's your life, our life, that is on the line. I want to be there for you, I love you and I know how hard this has been for you, but I'm still trying to make sense of it all, what happened to Tracy, this, everything."

Steven could hear the anguish in her voice and it broke his heart, but at least she sounded more grounded, like she *wanted* to believe what he had said and to understand what he was doing. It was too much to ask of her on their first conversation, but he just didn't have the time to work her through all of it. He needed to end the call, but he didn't want her mind wandering, coming up with her own notions or ideas of what he was doing.

He wanted her to understand the science the same way he had, so he came up with the best thing he could think of to do both. "I'll tell you what, I will send you the research I've done, the links to the websites and blogs and to the academic papers. You can read through all of it and that way you'll have the same information I had when I made my decisions.

"I know it's too much to ask you to understand everything in just one call, honey, and I'm sorry I didn't do a better job of bringing you along when I was making my decisions, but I just didn't have things clear in my own head until a few days ago.

"I have to go now, but I promise I'll send everything and once you've had a chance to look at all of it we can talk again. I love you, Beth, with all my heart. You are the best thing that ever happened to me, you and the kids.

"I'm sorry for putting you through all of this and I promise I will do everything in my power to get our life back again, but I need to do this, babe. I may not have started this, but I have to finish it, to make it mean something more."

Beth, now unable to control her emotions, responded in a quivering voice, "I know, Steven, I know you do. I will try to understand this better, to understand it the way you do. I love you and so do your kids. Whatever else happens, please don't forget that."

Steven's eyes welled up and he needed to say goodbye before she could hear it in his voice, "Thank you, Beth. I love you very much and I'll call you as soon as I can. Bye, honey."

With that he hung up the phone. He remained in the chair for a couple of minutes, getting his emotions back under control. It was the hardest thing he'd had to do so far, but he knew there might be even harder things to come. He wiped his eyes with the handkerchief in his pocket, let out a deep breath and stood up, ready to get on with the rest of it.

Zeidler and Drew Willis were waiting for him in the lobby by the conference room. Zeidler motioned for Steven to lead the way, "Are you ready to go, Steven?" Loomis, now composed, simply nodded and went to the elevator bank.

Chapter 18

Robert Grady and Mark Mullins were sitting in Grady's office waiting for Loomis. They both had what felt like their tenth cup of coffee in front of them, three or four having been poured in the last hour. Consequently, they were two bundles of nerves. They had sat in the office since the call, talking and tapping their feet. Both were nervous about the whole situation and had agreed that it should be Grady that led the interrogation.

Mullins said, "He said he had to speak with his people first, I bet you he walks in here with an army of attorneys and that we don't get shit."

Grady looked at him and then out the window, "No, I think he'll say what he's coming here to say, even if his lawyers tell him not to say it. He wants to talk, shit, if he could have, he probably would have told us he was going to do it before he did it."

Mullins looked at Grady with an unbelieving look, "You mean he's been planning this for a while? C'mon, that doesn't make sense."

Grady looked back at him, "You know, Mark, there's a shitload of things that make no sense about all of this, not to me anyway, but

Loomis deciding he was going to take out his daughter's butcher is not one of them."

Mullins went on, "You mean you saw this coming way back when?"

Grady was honest, he knew this room and this man would be the only opportunity he would get to speak his mind, "Aw, c'mon, you can't tell me it didn't occur to you at some point, especially after the warehouse. The guy is a professional operator with dozens of black ops under his belt in some of the most godforsaken places on earth. You really didn't think he might consider something like this?"

Now it was Mullins' turn to look out the window in introspection.

He finally hung his head and smiled sideways at Grady, "Yeah, I suppose you're right. I think it was always somewhere in the back of my mind, I just decided to ignore it…couldn't imagine him actually doing it."

Grady nodded, "Exactly, it was pretty much the same for me, but now you see why it wasn't a big surprise." Mullins just nodded without saying anything.

In the sedan driving them to the precinct, Zeidler was still on the phone orchestrating everything surrounding the case, a public statement, who would be part of the trial team, who would be in charge of researching what. Drew had to be impressed. He had figured Zeidler would delegate everything to delegators who would then delegate it on down the line. The truth was that the old man was still the ringmaster. Nothing happened without his explicit approval and nothing was decided without his say-so. Drew wondered how he was going to manage this type of micromanagement. He was used to being his own boss and doing things his own way, and although he knew he didn't have anywhere near the experience Zeidler did, he did consider himself a smart and seasoned attorney.

Drew stopped listening to Zeidler and looked at Steven Loomis. The man was remarkable. He was looking out the window, clearly arranging his own thoughts, oblivious to the conversations going on around him, hand supporting his chin, simply a man at peace with his decision. It wasn't that Loomis didn't likely betray some human emotions, especially when he was thinking about his family. Even then, though, he held his emotions in check and Drew could see that he was being very deliberate in what he would allow to affect his actions.

Drew decided to engage him. He wanted to get a sense of what he was planning on saying at the station. "So, you know what you're going to want to say?"

Loomis looked at Drew with something akin to curiosity with just a bit of frustration thrown in. "I think I've been pretty clear in what I am going to say. I am planning on letting the officers that I have worked with know that I am responsible for the shooting at the courthouse."

Drew pressed on, "That's it? Are you sure, Steven, because you know these guys are going to want to know a lot more than just the fact that you did it. They may not even believe you. There are lots of wackos that are probably, as we speak, taking credit for the shooting."

Steven gave Drew a tired grin as he answered, "I've interrogated my share of people, Drew, and I am fully aware of what the police will want to know. I am also quite aware that there are nuts out there who probably take responsibility for any crime they might want to be proud of, whatever it happens to be this week. Don't you think I've thought about all of this?

"I already explained to you exactly what I am going to say and who I am going to say it to. I will have nothing else to say at this time. I have also explained that I will share details that will unequivocally prove that it was in fact me who pulled the trigger, details that only the shooter would know."

Drew nodded. There really wasn't anything else to say. The guy knew exactly what he wanted to do and he knew the role he wanted his attorneys to play. Drew was already taking Loomis's plan in stride, but he was concerned about how Zeidler might react to it. He was already far down the road preparing not only the defense but the story and how it would be spun for the media, which he knew would be all over the story for weeks if not months to come, especially once the shooter was identified.

Zeidler finally got off the phone, "Alright, we're starting to work on a statement for when this breaks. Basic stuff, 'No comment at this time,' 'We'll wait to try this in court,' 'Mr. Loomis is innocent until proven otherwise,' and on and on. We'll basically tell them nothing other than what they're already going to have."

Steven had already figured this would be a media circus, but now that it was beginning to unfold he had to admit that it was somewhat unnerving. He had been and still was clear on his objective and his commitment, but everything that came along as a consequence of that commitment was something he was going to have to learn to deal with as he went along. He only hoped these men would be able to guide him through it and take some of the pressure off. So far, in spite of Zeidler's showmanship, Steven felt this was the right group of people to help him through this. He was particularly impressed with Drew Willis. In spite of his age, the charismatic young lawyer was self-assured and seemed to have a solid moral compass, two things that Steven valued greatly.

The sedan arrived at the police station and double-parked while Steven, Max and Drew got out. Max stuck his head back in to tell the driver to circle the block until he found somewhere nearby to park or until they came out.

The three men, dressed in overcoats and suits, walked into the precinct. As soon as he saw the watch sergeant, Steven raised his hand. The man had seen him enough times and raised his hand in return, "Mr. Loomis, been a while. Looking for Grady?"

Steven stepped up to the desk with Max and Drew close behind, "That's right, sergeant, I think he and Mullins are expecting me."

Sergeant Simms picked up the phone, "Hey, Bob, Steven Loomis is here with a couple of other guys…okay, you want me to…the conference room? Alright."

He looked around and found a young uniformed officer, "Hey, Patrick, can you take these guys back to the conference room?"

Patrick came around the desk, "Sure, Sarge. Follow me, gentlemen."

The four men proceeded down a long hallway. Sergeant Simms watched them turn the corner and picked up the phone, "Hey, you might want to head down here, something's going on. Loomis and two guys that were obviously lawyers just came to see Bob Grady…yeah, he was expecting them. I don't know what's up but I'm thinking it may have something to do with the whole courthouse deal…yeah. Okay. And hey, Felix, I don't know who else might have made some calls, but you know to keep this tight, right? Don't let me down, kid."

Simms hung up and almost immediately second-guessed his decision. He liked Felix Garcia, and the kid had proven to Simms that he had common sense and that he could really keep his sources clean, but this felt to Simms like it might be a big deal and big deals tended to throw off the judgment of even seasoned reporters. It was too late now. Simms would just have to trust that the kid would keep his word and his common sense.

Robert Grady and Mark Mullins were waiting in the conference room. Just five minutes earlier, they had finished arguing with Captain Freeman in this very conference room. In spite of Loomis's request, Grady had no choice but to tell Freeman, even though he knew what the consequences would be. In fact, the actual exchange had been worse than either Mullins or Grady had anticipated. They had both expected that Freeman would insist on being in on the interview, but neither had thought he would come as unhinged as he did upon being told the subject of their investigation would only speak to Mullins and Grady.

Freeman wanted to have his finger in everything of substance going on in the precinct. It gave him the sense that he was in control, and finding himself on the outside looking in on the biggest case the precinct had ever caught was something that Freeman just couldn't reconcile himself with. Grady had finally gotten him to calm down by explaining that he and Mullins were planning on coming at Loomis hard and they needed to have someone in charge outside the loop, so when Loomis and his attorneys wanted to go up the chain of command, Freeman would be there to catch them. It made sense and wasn't entirely untrue, but it was something he had come up with on the fly. Now that they were waiting for Loomis, Grady was thinking that it was actually a pretty good idea. He had diffused the situation and at the same time he had made an ally of Freeman, which could come in very handy if they did indeed have to get a bit ugly with Loomis or his attorneys. Grady had a very hard time believing that Loomis would lose his cool or that he would hire obnoxious mouthpieces; he seemed too controlled for that. Still, you never knew and Grady had seen weirder things in his time.

He and Mullins hadn't really talked about how to go about this. They had both done hundreds of interviews and had heard more than their share of confessions, but this case was completely different than anything either man had dealt with. In addition to the fact that Loomis was different from any other defendant they had talked to, there was the matter of the warehouse and the way in which Riche had been discovered. Grady doubted that Loomis would play that card, but men changed when they were facing the loss of their freedom or having to hurt their families. They also had to consider the fact that Loomis wasn't coming in alone, he was coming with what was probably the best legal team money could buy, a team that was unlikely to sit idly by and watch their client spill every bit of information that would make the prosecution's case. It was crazy to speculate on all the possibilities; there were just too many variables. In spite of all of this, Grady still felt good about the interview and he was still glad that things were unfolding this way. He knew he and Mullins might still have to deal with some tough questions about the warehouse, but clearly it was much better than having to go upstairs and let them know that they had given Steven Loomis information about the case and that he had most likely orchestrated the incident at the warehouse. Whatever way this was going to unfold, it was going to happen in the next two minutes.

The young officer led the three men through the hallways of the homicide unit and to the conference room where Mullins and Grady were waiting. As they were walking to the conference room, it occurred to Steven that he would most likely not see daylight again for a few days, if at all. He was confident of his actions, but the fact remained that if the prosecution chose to make an example of him, he faced serious time in prison. And while he had thought about that quite a bit, walking down this hallway and into a place where he was going to admit what he had done still gave him pause.

Once they got to the conference room, Steven wanted to make sure that he didn't let Zeidler control the meeting, so he went in first and immediately walked up to Grady.

"Hello, Detective Grady."

Grady stood and shook his hand, "Hello, Mr. Loomis."

Loomis also shook Mullins' hand and introduced his attorneys, "Detective Mullins, good to see you. This is Max Zeidler and Drew Willis, they are my legal representation."

Grady and Mullins shook both men's hands.

Grady had to grin at the sight of Zeidler, "Max, good to see you. Mr. Willis, nice to meet you."

Max also smiled, "Bob, been a while."

They shook hands. Both Drew and Steven were a bit surprised by the exchange.

Drew asked, "You two know each other?"

Max answered the question, "Yes, we do. When you've been in the business as long as Detective Grady and I, you can't help but run into each other."

Grady also responded, "Are you kidding? What cop in town with any time in the vice or homicide squad hasn't heard of Max Zeidler."

Thinking about it, Drew felt a bit silly being surprised by that. Zeidler was a fixture and one of the most unique characters in the New York legal system.

After the introductions, Loomis wanted to get this done as quickly and efficiently as possible, "Well, shall we sit down and have a chat?"

Grady motioned to three chairs and sat down across from the three men next to Mullins.

Both officers pulled out notes pads and Grady pulled out a tape recorder, "Mr. Loomis, we need to record the interview, do you have a problem with that?"

Loomis went to answer, but Max beat him to it, "Detective, we thought this would be an informal fact-finding interview. We don't need to have a recorder in order to do that."

Loomis turned to look at Zeidler. It was clear he hadn't been expecting him to interrupt with this statement and was annoyed by it.

He took the opportunity to assert his intentions regarding this process, "No, Detective Grady, I don't mind if you record the conversation."

He said this while giving Zeidler a subtle look that said 'This is my meeting.'

Zeidler was taken aback and began to protest, but Drew reached out and grabbed his arm. Max looked over and Drew shook his head almost imperceptibly. Zeidler backed off. Grady proceeded; he began by stating the names of all present in the room, the date and time, then asked Steven if he was ready to begin with the interview.

Loomis, hands folded in front of him on the table, simply answered, "Yes, I am."

Grady continued, "Mr. Loomis, I am sure your attorneys have advised you of your rights, but I am required to tell you that anything you say can and will be used against you in a court of law. You have exercised your right to have an attorney present at this meeting. Are you satisfied that you understand your rights?"

Loomis once again responded simply, "Yes, I am."

Grady went on, "And you are willing to move forward to make a statement?"

Loomis leaned back ready to get this done, "Yes, I am."

Grady leaned forward and the interview officially started, "Alright, where would you like to start, Mr. Loomis?"

Loomis knew this was outside of interrogation protocols. Grady and Mullins' job was to take charge of the interview and direct the questioning. Two seasoned homicide detectives did not normally politely ask a suspect where he would like to start.

Loomis folded his hands on his lap and began talking, "Well, gentlemen, as you know, my daughter was one of the victims of Donald Riche. You both were involved in the investigation, and during the course of that investigation I had the fortune of getting to know you, which is the reason I requested to speak with you only."

Grady was taking notes, but he was getting nervous about where this conversation was going. Loomis looked to be heading down a path where he was getting into their personal relationship, and that was not an area Grady wanted to get into, especially here, but he simply nodded in response.

Steven continued, "You also know that while he was at the courthouse building being arraigned, he was shot in the head as he was being transported."

Everyone in the room except for Loomis was taking notes. It was a charged atmosphere, everyone knew what was coming, but nobody wanted to rush it.

Loomis never broke his tone or pace, "I am here to let you know that I shot Donald Riche. I shot him from an office window in a building two blocks away."

The men continued taking notes, also seemingly unaffected by the news. Grady gave Loomis a few seconds to compose himself, although he clearly was the one who needed composing.

Grady wanted to get a detail that had been bothering him quite a bit, "What about the meeting that you were supposedly in? We have a time-stamped video of that meeting, a video that your company provided."

Loomis listened impassively and when Grady finished, he answered the question, "I utilized a simple video editing program to change the date on the video. I then asked an intern at the company, an intern I have no intention of naming, in case you were planning to ask, to take the actual video of the meeting and change it with my doctored copy. That meeting takes place regularly and includes the same people almost every time so it was not difficult to do."

Grady wrote everything down. He was waiting for Steven to explain why he had denied having shot Riche instead of doing this back when it happened.

When it appeared that Loomis was not planning on moving on, Grady asked the next question, "Okay. Can you tell me the reason you decided to shoot Donald Riche?"

Loomis looked at Grady with no expression. He simply answered the question, "No, detective, at this time I do not care to explain why I shot Donald Riche."

Mullins jumped in at this point. He had been quiet the entire time and he wanted to make sure that he was a part of the interview, even if it was to a lesser extent, "Mr. Loomis, I think it would seem obvious why you shot Donald Riche, so why not just deal…"

At this point, Max interjected and Loomis was actually thankful for it, "Detective, I believe my client just explained that he does not want to explain the reason he did what he did."

Mullins turned to Zeidler and snapped, "I understand, Mr. Zeidler, but your client just admitted to shooting Riche in public, in broad daylight. I think at this point we need to clarify a few things."

Max countered, "I should remind you that we are here voluntarily and that our client is making these statements of his own free will. He has a constitutional right to stop talking any time he wishes."

Grady intervened quickly, the last thing he needed was for this to turn into a pissing contest, "Alright, alright, we don't need to jump ahead. Mr. Loomis, can you give us any information about how you shot Donald Riche?"

Max now turned to Grady, "Detective, I just explained that my client doesn't have to …"

Grady interrupted him, he was willing to let Loomis do this his way, but he still had to get certain information, "I am fully aware of your client's rights, counselor, but you of all people should know that we hear confessions all the time from people that weren't within two blocks of the crime they are supposedly confessing to.

"And you know something like this is going to bring the nuts out in force. Already has, actually, so although I do not want Mr. Loomis to say any more than he is comfortable saying, I do need to get enough information from him to verify that he did in fact do this. In order to do that, I have to get information that only the shooter would know."

Max was about to start up again when Loomis put his hand up, "That's alright, Mr. Zeidler, I don't have a problem telling detectives Grady and Mullins what they need to know. I understand what you are asking, detective, and hopefully what I have to say to you will provide that confirmation.

"Donald Riche was shot with a cutting-edge sniper rifle, a CheyTac M200 Intervention with a custom .408 round. You will find that the rifle was taken from the weapons storage of Globalview Intelligence Consultants and you will find that the serial number comes back to that same company.

"You will find the rifle tucked behind a water pipe in the emergency stairway at 1720 East 5th Ave. The shot was taken from the second-floor window at the northeast corner of the building. It was an empty office and the door lock has been picked, so your forensic team will find striations from a metal tool.

"I'm sure you already knew the caliber of the round, but the CheyTac M200 Intervention is a relatively new and not widely available sniper rifle. The round I used has a standard ballistic coefficient of over 3500 yards and a muzzle velocity of 3000 feet per second, but I modified it to make it subsonic in order to help with sound suppression. Is that specific enough, detective?"

The question was asked without sarcasm. Grady had been taking copious notes, along with Zeidler and Mullins. He already knew the caliber of the bullet and the weapons it was likely fired from. Although most of the SWAT guys he'd talked to thought it had probably been fired from a Barrett, they wondered whether a suppressor had been used. You could not mistake the bang from a Barrett. They were still doing 3D renderings of the scene to calculate where the shot had come from exactly, but the crowds and onlookers had made it difficult. Now they knew.

He looked up and also without sarcasm answered, "Well, Mr. Loomis, if we are able to verify that, then yes, it is specific enough for us to believe that you shot Donald Riche."

There was a pregnant pause where everyone in the room was waiting to see who would speak next.

After a few seconds, Max spoke up, "Okay, Mr. Loomis has made his statement, so I would suggest that we move on to whatever is next."

Zeidler knew what would be coming next, but he had to get it on the record and he had to take control of Loomis's statements and movements from this point on. For his part, Loomis truly seemed relieved. His posture and his entire countenance were tangibly changed. To Drew Willis, he now really looked like a man at peace. It's not that he did not realize or understand what was happening around him, he clearly knew what he was involved in, but it was also clear that he was relieved to get this part of it off his chest. Drew didn't know what it was about, how Loomis was acting, but he was getting the idea that he was protecting someone. It made sense, he had to have gotten help from someone within his company and most likely from someone in the press or in the police department and by confessing to the shooting, he preempted the necessity for an exhaustive investigation that may have put some people in uncomfortable situations.

Grady and Mullins stood up, picking up their notepads.

"We have a few calls to make. We have to call the district attorney's office and the lead investigator from the courthouse. They are probably still in the process of analyzing evidence. This will save them a lot of time and resources. We also need to have them go to the building Mr. Loomis has identified to pick up the rifle and collect whatever is at the office he shot from," Grady said.

Mullins turned to face Steven, "Mr. Loomis, you do understand that given your statements you will be detained here at the station and that once we confirm everything and the DA is informed of this, you will be placed under arrest."

Zeidler answered for Steven, "Yes, detective, we do understand. I will be contacting the DA myself to discuss bail for Mr. Loomis."

Mullins nodded, "I understand. He will probably be in front of a judge tomorrow for the bail hearing, but I have to tell you, given the nature of the case and the media attention, it might not be until Wednesday."

Max was already taking his phone out of his pocket, "Oh, don't worry, detective, we'll be in front of the judge tomorrow, but actually, I am going to see if we can get him on the bench tonight."

Before walking out of the room, Grady also turned to look at Steven and his lawyers, "Make yourselves at home. I will have a uniformed officer stationed outside. I figured this would be better than one of the holding tanks. I'll be back in a bit. If you need some water or coffee, please let the officer outside the door know."

He and Mullins walked out of the room and on the way to Grady's office decided what each would do.

Grady started, "I'll call the district attorney's office, you call the team from the courthouse and let them know what they should be looking for and where they need to look."

♦

Bart Logan was still feeling shell-shocked, even though it had been a few days. The Donald Riche case was going to be his first exposure to a high-profile case, even if it was going to be as assistant counsel. He was also going to be able to work directly with David Neill, the district attorney. In the span of days, that opportunity had been erased, vanished. He was sitting in his office going over the Riche case files, but more than anything he was trying to figure out what his next move should be. As soon as the DA's office had found out that Loomis had turned himself in, David Neill had quite neatly and ruthlessly ambushed him and Melanie Farris. Of course, he had positioned it as wanting to give Logan another chance at a big case, but the reality was that it had gone from a slam-dunk case to a no-win case in a matter of minutes. He had gone from being a part, a small part, of the prosecution team putting away a hated serial murderer of children to leading the case against the father of one of the victims, an all-American Navy hero who had killed that hated serial murderer.

He was basically going to be a lead prosecutor against a defendant that had been hailed a hero before, would be hailed as an even bigger hero now, and who had lost his daughter to the 'victim' in the case. If he convicted Loomis, it would be no big deal, the guy had confessed after all, but if he somehow lost the case, something that was a possibility, a remote one to be sure, but one that the OJ verdict had made possible decades ago, his career with the DA would be over. You just never knew what a jury, a sympathetic jury, a particularly sympathetic jury in this case, might do. If all that weren't enough, he would have to do it while dealing with Melanie Farris. She was competent enough, a little too zealous at times, but she was a hard-ass in the office and seemed to always be on guard against her male colleagues. He was in it now, though, and if he wanted to hold his position, he would have to do this by the book, no more, no less. Truth was that he had been glad when that monster had been shot. He believed in the justice system and would uphold the law no matter what, but there were times when whatever the justice system had by way of punishment seemed inadequate, and this had been one of those cases.

Neill had said he didn't want to seem insensitive to the circumstances, so he wanted everything handled carefully, 'by the book' he said, and by the book was exactly what he was going to get. He had also warned both of his deputies not to say a word to the press, he would 'handle them'; he had said it as though he was a strong parent protecting his two vulnerable children. The fact was that he wanted all the media attention that was sure to come after this. Bart was more than willing to let him keep babbling his clichés as much as he wanted to. This was a case where he wanted nothing more than to do his job and keep his head down, and while he didn't know it yet, soon everyone involved with the case would want nothing more than to do exactly that.

Chapter 19

API: Manhattan, New York

January 12, 2012 by Felix Garcia/New York Chronicle

Prosecutors have announced that they have a suspect in custody for the shooting death of Donald Riche. Riche was shot as he was being transferred at the superior courthouse last Wednesday at approximately 2:30 in the afternoon. Riche was being arraigned for the torture and murder of nine girls from across New York's five boroughs. One of Donald Riche's victims was Tracy Loomis, age six. The man in custody accused of Donald Riche's murder is Steven Loomis, Tracy Loomis's father. Loomis is a senior executive with Globalview Intelligence Consultants, an international security firm under contract with the federal government. Loomis was in the Special Forces, having served in the Gulf, Bosnia and Afghanistan as a member of the Navy's elite DEVGRU SEAL team, better known as SEAL Team Six. Sources within the police department and the district attorney's office have confirmed that Loomis walked into a police station and confessed to the shooting. "He made a brief statement accompanied by his attorneys. That is all we can say as we are in the middle of an investigation," confirmed Detective Robert Grady, a lead investigator on the Donald Riche case and one of the detectives that took Steven Loomis's confession. Loomis is scheduled to be arraigned tomorrow at downtown superior court, the same place where Donald Riche was shot. It is expected that the district attorney will ask for no bail for Mr. Loomis, as according to the district attorney's office he poses a serious flight risk. Steven Loomis is represented by Max Zeidler and Drew Willis of the firm of Corliss, Zeidler and Kirk. Mr. Zeidler is confident that his client will be able to remain free on bail during his trial, "Mr. Loomis has been an upstanding member of society who has served his country with honor and who has a loving family that supports him. We are confident that a reasonable bail will be set." Although neither side would confirm it, there is strong indication that there will be a motion for a speedy trial, as the key facts of the case do not appear to be in dispute. In his statement to the press, District Attorney David Neill said that while the case was tragic in many ways, the district attorney's office would pursue the case by the book, "I think we can all sympathize with Mr. Loomis and what he and all of the other families were put through, but in the end we are a nation and a state of laws, and we have always allowed those laws to dole out justice whenever it is needed. The people of the state of New York expect this office to uphold the law and that is precisely what we intend to do. Irrespective of how we pursue the case, we will not forget the tragedy that has led us here." Authorities had cleared Steven Loomis after receiving a video of a meeting he had been in at the time of the shooting, but during his confession Mr. Loomis revealed he had doctored the tape. Barton Logan and Melanie Farris will be the deputy district attorneys handling the case for the prosecution.

Steven was being held at the holding tank at the courthouse. Zeidler and Willis had come to see him shortly after he had been brought there. They briefed him on how things were going to be moving from this point on but held off discussing anything of substance about the case until after the arraignment and the bail hearing. The arraignment and bail hearing were closed to the media and thus did not become the media spectacle everyone expected. There really wasn't much by way of legal wrangling, as the core facts of the case were not in dispute. When it came to setting bail, Bart Logan made a solid argument against setting any bail, but in the end Loomis's record and support from family and friends convinced the judge to set the bail at $1 million. Zeidler had more than that amount in the escrow account that the General had set for just such an instance and went about posting the bail immediately.

Upon being released from jail, Steven went directly home. More than anything he wanted to take a long, hot shower and to prepare himself something to eat at his own house. Zeidler had wanted to meet at the firm to talk about the case, but Steven had not budged, so they would be meeting in his living room. Now, with cold drinks in front of them, Zeidler, Drew and Steven prepared to discuss the nuts and bolts of what would be Steven's defense.

Max began, "Well, Steven, I think we are all in agreement that the crux of this case is going to have to deal with your mindset at the time the crime was committed. You've confessed to the shooting, the method and the intent, so for all intents and purposes, we can almost stipulate to all of that so we can get to the matter at heart."

Steven took a sip from his iced tea, "And what do you think is the matter at heart?"

Max looked over at Drew for some help, but got none, "The matter at heart is the why. The motive is clear, going through what you went through, but what made you take matters into your own hands and kill Riche is what is at the heart of this. We have been researching temporary insanity defenses, heat of passion defenses, and not guilty by reason of insanity.

"Your behavior after the shooting makes for a great foundation for making any of those arguments. The things you saw, the loss of your daughter, all point to the fact that you snapped and lost touch with reality, but believed you were doing the right thing all along."

Zeidler was standing and pacing now. Drew and Steven were just watching him.

He was on a roll, "That's why you came in and confessed. It fits perfectly."

Loomis waited for Zeidler to finish, put down his glass, and asked, "So if I understand what you are saying, you want to mount a defense where experts will get up on the stands and say that because of everything that happened to my family and me, I lost track of reality and that while I was in this state of 'temporary insanity' I shot Donald Riche, but afterwards, once I came out of it, I was the same great guy I have always been. Does that pretty much cover it?"

Zeidler had stopped pacing, "There are many nuances and technical aspects to it, but yes, that's what we will be arguing."

Steven looked down at the coffee table and then back up, "Mr. Zeidler, Max, I appreciate your expertise and your efforts, but I have no intention of claiming that I was insane while I did this, temporarily or not. I have no intention of saying that I did not know that what I was doing might be breaking a law.

"I plan on stating that it was my full intention to shoot Donald Riche in the way in which I did and that it was my intention to kill him.

"I also plan on stating that I planned on doing this in advance and made arrangements to procure the weapons to do it with.

"I plan on stating that I did all of this by myself with no assistance from anybody, and I plan on stating that throughout the entire episode, I did not have a single break with reality."

Zeidler's mouth dropped open as if he was about to say something, but no words came out. Drew sat motionless, stunned. This had to be the only time he had ever seen Max Zeidler left speechless.

He jumped in, "Steven, what you are basically saying is that we won't be having a trial to argue anything, that you are guilty of every one of the charges the state is accusing you of, and that the only thing for us to do is to try to argue to get the lightest sentence possible.

"You have basically taken every element we could have made an argument about out of play and left us with absolutely nothing to present to any jury to convince them of your innocence, actually forget about innocence, to convince them that there might be mitigating circumstances! If we do not bring in your state of mind, then it is very likely that the judge would not allow us to bring in anything relating to what Riche did to your daughter or any of the other little girls."

Zeidler was still perplexed, "What did you want an attorney for? To hold your hand while you said 'Yes, I am guilty of first-degree murder'?"

Steven listened to both of them with a touch of amusement. Truth be told, he should have been more forthcoming with them, but with everything else going on, he needed them to at least get him through the arraignment and the bail hearing.

"Gentlemen, please sit down. I understand everything you are saying, but you are mistaken. I do intend to fight these charges through a jury trial and I do intend to claim that I am not guilty of first-degree murder. This is not a pipe dream or some sort of a delusion. I have thought about it very carefully and I have done the research. This case is winnable."

Drew and Zeidler looked at each other and wondered whether their client had lost touch with reality.

Very gently, Drew sat next to Steven and spoke to him, "Steven, how exactly do you figure you can argue you didn't do it when you walked into a police station and said that you actually committed the murder of Donald Riche and you are now telling us that you meant to do it and that you planned for it?

"All of those things, Steven, are precisely what make you guilty of first-degree murder, so how exactly would you expect us to argue that you are not guilty?"

Now it was Steven's turn to stand, "Incorrect, Drew, incorrect! I most certainly did not state that I was guilty of the murder of Donald Riche, I made a statement that I had been the one that had shot Donald Riche."

Drew was now more confused, "Okay, so you are saying that you confessed to shooting and killing Donald Riche, but that it doesn't mean you committed murder? Well, Steven, I'll bite, what the hell are you saying, exactly?"

This was the essence of what Steven Loomis had set out to do, so he had to be cautious to explain it exactly as he had thought it and researched it.

"In order to be convicted of a crime, all of the elements of that crime have to be present, correct?" Drew nodded,

"That's right." Steven went on, "So to be convicted of first-degree murder, according to how the law is written, one human being must intentionally kill another human being with malice aforethought or premeditation. If any of those elements are not met, then you can't be convicted of that crime, is that right?"

Zeidler was still in shock, Drew was nodding, "But that's precisely our point, Steven, you have voluntarily fulfilled all of those requirements with the statements you have made, do you understand that? If we don't talk about your state of mind, there isn't anything to talk about, nothing to argue."

Steven took a couple of seconds. He knew what he was about to say was going to really cause a reaction, "No, Drew, that's not exactly right. I believe that I am not guilty of first-degree murder because *I do not believe that what I shot was a human being.*"

He said it calmly and completely deadpan, looking directly at both lawyers. Max and Drew just stood and looked at him, neither one knowing how to respond. Both of them were clearly looking for something to respond with.

It was Max to speak first, "Excuse me? Did you just say that you don't think you are guilty because you didn't kill a human being?"

Steven answered, "That is exactly what I am saying."

Now Max broke out of his trance, "Well, that's it, that proves that you were temporarily insane when you did it. That is exactly what we will argue, that you were so affected that you believed you weren't killing a human being."

Steven remained calm and once again tried to explain, "I don't think you understand, Max, that is what I still believe now. I was not and I am not insane, I simply intend to argue that Donald Riche was not human, and if he was not human then I can't be convicted of murder, that's what I was asking about just now. If all of the elements of the crime aren't there, then I can't be convicted of it, you just confirmed that."

Now Drew jumped in, "Steven, you are right, if all the elements are not there, then you can't be convicted, but that refers to those things that can be in dispute: Were you the human being doing the killing? Was there premeditation? Was there intent? What was the motive?

"All of these things are the things that are argued in a trial. They are things that after hearing the evidence a jury can decide on. What you are talking about is a concrete fact, it is not something that a jury can decide on."

Now it was Steven's turn to get animated, "Why the hell not? I have done the research and I had people help me do the research, and there has never been an argument in court about what constitutes a human being in this context, so there has never been a legal finding in this context."

While Drew and Max were still in shock, he proceeded to explain the science, his conversations with Leonard, the research that Schultz had done on the involuntary human responses to lying, everything. When he was finished, he sat back down and waited for Drew and Max to respond.

Max was the first one to speak, "Well, it's original, I'll give you that. Do you have anything stronger than iced tea somewhere? I think I need a drink."

Steven smiled and walked over to the wet bar where he got a bottle of single malt Scotch and brought it back to Max, who thanked him and poured himself a healthy drink. Drew had been contemplating asking Steven whether he was joking when he'd started explaining his position, now he was glad he hadn't. He wasn't quite sure how to proceed, but he did know that this was not their average defendant, not in the least. This was an intelligent, successful, senior executive who also happened to be an ex-Navy SEAL, not to mention a top 10 percent graduate from Annapolis, and if he believed he had enough information to make this argument, Drew was willing to cut the guy some slack.

"Steven, do you understand what you are saying? You saw the man, you know he was alive and that he was physically human, that he reasoned. You know that he was born and grew up and became whatever he became the way you and I became what we became.

"You can't expect that anyone is going to think of him as anything other than human. It just hasn't happened, even with all of the other people that have done horrible things before him. As demented as their acts have been, they have been tried and punished as men, as human men."

Steven was resolute "I understand that, Drew. I'm not stupid and you don't have to talk to me like a child. You've now spent some time with me, you know my past and you know about my family. Do you really think I would do something like this without thinking about it, without doing research?

"I know this isn't something that has been done before, but that doesn't mean it shouldn't have been. And I also know that the determination that what we consider to be human is no longer human is made every day. Every time someone whose heart is still beating and who is still breathing is unplugged from a machine keeping them alive. Someone is making that decision, family, doctors, judges, and every time that decision is made it is a human being making it about someone they no longer consider to be human."

Zeidler broke in, "But they are doing it because they are dead! Because their brain is no longer functioning, whatever made them human is no longer there."

Steven became more animated, "Exactly! So we can agree that whatever it is that makes us human is not held within the physical body, that it is held in the brain and it controls how we live our lives."

Drew answered, "Yeah, I think we can all agree that once the brain is dead, what is left is just a collection of organs. But you do know that there are those who don't even believe that the human soul is gone even though the brain is dead and that they protest and condemn those who they consider to be taking a human life."

Zeidler was now visibly shaken. In all the time Drew had known him, he had never seen Zeidler lose his composure, but he was clearly losing it now.

"What the fuck are we talking about? What does any of that have to do with what you are saying? Riche wasn't brain dead and there wasn't any determination made by any family or doctors to end his life. You blew his goddamned brains out from two blocks away! He was walking and talking before you did it! In our society, in our world, that is murder!"

Now it was Steven's turn to get more animated, "No, it isn't! That's exactly what I'm saying! It can't be murder if what I killed wasn't human, and I will go to my grave believing that! I have put my life and my family's future on the line to prove it in a court of law, and if you can't or won't accept it, then I obviously need new attorneys.

Drew interceded, "Alright, Steven, alright. Let's for the sake of argument assume that we move forward with this argument. How exactly do you think we are going to get in front of 12 people and argue this? How do you think we are going to shape a legal argument?"

Zeidler calmed down a bit, "Listen, kid, this is a bit too much, even for me. If you want to take this on, I will back you, but it's going to be you out in front, and I think we can both agree that if this turns into a fiasco, we're going to have to part ways when it's over."

He didn't say it as a threat, and Drew didn't take it as one, "Fair enough, Max."

He turned back to Steven, "Alright, Steven, so you were going to explain to me how exactly you think this argument can be made."

Steven went on, "There's not much to it. I told you, I believe that there is enough science to put in front of 12 people to make this argument. I'm not saying they're going to agree, gentlemen, I'm simply saying the argument can be made. The law is a fluid thing, changing almost every day. I'm sure that there are precedents set every day, and I'm sure you have both been a part of cases where you knew it was a long shot to take it to trial, but you did it anyway."

He had them both on that one. The fact was that he had probably picked the perfect team to make his argument and every one of them knew it. They were the perfect mix of brilliance and experience and of dash and strategy, and they were both charismatic as hell.

Max, engaged again, spoke next, "Alright, Steven, we're going to back you up on this, but first we have to agree to a couple of things. First, we're going to speak with your guy at Queens College and whomever else we can find to learn more about this science, and if we find serious issues with it or if we learn any of these people are quacks or nuts, you let us handle it our way. Second, if the judge makes the decision to not even allow this argument to go forward, you let us handle it our way."

Steven nodded, "As long as you present the argument to the judge and give it your best shot."

Max stood up to leave, "Wouldn't do it any other way. Okay, kid, we have a lot of work to do. I'm going to call ahead and get our people on this and see what they can find out. You look up any cases dealing with anything remotely similar. Steven, we'll be in touch."

Steven got up with them and as he was walking them to the door, gave them another heart attack, "Gentlemen, I would also like to put out a statement about what I am planning to argue."

Both lawyers stopped in their tracks and Drew asked the question for both of them, "You mean you want to put out a press release?!"

Steven smiled, "No, nothing like that. I want to explain everything I just explained to you guys to someone who will tell the story straight, no spin, no angle, just the science and what I am arguing. You know what the press has been like since I made my statement to the police, you saw them at the courthouse. Can you imagine the stories that will come out once I let the world know what I am thinking?"

Drew and Max looked at each other. It wasn't a bad idea. It would at least get people talking and the court of public opinion giving their verdict every single day, a verdict that was very likely to favor them.

Max spoke next, "Do you want me to make some inquiries with some of my media contacts?"

Steven shook his head, "No, I want this to come from me, to not have anything to do with your firm. Otherwise it will seem like just some legal stunt. It's probably still going to be taken that way, but I don't want it to be any worse than it has to be."

Both lawyers nodded, shook his hand and went on their way.

◆

Everything happened much faster than he had ever expected. He had called Grady to ask him about any reporters that he had worked with before and that he trusted. He had told the detective he wanted a print reporter, it didn't matter if they were staff or freelancers, he just wanted someone who could write a story without spin and without trying to sell it, simply telling the story. Grady had given him Felix Garcia's name. He'd been a bit wary about Garcia's age, but after he had read some of his stuff, including what he had written about Riche and the shooting, he knew why Grady had recommended him. He wrote well, not too dry, but not too flowery either. He had a keen ear and paid close attention to details, details he used to make sure that in the end, once the piece had been read, it hit home, and he did it all with no unnecessary spin or angle.

Loomis had met with Garcia two days after his meeting with his attorneys. They'd had lunch at Loomis's condo, where Felix had basically pushed his way through the throng of reporters, cameras and trucks amassed in front of Steven's building. They'd spent four hours talking, sometimes about the case, about his daughter and the shooting at the courthouse, and sometimes just talking about each other's lives.

By the time they were done, Steven knew he had made the right decision. Felix had been earnest in his questions but not too solicitous.

He was a professional, a rising star in his field and it showed, but he was also human and that showed too. He had shared parts of his life with Steven, not to curry favor or to try to get him to say more than he was comfortable saying, but simply because that's where the conversation led them. He knew he had chosen well because of the young man's competence, but more than that because at the end of their time together, Steven liked him as a person and that was no small compliment.

Three days later, when the feature story had been printed on the front page, his opinion had been confirmed. The piece had been complete, it included the basic story about the Riche case, the shooting, what Steven had explained about his reasoning and the science behind it, all well-researched and with enough details about him and his family to make the story human without making it sound sappy. The resulting fallout from it had taken everyone by surprise. The amount of media coverage that resulted shocked even seasoned players like Zeidler and District Attorney Neill. Virtually every newscast and talk show around the country had covered the story since it broke, but now it wasn't a daily thing, it was an hourly thing. Every conceivable form of media was represented. Twitter had no fewer than 13,000 hashtags about the story with more than 300,000 tweets an hour flying in every direction. The media blanketed his house, the law firm, the courthouse, every location even remotely associated with the case.

As was to be expected, opinions ranged from complete disbelief and a certainty that this was some sort of stunt to complete acceptance and a definite opinion that this had been a long way in the making. Scientists, lawyers, pseudo-experts and laymen alike ranged across the entire gamut of opinion. Whatever the experts might say, public opinion in general was decidedly in favor of Steven, even if it was spilt almost down the middle as to whether his legal argument had any merit. It was a dichotomy. People considered him a hero, but they were not so sure whether his legal argument had any merit or would hold up in court.

Steven had called his family to give them notice that the article would be coming out, and they had decided to make their way to his in-laws' summer house where any stranger would be immediately spotted and sent on their way. The property had been in the Delaney family for three generations and they were well liked by the locals. Steven knew they'd be safe there from the glare of the media. The only individual to make any statement to the media had been David Neill, who had spoken in platitudes about 'being sensitive to the horrible events' that had led to this point and 'upholding the law, as he had been elected to do,' but said nothing of consequence or any real insight. Even Max, who was used to this type of media attention, had demurred. He was a savvy veteran and knew how to use the media to his advantage, but he was in unchartered waters here and he'd told Drew he was going to be out front.

After the first two days of being chased, hunted really, by every form of media, Willis understood why Zeidler had deferred to him. Steven had gone online a few times, just to get a sense of what was going on out there. He was amazed to find 1.2 million more new results for him and the Riche case than when he'd begun. Everything from new blogs about the real Boogeyman to the expected mentions of 'The X Men' science to real scientific blogs and posts that mentioned Leonard, Grossman, Schultz and many others he had not heard about. He was amazed by how many newly minted experts seemed to be coming out of the woodwork. He knew very well that Leonard and many of the other pioneers had been ridiculed in scientific circles for their work. Now, with the possibility of CNN, the BBC, and every other form of electronic and broadcast media interested, people with dubious credentials were coming out from every direction with an opinion or insight.

Steven had also been concerned about Leonard and Scoma and the other legitimate experts, the people who really had dedicated their careers to this. He had not had the opportunity to call them and warn them about the article coming out. His concerns were put to rest, however, when he saw both Leonard and Scoma on television, clearly energized about the attention their discoveries were getting. Leonard, especially, seemed even more charismatic on television than he had in person, if that was even possible. He was gratified to see that the scientist was in high demand and that even with all the other jokers out there proffering their opinions, the real science was getting more attention than it had ever gotten in the past.

As far as Steven was concerned, he had already won. He had brought attention to something that could in fact represent the most dangerous and real threat to humanity since the Black Plague. These beings were far more dangerous, in fact, than any known pathogen. They could utilize intelligence to lull their prey into complacency, to engender trust, even affection, in order to do nothing but victimize, to hunt.

The term 'Apex Predator' had been used countless times as the media covered more and more of the science, but Steven doubted if anyone who used it or heard it could comprehend exactly what it meant. 'Well,' he thought, 'if they didn't understand it before, they will understand it soon.' The truth was, however, that those that had in fact fallen prey to the new species, that had felt the destruction, fear and devastation that they could deliver to anyone at any time, would be the first to understand it.

For their part, the DA's office had released a statement about his position and his planned defense. It hadn't been unexpected, but it was still troubling. It explained that the DA's office considered all of the science, the claims, and the proposed defense as nothing more than a stunt aimed at deflecting attention from the facts of the case. They went on to elaborate on the fact that such a claim had not been litigated in any court anywhere in the country and that it would not distract them from pursuing the charge of first-degree murder as prescribed by the laws of the state of New York. He knew it would come, but it was still difficult to hear the office that would be prosecuting him articulate it in a statement.

He had been bombarded by interview requests from every direction. Once he had given Garcia the initial interview, it was inevitable. Everyone at GIC knew the situation, and the company had been put on lockdown. No one was to speak to the media or make any statement without running it by the CEO himself. That was the reason Steven had been so surprised to hear from Stephanie, his assistant. She had told him that a Dr. Nigel Barlow had been calling every day, twice a day, requesting an audience with Mr. Loomis. Along with that call, he had heard from Max and Drew. They had found a case in Tennessee where a man accused of three counts of murder had used genetics to mount a defense. They told him that there had been a mountain of evidence against the man and that he had been looking at the death penalty. The defense had argued that because of his genetic makeup, the defendant had been predisposed to acts of extreme violence. In other words, he was born with that gene and could not be held completely accountable under the law. His attorneys had just been hoping to avoid the death penalty with the argument, but what theyd gotten instead was a guilty verdict for voluntary manslaughter. Drew had explained that this was the first recorded case where forensic genomics had been used in a courtroom setting. So there was a precedent, perhaps not exactly the same, but in the same context at least. Now there was a legal precedent where who had done it and how they had done it had not been at issue and where the defendant had not claimed insanity, temporary or otherwise.

Steven had not thought about how the science he was planning to cite would be used in another context, by people like Riche rather than people like him. He imagined that if Riche had gone to trial and his defense team had gotten wind of the Tennessee case, they might have argued the same thing. No use worrying about it now. It was good news for his case and now he knew that what he had thought was true, that unless it was a case like this one, with these facts, in this city, the world would remain ignorant about the science and its consequences. He'd never heard of forensic genomics before his situation and doubted most people had heard of it either.

He hadn't been out of his house since being released on bail and he was a getting a bit stir-crazy. It was after hearing the good news from Drew and being in his house without leaving for over a week that Steven had agreed to meet with Dr. Nigel Barlow. He'd told Stephanie that he was interested in speaking to Steven about the case and the science of his proposed defense. He was most likely another researcher or scientist who had heard about the case and wanted to learn more about his defense from a scientific perspective. He would just have to tell the man that he would only speak to him if he could agree not to print or publish anything about his case. The last thing he wanted to do was to encourage any more interview requests from the media. Stephanie had asked Steven if he wanted to meet with the man at his home and Steven told her that he would meet with him at his office. He didn't think Barlow would become a pest, but the man had been very persistent, and he didn't want anyone he didn't know intimately in his home. Stephanie had set the appointment for 8 o'clock the following morning, per his instructions. He wanted to be able to leave the building without a throng of reporters and photographers following him and he thought that time would be better than in the middle of the day when all 'live reports' and 'man-on-the-scene updates' would be in full swing.

Chapter 20

At Max Zeidler's office, there was an air of charged expectation. Everyone was acutely aware of the implications of the case they were working on and what it would mean as a legal precedent. It was pushing the envelope, something they were all quite used to doing, but none were used to doing it to this extent. This was groundbreaking stuff, something that would forever change the way criminal defense and the legal system itself viewed murder and all of its included related offenses. If a man who was by all rights completely guilty of murdering not one but three people, could get convicted of voluntary manslaughter using science, then Steven Loomis and his defense had a shot, a real shot, at beating the first-degree murder charge against him.

A case in a small, obscure town in Tennessee didn't hold a candle to New York, not when it came to public perception and not when it came to media attention. As far as Americans were concerned, New York was the capital of the world, period. All of this meant that everyone involved, from clerks to paralegals to research and appellate attorneys, was on their A game. This was the type of case that could make someone's career, and everyone knew that as well.

Drew was in his office, still going over the transcripts of the case in Tennessee. He was absolutely fascinated. The man, Louis Norton, had been charged with killing three women. His defense had absolutely nothing to work with and yet an early report by a sharp psychiatrist had engendered enough interest in one of the court-appointed attorneys to have them look into the possibility that Louis had been *born* with a predisposition to extreme violence. This predisposition coupled with some childhood abuse almost assured that Louis would grow up to do exactly what he had done.

The defense had concentrated on his childhood and teen years and had brought a number of witnesses to testify to the abuse. The testimony from the experts, two geneticists from the University of Tennessee, had provided highly technical and complex testimony about the effect that what they called the "Warrior gene" could have on whoever was born with it. Drew doubted that the jury, a jury from small-town Tennessee, had the requisite understanding of genetics, biology, evolution and so on to make a decision as to whether it was solid science or not. The prosecution had blundered in that they had not put on any rebuttal witnesses with the experience and expertise to discredit the science the defense presented. That and the defense's closing statement, where they put the science in terms that the jury could understand, had obtained the final verdict. It had been brilliant: Louis Norton was born an innocent, the way we all are, but he'd been born with a body that was predisposed to do harm to others; it wasn't something he'd decided to do out of the blue, it was something he was predestined to do. They'd explained the abuse in his early life and how that abuse made sure that Louis had no chance to avoid doing what he did. They wouldn't hold a man with only one arm responsible for not being able to hold on to a lifeline for a drowning man, would they? Would that man be faulted if he let go of the rope? No, everyone would understand that he was physically unable to do it. And that's what the case was here; Louis was simply not physiologically able to avoid doing what he did. It had been wrong and he knew it had been wrong, but he shouldn't be held responsible for something he'd had no hand in.

Drew thought the parallel the defense had drawn was a bit of a stretch, but it had been a brilliant stroke. The defense lawyer had known his jury, had known the respect they had for how someone was born, for 'God made every one of us,' and he had used it to his full advantage. Brilliant!

Drew had watched an interview with the lead attorney and he had gotten the distinct impression that the man was a bit uneasy with the verdict he had gotten. He had just been looking for a way to keep his client from getting the death penalty and he'd never expected he would only be convicted of manslaughter. Now that it had happened, it was clear that the attorney believed that his client should be held for as long as the law allowed, either in prison or in another appropriate institution. He'd never said that, of course, but the tone of the interview and his own knowledge let Drew know that's exactly what was on the man's mind.

As he was reading the transcripts of the sentencing hearing, Max came into his office looking pensive, which was pretty rare for the man. He was usually giving instructions, explaining something or otherwise being loud in some way. Now, he sat across from Drew and looked like he was trying to find an answer to some complex riddle.

"Listen, I've been thinking about it and I think we need to bring someone else into the case."

Drew leaned forward on his desk, surprised and a bit offended, "What? Why? Listen, Max, I know I don't have anywhere your experience in high-profile cases, but I know what I'm doing and I'm a good litigator, you know that."

Max smiled, leaning back in his chair, "Relax, kid, I don't mean for you, I mean for me."

Drew, now leaning back himself, was confused, "What are you talking about, Max? You said you'd back me up on this."

Max stood up and paced, "I am backing you up and I intend to stay with the case, but I think we need an older, seasoned attorney who's not attached to the firm to be a part of the defense team."

Drew started to say something, but Zeidler raised his hand, "Listen, we need someone who can be seen by the jury as being experienced and credible without seeming too flashy. I don't fit that bill, unfortunately. I'm too well known, I have been in the public eye for a long time now and most people think of me as a flashy, no-scruples old hand who defended the mafia dons back in the day, and that just won't work. It'll seem like it's some sort of publicity stunt, no matter how much we explain the science and our position. No, we need someone who will come across like a wise old man, like that wizard in the *Lord of the Rings* movie."

Drew chuckled, "Gandalf?"

Max turned, "Yeah, that guy. We need him to be the Gandalf of the case. He only needs to handle the scientific testimony from our experts. I know it's a crucial part of our case and that's the reason I think we need someone to do it who will be seen as credible and not the least bit flashy. Someone people will think would never be involved in the case if it didn't have merit, and that, my young friend, is not me."

Drew thought about it. He could see what Max was saying and it made sense. People in the media were already making statements about his involvement in the case and how Max had most likely concocted the story about a new species in order to try this in the media instead of in the courtroom. The more he thought about it, the more he agreed with his partner's position. He had someone in mind who might fit the bill, but he wasn't sure if Max also had someone in mind. If he did, Drew would defer to his judgment.

"Do you have someone that fits that description?"

Max stopped pacing and put his hands in his pockets, "Not yet. I'm thinking, but everyone I know just doesn't seem right. They're all high rollers and more likely to engender contempt rather than people thinking of them as Gandhi or Gandolfini or whatever that guy's name is."

Drew smiled, "Gandalf. I have someone. His name is Ray Gretche and he's prefect. Late 50s, tough as nails, and an incredible mind for controlling law and precedents. I represented one of the defendants on a huge drug case and he defended another one.

"He is incredible in cross-examination, made a senior vice detective look like a bumbling rookie patrolman and did it with style. He looks like the wise old man, like he's seen everything and knows best. I swear he looks like a sage grandfather imparting wisdom."

Max narrowed his eyes as he searched his memory.

All of a sudden his eyes widened, "You mean Big Ray? I know him, know him well, actually. His last name is Gretche? I didn't know. I've just known him as Big Ray for as long as I can remember. He's older than his mid-50s, though, quite a bit older, actually. He'd already tried a number of high-profile murder cases by the time I started practicing law. You're right, he is perfect. Alright, do you want to contact him or do you want me to do it?"

Drew thought for a couple of seconds, "Why don't you let me contact him. With everything being covered in the media, he might think it really is a stunt. If I contact him, he'll know we're on the up and up."

Max nodded, back to his perpetual-motion, good-natured self. The weight was off his shoulders, "Fair enough. If you need a hand with it or if you want me to go with you, let me know."

He turned and left leaving Drew almost talking to himself, "I'll do that."

◆

Steven had gotten into the building before seven that morning and as he had thought, there weren't more than a few news trucks outside, no reporters and a handful of photographers hanging out around the building. He knew that would change before too long. He was still amazed that there was that much media interest a week after the story had come out in the paper. He was starting to realize that it was not likely that the media attention would die out. If anything, it was beginning to sink in that this was just the beginning, that it would only get more intense from here.

He was going over some of the deals he had put together that were now being handled by his VPs. It vexed him to not be able to finish what he'd started. He had seen every single deal to its conclusion since he had come onboard at GIC. Part of the price he had to pay.

Stephanie got in about 30 minutes after he had gotten there. After giving him a hug and a once-over, she had gotten him a cup of coffee just the way he liked it and left him alone to continue his work. She knew him better than almost anyone else and knew that what he wanted more than anything was for things to be normal again, so she had known to just let him do his thing, the way she had done many times before.

At eight in the morning she went into his office to let him know that his appointment had just arrived, "Steven, Dr. Barlow is here."

He looked up from his desk, "Please show him in, Steph." He closed the files on his desk and stood up to greet his guest. Dr. Nigel Barlow looked like the stereotype of an academic. He was in his 50s, about six feet tall, thin and athletic, Steven thought. It looked like he kept himself in pretty good shape. He was impeccably dressed in a three-piece suit with a nicely matching, small bow tie. He was almost completely bald, with only a neatly cut band of gray hair surrounding his head. He wore round, stylish glasses and had an air about him of someone who was in a moderate state of anxiety. Steven made all these assessments as the man came over to shake his hand. There was something that made Steven uneasy about the man, although he couldn't quite put his finger on it. He was definitely nothing like Tyrone Leonard. He didn't have the same charisma or the presence that Leonard had. The look Steven saw in him was more like what? Hunger?

He put the thought aside and greeted Barlow, "Dr. Barlow? It's a pleasure to meet you."

Barlow pumped his hand up and down as they greeted, "Mr. Loomis, quite the contrary, the pleasure is certainly mine. Quite an honor, indeed. I am much obliged that you agreed to see me."

Steven detected a faint British accent. Barlow had obviously been in the US for some time, but the accent still came through. There was still something that was bothering Steven and it was starting to send red flags up, but he'd be damned if he knew what it was. Maybe he was just on edge, wary of people he didn't know. He didn't think so, that had never been the case before, but then again, the circumstances had never been as they were now.

He held his hand out toward the small round table in his office, "Please sit down. Can I offer you some coffee, water?" Barlow walked over to the table, set his briefcase down next to the chair and sat down, "Most kind, no, thank you, I'm fine for the moment."

Steven now sat across from the man. He wanted to just lean back and relax, listen to what the man came to talk about, but he found he couldn't do it. He was uptight, edgy, the way he felt before an operation and it was a strange enough feeling that, given the circumstances, he found he couldn't just relax.

He leaned forward, elbows resting on the table, and started the conversation, "What can I do for you?"

Barlow, sitting back in his chair with his legs crossed and his hands on his lap, proceeded to let Steven know why he was there.

"First of all, Mr. Loomis, let me apologize for my insistence on seeing you. I dare say I made a most annoying pest of myself with your assistant, but what I want to discuss with you is of the utmost importance, you understand. I also wanted to say that I am most sorry for your loss and for your other…difficulties."

This last part he said with something akin to annoyance, as if it had been something he knew he had to get out of the way but didn't really care for. Steven nodded and waited for him to continue.

Barlow went on, "You see, I am a criminal profiling consultant. I work with the FBI, have now for some years, and I am very interested to learn as much as I can about Donald Riche and his actions, how he came to do the things he did, his motivations, that kind of thing."

What Barlow had said was in no way remarkable, it was something that someone in his field would most likely say, given the situation. What was odd was the way in which he said it. There was no gravity, no sense of professional detachment in what he said. He sounded and looked more like a kid talking to someone who'd played with Michael Jordan wanting to know what it had been like to play next to him. There was an eagerness, a sort of… there was that idea of hunger again. Steven's unease continued to grow. He gave up on trying to understand the reason for it and simply decided he would try to let his instincts guide him. They'd never let him down before.

He gave Barlow a puzzled look and decided to play dumb, "I don't understand, Dr. Barlow, surely you have access to more information about those things than I do. I'm not sure that I can be of any help to you."

Barlow's countenance had shifted slightly. No longer the eager and obsequious guest, he now looked at Steven with an intensity that hadn't been there before.

His tone also changed. He now had a more purposeful set in his voice, "On the contrary, Mr. Loomis, I believe it's you and only you who can provide the insights I need. You're right, I do have the details, the information about Mr. Riche and his actions. I do, after all, consult with the FBI. As you can imagine, however, everything I've reviewed is provided in reports, photographs, written statements, that sort of thing. It is all very detailed and complete, but it lacks the most critical element."

Steven now leaned back into his chair and took on a different tone himself, more guarded and careful, "What element would that be, doctor?"

Barlow noticed the change and once again tried to take on the simple, curious tone he'd begun with. He tried but just couldn't pull it off, "The intimate element, of course. I want to understand the motivations and the thought processes that led Mr. Riche to engage in his quest, his journey. Those are things a report simply cannot convey, Mr. Loomis. I am interested in understanding the inspiration that took Mr. Riche down the path he chose."

Steven's instincts were now on full alert. There was something most definitely off about Barlow. The deferential, almost wistful tone with which he referred to Riche's 'quest,' the eager, hungry way in which he said he wanted to understand the 'inspiration' that had driven Donald Riche.

Now, with his instincts and every one of his senses fully engaged, he finally got what it was about the man and their initial greeting that had such a powerful effect on him. It was a faint but distinct scent. Steven had smelled it when the man had first come in. It had been so faint and so strange that he couldn't identify it. He now knew what that scent was, it was the acrid, metallic smell of blood and some sort of astringent, some sort of an astringent cleaner. The man was a doctor and probably had been exposed to blood and to a cleaner designed to remove the smell of it. Steven tried feebly to hold on to that thought because the alternatives were simply too disturbing. He wanted to get more from Barlow, to form a better idea of what the man was about and what he was looking for, so he held himself in check, remaining completely impassive and under control as he sat across from him, his mind racing to get a bearing.

"I don't know that I can help you with any of that. I know as much about Riche as you, probably less, actually."

Barlow gave him a thin, knowing smile, a smile that chilled Steven to the bone, "Come now, Mr. Loomis, as I understand it, you were there, you were in his studio, you experienced everything firsthand, before it was corrupted by all the technicians and investigators."

Now Steven knew that Barlow had absolutely no interest in the science and he was not engaged in any sort of research. His interest was personal and 'intimate' and given his continued references to Riche's 'studio' and the scene being 'corrupted' by the technicians, Loomis now understood much better what it was that Barlow was looking for.

"Dr. Barlow, I'm not quite sure what it is that you think I can tell you or share with you. Whatever it is that I saw or experienced at that warehouse is of a very personal nature to me, and as you can imagine incredibly painful, so I have no intention of reliving the experience, whatever the nature of your inquiry happens to be."

As he progressed through the statement, the intensity in Steven's voice grew and his eyes began to reflect a quiet anger that visibly affected Barlow. However fit the man was, he was clearly no match for Steven. As someone schooled on human emotion and reaction, he became immediately aware of the fact that he had completely misread Steven Loomis and responded accordingly, "A thousand apologies,

Mr. Loomis, it was not my intention to upset you in any way. I am very sorry for being insensitive. It is just that I have been a keen observer and longtime researcher of this type of behavior."

Barlow was almost theatrical in his apologies, trying to physically communicate just how sorry he was.

It all gave the situation an almost surreal tone, "You see, I was, and I don't want to sound insensitive again, looking forward to being able to better understand what drove Mr. Riche. A trial, the resulting interviews and interrogations, would have given me an excellent idea of what it was that Riche's grand plan was.

"Once you...once he was shot, all of that disappeared. Oh, of course I have access to all of the written reports and the pictures and the few statements that he made, but none of that, none of it at all, communicates the true insights into his mind."

Steven was now in information gathering mode. The entire exchange had revealed what Steven had intuited in the beginning. Nigel Barlow's interest in Donald Riche was the same type of interest that a professional had in how an amateur, a talented amateur, practiced his craft.

He wanted to understand what he was dealing with, so he went along, "And what grand plan is it that you think Riche was following?"

Barlow looked surprised. He had not expected the question and now that it had been posed, he responded immediately, without taking the time to figure out how to edit his response, "What plan? Well, I don't know, that's what I wanted to find out, to glean from your experience. It will almost be impossible now, without his input, without his insights.

"The world will see this simply as a mass murder committed by a madman, Mr. Loomis. They will air their stories and get their rating and their experts will go on and on talking about things they simply do not understand. No one, not one person, will understand the kind of planning, the kind of careful consideration it takes to do what Riche did. None of the experts will ever address or even mention the kind of meticulous thought processes that are required to execute that kind of enterprise.

"I think what you have done is wonderful, sir, and I commend you for it. I think it is time that the world understood that there is now a more advanced being, what I call a Prime Force, on the face of the earth."

As he listened to Barlow, Steven noticed a distinct change in the man. He was indignant, upset about what he saw as inferior creatures trying to pass judgment on the deeds of a more advanced intelligence. His whole countenance, the way he punctuated every point with his hands, how flush his face looked, the rising volume of his voice, all spoke to indignation. Steven now believed this was a man who had been looking forward to perhaps interviewing Riche and, God help him, talk shop. His was not the same type of interest that Leonard had, a professional interest in a scientific breakthrough. Barlow's interest had to do with feeling *kinship* with Riche.

Loomis had wondered if he had come face-to-face with a *Homo sapiens predaer* in Riche. He'd also wondered whether he would come face-to-face with one again. Now he thought he had his answer. He wanted to understand them better, but he was also starting to feel something else. What was it? Not fear, he wasn't afraid, it was more like feeling overwhelmed, like someone who'd read about sharks, who'd lost a loved one to a shark and who all of a sudden was in the water with a shark with no protective cage in between.

As much as he wanted to learn more about Barlow, he couldn't risk more exposure for himself, his case and, most importantly, the people he loved.

Still, he couldn't pass up one more question, "And have you done much work with people like Riche? Is that the kind of work you do?"

The question brought Barlow back to the moment, snapped him out of his tirade, but not completely.

He'd been talking more to himself than Loomis. Now that he realized Loomis would have questions of his own, he was more engaged than he had been, "Yes, quite a bit of work, actually. There have been instances such as these for some time now, Mr. Loomis. I dare say they've been occurring throughout history. And they've been vastly misunderstood, misjudged."

Steven wanted him to be clear, specific, "You mean other murderers? Other rapists and murderers of children? Is that what you mean when you say other instances such as this?"

Barlow paused briefly, with a startled look on his face, "What? No, of course not! But, Mr. Loomis, I think you and I both know that Mr. Riche wasn't just an ordinary murderer, don't we? No, what I mean is that there have been many more instances before, even before a record was kept, where something else, something far beyond the crude vulgarity of a mere murderer undertook a task they could not complete. Instances where sad souls, tortured by conflicting emotions and the inadequacies of the human mind, decided to embrace their nature.

"Murderers, psychopaths as you call them, Mr. Loomis, those that don't murder out of greed or jealousy or other simple human failings, are most likely half-breeds, individuals who have not yet evolved into something beyond human, but who feel the same needs, the same hunger, that those that have evolved feel. They don't have the tools required to satisfy that hunger, to understand who and what they are and they simply act on their instincts.

"What I am talking about, Mr. Loomis, is perfect predators, engineered for their purpose. Their intellect, their ability to blend in perfectly into their surroundings, the meticulous nature of their planning and their execution, those are the things I am interested in.

"I have had the privilege to hear of their activities, to listen while they impassively and naturally explained their purpose, their ultimate plan. No emotion, no anger or rage to be found, highly developed intelligence devoted to a single purpose with no ulterior motives, no agendas. That, Mr. Loomis, is what I am interested in.

"You have pulled back the curtain and you've let the world in on *their* world. But, Mr. Loomis, I wonder if you understand what you are in for. The world is simply not ready, you see, to accept that they exist because it would mean accepting that humans are no longer at the top of the food chain and that, my dear sir, is not something the world is ready to accept."

Steven was now certain that he was speaking to one of them. Barlow had been speaking of his interests, but he was really referring to himself and to others like him. Steven was now aware of a different feeling, rage. Rage at what was in front of him, rage at what it represented and rage that he could refer to his daughter and the rest of the girls as so many leavings, byproducts of some higher purpose.

He was afraid of what might happen if he let Barlow continue, but he also wanted to make sure he knew exactly where they stood before he left. "Maybe, maybe that's true, maybe the world is not ready, but now they'll have no choice but to take notice, to acknowledge that these things exist. Perhaps the system will continue to deny it, but people, everyday people, will know and they'll prepare as best they can, do what they can do to protect themselves and their children.

"I believe we are done here, Dr. Barlow, I have nothing else to say to you and I would advise you not to say anything to *me*. You're right, I have felt it, I have felt what you are talking about, the intelligence behind it, the careful planning, and the absolute and complete lack of anything human behind it. I know when I am in its presence again. It's not something I arrive at using my reasoning, it's something I *feel*.

"Now, I'm busy and I need you to leave, but before you do, I want to make something perfectly clear to you and I would counsel you to pay heed. If I see you anywhere near the trial, anywhere near this building or within 10 square blocks of my house and my family, I will kill you."

Steven was speaking in even, reasoned tones, but his eyes were narrowed into an intense, direct stare that looked into and through Barlow. His body was now tightened into a pitched, hair-trigger tension, a tension that many adversaries had experienced right before they had died. Barlow listened, a fascinated expression on his face. Loomis knew what he was and why he was here, truly remarkable. This had not been a part of any of the things Barlow had expected. He had expected grief, sadness, perhaps some outrage about his inquiry, but he had never expected to be made. Loomis had in fact felt what he had been amongst, knew exactly what he had been a part of, fascinating. Still, Barlow could sense the danger he was in. That was also something he had never faced before and never expected. He had never done this with someone who had taken as many lives as Loomis, who was as familiar with death as he was. Every time he had done this before, he had gotten what he wanted, the men and women with whom he had spoken had not known it, but they had always given him what he had wanted, the confirmation he longed for. Never like this, however, good lord, never like this. He did not respond with feigned outrage at any accusation or threat that Steven had leveled at him, but both men knew they were far beyond that.

He smiled a satisfied smile and cocked his head to one side, like a dog listening to high-pitched sound, "You would, wouldn't you? You would kill me with no hesitation, fascinating, most fascinating indeed. You won't be bothered by me any further, Mr. Loomis. You have nothing to be concerned with at all, not from me anyway.

"I am most grateful for your time, most grateful. You have given me much more than I could have ever hoped for, far more. Goodbye, Mr. Loomis. I dare say we may cross paths once again."

Neither man went to shake hands. Barlow simply stood up and walked to the office door. Steven stood up but did not move from where he was.

Before he opened the door to leave, with his hand on the doorknob and without looking back, Barlow said one last thing, "It's simply nature, Mr. Loomis, simply nature moving forward. Nothing evil or forbidden, just nature."

And with that Barlow walked through the door, closing it behind him. Stephanie came into the office once the man had left. Steven was sitting at the table with one hand over his mouth, clearly deep in thought. Stephanie became instantly concerned. She had seen the look before, never because of something good.

"Are you alright? You're a bit pale."

Steven looked up at her, "Huh? Oh, yeah. Just thinking, just thinking."

Stephanie decided to leave it alone. He would have told her if it had been something he wanted to talk about, always had.

"I'm going home, Steph. I just came in to talk to him, but I have to get back home."

Stephanie watched as he picked up his things and got ready to leave, "That man gave me the creeps. I don't know why, he looked nice enough, but he just had this little grin on his face while he waited for you. Just sat perfectly still with his hands on his lap and that stupid grin."

As he was walking to leave, Steven looked at her, gave her a sad smile and a little kiss on the forehead, "Yeah, I know what you mean. I'll see you, Steph."

He went down into the garage where the driver was waiting for him. On his way home, his mind was racing with possibilities. He should have checked the man out more thoroughly before agreeing to meet with him – damn that had been sloppy – but he had been happy about the news Drew had given him and he wanted to get out of the house. Besides, he would have most likely run into mentions of Barlow in his capacity as a profiler and would have still met with him. Now, with the weight of the trial looming over him, he had to concentrate on the case, put everything else out of his mind. He knew he had to do it, but he also knew, with absolute certainty, that he would never be able to put Barlow out of his mind. If there was one thing he had learned from Tracy's disappearance, it was that hard as he might try, he was just not capable of lying to himself. Once he got home, the first thing he did was to call Beth. He missed her, missed the sound of her voice. He would never tell her about Barlow, about what he was or that he had met with him.

After asking about the kids and her parents, Steven explained to Beth that right now they were in 'wait and see' mode. The DA was analyzing the case and weighing his options, that's what Drew and Max had said. They had also said that there would most likely be an evidentiary hearing to determine whether the court would even allow the defense to move forward. They had explained that the DA would be asking the court to find, as a matter of law, that Donald Riche was a human being. That had started another round of pundits and legal experts proffering their opinion on the matter. It was on every single news channel and there were millions of results online.

Steven and Beth had almost gotten into a fight when she insisted on coming to New York to be with him and he insisted that she would be far better in a safe place, somewhere they couldn't be accosted by a mob of reporters. In the end Steven had won, his had been the most reasoned argument and she knew it, but she was still upset.

The truth was that Steven needed elbow room. He had to figure out what to do next. As soon as he got off the phone with his wife, he went online to research Nigel Barlow. He found hundreds of hits from all across the country. He had been telling the truth, he did profiling work for the FBI and various other law enforcement agencies. It was obvious the man worked all over the country. The most recent cases Steven had been able to find were in California and Utah. In both of those instances, there were several people missing and in both, law enforcement was treating them as missing persons but were almost certainly also treating them as murders. Barlow had been a consultant in both instances and no suspects had been apprehended. As he was looking through the information, Steven also found three cases where Barlow had not been a consultant, but rather the therapist that the accused murderers had been going to before their crimes. Steven knew that he would never be able to testify to anything that the accused had said to him during their sessions, but the defense teams in each of the cases had brought him up to support their claims that their client had been under treatment. In each of the cases, the defense had made a claim of diminished mental capacity or insanity, and in each of the cases, the defense had failed and the accused had been convicted of multiple counts of first-degree murder. After staring at the computer for three hours, Steven had a clear picture of who, of what, Barlow was. In every single case he had been involved in, it had been young, college-age men that had gone missing. All of them had come from well-to-do families, all of them had gone missing without a trace and none of them had been found. Barlow had consulted with the FBI and the local police. In every one of the cases, police had not been called initially because it had taken a while for the men to be reported missing.

As he kept reading, Steven noticed that the murder victims in each of the cases where Barlow had been mentioned as having treated the defendant also happened to be young men. A picture was beginning to emerge, a picture that was almost too hard to fathom, but given what he now knew, what he had been through, it was a picture he could not ignore. He believed that Barlow was a *Homo sapiens predaer* and that he had been responsible for the disappearances. Either he had done it himself or, more than likely, he had directed others like him to do it. He could not imagine the horrors those men had faced at the hands of one or maybe more of these predators. The information Steven had found went back a full 10 years and in that time Barlow had been on the move almost constantly. He knew these things because of what he had been through, but he was also aware that to anyone looking in from the outside it might look like the paranoid mind of someone who has suffered a great loss and who had faced unimaginable evil. He needed for a fresh set of eyes to look at this, at everything he had found about Barlow and to have someone else's opinion, and he thought he knew who he would call on.

Chapter 21

Cecil and Thurman Meeks were identical twins. They had served under Steven the last three years he was with the SEALs. Both men were just about six feet tall, slender, but with broad shoulders and powerful legs, always dressed in identical Armani or Hugo Boss suits, but different-colored ties. The Twins, as they were known, were black with light blue-green eyes and the only way to tell them apart was how they wore their hair or, as was most often the case, how they wore their facial hair. Both men's heads were shaved to a smooth shine. Cecil had a goatee while Thurman was clean-shaven. Steven could also tell them apart because of the small, almost imperceptible scar that was just behind Thurman's ear, a scar courtesy of flying shrapnel from an IED. The Twins had left the service at the same time that Steven had and while he went the corporate route, they went into business for themselves. They had enough contacts around the world and the skills necessary to ensure they would never be out of work. Steven knew that the General called on them from time to time for 'off the books' operations. His boss had never offered and Steven had never asked, but he knew that they were called when there could be no trace of company involvement in whatever it was they were doing. They were two of the best operators that Steven had ever worked with and they did everything with one prime, underlying principle: loyalty. The Twins were loyal to those they respected and no amount of money or influence would ever change their zeal. The other thing that Steven knew he could count on was discretion. No matter what it was that he would ask them to do, he knew it would never go beyond them, ever.

He'd asked both men to come to his house to discuss what he needed done and that they do so as discreetly as possible. Both men had arrived in a furniture moving van wearing overalls with the company's logo on them. Cecil was also wearing a Yankees baseball cap.

As soon as he opened the door and saw both men, Steven took Cecil's outstretched hand and pulled him in for a hug, "Look at you, you guys went into the moving business? I knew there was a bright future ahead for you two."

Cecil returned the hug and chuckled at the joke, "You know us, anywhere we can make a buck."

Thurman, the quieter and more pensive of the two, also gave Steven a hug, "It's been a long time, brother, we're really sorry about everything you've had to go through."

Steven thanked him for the thought.

Cecil also took on a more serious note, "Yeah, man, we wanted to come by and see you, you know, just to make sure you were doing okay, but then we thought maybe you'd want to be alone for a while."

Steven motioned for them to follow him to the living room, "Thanks, guys, I appreciate it, and for what it's worth, you were right. For a while there, I needed to be alone, to figure things out."

Steven didn't want to get into everything that had happened, it had been all over the news and just like everybody else, the Twins were well aware of what he intended on arguing.

Never one to dally too much, Thurman got right down to business, "Well, you know you can count on us for anything you need."

That was his way of asking what they could do for him. Steven explained everything that had happened, the media and all the attention his case was getting. He also explained how he had come to meet with Barlow, how he'd thought he was another researcher, a scientist interested in the case. That was where it had gotten interesting, he couldn't tell them what he thought he knew, what he thought Barlow was, but he needed to give them some explanation for what he was about to ask them to do.

"After I met with the guy, I looked him up. It's something I really should have done before agreeing to meet with him, but you know how it is, you get complacent. Anyway, after I met with the guy, I did some research and found out the guy has been a part of more than 12 multiple murders or missing persons cases over the past 10 years. He's been doing his work for longer than that, but I only went back 10 years.

"Not only that, he was the therapist for three guys that were all accused of murder in three different states. As their therapist, he couldn't testify in their trials, he could simply acknowledge he had been treating the defendants, and that was how he came to be mentioned in those cases. I'm not sure what the chances are, what the actual statistical odds are that he just happened to be the therapist for three different murder suspects and that he also happens to be a criminal profiler in at least 12 cases, cases where no body has ever been found and where they have no suspects. I'd be willing to bet they're long odds, though.

"The thing is, he's constantly on the move; therefore, the cases are in different states and different jurisdictions, so no one has ever put it together."

There it was, that was as far as Steven was willing to risk it. He had not given them any sense of what he'd been thinking. He had simply let them know why it was he was interested in the guy. Cecil and Thurman looked at each other. With that look, they let him know that they didn't know what the odds of such a coincidence were, but they too knew they were long odds indeed.

Thurman was the first to articulate what they all knew should come next, "We'll get into the guy. Find out where he lives, what his patterns are, you know the drill. If he moves around as much as you say he does, he probably keeps more than one house. We'll get into that first. C, I'm sure this cat has passwords for his passwords wherever he lives, so we'll have to get the Russian on it."

Before Steven could protest about bringing someone else into this, Cecil interjected, "Don't worry, bro, this guy is a Russian outfit guy and he operates out of Lithuania. He's as off the grid as you can get. He has enough computing power to bring down the servers at companies like Visa and American Airlines, he's actually done that, wiped the American Airlines reservation system and he did it because they lost his luggage. Whatever this guy's security measures are, the Russian will get through them."

Steven nodded, a thought occurred to him all of a sudden, something he hadn't thought before but which was a possibility, "You know, it may be that he doesn't have any extreme security measures. I mean, why should he, right? Maybe to hold patients' confidential files, but that shouldn't be anything more complicated than a small safe."

Thurman nodded, "You may be right. All the better that way. Less time to get what we are looking for."

As that was Thurman's way of asking what exactly it was they were looking for, Steven obliged. "I just want to know what this guy's real connection to all these cases is. Maybe it is just coincidence that every case he's consulted or been the therapist in is a case where young men disappeared or were murdered by one of his patients.

Maybe he specializes in missing young men situations, maybe, but doubtful. I just want to know what is underneath the façade he puts on."

Thurman and Cecil listened carefully, they understood what it was Steven was looking for, but they also had questions of their own and there just wasn't an easy way to ask them.

Once Steven finished, Cecil asked, "You know you can count on us, Steve, you always will, but we got to know, is this something to do with everything else going on? With your case and all that?"

Steven knew the question would come sooner or later and he wasn't sure how he would handle it until the very moment when they had asked the question, "Yeah, it's something to do with the science, with the argument I will be presenting as a defense. But it isn't related to the case at all, I haven't spoken with anyone about Barlow and I plan on keeping it that way.

"You two are the only ones I have spoken with. I wish I could tell you guys more, but honestly I don't even really know what it is I'm looking for. I just have a feeling about the guy and maybe I'm paranoid, or maybe I'm looking for monsters under the bed where there aren't any, but I need to know what this guy's about."

Both men were nodding as he was speaking. These were men that had been in some pretty dicey situations under Steven's command and they had learned long ago to trust the man's instincts. Those instincts had saved their skin more than once.

Thurman got up and Cecil followed, "No worries, man, sometimes you don't know what you're looking for until you find it."

Steven hugged both men and sent them on their way. Now it was just a waiting game. Once he'd seen them off, he made himself a quick bite and washed it down with water. He hadn't known just how hungry he was until he had finished his sandwich. He called Beth to check on her and the kids. As he had suspected, mainstream media looking for an angle had flooded the town, and as he had hoped, they had not been welcomed nor assisted by the small Vermont community of Queensbury.

After hanging up with Beth and as he was getting ready to go to bed, he got a call from Drew. "Steven! Where the hell have you been? Don't you ever check your messages?"

Steven had to smile, "Only the messages I want to get."

Drew didn't pay attention, "Well, I've been trying to get hold of you. We have a hearing the day after tomorrow. Just like we told you, the DA has asked that the judge decide as a matter of law that Riche was a human being. That means that the judge could basically crush our defense before we even get off the ground. Basically, he would be deciding that Riche was human before we ever present any of our evidence.

"Max, Ray and I don't think that will be the case, we have a defense-friendly judge, and we have enough solid science to at least present the argument."

Steven interrupted, "Ray, who's Ray?"

Drew sounded impatient on his end of the phone, "Ray is an attorney that Max and I brought in for the case. Trust me, we need this guy. He's an older guy, old-school attorney, not too flashy and a great litigator.

"We need him because when we put the expert witnesses on the stand it, the one who conducts the direct should be someone who comes across as a wise old hand, someone who has seen it all. We need for the jury to listen to this guy and to feel like they've been listening to a story while sitting on grandpa's knee."

Steven chuckled on his end, "Okay, okay, I get it, you recruited Santa Claus to be on our team."

Now it was Drew who chuckled, "That's right and who better to know who's been naughty or nice."

"Ohh, that was awful," Steven winced at the cheesy reference.

Drew went on, "Anyway, you need to come in sometime tomorrow so you can meet Ray and so we can go over all of the evidence we'll be presenting. It's an evidentiary hearing, so the lawyers will do all of the talking. We're going to get started early, so just come when you're ready."

Steven agreed to be there, hung up the phone and went about getting ready for bed. Before going to bed Steven sat in front of his laptop trying to find whatever additional information he could about Barlow's education and early years. He graduated from UC San Diego with a double major in chemistry and pharmacology, then he got his medical degree at Harvard and interned at Johns Hopkins and at USC Medical Center. He started a neurology practice early in his career, but that hadn't lasted for long. After he closed his practice, there was no information on the man for six years when he showed up as a profiling consultant for the San Bernardino sheriff's office. After that first case, Barlow showed up all over the country, always as a consultant or a profiler. In every instance, the case had to do with young men going missing and in every instance, a suspect was never developed. He had also shown up in three cases where his patient had gone on to commit several murders. The mentions were brief as it related to Barlow. He was simply mentioned as one of the doctors that had treated the suspect. No authority or reporter had made the connection given the fact the cases were in completely different states and jurisdictions. Steven finally closed his laptop, his eyes were dry from staring at the screen and he had to get up early.

The next morning, Steven showered, dressed and went to sit at the kitchen table to drink his coffee and read the newspaper. As he expected, his story was the cover story on the front page, as it had been for the past week, and as it would probably be for the foreseeable future. He put most of the paper aside and just read the sports pages. At least there he knew he would not be reading about himself, but he would be reading about the Knicks and how horrible they were this year. He finished his coffee, got his coat from the front closet and went downstairs where he knew there would be a sea of reporters waiting for him, just like there had been all week. He waited in the lobby of his building until he saw the Town Car, and when it was directly in front of the door, he went out.

As he was quickly making his way through the reporters and the security staff in front of the building, he ran straight into a woman who had her arms loaded with packages and was also trying to make her way through the crowd as she walked down the sidewalk. They bumped into each other with some force. Steven moved people aside to help her pick up her packages. The woman was also trying to pick up her things, but the commotion and the pushing and shoving from the reporters made it difficult. Once she had her packages back in hand, she thanked Steven and went on her way. Steven jumped into the waiting car and got on his way.

As soon as he settled in the car, he noticed that it was not the same driver that had been driving him, "Where's Manny today?"

The driver looked in the rearview mirror and responded, "Took a sick day. Must be coming down with something."

As he listened to the man, Steven felt strange, as if he were hearing what the driver had said through a thick glass partition. He looked out the window and blinked several times, trying to get his eyes to focus on something, anything, but he just couldn't do it. As he leaned back in the seat, he realized he was fading and fast. With his last remaining bit of consciousness, he tried to grab the door handle to open it, but he just didn't have the strength. His last waking thought was of the woman with the packages…

When he finally opened his eyes, he was sitting in the middle of a drab, nondescript room with a bed, a small desk and a television. It looked like any one of thousands of rooms in small motels all over the country. He hands and ankles were cuffed to the chair he was sitting in and he had a piece of duct tape over his mouth. At first he thought he was alone in the room, but then he heard the faucet run in the bathroom. He couldn't turn his head far enough to see who was behind him, but he knew whoever it was was standing at the threshold of the bathroom because the light was projecting their shadow on the floor. Steven looked around the room to try to get as much detail as he possibly could about where he was. There was nothing in the room that could tell him where he was. He could hear the rumble of big 18-wheelers roaring nearby, which meant this was exactly what it looked like, a little motel on the side of the interstate, somewhere where tired drivers could put their heads down for a few hours or where weary families could stop and rest on their way to grandma's house.

Loomis tested the cuffs on his wrist and on his ankles, there was absolutely no play in either, they were firmly on. Finally, a voice came from behind Loomis. He recognized it immediately.

Barlow walked from the bathroom and sat on the bed directly in front of Steven, "I'm sorry for the extreme measures, Mr. Loomis, but I'm sure you can understand that I simply could not have you free while I talk to you. I hope you can appreciate the risks that I took in order to make this little meeting possible. Switching cars was easy enough, but to administer the sleeping agent and to do it in the middle of a crowd of reporters, now that took some finesse.

"After our last meeting, I was quite interested in you, far more than I would have believed. My initial interest had to do with young Mr. Riche's exploits, but after talking to you, after observing you, my interests have grown much further than they had been originally. Even so, I was prepared to simply observe you from afar, to do research on you through my usual sources. But then you were also clearly interested in me, so interested that you sent people to look into my background, to go in my office and into the home I keep here in New

York." Steven didn't move or react in any way, but his eyes moved when he heard Barlow talk about being tailed.

"Oh, yes, Mr. Loomis, I know all about your interest in me. Your people are good, very good actually, but then again, so am I. I have to be, you see. My work requires supreme vigilance, redundancy on redundancy, isn't that what they teach you in the military? Your friends almost went undetected, but in all fairness, I am certain they never expected to run into some of my countermeasures. They got nothing of value, I assure you. I don't keep my work anywhere near where I live.

"Now that we both know just how interested we are in each other, what do you say if we get down to where the rubber meets the road, as you Americans are fond of saying. I have done work, important work, for more than two decades now. It has not been easy, I have had to hide my true work by engaging in activities that fit within what society finds acceptable. It is a hard and tedious labor, Mr. Loomis, but a necessary one. Each of my subjects has contributed immeasurably to the understanding of the human brain, its capacity to adapt, to rewire itself, to evolve.

"Nothing that could be done in a laboratory or in some other artificial setting can compare to how the brain reacts to true horror, to the almost certain realization that death is imminent. It is truly fascinating. It is also fascinating to understand the flaws in the human psyche, the weaknesses that are caused by early trauma or perhaps by a natural genetic deficiency, and how those flaws and weaknesses can be manipulated, can be exploited to any purpose.

"You are quite right, Mr. Loomis, quite right. There are beings out there that are not human, beings that were born to be perfect predators, that were born with an innate desire to hunt and with the intelligence and ability to do exactly that – hunt. You didn't think Donald Riche was the only one, did you, Mr. Loomis? Surely you must have realized that he was but one of thousands, maybe millions, of others out there."

As he was listening to Barlow, Steven continued to look around the room for anything that he could identify, for anything that would tell him where he was. For his part, Barlow appeared to be enjoying this immensely. It was as though the man had finally found a kindred spirit, someone in whom he could confide.

"I have been interested in them for more than two decades. I followed Tyrone Leonard's early work, his and others' doing research on the possible existence of these individuals. Once I learned about Riche, I came immediately. His promised to be a most interesting case. There was so much I was looking forward to learning from him, but alas, I was never able to learn very much. You see, some of my most interesting work arises from studying those who undertake their projects with no sense of who or what they are. As I am sure you know, most serial killers are in fact psychopaths, humans whose minds are flawed and who are triggered by some form of psychological or physical trauma. My interests lie beyond that.

"Young Mr. Riche had not suffered any sort of trauma nor had he shown any sort of mental deficiency in his early years, so it was likely that he was the type of subject in which I am interested. Instead, you came up, and I must say it has proven to be a very handsome trade-off. I learned nothing from Riche, but now I have you to learn from, to observe and to follow.

"Did you think I would come to see you without first researching who you are? When you took ownership for Mr. Riche, I immediately obtained access to your records, Mr. Loomis, *all* of you records, going back to your time in the Navy. As you know, I do quite a bit of work for the FBI and I am able to obtain any record I choose. I do have to admit that some of your records were more difficult to obtain than I had anticipated. You were involved in some interesting operations.

"Believe it or not, Mr. Loomis, my interest in you is purely scientific, nothing personal. Leonard and the others research this as a science, as a laboratory experiment, but they have no idea what it is like to be in the presence of them while they are free to hunt, to explore their minds while they are in the middle of tracking their next prey. To guide them as they develop into what they truly are. The world does not have the stomach for the kind of research that is required. But things will change now; you've made them change.

"As much as they'd like to, they won't be able to ignore the fact that they are no longer at the top of the food chain. They are afraid because it is something they have no control over. Have you heard the talk shows, the newscasts? They are terrified, and they should be; they have no idea what these individuals are capable of, how good they are at what they do. They don't know, but you do, Mr. Loomis, you do and that makes you frightening to them as well. I know you don't see it now, but you will. Whether you win or lose, Mr. Loomis, what you've done has changed things, and I for one am extremely curious to see where it will all lead.

"You have no idea what you have managed to involve yourself in, the enormity of it, and how far and high it reaches. You don't yet, but I suspect you will, Mr. Loomis, I suspect you will. Some things you simply cannot unknow. Do you have any concept, any idea of where some of these individuals are, where they *hunt,* the influence they wield? Not all predators hunt the same prey, Mr. Loomis, or the same ground, and they most definitely do not use the same methods. Politicians, captains of industry, media moguls, energy giants. Can you imagine, Mr. Loomis, what these individuals are able to do? The many ways in which they can manipulate the world around them to satisfy their predatory instincts? It is astounding, Steven, absolutely astounding. Believe it or not, most of them go their entire lives not knowing what they really are. They are born, grow up and make a life for themselves, believing there is something wrong with them, believing they are flawed humans instead of what they really are, something far beyond human.

"I know it's hard to understand, truly I do. I'll try to illustrate it for you. Imagine that you take a young wolf, a cub, and you place it into a litter of young Huskies or Malamutes. They look similar, almost identical, to each other. You raise them equally and allow them to grow surrounded by the same environment. Now imagine that young wolf grows into a large, healthy male. Remember, they would all look very similar to each other and would likewise behave similarly. Now imagine that you stop feeding them one day. What do you suppose would happen? It is simple, natural, right? Brutal, but natural. The wolf would kill and eat the dogs it grew up with. To anyone witnessing the scenario, it would seem tragic, cruel, a littermate, a member of the pack eating his peers, but nature, Mr. Loomis, has no moral boundaries. He would eat them because he was born a predator, because he was stronger and faster, and like every other living thing, he needs to eat to survive. That, Mr. Loomis, is a gross over-simplification of course, but it is a quite poignant example of what you've run into. Creatures that look like those around them, grow like those around them, but sense they are different, sense they are stronger, smarter, more powerful than those around them. Context is everything, Mr. Loomis, I can assure you of that.

Steven's eyes had narrowed at the mention of wolves. It was the same example Leonard had used. Barlow caught it and smiled.

"What do you suppose it is like for the CEO of a mass communications company to discover that his…urges, his needs are because he is a part of a different species from humans and not because he is a flawed human? It is liberating! It is as though he is born again! I have watched it happen in these beings, Mr. Loomis, right in front of my eyes, they transform from defeated men into a powerful force. They understand how they can wield the vast power they hold in their hands. It is the same with politicians or those in the military." Steven's eyes widened at the mention of the military.

Barlow chuckled, "Oh, I see I hit a sensitive area for you. Of course, some of them are part of the military, why would they not be? Now you understand? Now you see the depth and the immensity of what you have brought to the world's attention? No matter. Trust me, Mr. Loomis, once your trial is over and done with, the world will once again forget. At your office, you told me it wouldn't matter, that the world would know and would be better prepared. It is a noble idea, but a farfetched one, I assure you. People, Mr. Loomis, like their safety, they like their security and knowing that the sun will rise every morning and they will simply adapt to a new reality, a reality where they are the prey and something else is the hunter. And they'll forget."

Barlow had started to pace, "But I digress, I brought you here so we could have this little chat and we could come to an understanding. I am quite aware that you know who I am and I am fairly certain that you also know some of what I've done, about my work. You sent your people in for a reason. So now you know who I am and some of the things I've done, and I know who you are and the things you've done. I will leave tonight to carry on my work elsewhere and I would strongly suggest that you concentrate on what is in front of you, your trial, your family, all the things you hold dear, and that you forget me and my work. We will part company never to engage in a conversation again. If you can do that, I can promise you that I will in no way bother you or your family.

"Should you decide to pursue me any further, to try to get more information about me and my work, then all bets will be off, as you Americans are also fond of saying, and I will make it my purpose to make sure you feel loss like you have not known, not even the loss of your daughter will compare. I took these drastic measures, Mr. Loomis, because I wanted you to understand that like you, I am a resourceful man with a lot of means, means I am more than willing to use to accomplish what I have set out to accomplish. But we mustn't assume there will be unpleasantness, that would be uncivilized and roguish, and I for one despise wanton violence."

Barlow walked into the bathroom where Loomis could hear him running the water and washing his hands. He came back out and stood in front of Loomis. Loomis was calculating how far it was to the man and whether he might be able to make it if he used his weight to propel the chair.

Barlow saw him and smiled, "I can see what you are thinking, Mr. Loomis, and let me assure you that it would be a most unwise decision on your part. Even if you were able to knock me down, your wrists are cuffed and so are your feet. I may be old, but I am certainly young enough to overpower a man in shackles, even as formidable a man as you.

"I suppose there is always the possibility that you will tell the authorities about this little impromptu meeting, but then again, how would that sound on the eve of your trial. How will it look if you accuse a known profiler, someone of stature who works with law enforcement to help catch criminals, of kidnapping you and holding you against your will while he talked to you and then let you go? I suppose they might investigate it, but I also suppose that they might think you are seeing monsters under the bed and that perhaps your sanity is compromised, and I am most certain that is not what you want the world to think, especially when your trial is about to get underway. Especially with the media all over, covering your every word.

"No, Mr. Loomis, I am very confident, very confident indeed, that you will not mention our little meeting to the authorities. So, let's agree that you will stay out of my business and I will return the favor and stay clear of yours, and let's agree that you will not mention our little meeting and nobody will ever know about it. You have much more on your plate at the moment and much more to lose. Whatever your interest in me might be, I am certain you will be much more interested in making sure that the state of New York does not put you away for the rest of your life.

"Like you, Mr. Loomis, I am very good at what I do, and I am very careful in every aspect of my work. You are in the security business, so I don't need to tell you about the technology and resources available to someone with means who wants to keep their work secure. I suspect you have infinite confidence in the gentlemen you sent in to dig into my business and thus can appreciate the level of care in my precautions given the fact that they were detected. I believe I have made my point, and I believe we understand each other, nod if that is the case." Loomis nodded; there was simply nothing else he could do.

Barlow smiled and went to the door, "Excellent! I knew you would understand my position and that you'd understand my reasons for doing this. Now, I will leave, and in 15 minutes a young man will come into the room and release you from the handcuffs. This young man will be paid handsomely to do exactly that, release you and walk away. He will be told in no uncertain terms that he is not to mention anything he sees to anyone. The consequences of any transgression on his part will be also be made perfectly clear. I must be on my way. I hope we do not see each other again. Godspeed, Mr. Loomis, and I wish you success in your upcoming trial. I shall be following it closely."

With that, Barlow turned and left the room. Loomis sat in the chair and looked around the room to see if there was anything he could use to break the chair apart, but there was nothing. He was certain that someone would in fact show up in 15 minutes to free him, but 15 minutes shackled to the chair seemed like an eternity. He had vastly underestimated Barlow. The man was much, much more than Loomis had ever imagined. He had obviously been involved in the disappearances he was helping to investigate, a perfect cover for what he was doing. Once he was called in to help with a case that involved the type of individual he was interested in, he basically had carte blanche to hunt at his leisure or to direct others to do it. He had also mentioned being able to look into the minds of these monsters, which meant that he had run into more than one and had either treated them, or more likely guided them, in their own twisted plots.

The enormity of all of it hit Loomis square in the face and he realized that what he had really done was to open Pandora's box. He had brought this to the world's attention, but now that he had, he understood the full scope of what he had stumbled into. Riche really was nothing, just the tip of the iceberg. He had believed that simply bringing attention to these beings would be enough; that once he had done that, he would be done, his final purpose accomplished. Now he understood just how wrong he had been. He realized that he had been simply coasting into his trial, that since he had accomplished bringing attention to the science, the outcome of the trial was really secondary, regardless of what he had told Beth or his defense team. Now he knew with every fiber of his being that he had to win the trial. He had to figure out a way to get past his legal issues without going to prison for God knew how many years. Barlow was right, the world would eventually forget and go back to living their lives oblivious to the new danger. They like their safety, Barlow had been right about that too. He thought of Beth and the kids and realized that, even though they would be taken care of, they would never be safe, not without him there to make sure they were. Barlow had also made sure he understood that, regardless of what he had said.

As he was trying to process everything, a young man came into the room. He looked like any number of lost men, hanging around the corners of any number of big cities, half gone from alcohol or drugs.

He came into the room and without hesitation walked over to where Loomis was shackled. He looked like he was purposefully trying not to look at Loomis or anything else in the room. He fumbled with the keys for a bit but was finally able to release Steven after a few seconds. When his hands were free, Loomis took the duct tape off. Once the man released him, he went to leave the room immediately, but Steven shot up, his old reflexes coming back, and grabbed the man by the arm.

Feeling Steven's grip, the man recoiled, "Hey, man! I don't know anything, alright?! I didn't see anything and I don't know anything."

Steven loosened his grip on the young man, shut the door, walked him over to the bed and sat him down. The man looked past him at the door, then back at him, weighing his chances of darting past him and out the door. He came to the conclusion that he had absolutely no chance and simply hung his head, his arms resting on his knees as he sat on the bed.

Steven got to the point, "Who paid you? What did he say?"

The young drifter, still keeping his gaze down, responded, "He pulled up in a limo, but that's nothin', man, there's lots of dudes come down here to get some…to have some fun. Most are lookin' to score, you know, smack, coke, meth, whatever, but some come down to get some a…for a different kind of fun."

He said this last part with a cynical tone, "This dude came to the corner and asked if I wanted to make $500 bucks, $500 bucks, man! That kind of shit never happens around here, so I get in the limo, and I'm about to unzip my pants when he flashes the cash and tells me that he wants me to come to this shithole, to this room, and to unlock the cuffed man in it. He tells me I just have to come in and let you go and leave. He told me not to look, not to say anything, not to do shit, just let you go, and that's what I was tryin' to do, man, just let you go and not do nothin' else, and then you fucking grab me and here we are."

Steven listened to the man and tried to figure out what his next move should be. Whatever it was, he had to get out of here and back to Manhattan, still he had to get some answers. "Did he say anything else? What did he look like?"

The man now looked up at him and gave him an odd little smile, "I don't know, man, he looked like another john, you know, just another Wall Street prick looking for action as far as I could tell. Suit, tie, cufflinks, you know, the Wall Street uniform. He didn't say nothin' else, man, he just said what I already told you, and he said if I tried to just take the money and bail, he'd know and he'd hunt my ass down and would take the $500 out of me in blood. Just like that, too, that he'd take it out in blood, and I believed him, man, when I took the money he had this little smile on his face and I could see he was strapped.

"Look man, I don't know what kind of shit you are involved in and I don't care, I just want to take my cash and get the fuck out of here, you feel me? I don't want any problems, man, I didn't see nothin', didn't hear nothin', alright? So just let me get out of here."

Steven was about to let the man go when he thought of one more thing, "Was this guy an older guy? I mean like my age or was he younger? Did he have hair?"

The man thought for a second, "No, man, he was younger than you, definitely younger. He had this little moustache and a ponytail."

So it hadn't been Barlow himself who had gotten this guy, it had been someone else that had to be with him, which meant that he might have other people watching him right now. It sounded like the driver that picked him up.

"Alright, get out of here and remember what you were told. You didn't see anything and you didn't hear anything. Fuck that up and you'll never be found, you understand?"

Steven felt bad about referencing the threat, but it hadn't been him who had made it and he was sure the guy had gotten a good look at his face. Even if he didn't know the details of who he was or what he had done, Steven's face had been plastered on the news around the clock for weeks now so it was likely the man recognized him.

The man got up from the bed and left immediately. Steven looked at his watch for the first time. He'd been gone for about four hours. Willis and Zeidler had been expecting him to come by the office and were probably going out of their minds with worry. He looked at his cell phone and saw he had more than a dozen missed calls and texts from them. This first thing he had to do was to find a way back to Manhattan, a way that at all costs would avoid being spotted. He was about to use his phone to make the call when he reconsidered. It was possible, probable even, that Barlow had tampered with his phone and would try to track his calls. This was his everyday cell phone and while it was more secure than standard cell phones, it was not encrypted and could be easily cracked.

He called the front desk and asked if he'd be able to make a call to Manhattan. The man at the front desk told him he could make a call to wherever the hell he wanted to call as long as he gave his credit card number for a deposit. Steven complied and gave the man his credit card information. He'd have to remember to report the card as stolen as soon as he was back in Manhattan. He called Drew's cell phone, which was answered on the first ring.

"Drew, it's Steven. Listen, I need a car to pick me up…"

Before he could finish, Drew interrupted him, "Steven! Where the hell have you been?! We've been calling you for hours! Do you not pick up you messages or what?! You know you can't pull this disappearing act shit right now, man! We have a hearing set and a trial after that and…"

Now it was Steven who interrupted him, "Drew! Listen, I will explain everything to you when I see you, okay, but right now I need you to arrange for a car to pick me up at…"

He realized he didn't know where he was and rummaged through the desk in the room to find where he was. He finally saw a book of matches and read off the address to Drew.

"New Jersey! What the hell are you doing at a motel in New Jersey?!"

Steven did not want to get into it over the phone, "Drew! I can't get into it now!"

Drew checked himself, "Right, you'll tell me when you see me. Okay, let me arrange for the car to pick you up. In the meantime, please try to keep a low profile if at all possible, please. The media and paparazzi are 20 deep in front of the building here, and I can't imagine they are too far away wherever it is you are. I don't know how the hell they get their information, but they seem to always be one step ahead."

Steven hung up the phone and began pacing the room. He tried to backtrack and figure out when he had been drugged and quickly got his answer. The woman. She had bumped into him pretty hard and the presents falling all over had been a perfect distraction. She probably had a subcutaneous syringe, like those diabetics use, and administered whatever chemical agent they had decided on when she crashed into him. Very smooth and completely unnoticeable to those watching. So that meant that in addition to whatever goon Barlow had in the limo waiting to drive him, he also had a very skilled female operative working for him. Former CIA was his guess, although there was plenty of other talent to be had if the money was right. The CIA, Mossad, MI6, and even the Russian KGB had yielded plenty of former agents and case officers who, with the end of the Cold War, had become obsolete and were looking to pad their pensions.

He sat down on the bed again and began to consider his next move. The real question, the question that would most likely determine how things would unfold, was who he was going to tell about all of this, specifically whether he would tell the old man about it. Steven knew that once he told him, certain things were inevitable, regardless of what he wanted the General to do or not do. He put his head in his hands and rubbed his temples to soothe the massive headache that was building and to consider that point carefully.

Chapter 22

T wo blocks away, Peter "Fast Pete" Gibson was walking down a dirty and unlit alley in Jersey City. The first thing, the only thing, he'd been thinking about since leaving the motel was scoring some smack. It had been eight hours since his last fix and he was most definitely starting to feel the nasty symptoms of withdrawal. He had not had the money to get the drug before now and was much too weak to try to scam some from his usual dealers. Usually when he started feeling sick, he might go to one of them, cop a fix and then take off running, hence his nickname. The dealers would pursue initially, but it would usually be only about $20 in drugs that he'd steal so they would drop off yelling and promising revenge. The only reason that Fast Pete had made it to the ripe old age of 28 was because he usually came back to these same dealers and paid them for the drugs, usually with 10 bucks thrown in as interest. He was on his way to do exactly that, pay his tab and score drugs with the $500 he had, when the car dropped in behind him. He was sick and concentrating on keeping his money safe, so he didn't notice the car, which was driving slowly with its headlights turned off. The loud music coming from various doorways and windows drowned out the sound of the engine. Before he was able to get to the end of the alley, the car pulled up slowly, coasting easily next to him. He turned, saw the dark windows and stopped. Just as he had explained to Loomis, Fast Pete expected this to be someone looking to score drugs or a blowjob.

He didn't have drugs to sell and he didn't need the money, so he didn't have to turn a trick either, but force of habit brought him closer to the window. When he was standing next to the car, directly in front of the rear passenger side window, the window began to come down. Inside, he saw an older man, well dressed, probably one of the sick fucks that came down here looking to satisfy some perverse sexual fantasy or another. He was about to tell the guy to fuck off when he saw the cylindrical shape come up from behind the glass. His mind had time to register what it was a fraction of a second before the small flash and metallic sound sent him off to a permanent sleep. The window rolled up and the car drove slowly to the end of the alley and into the New Jersey rush-hour traffic.

In the car, Nigel Barlow sat back in his seat. Long ago, when he had procured the suppressor for the weapon, a small .22, he had wondered whether he would ever need it, whether he would ever actually use it. After all, his methods were much more subtle and meticulous. Back then he had known that someday the silencer would prove to be useful and tonight he had discovered that he had been right, just like he had always been right about every countermeasure he had ever acquired. He had gone on with his work all these years undisturbed and undetected, because early on he realized he must be supremely cautious in everything he did and he had understood that he had much to learn about the necessities his work required. Over the years, he had refined his security and recruited the best security and intelligence talent to be had, because he knew that for him to continue with his work he would need help.

The scientific community had shunned him outright when he had first speculated on his theories and they had found out about some of his research methods. None of that mattered now, of course, he had made his own way and had accomplished everything he had on his own. He didn't have any colleagues with which to consult and his work ensured that all of his findings, his hypotheses would remain unknown for some time. No, he didn't enjoy the support of anybody, but he had means, and that above all else got him as much support as was needed.

He had no doubt that Steven Loomis would say nothing of their meeting, not initially. The man was a professional and a former special operations officer; he wouldn't act rashly, especially with the world's attention focused squarely on his shoulders. But Barlow would definitely need to keep an eye on him and his case. He had caught the man flatfooted, but he doubted that would happen again, and even though he was almost certain that Loomis would not follow him now, there was no telling what might happen once the case was over. He had not gotten to this point by being lax in his security. His countermeasures had detected the operatives that Loomis had sent, but he suspected it had been because they had underestimated him and his resources, and that was also unlikely to happen again. His sense of self-preservation had been honed to a point over the years, and right now it was telling him to keep a low profile, perhaps disappear for a few months. The more Barlow considered it, the more it seemed like the right thing to do. Loomis's trial was likely to take a few months at least. Plenty of time for him to regroup, observe the proceedings and draw up his next endeavor. He smiled as he relaxed further into the plush back seat. He had arranged to keep in contact with a few of his current projects, but he wouldn't take on anyone new.

This time off would also allow him to do a full workup on everything he had accomplished in the past couple of years. Truth be told, he had not had time to do it before now because he was always on the move, always in a hurry to his next project. Early on, he had realized that if he was to truly understand these beings, he had to be willing to move fast, to follow wherever they led. Over the years, he had been able to sharpen his skills so that now he didn't move until he was certain of what he was dealing with. In the beginning, he had followed anything that seemed like a promising subject, often finding himself dealing with a brutal and clumsy psychopath, nothing like what he had been expecting. Now he never went anywhere unless he was certain, unless he *knew* beyond a shadow of a doubt what he was dealing with.

He remembered fondly his first encounters with true specimens. At first he had simply observed from afar, just watching them operate, marveling at their skill, their intelligence, the brutal yet beautiful efficiency with which they hunted. In time he had approached them, not sure where it would lead. He had let them know that he understood, that he knew what they were, what nature had intended them to be. It had been almost too easy. After lifetimes of confusion, of not being certain of the reasons they felt the impulses, the urges they eventually succumbed to, they were more than willing to have someone with authority and knowledge guide them through their efforts. They were hungry to have a better understanding of who they were and the reasons they did what they did, and Barlow had been there to guide them and teach them and encourage them. Sometimes, they came to him looking for counsel, for help understanding the reasons they felt the impulses they felt and the reasons they never seemed to fit in. Les Martin, his current project, was shaping up beautifully. He had been a shell of a man when he first came to Barlow, confused his whole life because of his natural impulses and inclinations. Barlow had shown him the light, had let him know there was nothing wrong with him and that he was in fact a superior being. He would have to put Les on hold while he kept a low profile and hope that he had taken his advice to be patient to heart.

Yes, his had been a long and difficult journey, one filled with disappointment and frustration at times, but it had also been an incredibly fulfilling one. Fulfilling his own urges and desires had gotten him through some of the worst of it and had helped to bring a clearer understanding of his own role in nature's plan. If he was to be completely honest, those indulgences had also brought him enormous pleasure. There was nothing wrong with enjoying one's work and taking the time now and again to keep the mind sharp while satisfying one's urges. Yes, he would keep his head down for a few months and watch Loomis's trial from afar. He had not been lying to the man when he explained that things would never be the same and now that the world's attention was firmly on the science, things would most definitely change for a great many people.

Barlow suspected that Steven Loomis still did not quite grasp the magnitude of what he had uncovered, but he was likewise convinced that the man would figure it out before it was all said and done, and who knew what would happen then. This last idea gave Barlow some pause. After all, having a former military commando sniffing around came with some serious dangers, but it also came with some rewards. He had been able to carve his path unopposed all these years. The capabilities of those that might at some point become adversaries were pathetic. They were putty in his hands and unsuspecting prey for his subjects, but not Loomis. He seemed like he might prove to be a very formidable opponent, very formidable indeed, and while that brought some concern to Barlow, it also brought some excitement and anticipation. Finally, someone that Barlow could measure his skills against, someone that might test not only his own hypotheses but would stop at nothing to find answers. As he looked out at the city, his smile broadened. All these years, all this research and preparation. He had always believed it was all being done for a purpose, and now he knew what that purpose was and who stood on the other side of the line. That, more than anything else, made Nigel Barlow happier than he had thought he could ever be.

◆

After almost two hours, Steven finally saw the car pull into the parking lot and, as agreed, flash its lights three times. He wiped everything in the room for prints and made his way to the car below.

Once inside, he immediately engaged the driver, "What took you so long?"

The driver, a regular at Zeidler's firm, was taken by surprise. Loomis had never addressed him directly. "Sorry, Mr. L, Mr. Willis had to get three cars so we could confuse the paparitzis or papa... whateverthefuck...you know, the photographers in front of the building. They follow everyone that comes out of the building. I kid you not, Mr. Loomis, even the freaking trash men. I swear to Christ, those vultures would sell a picture of their mother naked to make a buck."

The man's candor and his heavy Brooklyn accent made Steven grin in spite of himself. He hadn't thought about that before now. With the trial looming and everything else that had happened, it was going to be next to impossible to do anything now without a long tail of photographers following. The time waiting had actually proven to be useful as he had been able to consider what to do next. The first thing he had concluded was that there was no way he would tell the General about any of this. He knew if he did the old man would insist on a security detail, not like the one that Drew and Max's firm had retained, but operatives, men that would never be seen and would always be around. Besides the security, he would most likely insist on following up on Barlow and on building a file on the man, and if Steven told him he didn't want that, the old man would agree, and then do it anyway without him knowing. He couldn't take the risk.

He didn't know why and how, but he was completely convinced that Barlow would keep to his word and forget about him and his family so long as Loomis did the same. It had been a brilliant stroke, really. As soon as Barlow heard about what happened to Riche and the background of the person who had done it, he believed his own work might come under scrutiny and authorities might want to revisit some of the unsolved cases where young people or children had disappeared. Loomis had done what he did because of his daughter, she had been his connection to the whole thing, but once he made public his reasoning and his defense, Barlow had quite correctly assumed that Loomis had done extensive research.

If Loomis had come across Barlow's name or come to any conclusions about other cases of serial murders or disappearances, Barlow didn't know that. So he had paid Steven a visit, perhaps to probe and find out more about Riche, but more likely to see if there was any recognition of him and his work on Steven's face. After they had parted company, Steven had sent the Meeks brothers in to find more information and Barlow had sniffed them out. That meant that either he had much more sophisticated security measures than they had given him credit for all along or he had gotten such measures after their meeting because he knew Steven would follow up on him and try to get more information. Either way, the man was not to be trifled with, especially now, with the world watching and with Steven about to go to trial.

So not telling the old man about it had been an easier decision than he had anticipated, but he had also come to the conclusion that whether he wanted to or not, there were people he *had* to tell about this. He had to let the Twins know that they had been made, something he was not looking forward to doing. To his knowledge, they had never been detected before, and something like this was bound to sting. He also had to tell Max and Drew. They were his attorneys and therefore bound by the attorney-client privilege. They would not repeat anything he told them even at the risk of going to jail, and they were going to be working closely together for months, so they had a right to know. Now that Loomis had a better idea of Barlow's capabilities, he had to consider the possibility that their offices might be bugged and that they might be followed. He would tell them, but he had to make sure they wouldn't overreact and do something dumb like insist on calling the FBI or other law enforcement organizations.

From now on, they would be escorted everywhere by a security team, not the security that Drew had arranged for, which was more concerned with photographers and religious nuts, but a hand-picked detail, professionals trained in the craft of counter-surveillance, personal security and close-quarters combat. He would also have the law offices and his own condo swept for bugs, something that would be much easier with Beth out of town. He knew the people he wanted on the team and would talk to the General to clear it as soon as he got to Max's offices. He didn't want GIC people, as that would draw too much attention and unwanted scrutiny to the company, but every one of the people that he was thinking about for this was a GIC contractor and every one of them had extensive experience watching the backs of some very important people around the world, people who more often than not had a bull's-eye on their back. He would have to explain to the old man that the media was getting more intense and they were using high-end technology to track his and his lawyers' movements. It wasn't a lie, that was exactly the case, but it wasn't the complete story either, and he was afraid that his boss, with his keen ability to read people, would see through it.

As they finally got to the building, Steven was completely blown away by the number of news trucks, antennas, photographers and reporters. He had thought that the media covering the finding of the warehouse and the girls and then the shooting was on a scale he hadn't seen before, but this made that look like a press conference for a small-town politician. The car drove into the building's basement, but before the automatic gate could roll down an adventurous photographer rolled under it and ran after the car. He was met by the building's security, which had been put on alert for just such a thing. Drew and Max were waiting for him as soon as he got out of the elevator. He had barely stepped into the front lobby when both men came up at the same time.

Drew was the first to reach him, "Steven! What the fuck is going on?! Are you alright? What were you doing in New Jersey?!"

Max got there a step behind Drew with his hand outstretched, "Easy cowboy, let the man breathe."

Steven shook Max's hand and then turned to address Drew, "Is there somewhere secure where we can talk?"

Drew turned to Max, "I don't know, is there?"

Max smiled, "Sure, I told you before. We can use my office. We have it swept monthly. Lots of pretty sensitive negotiations on a lot of sensitive clients. We've actually found a few bugs over the years."

Drew stared at Max, "Are you kidding? Bugs, as in electronic monitoring things, those kind of bugs?"

Max answered the question as the group started walking to his office, "I know it's hard for a straight-laced, do-gooder type like you to imagine, but high-stakes law is just as vulnerable to industrial espionage as the best R&D shops. Lots of people would love to learn ahead of time when we are going to settle a case."

When they got to Max's office, Steven took the sofa while Drew repositioned a chair to sit in front of him. Max settled on the other end of the sofa. It was clear that Drew was itching to hear the story, but Steven had to take a moment to settle down, and he needed a cold drink because his throat was parched.

"Max, would you mind grabbing me a bottle of water?"

Drew beat him to it and went over to the fridge to get the water.

Max took advantage, "Would you mind pouring me a glass of the Scotch that's on my desk while you're up?"

Drew smiled, "Anything else while I'm up?"

Steven shook his head. He was clearly more pensive than usual and he had a slight frown on his face, something that wasn't lost on Max, "So what's up, kid? What the hell happened to you?"

Drew came back with the drinks and handed the bottle of water to Steven, who opened it and took three long pulls from it. He took a deep breath, leaned forward so his arms were resting on his knees and began telling the story. He explained the meeting with Barlow at his office, how he had sensed there was something iffy about the guy. He told them about his own research on the man and that he had contacted some people to look deeper into his background, although he omitted just how deep those people were going to look. He told them about his run-in with the woman as he was getting in the car and how he believed it had been then that he had been drugged, that there really wasn't any other way it could have been done, unless Barlow had somehow rigged the car so he could knock him out with something in a gas form, but there hadn't been any smell that Steven could detect. He finished by explaining to the two attorneys that Barlow had promised to stay away and leave him and his family alone if he was willing to do the same and simply leave Barlow alone.

"I believe him. He's not interested in me or my family as a part of what he termed his 'work.' He did what he did because I went after him and started digging. My people are the best at what they do, so for him to have detected them it took some pretty serious equipment and other countermeasures, stuff that he probably didn't choose himself, which means that he's got people working for him."

Drew fell back into his chair and let his arms dangle as he tried to absorb everything he had just heard. His mouth was slightly open and his eyes were wide. He looked exactly like he should, like a criminal defense attorney who'd just heard that his client, a client he was defending for first-degree murder and who was making the claim that what he had killed was not a human being, had been abducted in broad daylight, taken to a dirty motel in New Jersey and told not to keep digging into his abductor's business. Max looked at Steven for a long time after he finished telling his story and gulped his Scotch down.

He too looked perplexed, but he'd been an attorney far longer than Drew and had seen some pretty weird things along a colorful career. "Christ, Steven, what are you planning on doing?"

Steven stood up, walked over to Zeidler, took his empty glass and walked over to the desk to pour him another Scotch. "As far as Barlow, nothing. I believe him when he says he'll stay away as long as I stay away from him and his work. Whatever it is he's been doing, he's been doing it for a long time, and he's afraid that all of it will have been wasted if he gets found out.

"I'm going to put together a team to run counter-surveillance during the trial. I don't think he'll try to do anything, but I don't plan to be unprepared in case he decides he's suddenly interested. I underestimated him once and I don't intend on doing it again."

He didn't tell them about the other security teams he planned on putting together.

Drew, finally out of his trance-like state, got up and chimed in, "Am I hearing this correctly? A man kidnaps you in front of your house, takes you to some shitty motel in New Jersey and sweats you while you're handcuffed to a chair, and you're not going to do anything?! Are you fucking kidding me?! Steven, we have to tell the authorities, we have to tell the FBI, the DA, somebody!"

Steven now poured another glass of Scotch and walked over to the two men, handing each a healthy shot. Max understood the younger lawyer's reaction, it was perfectly normal and to be expected, but he needed for him to think carefully and not overreact.

He answered for Steven, "Drew, calm down and think about it. What exactly do you think Steven would say? 'Yes, officer, I was taken to a shitty motel somewhere in New Jersey and handcuffed to a chair while this well-respected FBI profiler, who, by the way, I believe is responsible for dozens of murders and disappearances, warned me to stay out of his business.' Do you see how ludicrous that sounds? And let's not forget, Steven's face is plastered on every newscast and newspaper in the country and he's been indicted for first-degree murder.

"Even if that wasn't the case, though, it would still be a pretty far-fetched story. The cops or the FBI might investigate it, just so they can say they're doing their job, but you and I both know they'd be thinking that Steven was nuts, probably lost it because of what he's been through. No, I think Steven's right on this one, he keeps his mouth shut, arranges for security and gets ready for his trial."

Drew sat back down and ran both hands through his hair. He knew Max was right, everything he said made sense, but the whole situation was too surreal for him to reconcile. Kidnapping? Getting knocked out by women with presents? Deranged doctor victimizing innocent people? It all sounded like so much Hollywood bullshit. These kinds of thing just didn't happen in the real world, they just didn't.

Steven was thankful for Max's intervention. He was on edge himself and would have more than likely snapped at Drew as he explained the situation. Now that he'd had some time to consider things from afar, he had to admit that the whole thing did in fact sound like some bad movie of the week, something starring one of the original *90210* actors. And it wasn't just Barlow that made it so, it was the whole business, Riche, the shooting, everything. Well, they were in it now, Steven more than anybody else. He asked if there was a secure phone line he could use, and Max told him he could use the phone in his office as it had also been swept for listening devices. Max walked over to Drew, who was still shell-shocked, and led him out. The first thing Steven did was to call Beth to check on her and the kids. She sounded good, stronger than she had sounded just a couple of days ago and that was good news, it meant that she was healing and that gave him a great deal of comfort. She was a bit upset with him for not calling before now, but she also understood that he had a lot on his plate.

After he hung up with Beth, he called the Twins at the agreed upon number, "CECIL."

Steven, sitting in Max's chair, began to doodle on a pad, "Hey C, it's Steven. Listen, I don't want to spend too long on the phone, but I needed to call you guys. You've been made, the bastard had some countermeasures and he made you guys."

There was silence on the other end of the line as Cecil processed what he had just heard.

After a few seconds, Steven could hear him talking to who he assumed was Thurman, "We were made. Steven says the guy had countermeasures."

He heard Thurman's reaction over the phone, "Shit, I knew we shouldn't have used that guy, I knew it!"

Cecil came back on the line, "Sorry, Steven, Thurman's not taking it well. The Russian was busy, so we used a new guy for the hacking, someone referred by some of our folks at NSA. He's good, but he's not used to this type of work, and he probably figured this guy was just another egghead who had no clue about digital security. It had to be the hacking end of the job that gave us away. Thurman and I did our end clean, no traces and no blowback."

Steven had guessed as much, he knew the Twins too well to believe they had made a mistake, "Well, it's done now. Can you guys get a few more people and put together a security detail to cover my family and another to cover my legal team? No affiliated people, contractors, and they need to be discreet."

Cecil thought for a couple of beats, "I think we can handle that. Are you thinking this guy is going to come after you? Hey, now that I think of it, how do you know he made us?"

Steven thought about the question. He had to be careful about what he told them. He knew he had to tell them about his conversation with Barlow, but he also knew he couldn't tell them the whole story. Cecil and Thurman were as loyal as anyone in this business could be, but they, like him, owed a lot to the General and they genuinely cared about Steven, so as much as he wanted to tell them everything, he didn't want to put them in the position to have to lie to the old man, and Steven knew that once they talked to the old man about the extra security, he would start asking questions.

"Barlow told me himself. We had a nice conversation where he let me know that his security had detected someone digging around. You're probably right, it was the hacking end of the operation. He didn't say anything specifically, but it makes sense."

There was another brief silence on the other end of the line. Steven was guessing that Cecil was probably thinking things over and trying to figure out exactly what was going on with Barlow and himself.

As if to confirm it, Cecil had more questions, "Wait a minute, what do you mean you 'had a nice conversation with him'? When exactly did that happen? We've been watching his place around the clock."

Steven knew they would ask the question and he thought he knew what he wanted to answer, but now that they had asked he was once again trying to figure out how to answer it. "Yeah, we had another brief meeting and he let me know. He must have made it past you in a delivery truck or maybe he was wearing a disguise. He might not have spotted you, but when he found out about the hacking into his information, he probably guessed he was being watched."

Cecil thought about that. His people had been tailing Barlow around the clock, but the truth was that, like Steven, they had simply underestimated the man.

Steven went on, "He also let me know he had no interest in me or my family as long as I stayed out of his business, and for what it's worth, I believed him. So, you and Thurman need to stay clear, please."

Cecil replied instantly, "What? Steven, c'mon man, this guy got your attention for a reason. Now you're just going to let it go because he came and told you to stay out of his business? That doesn't sound like you, man."

Steven didn't have time to get into it with Cecil and he let him know it, "Cecil, I appreciate it, brother, but I have way too much on my plate to get into it. You're right, he did get my attention, and under different circumstances I'd go after the guy, but right now I'm facing murder charges, the entire world is scrutinizing my every move, and I just don't have the time or the inclination to get into whatever this guy is doing.

"I also have my family's safety to think about. There's no way I can do anything without knowing I'll be there to protect them, and I won't know that until this trial is over. Do you understand that?"

Cecil listened. He knew Steven was right, everybody and their sister was only too eager to get as much information on Steven Loomis as they could possibly get. Even under optimal circumstances, going after someone like Barlow required the right technological resources, preparation and planning, and Steven could not do any of those things right now.

Cecil finally got it, "I hear you. I guess you're pretty jammed up right now."

Steven thought to himself 'you think' but to Cecil he said, "That's right, and I need to know that you guys are not going to go rogue on me and try to get more information on the guy on your own. I'm serious, Cecil, no freelancing."

Cecil got the point, "Alright, alright, I got it. Have you told the old man yet?"

Steven also knew they would ask that question, "No, and you won't either. You know what would happen if I told him. He would smile and pat me on the head and tell me that he was going to keep away from the guy, and as soon as I left the room he'd do it anyway.

"No, right now I have to shelve this completely. I have a trial to get ready for and that's going to take everything I got. Let me know when you have the teams picked out…oh, and tell Thurman not to be too hard on the new guy. Hell, we all thought he wouldn't have very sophisticated security, remember?"

Cecil sighed, "Yeah, I remember, but still, it stings like a motherfucker to be made like that, especially by a guy like this."

Steven could hear the strain on his voice. Professionals always took it hard when they failed. Steven finally ended the call and went to find Max and Drew. He walked down the hall to Drew's office, but before entering he looked over the sea of cubicles in the middle of the floor. It was a swarm of activity with what had to be 30 associates and paralegals walking back and forth and carrying stacks of reference materials. It was clear they were all in the middle of doing research for one case or another and he was impressed by their intensity.

He walked into Drew's office where he found Drew, Max and a man he didn't recognize. He looked to be Zeidler's age, although he was much taller and heavier and had far less hair. He was also dressed in a very different style from what Max normally wore. While Max favored two-thousand-dollar Hugo Boss tailored suits, usually charcoal grey or pinstriped navy blue, this guy was wearing a dark brown, off-the-rack suit and his tie was too short for how tall he was. He had a pleasant manner about him, a wise-old-man quality that was hard to define, but which came through in spades. They all turned in his direction as he walked into the office.

Max came over and pulled him further into the office, "Steven, did you take care of what you needed to take care of? Good. Allow me to introduce you to Ray Gretche. This is the attorney we told you about. He'll be joining Drew and me as part of the defense team."

Gretche walked over to Steven, hand outstretched, "Mr. Loomis, it's a pleasure, it really is. I think what you're doing is remarkable and quite unprecedented, and I for one am looking forward to being a part of it."

Steven shook the man's hand and couldn't help a small grin. The man's enthusiasm was completely genuine and it showed. "It's Steven, please. So, you think we have a shot here?"

They migrated over to the sofa and chairs in Drew's office. Now sitting in one of the big chairs, Gretche took a couple of seconds before answering.

That was good, it meant the man was considering the question carefully and not just blowing smoke up his ass. "Well, I'll tell you, if we can put on the defense and bring the witnesses we want to the stand, then yes, I think we have a pretty good chance. Juries are a very complicated animal, Mr. …Steven. You never know what a jury is going to do until they send the note out to the judge. I've argued in front of enough juries to know that just when you think you've got them figured out, they pull a fast one on you.

"What we're going to be asking them to do here is to define, legally define, what a human being is. That's the bottom line, that's the heart of the case. What is a human being, legally speaking, and does Riche fit that definition. The one thing we have going for us, and it's no small thing, is public opinion. I don't mean to seem insensitive, but we have the perfect set of circumstances here, a 'victim' who was indicted for the disappearance and murder of nine young girls, a defendant who is literally the epitome of the American success story, and a groundbreaking legal argument based on cutting-edge science. It could not be better."

Steven was nodding slightly, "You make it sound like it's in the bag."

Ray chuckled, "Perhaps, Steven, perhaps. But remember that I said *if* we're able to put on the defense, and that's a big *if*."

Drew, now sitting on the other side of the sofa from Steven, jumped in, "And that brings us to tomorrow's hearing with the judge. He's called the meeting in order to get a read on the defense we will be presenting. Just as we expected, the DA wants the judge to make a ruling on the legality of our argument. In other words, he wants the judge to find that as a matter of law, Donald Riche was a human being. If that happens, we're done for, at least as it relates to this argument.

"I don't think that's going to happen, Judge Newman, the judge the case was assigned to, is a former civil rights and plaintiffs' lawyer fighting big insurance companies. He's a bit eccentric, but he's genius smart and pretty fair. He has a reputation as a defense's judge. Still, we're asking for him to allow us to present a defense that's never been presented, and defense judge or not, he's as concerned with advancement as any judge and will keep us from making our argument if he thinks it's some kind of a stunt."

Max jumped in, "Which is why we're going in loaded for bear. Every single one of the people you saw out there, paralegals, clerks, associates, is researching the science, the law and any relevant precedents, and they're putting together a file for us with all of it. I think Drew's right, unless we really screw this up, I think old Judge Newman is going to let us move forward with our defense."

Steven looked over at Ray, who was nodding his head emphatically as Drew and Max were speaking.

He still wasn't sure what his role would be in all of it, however. "So what do I do while all of this is happening?"

Drew answered the question, "Well, nothing really. You just sit in the courtroom while we argue our position. Depending on how the judge wants to handle it, we will either be arguing from the defense table or we'll be back in his chambers. I think he'll probably want to do it in his chambers, to be honest, more comfortable that way."

Max agreed, "I agree, the only way he is going to take the bench is if he finds in favor of the DA, and if he does that, well, then it just won't matter."

Steven nodded, although he still didn't understand all of the legal implications. As far as he understood, tomorrow, he and his defense team would find out if they would even be able to get their day in court. As had been the case many times before now, he was momentarily overwhelmed by the enormity of the whole thing. He still couldn't believe the amount of media coverage it had generated. It was much more than he had ever imagined, but as had also been true many times before, he simply resigned himself to the fact that he was in it now, there was just no going back, not that he would even if he was able to. He had done what he had done for a reason, a reason he believed in then and believed in even more now.

The playing field had changed drastically, however, and simply bringing attention to these creatures, to the science of them, would no longer be enough. Barlow had changed things, and now, rather than being content and feeling he had accomplished what he set out to accomplish, he needed to avoid prison at all costs. Whatever this was, he now knew it went much deeper and much further than Riche. Barlow had said that Steven didn't understand just how far this went, didn't know the extent of the power these creatures could wield and that they 'hunted' in different ways and different places. What the hell did he mean by that? Steven didn't know, and he couldn't get pulled back into trying to find out what he meant. No, he had to win the trial and avoid prison no matter what it took. The problem was that for the first time in his life, Steven Loomis would have to rely completely on others to step up for him and defend him, and he would not be able to do anything to help them. It was a feeling of helplessness and he simply wasn't used to being helpless.

The four of them spent the next three hours going over what the defense was going to present by way of evidence. It boiled down to the scientific research that Leonard and his colleagues had developed over the past 20 years. They did not need to prove to the judge that there was in fact another species, they simply needed to prove that there *might be* another species, that there was enough evidence of it to let a jury decide the matter. If they were able to do that, then the judge would most likely let them present their case and let the jury decide whether a new species did in fact exist. No need to show their hand to the DA if they didn't have to.

They adjourned at just before eight in the evening, and to Steven's amazement, everyone he had seen before was still there and they would most likely be there well into the night. Steven made his way home, exhausted from what had been a most unusual day. The media was gone for the most part, although the news trucks and photographers remained in place, just in case there might be a chance to get a good shot or a quick comment. It had been a long time since he had gone to bed in awe of what had transpired during the day. That very morning, he had been headed to his attorneys' offices when he was sidetracked by Barlow. It seemed like so long ago, but it had only been hours since it happened. Back when he had been in the field with the SEALs, he would go to bed most nights tired from a long day's work and amazed at the places he had been and the things he had done in just one day. He would get used to it again. He called Beth and chatted with her about the hearing and about his new attorney. Steven liked Ray from the get-go. The man was endearingly sincere about working on the case, and while Drew and Max were sharp and sometimes flashy bundles of energy seemingly juggling 10 things at once, Ray had more of a down-home quality about him. Drew had hit it square on the head when he said that Ray was like the wise old man whose stories everyone always wanted to hear. He was the perfect counterbalance to Max and Drew, and Steven was glad to have him on the team and told Beth as much. She filled him in on the kids. Bethany was missing him terribly, she had always been daddy's girl. Christopher was still too young to understand everything that was going on, but even at his age he had been asking about Tracy. When Beth explained that Tracy was with the angels, he got quiet and went off to play with his trucks. It had killed Steven to hear about what his kids were going through, but Beth had assured him that they were kids and that they would get over things, probably a lot quicker than either of their parents would. It had made Steven feel better, not necessarily because of what she had said, but because she was strong enough to say it, which meant that she herself was healing. Steven finally said goodbye and went into the kitchen to get a glass of milk and a few Oreos. It was a small indulgence, but it was something he had done almost religiously before everything had happened, and it was a modicum of normalcy.

Chapter 23

T he first thing the next morning, Steven headed to the law offices, before the media could get going in earnest. They had agreed to meet at nine, do a final review of all the research the paralegals had put together, and head to the courthouse at 11:00 for a one o'clock hearing with Judge Lester Newman. After discussing it for more than two hours, the team decided it would be Drew who would present the research and lead the defense in the hearing. Ray and Max would jump in if necessary, but they all agreed that it would be more effective for one person to present their position. It was likely that the DA's office would have two or three people arguing against them, and given what they knew of Judge Newman, it was a strategy that would most likely backfire. They all agreed that Lester Newman was too smart to believe an argument had more merit simply because there were more lawyers presenting it. It had been Judge Ito of OJ Simpson fame who had first sparked that tidbit of legal lore. Many legal scholars believed that the fact that the defense's case had been presented by the likes of Robert Kardashian, Barry Scheck and Johnny Cochran had influenced the judge and how he allowed the case to proceed. Lester Newman was an old hand and had sat for some of high-profile criminal trials with high-powered attorneys on both sides and had never batted an eye. He was no-nonsense and would slam anyone that he believed was trying to 'put one over' on him. All three attorneys had watched him do exactly that more than once, so they all agreed that only one of them should present the research and make their argument.

The key would be to convince the judge that there was enough scientific information about the new species to let a jury decide the matter. One key element that they had going for them was the fact that most judges would be hesitant to disallow a defendant to present the defense he or she wanted to present, especially in a case with serious charges. The American legal system was based on the premise that when one was charged with a crime one was free to present the most vigorous defense possible, as long as it was within the bounds of reason. In this case, the DA was arguing precisely that, that this defense was beyond the bounds of reason and it was up to the defense to convince the judge that there was enough science to establish that, while definitely unorthodox and unprecedented, their defense was within the bounds of reason. With that standard, all three attorneys were fairly comfortable they would be allowed to move forward. Still, one never knew and David Neill, the DA, was a skilled litigator and knew Judge Newman well.

As they were gathering their things to leave for the courthouse, Ray had a thought, "You know, it's actually a pretty good strategic move on Neill's part."

Max looked over from his desk, "What's that."

Ray explained, "Yeah, it's a pretty clever move if you think about it. I don't think Neill believes that the judge is going to throw out our defense outright, but by asking for a de facto finding, he's laying the groundwork just in case he loses the case. He can always point to the hearing and claim the defense should not have been allowed to move forward with this defense in the first place.

"More importantly, he's going to get a peek at the science we have and will know what our general approach will be ahead of time. He'll be able to prepare with more than just blind speculation."

Max mulled that over and finally nodded, "I guess you're right. We were planning on waiving the preliminary hearing precisely so we wouldn't have to show our hand at all. None of the facts of the case, the who, where and how, are in dispute so there was no need for a prelim. He probably figured that out and decided to ask for this hearing. You're right, it's a pretty good strategic move. Well, I don't think any of us thought Neill was an idiot."

The four of them picked up their coats and the three attorneys had a small stack of files each. They made it down to the garage where there was a black Suburban with tinted windows waiting for them. As they were leaving the building, Steven was blown away once more, not by the number of reporters and photographers parked in front of the building but by their tenacity. As the Suburban rolled to a stop before turning onto the street, several photographers launched themselves at the windows trying to snap a picture of its occupants. He also saw a number of news vans pull in behind them once they managed to get into traffic. Everyone rode in astonished silence on the way to the courthouse. Even Max and Ray, who'd had more than their fair share of exposure to media coverage, were struck silent by the extent of the coverage this case was generating.

◆

As they approached the courthouse, they could see that there were just as many news trucks there as there had been in front of the office and perhaps even more reporters, if that was possible. As the SUV pulled in front of the building, four large men in suits came close to the door and along with a few police officers pushed the photographers and reporters back from the back door of the vehicle. This was the security detail that Max and Drew had arranged for. They were competent enough, but they were definitely not trained for the type of security that Steven knew they needed.

As he and his defense team made their way up the courthouse steps, with reporters firing questions at anyone who might have an answer for them, he looked around trying to find Cecil and Thurman and the team they had put together. It wasn't too difficult for him to spot them. Unlike the security team arranged by the attorneys, the people he spotted were facing away from the group rather than facing them. As he scanned the crowd, he spotted first Thurman and then Cecil, both of them inconspicuous in their dress and demeanor, just a couple of curious bystanders. He saw they both had loose windbreakers on and knew that under those jackets were automatic weapons, probably fastened to a tactical vest. Although not available to the public, such vests were almost like a uniform for people in the business. Likewise, he saw that every one of the people on his security detail was also likely wearing a vest under their clothing. They were all positioned in areas that a potential threat might come from, and as he neared the entrance to the courthouse he also saw three pairs of binoculars located in three different buildings around the courthouse. It wasn't anything anyone not looking for it might spot, but he was in the business and it came naturally for him.

Once in the courthouse, the four headed to Newman's courtroom, which they found locked. A bailiff cracked open the door and when he saw them opened it enough to let them into the courtroom. The media that had been stationed at the entrance to the courthouse, and a few that had already been inside, parked themselves outside of the courtroom, many of them getting ready to go on air with a 'live update.' As soon as Drew came into the courtroom, he was greeted by Harryette Asher, Judge Newman's secretary. As old as Judge Newman looked, Harryette looked like she could be his mother. There were wrinkles on top of wrinkles on her face, but her eyes still had a sparkle in them and she had a sweet manner about her that he had always found endearing. It was this countenance that made it more entertaining when she unloaded on someone who according to her 'hadn't come correct.' This could mean someone talking on a cell phone in the courtroom, not being properly dressed or 'just plain behaving like an ass.' Harryette usually unloaded on rookies who happened to walk into her domain unaware. Once you got past that and got in her good graces, she was an incredible ally to have. She could get you an audience with the judge if you needed it or fudge the time stamp on a brief you might have turned in late.

Drew had brought her cranberry muffins, her favorite, on more than one occasion, so she lit up when she saw him, "Drew Willis! I heard you were on this case!"

Drew smiled, "Hi, Harryette. Looking beautiful as ever."

She did not have the same affection for the other two attorneys, so all they got was a nod and a curt, "Gentlemen." Max and Ray responded in unison "Harryette."

Looking back at Drew, she said, "Come here, let me look at you!"

Drew complied although he was thinking to himself that it had been just a few weeks since she saw him last. Both Max and Ray rolled their eyes.

She took his hand with both of hers when he made it to her desk, "Oh, if I were just 20 years younger…"

Drew had the exchange down pat, "I'd be in big trouble no doubt. Harryette, are they here for the meeting yet?"

Harryette whispered in a conspiratorial tone, "They sure are. Bart Logan and the Amazon woman."

Drew chuckled, "Melanie Farris."

Harryette nodded, "That's the one."

Drew was disappointed, he had wanted to see Judge Newman before the prosecution team got there. Oh well, they would just have to present the argument to all of them at the same time. Now that he was here, Drew started to get nervous, not fear, but a sense of anticipation and intensity. This was going to blow their top and, truth be told, he was going to enjoy watching Bart Logan and Melanie Farris blow a gasket, like he knew they would.

Before going in, Max whispered, "I'm surprised Neill isn't here himself."

Drew agreed, "I am too. He probably wants to hedge his bets in case things don't go his way. He wants to be able to point at the other members of his team to place the blame, nothing new for him."

He knocked on the open door and the judge stood up to greet them, "Gentlemen, please come in."

The three of them filed in and took the chairs the judge pointed them toward.

In the meantime, Steven sat down in the courtroom waiting for his attorneys. He was thankful that the courtroom was closed to the media. The only other people with him were the judge's secretary and the bailiff that had opened the door. He sat in silence, thinking about Beth and the kids and wondering what they might be up to right now. He had promised Beth to call her immediately after the hearing. He didn't know whether the judge would make a decision immediately or whether they would have to wait a while. He also thought about the General. He had been thinking about him a lot since his encounter with Barlow. The old man was paying for his defense, was taking care of his family, and had given him an incredible opportunity when he left the military and he felt horrible not being able to talk to him about Barlow.

As Steven sat in the courtroom waiting, the bailiff came over to where he was. He addressed Steven in a low, tentative voice, a complete contrast from his physical presence, "Uh, Mr. Loomis? I just wanted to give my condolences. It's a damn shame. Me and most of the guys are pulling for you, sir, we really are."

Steven gave the man a thin smile, "I appreciate that, officer, I really do."

The bailiff returned the smile, gave Steven a nod and went back to stand by the door. He had been so wrapped up in everything that he had not had the opportunity to consider the effect his actions had on the public at large. He had tried to avoid the media coverage as much as possible, but he was beginning to realize that the further they got into the case the harder that was going to be. The tidbits he had caught here and there had let him know that for the most part the public was firmly behind him. There were the usual crazies claiming that what happened to Riche should happen to all those that killed children and the religious zealots were also out in force claiming that he was playing God and was just as evil as Riche. For the most part, normal everyday people believed what he had done was an act of heroism. The legal experts he had heard on various newscasts and talk shows were also all over the place. Some believed that this whole thing was nothing more than a stunt cooked up by his legal team in order to get around his confession, while others believed it was a brilliant legal maneuver meant to blur the facts, facts that were no longer in dispute given the fact that he had admitted everything. It was amusing to think that he had actually had to talk his legal team into making the argument.

Well, now the only thing that mattered was what the judge thought. If he thought it was a stunt, they were dead in the water and could do nothing about it. Like most former officers, especially special ops officers, Steven always believed that he was in control of his destiny, that he could always do *something* to help his cause, whatever the cause might be, and here he was not able to do a single thing to help himself. It was something he would have to learn to live with, at least for a while. After just under an hour, Steven saw Drew, Max and Ray come through the doorway leading into the courtroom. The two prosecutors that would be trying the case followed them. He remembered them from his arraignment. They were both relatively young and did not look too happy, although he imagined that they probably always looked that way. His own defense team did not give anything away.

Drew walked over, "Alright, let's see if we can find a room where we can chat."

He walked over to Harryette and asked her if there was a room they might be able to use for a few minutes. The two prosecutors walked out immediately, and Steven could hear the reporters shouting out questions and he could see the flashes going off as what had to be more than a hundred cameras took their pictures. Harryette got up and went back the way they had just come out. She came back after two minutes and whispered something into Drew's ear.

He came back over, this time smiling, "I knew those cranberry muffins would pay off some day. She says the judge will let us use the jury room to chat."

They all got up and walked through the judge's hallway and into the jury room. There was no access to the room except through the courtroom. After Ray closed the door, they all sat down around the table in the room.

Max was the first to speak, "Well, we've got good news and we've got bad news. I know it sounds hokey, but it's actually true in this case. Don't get that look, it's mostly good news. Judge Newman is going to let us put on our defense."

Steven smiled, "That's great! I mean, that's what we wanted, right?"

Now Ray spoke up, "Yes, it is, and yes, it is a big win for us that he's allowing us to move forward, but there are some conditions. It's nothing that will really hurt us, but it will definitely make it more difficult to move forward."

Steven, now confused, looked at Drew, "What does that mean? What conditions?"

Drew explained, "It's nothing we hadn't thought about or considered before now, but we figured if the judge was willing to allow us to move forward we wouldn't need to deal with it. What the judge said is that we can move forward with our defense, but we can only bring in Riche's behavior as it related to Tracy. We can't bring in or make reference to all the other girls."

Steven's face fell, "What?! Why not? That's what made him a monster!"

Ray stepped in, "Relax, kid, it's not as bad as it sounds. The judge did the right thing. Remember something, Steven, it's you who is on trial, not Donald Riche. We may know what he did and what he was, but this case is about you committing murder, not what Riche did. Ironically enough, the fact that he wasn't tried for the charges means that he was never convicted of them, which means we cannot make reference to them because legally they are just allegations."

Steven stood up. He was obviously upset, he could not understand the legalese and was frustrated because of it, "What do you mean they're just allegations?! You saw the pictures, everyone saw the pictures! They're not just allegations, they're fact!"

Now Max jumped in, "Steven, relax, have a seat and listen. You're right, the world knows he did it, but this has to do with the legal system, *our* legal system, and as you know, our legal system says innocent until proven guilty in a court of law. *In a court of law*. A lot of people forget about that part. They are allegations because he never got his day in court, never had a chance to prove his innocence."

Steven, now sitting down, went to say something else, but Max held up his hand and continued, "No, let me finish. You and I and the rest of the world know that he would have been convicted had he gone to trial, but the judge can't go by what *would have* happened. He has to make his decisions based on the facts, and the fact is that the charges against Riche were never proven."

Now Drew piped in, "That's the bad news, but they're not as bad as you think. You see, the judge said *we* can't use any of Donald's atrocities unless they relate to Tracy, but that doesn't mean the rest of the world won't know what Riche did, everything he did. You've seen the media coverage of this case, you've seen the pictures and all the experts commenting on it and so has the rest of the world, including the people that will make up the jury."

Steven's face let them know he was not understanding what Drew was explaining.

Drew went on, "The jury will be made up of ordinary people, people who watch television and listen to the radio, people who will be more than aware of what Riche did. What we're not able to bring in because of the judge's ruling, the media has already brought in. When we are picking the jury, both sides will ask the potential jurors if they've heard about Donald Riche and what he was accused of doing. Most people will admit that they have heard of it, some will say that they haven't, but they'll just say that in order to get on the jury.

"The reality is that they would have to be dead in order to not have heard anything about it. The assistant district attorneys assigned to the case were furious that the judge allowed the case to move forward, because they know that there's almost no way we're going to be able to pick a jury that hasn't heard about Riche and what he did. We're in good shape here, Steven, we really are."

Steven nodded, he understood what Drew had explained, "Sorry, guys. I'm just a little on edge. I don't understand a lot of the legal details and I have to be honest, some of it seems totally counter to what I imagined it to be."

Max patted him on the shoulder, "Don't worry, kid, you're no different than most people. Drew's right, we're in pretty good shape. This is one of those cases where global media has done the heavy lifting for us. That's why the DA's minions were so pissed off. They made the argument to the judge that it was going to be impossible to pick a clean jury, and they're right. When the judge made his ruling, he explained to them that he couldn't allow his decisions to be guided by what the media decided to cover or not cover and he was right to do that."

Ray added, "So during the trial, we're going to bring in his actions as they relate to Tracy, but the jury will know she wasn't his only victim. Cheer up, Steven, this is about as good as we could hope for."

Steven, now more at ease, asked, "So what happens now?"

Drew answered the question, "Well, the judge set the trial for two weeks from today. He's decided to fast-track the case because of the media coverage. There really isn't any discovery – that's where the DA shares his evidence with us and we share ours with them – to be settled.

"The facts of the case are not in contention since you confessed to doing it and gave the police information as to the where and how. Between now and the trial date, we need to decide who we are going to put on the stand and what they'll be testifying to.

"There's a lot of complicated science that we're going to be presenting, so we really need to coach our witnesses up on how to do that in laymen's terms. Juries tend to go to sleep if you start presenting stuff that's too technical and scientific. We also need to decide if you're going to testify."

Steven interrupted, "I am testifying."

Max spoke up, "Listen, Steven, we have to think…"

Steven interrupted again, "No, Max, that's not up for discussion, I'm testifying. It was my decision to do this and it's my theory we're moving forward with. They need to hear me explain it. They need to see I'm not a wacko or a father driven to insanity. It's a deal breaker, guys."

Ray interjected, "He's right, Max. I think the one thing the jury will be looking for is for Steven to explain his thinking, why he's decided to defend himself this way. Hey, he talked you two into moving forward with this defense, he must have done something right."

Max was still not convinced, "Well, let's just start deciding on our witnesses and we'll see how things shake out."

Steven was fine with that. He didn't want to get into an argument with Max over this, not now anyway. The four of them got up, walked through the courtroom and out into the outside hallway, where there were dozens of cameras snapping pictures and reporters shouting questions. Judging by the questions that were being asked, the media already knew about the nature of the meeting with the judge and what the outcome had been. Steven was amazed at how quickly they had gotten the information and wondered where the leak was. It could have been anybody, the people at the DA's office, the bailiff, Harryette herself, anybody.

They were making their way through the courthouse, helped by their security team, when Max stopped and for the first time spoke to the media, "We intend on proving to the jury that the argument that Mr. Loomis is making is based on solid and proven science. It is not a stunt and it is not meant to deflect attention from Mr. Loomis's actions."

A reporter shouted out, "Max! Max! Is your client saying that Riche was some sort of alien? Is that what he means to say?"

Max responded, "No, that is not what he is saying. That's the type of story the tabloids have come up with. The science we are going to present is complex and detailed. We can't get into specifics at the moment. Thank you all, now if you will please let us through."

And with that the group made their way outside, where even more press was waiting. The security detail made a path for them to follow to the waiting Suburban. As he was walking, Steven noticed his own team, looking out into the crowd inconspicuously. He spotted Thurman and gave him a quick nod. They made their way back to the law offices, where they spent the rest of the afternoon discussing witnesses. The one they could all agree on was Dr. Tyrone Leonard. They would decide on the rest in the next couple of weeks. They agreed that Steven would visit Dr. Leonard to let him know he would be called as a witness and he would assess where the scientist's head was.

◆

Steven left the office just before eight that evening and headed straight home. When he finally walked into his condo, he immediately saw that there was something different. Things had been moved and lights that he knew he had turned off were now on. He stopped and reached into his lower back and pulled out his SIG Sauer P226. Max had warned him against carrying a weapon, but there was no way he would be caught unprepared again. He walked slowly in a crouch heading toward the kitchen where he could hear someone rummaging. As he moved from the living room and into the hallway, he stopped and from a low position peeked around the corner. What he saw surprised him more than if it had been some random intruder. Beth was standing in the middle of the kitchen. There was a pot on the stove and Steven, now completely relaxed, could smell the marinara sauce cooking. He opened the drawer on the small table in the hallway and dropped the gun into it. He walked out into the open, where she spotted him instantly.

"Hey, you! I'm glad I waited to put the pasta on, it would have been overcooked by now."

He walked all the way to her and took her in his arms. It felt so good to have her with him. He buried his head in her hair, inhaling deeply and taking in her scent. He had loved doing that since they first started dating. She also held him close, feeling his heart pounding against her chest. He turned his head and kissed her. It was a tender and warm kiss, but one that also held passion just under the surface.

He finally spoke, "Beth, what are you doing here? You should have told me you were coming."

Still holding on to him, Beth backed up enough to look at him face-to-face, "And have you tell me to stay away? No way, Steven, I know you. You would have argued until you got your way. We might have even gotten into a fight, just like the last time we talked about it, remember?"

He did remember and he also remembered that even though he knew the smart thing was for her to stay away, he wanted her with him.

He smiled, "You're right, you're right, I would have tried to convince you to stay away."

Beth smiled, "See, and I know that deep down you would want me to be here, but you're too stubborn to admit it. This way, there's no way you can convince me, I'm already here."

He chuckled, "So ask for forgiveness rather than ask for permission, is that it?"

Her smiled widened, "That's right. Now, why don't you go change, get comfortable while I finish with the pasta and open us a bottle of wine."

He did exactly as told and came back wearing sweat pants and a t-shirt.

She smiled from the kitchen, "Better?"

He smiled back as he poured both of them a glass of wine, "Definitely. God, that smells great. I've done alright on my own, but I do miss your cooking."

She joined him and took her glass of wine, "Done alright on your own? Ha, you mean you haven't burnt the frozen pizzas."

He chuckled, "Alright, you got me, but they're not bad, you know."

She went back into the kitchen and came back with the dish of steaming pasta and a small bowl with the sauce.

"Can you grab the rolls and the salads? They're in the kitchen."

They sat down to their dinner, drinking their wine and enjoying their food. For Steven, it was more about feeling normal again than it was about the food itself. They talked about the kids and what they had been up to since he left. Beth caught him up on all the family gossip. Her cousin was getting another divorce and another cousin had just been accepted to Yale Law School. They did not talk about the case until well after dinner, while they were doing the dishes standing next to each other.

He explained the hearing and what his lawyers had told him. "You'll like them, Beth, they're good guys, different, but good guys."

She went over to the wet bar and poured them two after-dinner drinks, Amaretto for her and Baileys for him.

He walked over to her and kissed her forehead as he took the glass, "Are you trying to get me drunk so you can take advantage of me?"

She smiled coquettishly, "Something like that."

He put his arms around her and brought her close. He could smell her lotion, lilacs, always lilacs. He brushed a lock of hair from her face, took her face in his hands and kissed her. A tender and loving kiss, but there was passion there, too, and as she felt it, she put her arms around his waist and allowed herself to get lost in the moment. Right then, right at that moment, they were just husband and wife again. Two people deeply in love, sharing each other's grief and loss and hope and trust. He pulled back and looked at her with the same wistful, content eyes he had looked at her with when they first met and remembered why he had done everything he had done. His family, his home, those were the things that drove him, and those were the things that would see him through everything that lay ahead of him. He remained that way, just looking at her for a full minute.

Finally she smiled, "What?"

He chuckled as he pulled her close again and rested his head on her shoulder as he spoke in her ear, "Nothing, I was just thinking about how much I love you, how much you mean to me and how far we've come. I love our family, Beth. I love you all so much, and sometimes I wonder whether the things I've done have been the right things, you know? Not just this, everything, all the years in the Navy going away for months at a time, years sometimes."

Now she took his face in her hands and held him so he was looking straight into her eyes and their noses almost touching, "Hey, hey, listen to me. Everything you've done has been done with love for your family in your heart, and that makes it right. Steven, you more than anyone should know that life never comes with a user's manual. We do the best we can with what we have and we try to do it with love in our heart. That's the best thing we can hope for, for our love for each other and our kids and our parents to guide the things we do. Sometimes it's hard and we falter or sometimes we hurt so bad that we can't see it, but we always come back to that, the love we feel for the people closest to us."

He gave her a smile that warmed and broke her heart at the same time, "I know, babe, I know, I guess right now I'm wondering if my pain, the sense of loss I feel, has blinded me to what you're saying. I miss her so much, Beth, I miss her so much."

He put his head back on her shoulder and sobbed. She just held him and stroked his head. She knew that unlike her, he hadn't had time to truly grieve. He had held it all in, too preoccupied with everything that had happened and trying to keep his family safe. He was the best man that she had ever known and she loved him more in this one moment than she had ever thought possible. When she was young, one of her aunts had told her that most women ended up marrying their fathers. She remembered that at the time she believed if that was the case she would never marry, because she didn't think she would ever find as good a man as her father, but she had. They remained like that for a few more minutes, her stroking his hair and him sobbing and releasing everything he had held inside.

After a few minutes, he looked up at her and smiled, "Sorry, babe, it just came up on me."

She smiled back, "Silly, silly man. You may not realize it, but these are the moments when I love you the most. Moments where you're not Steven Loomis, Commander SEAL Team Six, or executive god at GIC, moments when you're just the man I fell in love with and the father of my children."

He chuckled and gave her a big bear hug, "Executive god of GIC? Really?"

She chuckled in return, "It's what came into my mind, do you like it?"

He finally let her go and wiped his face with a napkin from the wet bar, "I do. I'll have to let everyone at the office know so they will know to worship me properly."

They both laughed at this, a sincere and healthy laugh. They stopped laughing, looked at each other and launched into laughter again. It was a laugh that carried with it the relief of being together, of being able to glimpse that maybe one day they would be able to go back to just being a family, nothing more. When they were finally composed and on their way into the living room with their drinks, the phone rang. They looked at each other with puzzled expressions, wondering who would be calling at that hour.

Steven answered. It was Danny, the night doorman, "Mr. Loomis? Yeah, this is Danny downstairs. There's a gentleman here to see you. He says you know him. An Art Goodman?"

Steven smiled, he should have known, "Yeah, Danny, let him up."

He walked over to Beth in the living room, "It's the General. He's coming up."

She looked at him still with a puzzled expression, "The General? At this hour?"

Steven nodded, "Yeah, he must have something important he wants to talk about. Other than the case, I can't think of anything."

Beth stood up, "Well, I'll finish cleaning up the kitchen while the two of you talk."

There was a light knock at the door and Steven, already on his way to the door, answered it, "General, it's good to see you, please come in."

The General came in and before he could say anything he noticed Beth going from the living room to the kitchen, "Beth? I didn't know you were here. If I'd known, I would have come some other time."

Beth looked over, "Hi, Art, don't worry, Steven was surprised too. Come in, please. Would you like something to drink?"

Steven took his coat and led him to the living room. "That would be nice. Scotch, maybe? Neat?"

She nodded and went to the wet bar, "You need anything, honey?"

Steven, sitting down next to the old man, shook his head, "I still have my Baileys, babe, thanks."

She came over to where they were sitting and handed the amber beverage to Goodman, "Here you go. Now, I am going to go run a bath for myself while you two chat and then I'm hitting the sack. It's been a long day."

Before she left, the General stood up and gave her a peck on the cheek, "I bet it has. Thank you, Beth."

She left and the two men took a sip from their drinks.

Steven spoke first, "So, to what do I owe the honor, sir."

The General looked at Steven for a couple of beats before answering, "I just wanted to check in with you, son. I haven't had a chance to speak with you for a while. Sorry to come at this hour, by the way, I had to wait until those vultures left. They're everywhere, even in front of our building."

Steven hung his head.

He knew that the media was camped out at the GIC building because of him and it annoyed him. "Yeah, sorry about that. You're right, they're everywhere. I knew this would cause a media shit storm. I just never in a million years imagined it would be to this extent."

The old man nodded thoughtfully and took a sip from his drink. Both men were reflective by nature and had always been comfortable with silence, and it was no different now. Neither man was the type to simply speak to break the silence and both thought carefully before they spoke. It had been that way since the time he started at GIC. Finally, Steven decided the best thing to do would be to update his boss on what was going on with his trial. He hadn't been able to speak to the man since he had confessed and explained to the world what his defense would be.

"We had a hearing today, as you probably already know. The judge allowed us to move forward with our defense."

Goodman took another sip and nodded, "Yeah, that. I have to tell you, son, I was genuinely surprised by the article in the newspaper."

Steven, both hands on his glass, nodded, "Yeah, I'm sorry about that, sir. I wish we could have talked before all that happened, but there just didn't seem to be a way for me to come see you before it happened."

The General waved his hand, "Oh, don't be sorry. I imagined you were probably being hounded by those jackals in the media. When you made the decision to take Riche out, I figured there was more behind it than just revenge. I think I know you well enough to know you're too measured to be taken by reckless sentiments. And you confirmed it when we spoke at my office. But I would be lying to you if I said I knew this was what you were planning. Talking to the media is a big step."

Steven nodded and took a sip from his drink. He waited a few seconds and finally turned to the old man, "And? What do you think about it, about the article and all the coverage?"

Goodman thought for a few seconds and answered, "Well, it makes sense. I mean, I think those of us who have had the opportunity to see the atrocities of violence up close have at one time or another asked the same question: What kind of animal does this? We all ask it, but we never expect to get an answer, because deep down inside, we know that no answer is going to satisfy us.

"Now, with this, you've made the decision to provide an answer. Whether it's *the* answer only time will tell, but it lets people know that if you chose to go down this path you must have had enough information to make the decision. All the so-called 'experts' and scientists are just putting their two cents in, but none of them really know what the hell they're dealing with. The reporter that wrote the article, Garcia, did a decent job of presenting your theory and your reasons for doing what you did, but some of the others writing and talking about it haven't been as straight, and it will only get worse."

Steven gave him a small, thin smile and took another sip of his drink. He went on to explain the details of the hearing they had earlier that day and what would be coming up in the next couple of weeks.

The man was footing his legal bills and had put up the money for his bail and Steven felt he had the right to know. Even if that hadn't been the case, he considered the old man much more than just his boss and he valued his advice greatly, so he would have told him everything, regardless. Goodman asked a couple of questions as Steven was laying everything out for him and Steven answered as best he could. After an hour together, the General stood up and drained the last bit of Scotch from his glass.

He grabbed Steven by the shoulders and looked straight into his eyes, "Well, son, you're in it now. Just remember, we're here for you, *no matter what happens*."

Hearing the emphasis on his last words, for the first time Steven wondered whether the old man knew about Barlow. The only people that knew about that were Cecil and Thurman Meeks, and he had a hard time believing that they had said anything.

He simply looked back at the General and said something he had been meaning to say for a while, "I know, I really do, sir. I want to thank you for everything you've done for me, for my family. I know there's no way I can repay that, but I wanted you to know how much I appreciate all of it."

The old man chuckled and walked toward the door, "Nonsense, you're family, and you know if it were the other way around you'd do the same thing."

Steven smiled, nodded and surprised the old man with a heartfelt hug.

The General chuckled as he too put his arms around Steven and patted his back, "You just take care of this business and know that your family is cared for, alright?" Steven nodded, let him go and bid him goodbye.

When he came out of the building and onto the street, a car with tinted windows pulled up to the curb and the old man got in. Once he was inside, the driver pulled away from the curb and into traffic.

Thurman Meeks turned to the old man and asked, "So, did he tell you?"

Goodman shook his head, "No, he didn't. I don't blame him. He's got a lot on his plate and he figures that if he tells me I'm going to want to take some action. He's probably right, about Barlow I mean, the only reason he took an interest in Steven is because of Riche and everything that's happened. He's not going to want to put whatever it is he is doing at risk by coming after someone he knows is an experienced Special Forces operator and has the resources to go after him.

"No, the asshole did what he did because he knew Steven would have to let it go for now, and he figured that would give him enough time to pick up and put the show on the road."

Meeks nodded, "I thought the same thing. If he was able to sniff us out then it means he's been expecting someone to sooner or later start digging into his business. He probably thought it would be later, and when we started digging and tripped a few of his countermeasures he got spooked."

The old man was looking out the window, clearly thinking about the situation, "Yeah, but even though he was spooked, he had the wherewithal and the resources to get Steven alone, which means he's been doing whatever he's been doing for a while and he's prepared himself for contingencies, and that makes this mutt much more dangerous than your average psychopath."

They drove in silence for a few blocks.

Finally, Meeks spoke up, "So what do you want to do?"

The answer let him know that the old man had been thinking about precisely that question, "We let the guy go, let him pull up stakes and get on his way. We keep Steven covered during the trial. Are the two teams at his in-laws' house still good?"

Meeks nodded, "Yup, all guys you know, all professionals."

The General knew that by 'professionals' Thurman meant guys that had serious experience in the field, probably ex-SEALs or Special Air Service, SAS operatives, Britain's version of the SEALs.

Meeks went on, "We also have the team that Steven asked for in place. The security detail his lawyers arranged for is dealing with crowd control and transportation logistics, which is good because it lets us concentrate on the important stuff, electronics detection, sniper counter-surveillance, the standard stuff."

The General still had some questions, "How good is their security detail?"

Meeks answered, "They're pretty good, for what they do. Former cops, all of them, two of them are former jarheads."

Goodman nodded, "Alright, we keep out of sight for the duration. When the trial is finished, I'll talk to Steven and we'll decide what we're going to do. If I know him, I think he's not going to just let Barlow disappear into the woodwork. I suppose it will all depend on how his trial pans out.

"Now he knows Riche was nothing, just one predator in a much bigger jungle. When he killed him, Steven swatted a mosquito and then realized the mosquito was sitting on an elephant's ass, and the son of a bitch woke up and charged after him."

Meeks chuckled. He'd always enjoyed the old man's way of putting things.

The General went on, "Now it's our job to keep that elephant off his back until after the trial, then it's his decision whether we go hunting or not."

Thurman nodded, "Yeah, and I think you're right, Steven's not going to let this guy just disappear."

They drove in silence all the way to Goodman's building. He owned a penthouse on the Upper East Side.

Before he reached for the door handle, Thurman grabbed his arm, "General, I told you about this because I consider Steven a brother, but it still bothers me that I betrayed his confidence, it bothers the hell out of me."

Goodman smiled, "Relax, son, you did the right thing. Sometimes we're so far in, so deep, that we don't realize when we need to call for cover. That's where Steven is at, he's looking at a murder charge and he's got the world's attention firmly planted on him. He's a good executive and he was a good officer because he knows what he doesn't know, that's why he brought you in.

"Just so we're clear, Thurman, we're all a part of a brotherhood, like it or not, and right now one of our brothers needs our help, even if he doesn't completely understand how much help he needs. You did good, Chief, trust me."

Retired Chief Petty Officer Thurman Meeks smiled, the General was the only one who called him that. "Good enough. Have a good night, sir."

The General stepped out of the car, patted the roof twice and turned to go into his building.

Chapter 24

The next morning, Steven got up before Beth, before the sun came up actually, made coffee, had a cup himself and left the rest for Beth along with a note and some fresh-squeezed orange juice. The previous day he had arranged for a car to pick him up precisely at six, before the whole world woke up. As he walked out of his building, he saw that his security detail had already pushed the media early birds out of the way. He went straight to the car, and one of the men of his security team got in behind him. This was something that his lawyers had insisted on. They didn't know about the SIG Sauer he had tucked in his lower back and he wanted to keep it that way. He didn't know how they would feel about their client, a defendant accused of first-degree murder, carrying a concealed weapon, but he was pretty sure one or all of them might blow their top. He knew he might be violating a condition of his bail, but under the circumstances he didn't care. The car drove straight to Queens College. The security guard got out first, scouted the nearby sidewalk and gave him a nod. He got out of the car and went straight into a building on his immediate right. He had been here twice before and knew the layout well. As he made his way through the building, he could sense the looks he was getting from the few people that were there that realized who he was. Most were students up before dawn cramming and others had been up all night studying, fueled by caffeine, so there really weren't that many who took any real interest. The school had been on high alert, as there had been a constant stream of media coming through campus since the shooting. He had seen a couple of the interviews Dr. Leonard had given, so he knew the man could handle himself. He finally got to the right floor and walked up to the same student he had spoken to before.

"Mr. Loomis! I didn't know you were coming, does Dr. Leonard know you're coming this morning?"

Steven nodded, "Yes, he does. I called him yesterday. He said to come by this morning. Is he free?"

She smiled and stood up, "Yes, he is, please come back."

When they were a few feet away from his office door she excused herself and went back up front. He knocked lightly on the open door as he stepped to the threshold.

Leonard turned toward him, a stack of blue test booklets balanced precariously on his desk, "Mr. Loomis! Come in, come in, please!"

He walked over to the small table in his office where there were even more booklets and moved a stack of books from the chair they were in to the floor. "I apologize for the mess. I keep meaning to get some of my graduate assistants to clean it out, but it seems I need everything here. I know it looks messy, but believe it or not I know where everything is, wouldn't know what to do with myself if it were all clean."

Loomis smiled and took the chair he had emptied. Leonard sat down across the table from him and with that beaming smile that seemed to always be parked on his face asked, "So, what can I do for you?"

Steven wasn't sure where to start. There was so much he wanted to say to the man, but he knew that now was not the time to say it.

He started with the main reason he was there, "Dr. Leonard, first of all I want to apologize. I know how busy you are and I know how difficult the media can make things. It seems like they're everywhere I turn these days and I know that it's probably the same for you. I am sorry for that, it's not what I intended and I wish I could change it, but I can't. That's the reason I asked to meet with you at this ungodly hour."

The smile on Leonard's face widened, "My dear sir, there's nothing to be sorry for! Are you kidding?! I've been toiling in obscurity for over two decades, hoping that one day what we've accomplished, the work we've done, would see the light of day, but knowing all the while that it probably would not happen in my lifetime. Now not only is the world interested in the work I've been doing, they want to know what's next! I'm scheduled to go on with Piers Morgan the day after tomorrow! No, Mr. Loomis, you don't have a single thing to be sorry about. As for the hour, I am usually in here before six, so it was no problem."

Steven smiled, honestly surprised by Leonard's response, "I suppose I hadn't thought about it that way. I'm glad, professor, the world needs to know about what you've done, the things you've discovered."

Leonard's face now took on a more serious expression, "I don't know what you've gone through, I really can't imagine, but I can assure you of one thing, Mr. Loomis, the world will know. I will make sure they know and so will all the other scientists that have dedicated their lives to this."

Steven nodded and went on, "I'm also here because, as I am sure you've heard, my trial starts in a few weeks and my defense team is planning to call you as an expert witness, and I wanted to personally give you the heads up. I hope that won't be a problem."

Leonard shook his head, "Not at all. I am assuming they will be calling me to testify to the work I've done and to go over my findings."

Steven nodded, "That's right, that's exactly what you'll be called to testify about. My lawyers also want you to review Donald Riche's file, you know, his history, his background and upbringing, and to provide your opinion."

Leonard's expression changed into one of concern, "Mr. Loomis, I can do a psychological autopsy and provide my point of view relative to it, but I hope you understand that there is simply no way for me to be able to determine whether Mr. Riche was in fact a *Homo sapiens predaer*. I just can't make that determination. I wouldn't feel right about doing that."

Steven explained further, "I don't think that's what they're looking for you to do, professor. I think the idea is that you do the psychological autopsy and then provide an opinion whether what you find might lead you to conclude that Riche *could have* been one of them. This whole thing professor is not about proving that Donald Riche *was* a *Homo predator*. I don't think anybody believes that you can say unequivocally whether he was one or not."

Leonard's smile returned, "That I can do. I've done quite a bit of that over the years, actually. Unfortunately, we don't always get to our subjects in time, and when that happens all we have is what's left in their profile file."

That settled, Steven debated whether to ask the scientist a question that had been bothering him for some time.

Leonard could see that the man was debating whether to ask something and decided to probe, "What's on your mind, Mr. Loomis? I have a feeling that there something else you want to say."

Steven smiled and shook his head slowly, "You got me. Yeah, you're right, professor, I do have something I've been thinking about."

Leonard just waited and Steven eventually broke down, "Alright, we've talked about this new species and you've explained that the reason you began to speculate that this was a new species in the first place was because they didn't conform to the norms that you and your colleagues and others had set for extreme aberrant behavior, that you made the determination that these things are the way they are from the time they're born, that they're not a product of education or environment, but how do you know?

"I mean to make that determination you would really have to start studying them before they are old enough to be affected by their environment, and I can't imagine that you've been able to conduct your experiments on newborn babies."

Leonard's expression lit up again. This was his field, what he'd dedicated a lifetime to, and it showed every time he was about to explain something. "Very perceptive, Mr. Loomis, very perceptive, but you see, while we can't research newborns, we can research babies before they're affected by any human norms or their surrounding environment. It's relatively new research, pioneered by the Infant Cognition Center at Yale University. They've been researching babies as young as three months old, researching whether altruistic behavior and cooperative behavior is something human children are born with, something innate."

Steven remembered the research Scoma had told him about, "Yeah, Dr. Scoma told me about some of it."

Leonard stopped and, with a glint in his eye, stood up, "You know what? Come with me. I think you'll find what I'm about to show you quite enlightening."

Steven followed Leonard out of his office and down a short hallway. They went into a room with several flat-screen televisions and some DVD players attached to them. He sifted through a small stack of DVDs sitting on a television before finding what he was looking for. He walked over put the DVD into one of the players, turned the television on and motioned for Steven to sit down. Steven watched as the study utilizing the puppets that Scoma had described unfolded. It was clear that most babies shown chose the helpful puppet in the scenario. The same scenario was repeated several times with various babies.

Leonard turned the television off and turned to Steven, "We duplicated that experiment many, many times and just as you saw in that video, more than 90 percent of the babies chose the helpful puppet. The implications were astounding. This meant that human babies were basically predisposed to do good, to be helpful. Other experiments with other children found that roughly the same percentage were willing to share without being prompted to and they were willing to be helpful, *even at their own expense.*

"All of this, Mr. Loomis, had led the researchers at Yale and at other similar institutions to conclude that human babies are basically born 'good,' that there is what we often call a moral compass that leads them to choose to do what we as a society have determined is the right thing. It is still a young science and there are many other experiments being conducted as we speak, but that's the gist of it."

Leonard, with a sparkle in his eye and back in his child-in-a-toy-store mode, went on, "So most of these researchers were testing the inherent goodness in humans, even at a very young age, but we were interested in the 10 percent that chose the 'bad' puppet. We retested them using different scenarios, and at first we found that for most it had nothing to do with good or bad, but rather a preference in color. They simply preferred one color versus another."

Steven jumped in, "You said 'most.' What about the other...."

Leonard held up his index finger in triumph, "Exactly! What about those who chose the 'bad' puppet for some other reason? We conducted other similar experiments with those babies and found that those that selected the 'bad' puppet in one scenario selected the 'bad' puppet in every other scenario we devised. We began to get excited, but we had to make sure, so we kept track of those children and brought them back when they were older, 12 to 15 months to be precise. We eliminated all the children that had in any way been exposed to any form of psychological or physical trauma or whose parents seemed unstable or whose life situation was otherwise compromised."

Leonard found another DVD and put it in. In the scene that started playing, an adult sat in a chair and there were two babies in the room playing with some toys. The adult then dropped a pen in such a way that the babies could see it. The adult attempted to reach the pen, stretching his arms and making gestures that showed he wanted the pen, but could not reach it. In the first group of toddlers, the two babies watched the adult struggle and after a short time, one walked over, picked up the pen and handed it to the adult. The same scenario was repeated with several children from the 90 percent group. In each situation, one or both of the babies tried to help the adult get the pen or they picked it up and handed it to the adult themselves. After repeating it several times, the experiment was conducted with one child from the 90 percent group and one child from the other group. Again, both toddlers watched the adult struggle and after some time the 'good' baby got up and got the pen while the other baby watched. The scenario was repeated several times with the same toddlers and each time the same thing happened.

Leonard whispered, "Now watch this."

In the next scene, the same situation unfolded, except this time when the 'good' baby got up to go get the pen, the other child walked over and pushed the helpful child down, walked over to the pen, picked it up and walked back to where he'd been playing, pen sitting right beside him.

Leonard pushed pause, "That same situation was replayed with several iterations, and in every instance the same thing happened."

Steven was not clear on what it was that he had seen, "So one baby wanted the pen for himself, is that it?"

Now excited, Leonard explained, "No, Mr. Loomis, the child did not know what a pen was or what it was used for. He waited until he *knew* that the pen had some worth for the adult and once he made that determination, he made the decision that he'd keep the pen for himself, even if he didn't know what it was.

"If you observe closely, he gets really interested when the other child delivers the pen. We were able to ascertain that the reason for that is because the child was calculating whether the adult could reach far enough to actually catch the child picking up the pen, and when he saw that the adult couldn't reach, he made his move.

"What you have witnessed, Mr. Loomis, is a 15-month-old child, not shaped by education or trauma or environment, making tactical calculations, assessing the worth of the object the adult wanted and finally deciding that it was important, which meant that it must have some value. The child didn't know how or why but he knew it was useful and valuable, and that meant that if *he* had it, he would have more than the other two players in the scene. Fifteen months, Mr. Loomis, fifteen months!"

They watched a few more videos and when the last one was finished Leonard turned off the television.

Steven was shaking his head, "Jesus, this is amazing. It's also scary as hell."

Leonard turned to look at Steven, "Yes, Mr. Loomis, it is. Now you understand why some of my colleagues and I have determined that they are the new apex predators of the planet. If they are capable of that at 15 months, what do you think they're able to do when they're older and more educated and perhaps in a position of power?"

Steven leaned back in the chair he was sitting. He knew what one of them could do with all those things, had thought he knew it when he found Riche's warehouse, but realized that was just the tip of the iceberg. Barlow had shown him that.

Steven thought of something he had heard Barlow say, "Professor, have you heard of a Nigel Barlow?"

Leonard's expression turned into one of curiosity, "Yes, yes I have. Why do you ask?"

Steven did not want to complicate his relationship with Leonard any further, "I came across his name while I was doing some of my research."

Leonard still looked puzzled, "Interesting. He hasn't been involved in serious research for some time. He does consulting and profiling work for law enforcement. I believe he also has a practice. He's a neuropsychologist."

Steven went on, "What do you mean he hasn't been involved in serious research? What kind of research has he done?"

Leonard looked uncomfortable talking about this. Steven could tell the man had come across Barlow at some point and had been affected by his dealings with him the same way he had.

Leonard was clearly being cautious as he answered, "What I mean is that he's not done the type of research that most academics engage in. Research that can be reviewed, duplicated and then reviewed again. He hasn't published anything in any peer review publication. He believed that we should simply observe them as they engaged in their atrocities. That in and of itself was enough to get him shunned by most of the scientific community interested in the science we were exploring."

Leonard shook his head slowly as he continued, "But then he began writing a manifesto, something out of science fiction. He believed these beings were superior to humans and should be nurtured, allowed to reach their full potential. He believed the only way humans would survive this species was by understanding them and then harnessing their natural tendencies to our advantage. That ensured he would never be taken seriously by anyone in the scientific community. Then he disappeared for a few years, and when he came back, he started doing the work I just mentioned to you."

Steven nodded. He didn't want to show any sign that he was interested in Barlow beyond just simple curiosity.

"Well, like I said, I saw his name in a few things I came across and just wondered whether you'd ever come across him."

Leonard nodded thoughtfully and responded, talking more to himself than to Steven, "Yes, yes I have. He's not the type of person you ever forget, if you get my meaning."

Steven simply nodded. If there had been even a shadow of a doubt or hesitation about what he had done, this had taken care of it. They went back to Leonard's office, where Steven thanked the professor for his time and called for his driver. He knew it would be about 20 minutes, so he sat down in the chair Leonard had cleared.

Leonard sat across from him, "So, I suppose now you and your legal team will go about getting ready." Steven sighed, hung his head and ran his hands through his hair. "Yeah, professor, that's right, although to be honest with you, I'm lost half the time when my lawyers start talking about it."

Leonard smiled, "I can imagine it's like listening to another language."

Steven smiled back and nodded. He thought about the change that had come over Scoma when they spoke and he thought of another question he wanted to ask Leonard.

"Professor, Dr. Scoma mentioned that the two of you had written a paper together. I know I came across it in my research, but for the life of me I can't remember what it was about. How did the two of you come together? I mean, I know how your work intersects now, but how did you meet?"

Leonard's expression changed. That semipermanent smile that always seemed to be parked on his face vanished. He regarded Loomis with a mixture of caution and compassion. That told Loomis that he was trying to decide whether to answer his question or not. That meant that the answer to his question was something far beyond 'our work brought us together.'

After a few seconds, Leonard let out a big sigh and proceeded to explain how the two scientists had met. "Jim Scoma is a brilliant mind, Mr. Loomis, absolutely brilliant, but he's also one of the finest human beings I have come across."

Leonard paused and Steven got the distinct impression that he was saying all of it to prepare Loomis for what he was about to tell him. He nodded but said nothing.

"Jim was about to get ready to begin his own work relative to the new species. He'd read some of my papers and had been at some of the conferences where I spoke and became interested in what we were doing." Steven just listened.

"Before starting his research, Jim thought it might be a good idea to establish a baseline for human physiology and genetics. He wanted to have something to measure his results against, so he tested himself in order to establish that baseline."

Leonard paused and Steven could sense where he was going. He now understood why Leonard had been careful about answering the question. He remained quiet.

"After he got the results of all his testing, he became extremely concerned. You see, Mr. Loomis, Jim Scoma's tests were almost identical to those of individuals that we'd come to establish as *Homo sapiens predaer*."

This last statement seemed to hang in the air as Leonard allowed Loomis to fully digest it. His mind was racing and he had a million questions he wanted to ask, but he settled for a much simpler, almost feeble response, "How?"

Leonard's smile appeared again, although it still did not have the brilliance in normally carried, "That was basically his question to me: How? He was confused, as you can imagine, and wanted to know how it could be possible.

"When we met, we went over all my findings and over his own measurements and quickly determined that while his physiology, genetic makeup and cognitive processes were a close parallel, there were some differences. Still, his results were definitely not within human norms. That was the reason he decided to research this from another angle, from an angle that did not concentrate on my end of the scale."

Steven nodded. He could now see what had started Scoma down the path he chose for his research; it made sense. Still, Steven still got the sense that this was not what was making both scientists uneasy. It might be part of it, but he sensed there was more. He still had that almost imperceptible sense of vertigo he got when there was something there, something he could almost put his finger on, remember, but not quite.

He decided to come at it from the only other angle he could think of, "He mentioned the paper the two of you worked on together, and as I said, I think, I'm almost positive I came across it, but I'd be lying if I told you I remember anything about it. He said it was a paper on how animals group together in order to protect themselves from predators."

Again Leonard's smile faded and again he debated on whether to say something in response. In the end, Leonard seemed to have decided that he had already answered Steven's most troubling questions, so he explained, "Yes, early on I did some work on how weaker, slower animals established some of their most effective defenses by grouping. You see, there are some scientists that believe that herds – schools of fish, flocks of birds, those kinds of groupings – were either following a leader or were engaged in a top-down migration where one bird or bison began a migration and the rest simply followed, top-down leadership.

"What we found is, yes, that is part of it, but a bigger part is more of what we would define as group-think. It is not a linear process. It doesn't go from one animal to the other to the other, but it is all of them as a group making determinations for the group. This type of behavior was incredibly difficult to establish because we simply could not model it, in other words, we simply could not get a group of animals to think as a group. With advances in computer science and other technologies, we are now able to model this behavior in computers. The latest artificial intelligence technology, Mr. Loomis, is not based on linear programming, as it had once been, but on parallel programming. Computers tasked with attaining an outcome after a number of conditions have been programmed in several parallels.

"So rather than one computer and one program acting on the conditions put in, it is several programs running in parallel to achieve an outcome. Over generations the program 'learns' what is most efficient and effective in achieving the goal set, because there are several 'parallel' programs working together to achieve it."

Leonard paused. He could see he was losing Steven. He smiled and continued, "I don't blame you if you don't quite get it yet. It is still difficult for me to understand, but Jim Scoma is a genius when it comes to this and that's why we wrote the paper together. I had been looking into this grouping behavior as a prey animal's best defense and wanted to see how it related to what I was researching. I wanted to understand how weaker and slower animals were able to survive, how certain species were able to survive in spite of physiological and cognitive disadvantages when it came to the animals that preyed on them."

Steven interrupted, "And? What was it you were able to determine?"

Leonard answered, "Remember that what I was, what I *am,* interested in is *Homo sapiens sapiens* and *Homo sapiens predaer.* What I found was that human beings have been able to not only survive, but thrive, because of their ability to utilize their intellect to build defenses. Weapons, buildings, fire, all of them, were humans' desire to survive, to protect themselves. As the environment has become exponentially more complex, so have our defenses. Home security, advanced weapons, sensors, all of it is a result of man's desire for security and for our species' continued survival."

Steven noticed that Leonard's demeanor was not easy and jovial as it had been when he was speaking about his research. This was an area beyond his immediate expertise and he now had an intense, focused way about him.

Leonard went on, "Our most effective defense, however, our most effective and lasting defense, Mr. Loomis, has been our ability to group, to gather around fires, to build society. If you haven't noticed, as far as our physiology, our physical ability to fend off stronger, more powerful predators, we are a pretty sad species. Without technology, a group of humans in the African prairie can still survive, even if it is just by grouping together. Predators will pause and often simply walk away when confronted with a large group of humans. In the same way, they will wait until a foal staggers from the herd rather than trying to catch one if the middle of a tight herd. But if a human runs into a pride of lions in the African savannah, it's pretty much gamer over, as I'm sure you'd agree."

He continued, "So the paper we wrote was about that. Specifically, we wanted to understand better how predators went about getting around these grouping defenses. My initial idea was that even though *Homo sapiens predaer* is superior to humans physiologically and cognitively, humans would still be able to survive and thrive because of these grouping mechanisms."

Steven could understand exactly what he was saying. He had watched a show about lions not too long ago. The memory brought with it a pang he wasn't ready for.

He had taken more of Leonard's time than he had intended to, but now he had a better understanding of what had brought the two scientists together.

"Professor, you've been more than kind with your time. I truly appreciate it. I'm sorry for the whole media thing, it's not something I can really do anything about. My lawyers' office will be in contact with details about the trial and your testifying."

Leonard waved his hand, "No need to apologize. As I said, the attention is worth whatever small inconvenience I might have to go through."

Leonard reached across the table and took Steven's hand in his. The almost haunted look on the man's face chilled Steven, but not as much as what he said, "Mr. Loomis, Steven, I'm grateful for the attention you've brought to my and others' life's work, but you have to know, you have to know because the price is very steep. Yes, your trial, what you've had to go through with your family has been a price almost too high to fathom, but what may still be to come may be higher still. Donald Riche was one individual, Mr. Loomis, *one*. But there are others, I'm sure you know that, and you've gotten their attention too.

"Our work is important work, it has been from the beginning, but the time is coming when it will not be enough, when simply bringing attention to them won't be enough. Technology has been our salvation across history. It has been what has kept us alive and what has made it an even playing field with predators that would hunt us without a care in the world. The problem, Mr. Loomis, is that these predators can use it too. They can use it to hunt the way we use it to stay alive. You need to be careful now. You need to understand how big this is and how dangerous it can be for you and your family now."

Barlow had said something similar, had told him he didn't yet understand the extent of what he now found himself knee-deep in. He wondered if Leonard had said all of this because he had asked him about Barlow. He wondered whether it was Barlow he was thinking of when he said what he said. There was something that Leonard was trying to explain without having to say it, but Steven was overwhelmed, he had too much to think about and process. He simply nodded and stood up, thanked Leonard for his time and went downstairs to wait for his driver. Once the driver arrived and again led by his security, who had been waiting for him at the outside door of the building, he made his way to the car rushing past the few photographers and reporters that were there waiting for him to come out. He jumped in and gave the driver his destination. When the driver heard where he wanted to go, he actually turned to look at the security agent, who simply shrugged.

◆

They made their way through downtown traffic to the GIC building, where once again they had to make their way through the media stationed outside, although there were not that many at that hour. He was surprised by how much time he had spent at Leonard's building. Once inside, Steven went to the man sitting at the information desk, who put down the paper he'd been reading and stood up as soon as he realized who it was.

Steven smiled at the man, "Ernie, how's it going?"

Ernie, a little flustered by the media outside and by the bear of a man accompanying Loomis, gave him a tentative smile back, "Mr. Loomis, I…"

Steven raised his hand and tried to put the man at ease, "How's Collette and the baby?"

Now a little more confident Ernie's smile broadened, "Fine, Mr. Loomis, fine. Hey, thanks a lot for the basket, my wife loved all those bath salts and lotions."

Steven, now standing in front of the massive marble desk Ernie was sitting behind, just nodded, "Don't mention it. It was just some things Beth thought she might like. Listen, Ernie, I know this is going to sound a bit out of the ordinary, but is there access to the roof of the building?"

Steven knew there was, but he wanted Ernie to feel like he was doing his job, "Jeez, Mr. Loomis, there is, but it's just for the maintenance folks. You know how it is, they're afraid some asshole might just decide to take a swan dive."

Steven nodded and leaned closer to Ernie, gesturing with his hand for him to move closer, and spoke in a low conspiratorial tone, "I know, Ernie, but you've seen what it's like out there. Fucking media everywhere. I just want a few minutes for myself, with no one around, you can understand that, can't you?"

Ernie nodded thoughtfully.

He had seen the ever-present throngs of reporters and photographers outside, "I can, Mr. Loomis, but I don't know, you know, it could mean my job."

Steven looked at him, still leaning over the big desk, "I know, Ernie, and that's why I'm asking as a favor. I just want to get my head together and just think, and everywhere I go everyone wants to know how I feel and to tell me they understand. And that's fine, for a while, but a man needs to think sometimes, just think without all the other bullshit. Listen, I'll only be up there 15 minutes. You can time me if you want. I would really appreciate it, man."

Ernie thought about it for a minute and then finally smiled, "Alright, you got it, but just 15 minutes, right?" Steven nodded.

Ernie called out to the other security guard on duty who was standing by the elevators, "Hey, Tony, I'm taking fifteen, watch the desk, alright?"

Tony held up a thumbs-up.

Ernie looked down at his console and pushed a couple of buttons, "Alright, the freight elevator goes up to the roof. You'll need this card to push the button to the roof. Once you get there, the code is 19943 and then the pound sign."

Steven took the card and walked around the main elevators down a short corridor and found the freight elevator. He pushed the button and waited along with his security for the elevator.

Once the elevator got to the lobby, Steven stepped in and when his security agent went to follow, he put his hand up, "Not this time, Lou, I'm taking this ride alone."

When the agent started to protest, Steven held up his hand, "Uh-uh, not this time, Lou, my ass, my building, my decision."

Lou thought about it briefly, nodded and took a position next to the elevator.

Before the door shut, Steven reassured him, "Don't worry, just need some alone time. I'll be back in fifteen."

He made his way to the roof and used the passkey to open the door. In all the time he had been at this office, Steven had never made it up on the roof. He didn't know what had possessed him to come up here, it just seemed like a good place to come and think and take in the crisp New York air and the sun coming up. He looked over at the railing overlooking Madison Avenue. He walked over to it and looked out over the city. Once he got over the initial vertigo, he enjoyed the view.

When he had first gotten to New York, he had wondered what all the fuss was about. People were not very friendly, most were outright rude, and they always seemed to be in a hurry to get someplace. He gripped the railing and took a few deep breaths, trying not to think about anything specific. He marveled at the enormity of the city. Down on Wall Street, fortunes were made and lost in the blink of an eye. People put their trust and their life savings in others' hands, men who would convince them that what they were doing was safe, and they were often rewarded with the loss of everything they had saved. Nature's perpetual dynamic of predator and prey was alive and well, even in this completely man-made, technological jungle.

But now he was aware that a different game was afoot and he had become a player in it. He had come upon it by chance and now he knew that he did not yet understand the extent of it. Leonard's last words and the look on his face had shaken Steven to the core. The man was a researcher, a scientist that looked at everything through the proverbial microscope of science, and he had looked afraid. Nothing Steven had been through, not even the warehouse, had cut through him the way Leonard had. Nobody else he had talked to about this had Leonard's background, his experience, and even though his interests were scientific, he understood the danger that these things posed to humanity. He understood it not as some experiment gone horribly wrong, but as what he considered to be the next logical step in purely Darwinian evolution.

The reason his visit to Leonard had had this effect on him was the videos he had seen and the conversation they had right before he left. Throughout this entire ordeal, Steven had been thinking about and dealing with adults – Riche, Barlow and even those whose names he did not know. As much as he had learned about this science, as much as he had read about these creatures, he had always envisioned adults. It was difficult to think about everything he was going through in the context of children. Children were innocent. They were at the mercy of those around them, their parents or others charged with taking care of them. So when they later became thieves or rapists or murderers, most of the time one could look back at those who had cared for them and raised them and see why it was that they turned out the way they did. That was how things were supposed to work: children grew to reflect the care and love, or the lack thereof, that they were given when they were growing up.

What Steven had seen today let him know that perhaps that was how *human* children worked, how humanity had evolved over time. He had seen that human babies, babies too young to be affected by the outside world, were born good, with a sense of fairness and altruism that had to be innate because they were too young to be taught. He watched as babies helped a stranger, even at a cost to themselves. But he also saw the other side of that coin. He saw babies observe and calculate and decide that whatever it was the adult was after must have some value. They didn't know what a pen was or what its value could possibly be, but that didn't matter, what mattered was that it had a value and therefore they wanted it. Some babies, young toddlers really, had actually used a toy they were playing with to strike the other child and then take the pen. Some showed delight when the other child began crying. It was innocuous enough, there was no grand gesture, nor was there some sort of punishment for those that did not do things correctly. It was the basic scenario of a predator observing its prey, making calculations in how to strike and finally moving in.

It had disturbed the researchers immensely, but, as Leonard had explained, their experiments were to delve into the goodness, the sense of sharing and cooperation that human babies were born with, so they just made a footnote about the other children's behavior. It had been Leonard who had sifted through all of it and compiled all of the video from the various studies, some from England, some from France and some from Germany, where researchers actually also took an interest in those other children and where Leonard had explained some of the most advanced research on the science that was being done. More than anything else he had witnessed or learned until now, that scared Steven Loomis to the core, because it truly meant that these beings were born that way and no amount of love or nurturing or care was going to change them.

Leonard had also pointed out something subtle that Steven had missed, but which was chilling to watch once he noticed it. In almost every one of those instances, the children doing the preying were much more agile and coordinated than the other child, who was the same age, gender and general size. They moved with more ease, with none of the clumsy struggle of a small toddler getting up and moving. Their pace was more determined and direct. Again it was all very subtle, but after once seeing those minute physical differences over all the studies it was hard to miss. Leonard had hypothesized that, although he had no way to verify it, those children's cognitive capacity was even more advanced than what they displayed.

The last video he had shown Steven had been of a simple auditory test designed to test the hearing range and capacity of 13 of those children. The sample was far too small to provide workable data, but it was definitely indicative of clear physiological and sensory differences. He had devised a test where children were shown a cardboard screen covering a cupcake, then a bell rang and the screen lifted to show the cupcake several times, and the children were allowed to eat some of the cupcake each time. Then the child was asked to turn around away from the cupcake, and when the bell rang they could turn around and get their treat. This continued with the bell reducing in volume each time until it was completely out of their hearing range and so they did not turn around. Every one of the 'human' children stopped hearing the bell within just a few decibels of one another. Some heard it for longer than others, but none could hear it past a certain point.

He did the same thing with the 'target' children, as he had dubbed them, and the differences were astounding. Every one of them could hear the bell at a level that none of the other 'human' children could. He explained that aside from showing clear sensory abilities the other children did not have, they also, once again, made connections, studied the situation and made the determination that they could get the treat without having to wait to hear the bell. What seemed to concern Leonard the most about all of this was that in every instance these 'target' children had parents who loved and doted on them as any parent would with their baby. He theorized that those emotions, the care they might be given, the love and support they would grow up surrounded by, might ultimately teach them how to be better hunters, how to mimic those feelings in order to get whatever they were after.

Leonard looked as scared as he did because he understood better than most the type of threat these beings posed. He had dedicated his life to researching them, but he had done it from behind a figurative glass, not really thinking of them as his neighbor or his mailman or one of his students. And now that Steven had done what he had done, Leonard had no choice but to see them as people he was living among, perhaps much closer than he imagined.

As Leonard had stood to bid him goodbye, there was a sense of urgency in his voice of some sort of timeline looming that Steven didn't quite understand.

Leonard had said something rather cryptic when he bid Steven goodbye, "Technology, Mr. Loomis, has kept us alive until now, but these beings, these predators know that and they will use it. Psychopaths troll the Internet for victims, but that is not where the true danger lies. My most fervent hope is that the attention you've brought to this, to the science, will be enough to warn the world.

"What you've done, Mr. Loomis, Steven, is to simply ask the United States legal system to legally define what a human being is.

Actually, you're going to be asking 12 of your peers, ordinary people, to do that. Whatever happens from here, what will not change is that the question has been asked. No matter what the verdict is, the world will keep asking the question, wondering whether this is real or not. I hope that will be enough."

Steven sensed there was something he was missing, something big just under the surface, but as had been the case many times before, he found he simply could not go deeper, not until his trial was over.

Steven turned his head, taking in the towering skyline, thinking about how New York had a way of growing on you. It had on him. He also thought about other places, other cities, each with their own charm, each with their own peculiarity and each with their own danger. He wasn't some kind of hero, some kind of savior ready to take on all the villains out there. He was just a man who loved his family and his job and wanted nothing more than to go back to both. But sometimes the fates had other plans, sometimes even when you didn't want to, you could be pulled into a life you had never imagined.

He remembered a time when he had been watching a show about lions on the National Geographic channel and Tracy had cuddled up with him. It had been just under a year ago and he had wondered then whether she might be too young to watch the show with him but decided that she was old enough to watch nature unfold. He kept glancing down at her on his chest and paid particularly close attention when the images of the lionesses in the pride hunting down a young, injured impala appeared on the screen. She had watched silently and when it was done, she lifted her head from his chest and asked him why lions were so mean. He explained about nature and the cycle of life and how the lionesses had to feed their own babies, too, and that in nature that meant that bigger animals would sometimes have to hunt and eat smaller ones. She laid her head back down on his chest, clearly thinking about what her father had told her and lifted her head a few minutes later to let him know she understood. Just simply that, she understood. He gripped the railing tighter, hit hard by the irony of the memory.

These things, whatever they were, did not see what they did as evil or depraved, it was just their nature, what they were made to do, just like he had told his daughter about the lions. Now, in the grip of his memory, he wondered with no small sense of irony what the impalas he had watched with his daughter would think about the lions hunting them. He had an idea now, they might think them cruel and cold and evil, as his daughter had thought they were. But the truth was that in the African prairies where the impala lived, the lions were apex predators, nothing more and nothing less.

His old life, the one he had procured for himself and his family, had gone the day Tracy had disappeared. He could have let it go and moved on to mourn his daughter and to pick up the pieces of his life, but that's just not how he was built. If he hadn't known it then, he certainly knew it now. What he had learned and what he had done had been nothing more than the primer, the trigger for what was about to come. Time would tell what his life would ultimately turn into, but right now he was enjoying the view from the top of his building and, just for a little while, just being a man.

As he stood gripping the railing and breathing in the cool morning air, Steven Loomis felt ready. There would be much more that he would have to face, that he would have to figure his way through, but his family was taken care of and his people were behind him. As someone who had faced death countless times, he knew these two things were what most often pulled a man through. As he started to head back to the door to go back down to the lobby and to think about the rest of his day, it hit him. He knew what it was that had been just under the surface, just out of his reach. It wasn't something he had been working up to or eased into, it came fast and hard, and it almost knocked the breath out of him. He now understood what Leonard had been so cryptic about, what he had been trying to tell Steven without actually saying it.

He now knew why Scoma had almost shut down and why Leonard had looked so haunted. He knew why Leonard had that sense of urgency in his voice. He thought he understood the gravity, the enormity of the threat humanity faced, and now he also knew Barlow had been right, he hadn't understood how far and how deep this went. He now remembered the paper he had seen that Scoma and Leonard had written together. Just as both scientists had explained, it was a paper about grouping behavior and how prey used it to defend against superior predators. It also explained how humanity had used it to survive, to defend itself against all predators, just like Leonard had told him. The focus of the paper was on the threat to these defensive mechanisms, how advanced or sophisticated predators understood these mechanisms and devised ways to defeat them, often turning these very defenses against their prey. What knocked Steven's breath out of him and brought his heart up into his throat was the specific topic of the paper, what was in fact on the title: *Homo sapiens predaer and Social Media.*

Chapter 25

After spending just under 15 minutes on the roof, Steven headed down the way he had come. Once he reached the lobby, his security guard fell in behind him. He walked over to Ernie, who was eagerly waiting for him to get back, "Thanks, Ernie, I appreciate it." Ernie smiled, clearly relieved, "No problem, Mr. L, I think there's some people that want to talk to you." Steven followed Ernie's gaze and saw that the media was now awake and present. The building's security had kept them from coming into the lobby, but they were three and four deep on the sidewalk. Steven shook his head, "Fucking vultures. I can't believe how many are out there." Ernie also shaking his head added, "That's nothing, Mr. L, just wait until lunch time, that's when they really get rowdy."

Steven had no intention to wait for that to happen, "Lou, call the car. Tell him to just pull in front of the building and wait there for us." Lou did as he was told and started toward the door, walking in front of Steven and ready to plow a path to the car if necessary. As Steven started toward the door, Ernie called out to him, "Hey, Mr. Loomis, I almost forgot!" Steven stopped as Ernie came around and trotted toward him with something in his hand, "A lady came by yesterday and left this for you. She said to give it to you in person, that's why I didn't send it to you by courier like other times. She said to just toss it if you didn't come in by this afternoon."

Steven took the sealed envelope with nothing written on the outside. He opened it and was truly taken aback by what he found in it. A printed note read: 'MEET ME AT BRUNO'S BISTRO. I WILL BE THERE UNTIL 3:00 PM ON WEDNESDAY. COME ALONE OR NOT AT ALL.' Steven had absolutely no idea who the person could possibly be. A reporter trying to get an interview maybe? But why the time limit? And why all the cloak-and-dagger crap?

He turned to Ernie, who was still standing there, clearly curious about the note, "What did she look like, Ernie? Was she old, young, what can you remember about her?" Ernie thought for a few seconds, "She was dressed pretty nice, you know, like in a business suit, nice watch, nice shoes, I don't know what brand they were or anything but, you know, you can tell they were some expensive shoes, nice watch too, a Rolex. She wasn't old, but she also wasn't too young or anything, you know, she was like your age, no offense or nothin'. She was looker, though, real sexy-like." Steven smiled, "None taken, anything else you can tell me?"

Ernie looked up at the ceiling, trying to remember anything else, "Hmm, let me think, yeah! She had like an accent, like she was from Europe or somethin'. I don't really know what kind of accent it was, but I know it wasn't a Spanish accent, my girlfriend is Puerto Rican and I know a Spanish accent, believe me." Steven, still trying to figure out who the note could have possibly come from, asked a final question, "Have you told anyone about the note, Ernie?" Ernie took on a puzzled look, "Uh, no, Mr. L, I didn't, was I supposed to?" Steven shook his head, "No, Ernie, not at all. Hey, do me a favor and keep this between us, alright?" Ernie smiled, "No prob, Mr. L, can do." Ernie headed back to his post and Steven stood in the middle of the lobby trying to figure out who the author of the note could be. It didn't take him long to figure out that it was definitely nobody he knew. No one in his family or professional circle would contact him in this way. Who then?

As Steven sat in the lobby thinking, Lou was already at the door and bracing himself to plow past the reporters blocking his way to the SUV waiting at the curb, "Hey, Mr. Loomis, the driver's here, we need to go." Steven looked over, nodded and got on his way. He had been lax in his personal security protocols before his encounter with Barlow, but now the old instincts kicked in. As he was walking behind Lou, he tensed his body and prepared to respond to anything that looked out of place, ready to engage immediately if he sensed something amiss. He walked firmly to the open car door, using leverage and pressure to move those that were impeding his progress out of the way. He didn't shove or push anyone, but he was firm in his handling of them as he made his way to the waiting car.

Once inside, with Lou sitting in the front seat, Steven resumed his thinking. He had already come to the conclusion that it had not been a reporter trying to get a story or someone he knew personally or professionally. He was completely at a loss as to who it could be. The note had said 'until 3:00 PM' and to 'come alone.' Could it be Barlow? No, Steven reasoned, Barlow was most likely on his way to wherever his next destination was, he had already delivered the message he needed to deliver. Who then? Steven had been tempted to simply ignore the message and go to his attorneys' offices to begin preparations for his trial. He knew that was the smart thing to do, but he could not help his curiosity. Whoever had left the note wanted to speak with him and wanted to do so in a place that would be private and away from the eyes of the media, his attorneys and his family.

Bruno's was a well-known mafia hangout in Little Italy. It had been the scene of multiple hits during the '70s and '80s and was still considered to be a dangerous place for anyone who didn't belong there. The note had said to be there before three, before the dinner crowd, which meant the place would most likely be deserted, except for those who had business to transact there. All of that told Steven that whoever it was who left the note was either a member of the mafia or had some serious connections to the mafia. Neither of those options made any sense, however. Steven had never had occasion to deal with or even come close to dealing with anyone connected to the New York mafia. He knew the smart thing to do was to ignore the note, but he decided that whoever had left the note might have some information or some message that might prove valuable. It was still early and he would have more than enough time to head to his lawyers' offices afterwards.

Drew's calls hadn't started yet, so he had an hour to go to Bruno's. His driver had been heading to the law offices, so when Steven told him where he wanted to go, the man had looked first in the rearview mirror and then at Lou sitting next to him. Lou simply shrugged his shoulders and the car changed directions and headed to Little Italy. When they got to Bruno's Bistro, Steven gave his driver and security instructions to stay in the car.

Lou seemed uneasy with the idea, "Mr. Loomis, I don't think that's such a good idea."

Steven knew Lou was just doing his job and that he didn't know what the note said, but the note asked for him to come alone, and while going in alone might be a bad idea, going in with Lou was a worse idea. Still, he tried to reassure him, "Don't worry, Lou, I won't be long. I doubt anyone is going to try anything here, they tend to frown on people trying anything that hasn't been sanctioned."

Steven knew Lou had been a cop with the organized crime squad, so he was well aware of what went on at Bruno's, and he knew Steven was right, other than a rival group trying to pull off a hit, this was a well-guarded place. The new mafia had morphed into an even more businesslike organization, engaging in cyber theft, massive pirating operations, and massive counterfeiting operations of brand-name handbags, shoes and anything else that might turn a profit. The days of hijacking trucks, stealing containers of cigarettes, and extortion of local businesses were a thing of the past for the old New York mob and more the purview of the Russian gangs.

Steven walked up to the door of the restaurant and saw there were a few people inside. One man was behind a long bar, obviously stocking its shelves, while another one was mopping the floor. Along with the two men working, there were two other men, one sitting at the bar reading a newspaper and the other sitting at a table near the door with an espresso next to him and seemingly enthralled by a crossword puzzle. The two men sitting were most definitely not restaurant employees. Both were wearing expensive suits rather than aprons. As he expected, the sign on the door said CLOSED. When he got near the door, the man sitting at the table close to it stood up, walked over and opened it before he could knock.

He looked Steven up and down with a frown on his face, "Yeah?"

Steven wasn't sure how to respond, so he simply pulled the note from his breast pocket, "Someone left a note asking for me to come here, so here I am."

Without saying anything, the man motioned with his head for Steven to come inside and closed the door after him. Once inside, he started to frisk Steven.

Steven took a step back, "Whoa there, I'm armed, big guy, and I'm not giving you my gun."

The crossword guy tried to step forward while the man sitting at the bar was now standing and moving toward Steven, who shifted his body in order to address both men. The two men paused in their movement, both of them considering what to do next. Although they did not know Steven, his face and his background had been reported almost around the clock in every medium imaginable. Both men were accustomed to most people yielding to their physical size and their threatening countenance, but Steven wasn't most people, he was an experienced former Navy SEAL and both men knew the reputation of the SEALs.

Before the situation could get any more heated, a woman appeared from a side hallway that led to a small private dining room next to the main dining room, "Paul, Sonny, it is okay, he is not going to cause any problems."

The two men looked at each other, gave Steven an angry, reproachful look and went back to their respective posts. Steven walked over to where the woman was standing. Before he could get all the way to where she stood, she turned and walked back to a small booth in the side dining room with Steven close behind her. Once they were both seated, Steven got a good look at the stranger. There was something faintly familiar about her, but even after he had scoured his memory he was still coming up blank.

The woman smiled, "Still cannot figure out who I am? Maybe you would have better luck if I were carrying a few packages."

Steven grinned, "That's where I know you from. That's why you looked vaguely familiar."

The woman's smile broadened, "I am impressed you thought I looked familiar, I took some pretty extreme measures to change my appearance."

Steven gave her a thin smile in return, "It's your walk. You have a unique gait. You did a good job, though. You didn't look familiar until I saw you walk just now."

She nodded thoughtfully, "I will have to remember that next time."

The woman sitting in front of him was slender, most likely in her early to mid-40s, with auburn hair down to her shoulders, and a handsome face with an olive complexion that gave her a Mediterranean look. She had brown eyes that could be mistaken for black in dim light. She moved with an easy and fluid grace that conveyed confidence, strength and training. The woman he had run into on the sidewalk was clumsy and awkward in her movements. The woman spoke with a very subtle accent, most likely Middle Eastern, but definitely not Arabic, which made her either Israeli or Persian.

She sensed him trying to figure out who she really was and decided to give him a clue, "This is nothing like the Mazar-i-Sharif, is it, Steven?"

By mentioning that site, she let Loomis know she had read some of the most confidential files on him, something definitely not easy to do. Barlow had let him know he had access to those records and here was the proof.

Although more relaxed now, Steven was still uncomfortable with the meeting and wanted to get on with whatever she had in mind. "Listen, I don't know what it is you want, but your boss already gave me his message. I got it, alright, I got it. I'd just like to get on with my case and back to my family, so you can let him know he's clear, I have no interest in whatever it is he's doing."

She cocked her head as she listened, the coquettish smile still on her face. When he finished, her smile widened, "I do not want anything, Mr. Loomis, and he is not my boss. He is a client, a good client. He calls when he needs my type of services and he pays incredibly well. I asked you here out of professional courtesy."

Steven chuckled, "Professional courtesy? So you asked me here out of the goodness of your heart, because you were worried about me? Come on, now, you can do better than that."

She looked at him, smile gone from her face, "Frankly, I do not care whether you believe me, I asked you here because I saw the operations you have been involved in and I know you have a family. I know what it is like to have a family you love and to have to split your life in order to engage in the types of operations we have to engage in. And I know of loss."

Steven's eyes narrowed, "*We* have to engage in? What exactly are you talking about? What types of operations have you engaged in?"

She pulled out a cigarette and lit it. Steven waved his hand at the smoke and saw an opening to get more information, "Why are we meeting here?"

She took another drag from her cigarette and blew the smoke at the ceiling, "A close friend and client owns this place, so I am allowed certain…considerations. Look, Mr. Loomis, I have no intention of sparring with you. I asked you here because I truly do not believe you know what you have gotten yourself into. I know Barlow spoke to you, and I have no doubt that by now you have done some digging of your own and you know he is much more than what he appears, but I do not think you understand the full weight of what you have stumbled into.

"Barlow has been doing his work for decades and has developed a network of resources and allies that rival some official intelligence services. He has a stable of contractors, such as myself, who are called in to do a specific job and then sent on their way. Only he knows his full objective or the reasons for engaging the contractors.

"He contacted me last week, flew me in, provided only the necessary information on my target, you, and gave me a task to complete. The shot I gave you was a combination of fentanyl and zolpidem that he put together. Once I completed my task, I went to a locker at the train station and picked up my payment. That is how every one of my previous assignments has worked. But this was different, your situation, the deal at the courthouse and what happened with your daughter made it different."

Steven listened carefully. It made sense, in order for Barlow to be able to keep his work private he had to compartmentalize every aspect of what he did. Still, the woman was obviously a trained operative and such people were careful about who they worked for.

There was no way that she had no inkling as to what he was up to, "I see, so he just gives you instructions, lets you know where to pick up your money, and off you ride into the sunset, completely oblivious as to what he does. Is that pretty much it?"

He had asked the question with a tone that could not be interpreted as anything but sarcasm. She looked directly at him, pondering what to answer.

They were both professionals and she knew lying or holding back would be useless, "No, I said that is how he likes to conduct business, I did not say that I did not do some of my own research. Before you ask, I do not know what it is he does, *exactly*. I have my suspicions based on what I have found and on some of the things I have seen.

"That is what I am willing to share with you, and I am willing to do that because, in spite of what you may think, I do have respect for the things you have done and because of what happened with your daughter. I am a professional, just like you, but even I have some lines I am not willing to cross."

Steven, now more attentive, responded, "So you are here out of what…concern? As a professional courtesy you said, right? That's what you said, right, professional courtesy?"

The sarcasm was not as marked, but it was still present in his tone.

She ignored it, "Call it what you want, I simply want to be able to tell myself that I did what I thought was right. Look, Loomis, the man has connections you would not believe – senators, congressmen, judges, highly placed agents at the FBI and the CIA. Some are his patients, he is something of a celebrity therapist among the elite. His practice is only made up of people that have been referred directly to him; he does not take any patients without a referral from another of his patients or contacts. He meets with them at odd hours, whether it is for a therapy session or something else, only he knows. Sometimes he meets with more than one person, but never with more than three.

"He is constantly on the move and has offices here in New York, in Los Angeles, Vail, Dallas and Chicago, and the time he spends in those places depends on who he is seeing. He also has a facility in Switzerland and another in Australia. He is incredibly well funded, and I mean *well* funded. With high-powered patients who look to him as something of a messiah, there is never a shortage of fundraising dinners.

"He has a foundation that he heads, but no one knows what it really does. I know that there are geneticists, physicists, anthropologists and biologists employed by the foundation, but what they do nobody knows. He has positioned it as a foundation dedicated to the better understanding of the human brain, but he never presents any details about what it does. Every single file relating to his work in any way is encrypted. I know you work in intelligence and security and that you know what the cutting edge of encryption technology is, but what he uses goes far beyond anything you have dealt with. Offshoots of the Shnorr signature and El-Gamal systems, stuff that hasn't even been sniffed by the NSA."

He raised his eyebrows and shook his head. She was right, he had no idea of what he had uncovered. The meeting with Barlow had brought him closer, but what this woman was saying brought it home. His only experience with the new species had been Riche and to a certain extent Barlow himself, but he had to concede the point that even though Barlow had hinted at the enormity of what he had stirred up, Steven had been unable to fathom that it went as far as this. Riche had been one individual, one predator engaged in horrible and sadistic behavior. Even so, he had single-handedly destroyed multiple families, not only here in New York but in some of the other places where he had been hunting to hone his skills. But if they were senators, judges, CEOs and, God forbid, people in high-ranking military positions – what kind of destruction and mayhem could they cause? How many lives could they destroy?

She saw that he was mulling over what she had just said and was trying to put it into perspective, "Do not try to make any sense of it, you will not. I have tried and it is just not possible. The man keeps everything he does completely secure."

He shook his head, "You work for Barlow and you know all of this, but you don't know exactly what he does? Sorry, but I don't buy it."

She smiled and stubbed out her cigarette, "Whether you buy it or not is not my concern, I just wanted to let you know what you have gotten yourself into."

Steven had already spent more time at the restaurant than he wanted to, "I don't know why it is that you and Barlow keep referring to 'what I've gotten myself into.' I haven't gotten myself 'into' anything. I took out my daughter's killer because I believed he was something other than human and I wanted to bring attention to the science, to give some meaning to her death, that's it. I'm not a defender of the weak or an avenging hero; I did what I did because of my daughter, that's it." The woman chuckled softly and cocked her head to the side as she had done before, "Oh, Mr. Loomis, you really believe that, you really think this is just about Riche and your daughter."

Steven now took on a more intense demeanor, "Yes, that's what I believe because that's reality, that's what motivated me to do what I did." The woman returned the intense look, "I have no doubt that is what made you shoot Riche and do the research you did, unfortunately for you; however, you stumbled onto something way beyond what you were expecting and that is why Barlow took an interest in you. I do not want to waste my time with you arguing about what you believe or do not believe. I wanted to meet with you out of professional courtesy, if you want to call it that, and because I believed, and now you have proven to me, that you really do not get what you have involved yourself in. I have done what I wanted to do, warn you about Barlow and the people he is associated with, so I believe our time together is up."

Steven shook his head, "Wait a minute, what do you mean professional courtesy, who the hell do you work for? I'm planning on just focusing on my trial and trying to get back to my family." She nodded, "I have no doubt of that, Mr. Loomis, but they will not let you simply go back to your life. Now that the world knows what you have found, those who *are* in fact part of what you have discovered will come knocking. Maybe they will not do it today or in a week or even a month, but trust me on this, they will come sooner or later, and if your family happens to be in their way they will not hesitate, not for a second. As to who I work for, I am a freelancer, Mr. Loomis, I think you already know that, and I am a professional, which means if I take a job I will do it and do it well, but I have limits, and involving someone's family is something I will not do."

As she finished speaking, Steven saw her pendant for the first time, a Star of David hung around her neck. He began to suspect she had probably worked for Mossad, the Israeli intelligence service, before going out on her own. She went on, "Barlow pays exceedingly well and he has access to very good talent, all the usual suspects, Delta, SEALs, SAS..."

Steven interrupted her, "Mossad?" She gave him a small smile and touched her pendant, "Even if I were, do you think I would tell you?" Steven shook his head, "You don't have to. So what is it you'd have me do? I have a trial coming up, and if you haven't noticed, the entire world is completely focused on my every move, so what exactly do you think I should be doing?"

She leaned forward, her elbows on the table, "You said it yourself, just concentrate on your trial, no more research or trying to dig into Barlow or anybody else. I know you are already doing that, but as soon as you are able to, you should try and send your family somewhere safe, somewhere where you can protect them from anything."

Now it was Steven who leaned forward, with a menacing look on his face, "Are you saying my family is in danger? That there's someone coming after them? Is that what you're trying to tell me?!" The two men in the main dining room got up from their respective seats and started toward the side dining room. She lifted her hand without breaking eye contact with Steven and both men sat back down. "No, Mr. Loomis, I am not telling you that anyone is after your family, I do not know whether that is the case or not. What I am telling you, have been telling you since we sat down, is that there are a lot of people out there that are very interested in you and your case, and you know that I do not mean interested like the rest of the world is interested. I was not lying when I told you that I do not know exactly what it is that Barlow does, but I do know whatever it is brings death and destruction wherever he goes. Not in huge numbers, not like a war or a famine, it is more subtle than that. Wherever he goes, people start locking their windows, holding their children tighter, streets once crowded soon go quiet. It is not noticeable, you see, unless you have followed him and noticed a pattern, and only people like us, Mr. Loomis, people 'in the business' as it were, notice those kinds of patterns. Is it too farfetched to think that there could be those out there who might come looking for you, for your family? Who might think that in some way you are talking about them when you talk about a new species? I know there is no way you have not thought about that before now. I am just trying to tell you that those things that you are concerned about might just be closer than you think."

She was right and Steven knew it. He had in fact thought about others that might be out there, but he had come to the conclusion that he couldn't do anything about them. There was only one that Loomis was concerned with, "I told you, I spoke to Barlow and he told me he'd stay away if I kept out of his business and I intend on doing just that. I have more than enough on my plate to worry about him." She shook her head, "Did you not just hear what I said? It is not Barlow you need to worry about. I agree with you, if you steer clear he will leave you alone, but he is just one person."

Steven had had enough, "Well, there's nothing I can do about others coming after me, is there?! If they're going to come, they're going to come, no matter what. I have people in place, but you and I both know that if someone is willing to sacrifice themselves, there's no way to stop them."

She nodded, "That is right, but I do not think anyone will be sacrificing themselves to get to you. These people, Barlow and those around him, do not do what they do out of a sense of duty or in pursuit of a cause. You have read about them, it is what your whole argument is based on. They are predators, predators with vast resources and connections and in positions of power whose ultimate purpose is to prey on others. I just wanted to leave New York with a clean conscience, and now I can. I advise you to send your family somewhere safe, somewhere you know and where they know you." She gave this last warning while holding Steven's eyes directly.

He knew what she was talking about; she was saying he should get his family out of the country and to somewhere familiar where he had people he could count on. Steven could think of a few places like that. Over his career he had visited hundreds of cities all around the world and he had made more friends than enemies, so there were plenty of places he could think of. The problem, and it would be a huge problem, would be convincing Beth to leave. He needed to think things over, but he was thankful to this woman for the warning, "Thanks, I do appreciate it, Ms. ...? The woman's smile reappeared on her face, "You can just call me Diana. And you are welcome. Good luck to you, Mr. Loomis." Steven nodded and got up from the booth.

He got back in the car and told the driver to head to his lawyers' offices.

On the way, he gave more thought to what Diana had said, 'send your family somewhere safe.' It stood to reason that if she had done the job for Barlow, she knew Beth was in New York and the rest of his family was in Vermont. The media made sure his location, as well as his family's, was known by all and she obviously did not think they were any safer in Vermont than they would be in New York. As he thought about the situation more carefully, he realized that the intensity of the media attention would actually help to keep his family safe. Whoever or whatever came for them would have a virtually impossible time going unnoticed. Still, she was right, if Barlow or someone like Barlow, someone with the kinds of resources she had mentioned, wanted to get to him or his family bad enough, there was no way he would be able to stop them, not with the trial going on and the eyes of the world on him.

Well, he couldn't do anything about the trial, but he damn well could do something about putting his family somewhere safe. Beth would just have to understand, he would make her understand, but to do that he was going to have to tell her everything, and he was truly at a loss about what she might do. He also knew that with all of this, with everything he had learned from Diana, he would have to tell the General. Damn, he hated being put in a position where he really had no choice, where he *had* to do something. Being a successful Special Forces officer meant having options, backup plans to backup plans, and right now he really felt like he did not have very many options, not options that made sense anyway.

As they pulled up in front of the building, Steven was once again completely blown away by the number of cameras and reporters in front of the building. Every time he thought there simply could not be any more, more appeared. The driver drove into the garage where security was situated in order to keep adventurous reporters from following the car into the parking garage. As soon as Steven got out of the elevator, Drew was already there, "Damn it, Steven, pick up the goddamned phone once in a while, will you?" Steven gave him a half smile, he was used to Drew's tantrums, "Alright, I will, but Drew, it's not even eleven. I wanted to sleep in today, alright?" Drew, now joined by Max and Ray, smiled, "Yeah, right, you know that's bullshit. I called your house and talked to Beth, she said you'd been gone since before she woke up." Steven, now smiling more broadly, headed to where he knew the coffee was brewing, "Alright already, you got me. I just wanted a few minutes to myself, just to get away from all of this for a while, okay?"

Now, with all four men in the coffee room, it was Max who spoke up, "I think we can all appreciate wanting some time alone, Steven, but with everything that's happened, you can't just disappear, you know what I mean? From this point forward, we all have to be like one, working together, strategizing, everything. If we are going to sell this argument, we all have to be on point all the time, okay?" Steven hung his head, "You're right, you're right, there's no excuse. It's just that sometimes I feel like every single little thing I do is blown up, analyzed and dissected, and I just wanted to breathe a little, but I will not disappear again, you have my word."

The four men walked into Max's office. Drew and Steven sat on the sofa in the room and Max and Ray sat in front of Max's desk in two chairs turned to face the sofa. Ray leaned forward, "So, Steven, we've been strategizing and we've decided that we're going to defer our opening statement in the trial." He let that hang in the air, expecting some sort of response from Steven, but getting none. Steven looked from Ray to Drew to Max, "I'm not quite sure what that means, guys. You need to give me a clue here." Drew explained, "At the beginning of the trial, each side gets to give an opening statement where each side explains what they will be looking to prove to the jury. The prosecution goes first and then the defense. That's how it normally goes, but every once in a while, the defense will hold their opening argument until after the prosecution presents their case. We think that's what we should do here, let the prosecution present their case and then we make our opening argument."

Steven nodded, "Okay, if that's what you guys think is best." Ray spoke up, "We do. I mean, think about it, when the prosecution presents their case, what is it that they'll be presenting? What *can* they present? The who and how are already well established, so they'll be simply trying to convince the jury about the why." Max went on, "It's true, all they will be able to argue is the why, but it will still be an uphill battle for us. I can guarantee you that they will move on with the argument that you did what you did in a fit of rage after learning about what happened to your daughter, and it will most definitely be a battle to convince the jury otherwise. They're human beings, Steven, and they will be thinking about how they themselves would react if one of their children suffered the same fate."

Steven was listening to his lawyers and trying to understand the subtle legal maneuvering they were making reference to, but it was hard to do so after his meeting with Diana. Still, what Max had just shared seemed like it would bode well for him, not against him, "Well, isn't that a good thing? I mean, don't we want the jury to feel sympathy for me?"

Now Drew jumped in, "Yes and no. We want them to feel for you, for what happened to you, but we don't want them putting themselves in your place, because if they do they will come to the conclusion that you probably did what you did out of revenge. That's what they would have done in your place. You have to understand, Steven, most people are not former Special Forces operators and senior executives at security firms. They do not have the self-control and deliberation that you have. Most of them are just regular people with regular jobs and regular lives, and those kinds of people would not have undertaken everything you did when your daughter went missing. They can relate to losing your mind and shooting your daughter's murderer because of grief, anger, revenge any one of the expected human emotions after experiencing something like this because that's exactly what they might have done. Our task is to convince those people that it was none of those things that drove you to do this, that you did what you did because of what you found in your research and that, Steven, is going to definitely be an uphill battle. We have to convince 12 people that Donald Riche was not a human being, that he was a part of the species you read about. In other words we will be asking them to put aside everything they've known about the human race and to accept that there is now a species higher on the food chain than humans."

Ray spoke up again, "That's not quite accurate, Drew, we need to convince these people that Riche *could have been* one of these things, which means that what we really have to work on is convincing them the species is real, that it exists. If we do that, then moving them into believing Riche could have been one of them becomes doable." Max was nodding, "That's right, and the way we are going to convince these 12 people that you didn't do this out of revenge or rage is by having you explain that if that had been your motivation, you could have done it and gotten away with it."

Steven was taken aback by this, "Wait, are you serious?! You want me to testify that if I wanted to, I could have gotten away with it?! That doesn't sound like something you'd want someone accused of murder saying, especially to the jury." Max leaned in, "You're right, in any other murder trial it would be crazy for a defendant to say that, but you have to, Steven, you absolutely have to. Think about it, how else are we going to convince these 12 people that you didn't do this out of revenge? The way we do that is by convincing them that if it had been revenge you wanted you could have killed Riche and walked away. You had an iron-clad alibi and the world was glad to see him go, so most likely you would have gotten away with it. That's true, isn't it, if you had wanted revenge you would have gone about it some other way, wouldn't you? You wouldn't have turned yourself in."

Steven considered that and nodded, "Yeah, you're right, I would have just walked and gone about solidifying my alibi, making it airtight." Now Drew jumped in, "That's right, and we will be asking the police how likely it would have been that they were going to catch whoever did it before you turned yourself in. I guarantee you, they will say that they had no solid leads, no suspects for the shooting. They have to because that's what they kept saying after the shooting, 'no solid leads' or 'the investigation is ongoing.' I can tell you right now that no policeman is going to get up on the stand and testify that they were on the verge of cracking the case when you turned yourself in, it'd be bullshit and they know it."

Steven understood the need for him to say exactly what they'd just explained, that he could have gotten away with it. Still, he wanted to make sure that the science, the work of Leonard and others like him, would be kept front and center, "I get it, I really do and I have no problem with testifying to it, it's the truth, but I want to make sure that the science, the research I did, will play a central role in my defense. That's the only way the jury will believe any of this. Look, I know you guys are trying to establish an angle and I understand that, but you also have to understand that a big part of what I did, a big part of the motivation, came from fear, from being in the presence of something so far removed from anything human that it grips your heart and fills it with fear. That's what being in that warehouse was like, like we were intruding in the lair of something unspeakable. There have been mass murderers before, we all know that, and there have no doubt been people that have committed similar atrocities, but this was different and everyone there could sense it. There was an intelligence and a deliberation there that spoke of very careful planning and execution. The fact of the matter is that Riche made a mistake, he took two girls that could easily be associated with each other, but what if he hadn't? What if he had kept taking girls from vastly different backgrounds and neighborhoods? The police would have admitted that a serial kidnapper, and most likely a murderer, was on the loose. People would have held their children tighter, they would have been more vigilant, but so would Riche. He would have been more careful, his plan would have changed to account for the additional vigilance. And he would have kept hunting. No, gentlemen, the only way we can convince these 12 people on the jury is by showing them the science of what these things are, by reminding them what for centuries society has deemed to be human and showing them how far from that these things are. Think about it, the bottom line is that if they find Donald Riche was human it would mean that he was a part of their species, the human species. If we give them a solid enough option, an option based on serious scientific research by authorities in their field, they'll take it."

The three men were nodding, they understood that as much as they could strategize on the legalities of the case, it was human emotion that had to come through and that human emotion would have to be fear. Ray spoke first, "You're right, only you can communicate that feeling, that fear, and we'll make sure to set you up to do it. As far as the science, we have to get with Dr. Leonard, Dr. Grossman at Columbia, Shultz to go over his involuntary indicators, and a few other scientists we've found who have also done good work, and we're going to have to prepare them to give their testimony in a way that is understandable to laymen. I think Leonard, Shultz and most of the others should be okay, but Grossman might be a problem. The guy has a stick so far up his ass he has trouble looking down." The group chuckled at the comment.

Max spoke up next, "Well, let's bring them in and take them through the case and make a decision then. It makes no sense to try and make decisions before we hear them on the stand." Steven wanted to know why one name was missing, "What about Scoma, Dr. Jim Scoma at UC Irvine? Aren't you guys planning on calling him in?" The three lawyers looked at each other, Drew spoke up for the group, "No, we weren't. His work doesn't relate to Riche or the case and we thought he might just end up confusing the jury."

Steven shook his head, "No, I don't think he will. I mean, I will defer to whatever you guys decide in the end, but the man is incredibly engaging and his work was a big part of what convinced me that this new species was possible. You're right, his work deals with other types of behaviors, but in the end it is still about something other than what we know as human beings on the face of the earth. Some of his work and the examples he gave me made a lot of sense, it had a balancing effect on me, to be quite honest." Ray looked puzzled, "What do you mean it had a balancing effect?" Steven answered, "What I mean is that I had doubts, I could not understand how a new species, something beyond human, could manifest itself only in the most deviant and horrible end of what we consider the human spectrum. I mean, think about it, a new species arises, a species more evolved than humans and that new species only manifests itself in the most horrible way imaginable, as a predator hunting humans. I just had a hard time believing that evolution only manifested itself on the evil end of the human spectrum, and Scoma and his work showed me that was not the case, that the new species also manifested itself in other conditions. Leonard was the first to catalogue the species and to name it, but Scoma is also working to define another species that does not manifest exclusively as predators. He hasn't named it and is still researching the similarities and differences with Leonard's *Homo predator*." The three lawyers were considering what he had just walked them through. It was clear they would talk about it again, but at least he had made his wishes known. The four men stayed in Max's office for the remainder of the day, strategizing about their case and preparing for what the prosecutor was likely to throw at them.

◆

Judge Denies Defense's Request
API-Manhattan, New York
By Felix Garcia/New York Chronicle

The judge presiding over the Steven Loomis murder trial has denied the defense's request to put Harvey Lynch, a well-known defense attorney, on the stand. Loomis is accused of the shooting death of Donald Riche, which took place as Riche was being transported to the central holding jail on January 17. Donald Riche had been arraigned on charges that he abducted and killed nine girls between the ages of six and eight. Tracy Loomis, age six, was one of Donald Riche's alleged victims. Steven Loomis eventually turned himself in and took responsibility for the shooting. He has since claimed that there is solid science that has classified another species within the same family as humans. His defense team will present a defense where they will argue that Loomis cannot be convicted of murder because Donald Riche could not be scientifically and therefore legally classified as a human being. Drew Willis, lead counsel for the defense, believes the science will prevail, "Mr. Loomis is a senior executive with a global intelligence firm and a highly trained Special Forces officer, he would not make this claim unless there was extensive, solid scientific evidence to support it." In a preliminary ruling, presiding judge, Lester Newman, allowed the defense to move forward with their argument but limited the evidence of Donald Riche's alleged crimes to those that involved Steven Loomis's daughter, Tracy. The defense wanted to put Harvey Lynch, the attorney who represented Riche leading up to his arraignment, on the stand in order to prove Riche was not in a delusional state and had in fact very carefully planned everything he was accused of doing. In his ruling today, the judge stated that attorney-client privilege applied even though Donald Riche is dead. District Attorney David Neill stated that it was a good ruling because it honored the most sacred duty an attorney owes to a client, "We feel it would have been a violation of what should be an inviolate duty, the duty of an attorney to keep every communication in confidence. Had the judge allowed Mr. Lynch to be put on the stand, we would have had a slippery slope where lawyers involved in a host of cases would have tried to claim some exception or another to put an attorney on the stand." Drew Willis was disappointed in the ruling but remained confident about the defense's case, "We are disappointed in the ruling, because we feel that Mr. Lynch's testimony could have provided some context for the jury, but we are confident that even without that Mr. Loomis's argument will still prevail." Max Zeidler, another member of the defense team and a well-known member of the New York legal community, was also confident their case was not harmed by today's ruling, "I don't understand how the judge came to this conclusion. When the person who can claim the privilege is dead, so is the privilege. Still, the science will be clear and undeniable once we are able to present it." Asked about Steven Loomis's defense, the DA reiterated that his office believes it to simply be a move of desperation, "It's the fourth quarter and they're down by six, of course they are going for the Hail Mary. We are confident, however, that the jury will be able to see past this and concentrate on the issue at hand: Did Steven Loomis kill Donald Riche with malice and premeditation? The answer is clearly a resounding yes." Barton Lewis, the deputy district attorney leading the prosecution team, says the jury will be able to keep emotions out of their decision, "We are all aware of the circumstances that brought us here and I think we would not be human if we did not sympathize, but we are also a nation of laws, and the people believe the jury will be able to keep that front and center as they make their decision." Some legal experts believe that the prosecution may be underestimating the potential effect that public opinion will have on the jury. Frank Mallory, a jury selection consultant, believes the evidence presented will have a powerful effect, "I think the prosecution does not realize just how far public opinion can move a jury. Of course everyone that will make up the jury pool will say that they can be fair and not take any of the other facts surrounding the case into account, but they're human and some of the evidence they will be looking at is going to move them." The trial is scheduled to begin in two weeks. Jury selection will begin on May 12 at 8 AM.

Not far from his law offices, Harvey Lynch was sitting on a stool at a greasy-spoon diner, enjoying his lunch, the meatloaf special. 'You're damn right I'm not going to testify' he thought as he took another bite of meatloaf and put down the paper he had been reading. He wanted nothing to do with Riche, Loomis, nothing even remotely linked to the case. He had taken on Riche as a client before his warehouse of horrors and the mutilated bodies of nine little girls had been found. When the shit hit the fan, he had no choice but to represent Riche. He had been almost ecstatic when Riche had been shot. 'Good riddance' he thought as he took another bite and shuddered at the memory of the things he had heard from Riche and the pictures he had seen of his client's exploits. He had not been able to get a good night's sleep for almost two weeks after that. He was still going to counseling and was only now able to get a few hours of uninterrupted sleep with the aid of a sleeping pill. He would never, not once, repeat what Riche had told him. Never. His law practice, which had been a general practice that included a fair share of personal injury and divorce prior to Riche, was now almost exclusively devoted to criminal defense. Criminals, it seemed, were impressed by the fact that he had represented a monster. They figured, quite correctly in fact, that by comparison their crimes were child's play. Lynch was thankful for the financial benefit this brought but was more than willing to give it up in order to pick up more cases that had nothing to do with criminal law. Unfortunately for Lynch, the same thing that brought the criminals kept the other clients away. Still, he couldn't complain. His practice was doing well and his life was just about back to where it had been before all this craziness. Next to him were other patrons also enjoying their lunch fare, burgers, ribs, pot roast, good old American food. Lynch smiled at the fact that this was not a place for vegans or health nuts, this was a true greasy spoon and he enjoyed his food immensely. The long counter where he was sitting accommodated another 20 stools. A refrigerated case at the end of the counter displayed a good variety of pies. Lynch had his heart set on coconut cream. Their coconut cream pie was legendary. Behind the counter waitresses rushed to pick up their orders, urged on by the short-order cooks who rang a small bell with their spatula every time an order was ready. It never ceased to amaze him how each waitress knew when it was her order that was ready, the cooks never called out a name.

Above and to the left of the opening where the cooks put the orders sat a flat-screen television tuned to CNN. There were no baseball games scheduled and the Jets and Giants wouldn't start their season for another few months, so CNN it was. The din of the lunch crowd drowned out the sound on the television almost completely. Not surprisingly, CNN was completely dedicated to the Steven Loomis case. It had been that way since the day Loomis had turned himself in. At first Lynch himself had hardly been able to go anywhere without someone trying to get a comment or an exclusive interview with him. Once the article that Felix Garcia had written was published, fewer and fewer requests came his way. He had been a part of other cases that had gotten incredible coverage, but this was ridiculous. Late-night talk shows, morning shows on television and radio, even freaking sports shows had something to say. The initial reaction was that Loomis had lost his mind because of what happened to his daughter. Most experts were of the opinion that Loomis's attorneys were setting up for an eventual temporary insanity defense. That had changed, however, when experts like Tyrone Leonard and others like him were interviewed. They had shared their research and their findings with the world and now public opinion was leaning toward Loomis's argument. As he sat cleaning the gravy on his plate with a piece of roll, Lynch listened to the two men sitting immediately to his left. "I don't buy it, you know what I mean. I mean, the guy's daughter was murdered by that animal, who wouldn't want to take the piece of shit out, but this, this thing about another species and all that crap is just bullshit. Y' know? I mean, he should just own up to it, you know what I'm sayin'? Just say, 'Yeah, I took the piece of shit out because he killed my daughter and what about it' or somethin' like that. People would understand that, not all this other happy bullshit they're sellin'. I bet it's the lawyers that are tellin' him to say that. Fucking lawyers, did I tell you about Gina's fucking lawyer? Alimony! Can you believe that shit?! She fucks Tommy Lagazzio and then has the fucking gall to ask for alimony?" The man sitting next to Mr. Alimony had obviously heard this tirade before, "Yeah, you told me already, like 10 times. And you know what? I don't believe the guy's full of shit. Have you heard about this guy? He was in the Navy, one of those SEAL guys, like the ones who killed Osama. I ain't shittin' you. Those guys don't fuck around, y' know what I mean. They are trained to kill in like a hundred ways without getting caught. They even know how to kill with a paperclip…"

Alimony interrupted, "Get the fuck out a' hea'! Paperclips!"

"I shit you not. Anyway, you think this guy would have gotten caught if all he wanted to do was to take that piece of shit out? There's no fuckin' way he gets caught, no way. No, you know what I think? I think that there's something to this whole thing about another species and about these new predators and all that crap they're talking about. Think about it, I mean, we're always talkin' about aliens and alien abductions and shit like that, and people go on talking about UFOs and all that crap."

Alimony guy turned with a look of disgust on his face, "What the fuck does that have to do with this? You're always bringing in that alien shit. I keep telling you it's just bullshit, it's a fact that they're just weather balloons or some asshole with a remote control. And what does any of that have to do with this anyway?"

Alien guy responded as if he were talking to a child, "What it has to do with it is that we're talking about something other than human, right? Some other species that looks like us and acts like us, but they're not us. So, maybe the aliens don't come from another planet, maybe they've always come from here, from earth, and we've been thinkin' they come from outer space, or maybe aliens came to earth a long time ago and they fucked some earth women and made this other species, that's what."

Alimony guy shook his head, "You and your freakin' aliens. But you may have a point, I mean, those scientists they have on the talk shows say that these things have been here a while. I don't know, I guess maybe they could exist, maybe, but I still think it's the lawyers that came up with that crap."

Lynch shook his head, took a sip of his coffee, ate his last bite of pie and went to pay the check, leaving Mr. Alimony and Mr. Alien to continue a new debate on Joe Namath versus Eli Manning they had started on before he got up. He himself didn't know what to make of Loomis's defense. He had done some research and knew he was solid.

He also knew Max Zeidler, and the man may be a lot of things but stupid wasn't one of them. There's no way Zeidler would let his client come up with some bullshit stunt of a defense. No, if Max was going forward with it, Lynch would bet money that there was definitely something to it. As he was walking back to his office, Lynch was approached by a man who looked a little like a thinner Sean Connery. Lynch was ready to give his standard 'No comment, call my office' response. He had been hounded by the media, just like anyone else who had been even remotely connected to the case. The man did not have a cameraman tailing him or a recorder in his hand, however, and he also didn't have the harried and pushy air of a reporter. On closer inspection, Lynch thought the guy looked more like Professor Xavier from The *X-Men* movies. The man stepped closer to Lynch, with one hand outstretched and a business card in the other, "Mr. Lynch?" Lynch, still cautious, held off shaking the man's hand, "Sorry, do I know you?" The man smiled and, realizing Lynch wasn't going to shake his hand, simply smiled, "Forgive the intrusion, counselor, my name is Nigel Barlow, Dr. Nigel Barlow." Lynch took the card from the man. He saw that Barlow was a criminal profiling consultant, "I see. What can I do for you, Dr. Barlow?"

Barlow now took on a conspiratorial tone, something Lynch didn't particularly care for, "Yes, you see, I am a researcher and criminal profiler. I do work for various police departments as well as the FBI and the department of defense. You are welcome to confirm my engagements with any of those organizations, if you wish."

Lynch looked at the card again and then back at Barlow, "Well, doctor, I don't remember coming across your name in any of the reports or profiles I've read." Barlow shook his head, "Forgive me, Mr. Lynch, I did not mean to imply that you should have. I was not involved in the Loomis case, you see. I am speaking to you in the capacity of a researcher. I am doing work for my profiling practice and a book I'm working on, a novel based on the case. I would very much like to speak with you, if you have a moment." Lynch looked at the card again, something about the guy was just a little hinky. Lynch couldn't put his finger on it, but his gut instincts were twitching just a bit, maybe it was the guy's British accent. Lynch distrusted the British just on principle, "Yeah, alright. Can you walk and talk, though, I'm heading back to my office." Barlow lit up, "Splendid! I truly appreciate it, but why don't we take my car? We can speak in more comfort and you'll make better time." Lynch saw the Town Car Barlow was moving toward and decided that riding back to the office in style did not sound bad at all, the meatloaf was sitting heavy today, "Yeah, alright, let's go." Barlow smiled.

In the end, Harvey Lynch did repeat what Riche had told him. He had shared with Barlow everything he could possibly remember, every single word. His last conscious thought was relief, blessed relief. Three days later, Harvey Lynch's wife filled a missing persons report.

Read an excerpt from the next book in the Apex
Predator series by J.A. Faura, *The Human Element.*

Prologue

MANHATTAN, NEW YORK

Felix Garcia finally had fifteen minutes to run downstairs and grab a hot dog from the vendor that was always in front of the New York Chronicle building. Garcia, a reporter for the Chronicle, actually ran a tab with the guy, he was there so much. He had been looking for some unique angle to cover on the biggest story in the history of New York, perhaps the US and maybe even the world. A criminal trial where what defines a human being would be litigated; a first-degree murder trial, no less. As he sat in the elevator Felix thought that it really did depend on how the audience thought about the case: if they believe the defense's argument that there was indeed another sub-species under homo-sapiens, then it was most definitely the biggest story in the history of the modern human; if they thought it was just some sort of ploy or gimmick the defense is using to get their client off, then it wasn't quite that big, but it was still the biggest story New York had ever seen for sure. It wasn't just the argument the defense was planning on using that made it a huge story, the facts of the case were simply sensational, even by New York standards: a father whose daughter is kidnapped and murdered and who is a former Navy SEAL, decides to take out his daughter's killer. After he does it, however, he does not claim insanity, temporary or otherwise and in fact declares that his motive for killing the man was to bring the world's attention to what he says is the most significant and real threat humanity has ever seen. It had everything, a sympathetic figure, a monster, a hugely divisive issue and some groundbreaking scientific testimony. It did not get any more sensational than that, it hadn't, ever, anywhere. So even if it wasn't the biggest case modern humanity had ever seen, it was definitely in the running. With that kind of case, the media attention had also been unprecedented and just kept getting even more frenetic, something that Garcia and most other reporters covering the story had not thought possible. He had almost given up on getting a scoop, when his local contacts at the courts building, the police department and strategically important law firms, came through for him. He had made the deadline last night and knew the digital version would be published any time and the non-digital would command the front-page headline in their evening edition.

The elevator light showed they were on the first floor, the door opened and he everyone in the elevator except for Felix and two other people, both of whom also worked for the Chronicle, stayed in the elevator. They knew that the first floor lobby was a chaotic and crowded space with reporters from other papers owned by the same group that owned the Chronicle parked on every square inch available in the building. With every office stuffed beyond capacity, they had migrated to the first floor lobby. Felix and the two other people, however, knew that if they went down one more floor to the basement of the building, they could exit without having to navigate equipment, people, tripping over cables or being seen. Felix was still the only reporter that Steven Loomis, the man accused of the murder, had spoken to, which now made Felix something of a celebrity himself. The three of them walked through some storage, past an electrical panel and out a side door, which locked once they were through. Felix pulled the collar on his coat up over his ears; it was still very cold, even though it was almost mid-March. As he walked to the vendor's cart, which had now morphed into three carts, all owned by the same family, he got a notice on his smartphone, the piece had hit.

He stopped, stood to the side and pulled up the story on the Chronicle's mobile app.

District Attorney will not pursue lesser-included charges

API-Manhattan, New York

By Felix Garcia/New York Chronicle

The District Attorney's office has confirmed that there will not be lesser-included offenses used on the Steven Loomis murder trial. Loomis is charged with the first-degree murder of Donald Riche, who was suspected of the kidnapping and murder of Tracy Loomis, as well as eight other girls between the ages of five and seven years old. Riche was shot while being transported from the courthouse to the holding facility. NYU law school criminal procedure professor and Chronicle legal consultant Hank Weller believes not including lesser included offenses is a very unusual step for a DA to take, especially in a murder trial of this nature, 'Normally in a murder trial you want to make sure to give the jury plenty of choices to convict, so you would include the charge of second degree murder, voluntary manslaughter, involuntary manslaughter, whatever is appropriate. David Neill is basically saying that he believes so much in the facts of the case that he doesn't need other charges as a choice for the jury'. While District Attorney David Neill did not comment personally, a statement from his office seemed to confirm Weller's opinion, 'The District Attorney's office believes that the charges in this case fulfill the precise requirements for first degree murder without question. This decision is not an attempt at making a statement or trying to influence the jury pool, it is a decision based on the facts of the case alone.' During a telephone interview Steven Loomis's lead attorney, Drew Willis, seemed unconcerned about the DA's decision, 'That is a choice every prosecutor is entitled to make, regardless of the facts of the case. As a defense team we cannot concern ourselves with every choice the District Attorney chooses to make, if we did that we might have to change our strategy every couple of weeks.'   Other experts interviewed also find the DA's decision unusual. Carrie Hutton, a senior attorney with the public defender's office, disagrees that it is not a decision meant to communicate a message, 'We see this kind of decision when the district attorney is absolutely convinced that the jury could not find otherwise, when the facts are so crystal clear and the evidence is so convincing that it is almost a foregone conclusion that the jury will find a defendant guilty. It is usually done to pressure a defendant into taking a deal and pleading guilty. I think this could backfire for the DA in this case. I don't think the facts are as clear as the DA thinks they are.' She went on to explain that while the facts of the case are undisputed, the science and other probable evidence makes it a situation where the jury could find for the defense, 'Consider, the defendant shot the victim in broad daylight, confessed after the shooting and clarified that he had planned exactly what he was going to do. By all rights that should not be in any way defensible, not unless there is a claim of insanity, which there isn't in this case.' Loomis's defense team strategy has been the focus of intense international media attention. The defense strategy is based on what they claim is solid and significant scientific research that points to a previously unclassified subspecies of homo sapiens, a subspecies they are calling homo sapiens predaer or homo predator. Hutton went on, 'That's why the defense's argument is so fascinating from a legal perspective. The human element is not something that has ever been litigated before. Not in this context at least.' Professor Weller agrees that it may be a wrong decision by David Neill, 'I think he's laying his cards on the table and simply establishing just how clear cut this case is, but it is far from clear cut. Juries can do a lot of things, as the OJ trial showed us. I think it is a strategic move designed to give the defense an incentive to make a deal with the prosecution.' Jury selection begins Monday, May 12 at 8:00 AM. The county information office confirmed that there will be a jury pool of approximately 100 potential jurors, far more than would be called in, even in the most visible and public cases. Weller, Hutton and other legal experts believe that jury selection may take as long as three weeks, far longer than for any other case that has been tried in the state and perhaps the country. It is widely believed that the outcome of the case will hinge on jury selection and the strength of both sides' expert witnesses, which is the reason many believe the jury selection will take so long. Hutton stated she believes it is going to be a much more contentious process than it normally is, 'I think both sides are doing some serious assessment of the type of juror they are looking for and they will go toe to toe to get the jury they want. They don't have to spend time litigating any of the facts other than what the defense is claiming, so they can focus on the jury they want.' She explained that each side is allowed a number of preemptory challenges, challenges where neither side has to give an explanation for why they are dismissing a juror, but she believes that each side will go through those challenges in the first week and will then need to challenge for cause, where they have to provide the court with a reason for dismissing a juror. The court is not obliged to accept the reason each side presents. Although it is extremely rare, the judge may decide that a juror can stay, even though one side or the other might have provided a reason for the request to dismiss.

Felix smiled; the story had probably hit the rest of the media like a lightning bolt. Even the most well-known reporters and their teams had not been able to get the information and had definitely been definitely looking. He had gotten the information before anyone else covering the trial because of his contacts and his absolutely relentless work ethic. That had also been the reason that Steven Loomis had only spoken to him, Robert Grady the lead detective in the case had given his name to Loomis when he had asked for an honest, balanced member of the media that he could trust with writing his story. It wasn't just his work ethic that had allowed him to scoop much bigger media outlets, it was also the fact that he had grown up on these streets, Spanish Harlem and the Bronx specifically. His grandfather had been a well-known hustler on those streets. Never into anything too heavy, just enough to keep his family covered, Augie Garcia had made a lot of friends in a lot of places; friendships that extended into family and that had been cultivated and maintained over the years. The 'grapevine' on the street was always the best source of information if you were really looking for the story, the true story. Any son of the streets of Spanish Harlem and the Bronx could tell you that. Garcia, walked up to the hot dog vendor who smiled at him, "Hungry big Felix?" Felix held up two fingers, "You know it Ali, hit me up with a couple." Ali started preparing the hot dogs, "Everything on them?" Garcia winked at him, "You know it."

Not too far from where Felix Garcia was enjoying his hot dogs, the District Attorney, David Neill, was in a meeting with the two prosecutors that would be handling the Loomis trial, Barton Logan and Melanie Farris. Bart would be lead counsel with Melanie backstopping him. She was actually more senior than Logan, more seasoned, which meant that if the trial went to hell she'd have more to lose. Both of them had been very cleverly manipulated, almost ambushed, into handling the case. Not that they really had much choice. When it was going to be a trial to convict Donald Riche, murderer of young children, Neill was going to handle the case personally with Farris as second counsel and Logan as the third-string sub. Bart would have more than likely been researching points of law and citations for them to prepare for the trial. When Loomis shot Riche the situation had gone from a 'can't lose' type case, to a 'can't win' type case. How do you prosecute a man who is an upstanding citizen, a decorated military commander serving in the military team that was literally made up of the best of the best? A man whose daughter the victim in this case had kidnapped and brutally murdered along with eight other girls and who knew how many other victims. How do you prosecute such a man? Very carefully, that's how. You make sure you don't attack him or who he is and you focus on the law, on establishing the elements of the crime and that's it, no judgment of the man whatsoever. His boss had called this meeting to go over preparations for the trial, but had instead been ranting about the article that had just been published by the New York Chronicle. David Neill was not a very amiable or charismatic individual; he was a dry, focused individual who had been born to be a public servant. He believed in the absolutes of the law and expected every one of his deputies to be the same way. There were no gray areas in the law for David Neill, something was right or something was wrong, period. He had used that complete commitment to the law and to catching and convicting those who broke it to get elected twice already. Right now, however, Neill was breathing fire about the article. He had lost it after Lucas Gordon, one of the chief deputies in the office, had notified him about the article. "I want to know who the fuck is talking to that little bastard from the Chronicle! That spic has been hanging around the courthouse and our office for years getting all kinds of information that nobody should be able to get. It hasn't really been an issue because the crap he usually covers is small-time, but this is different, this will literally make or break the careers of every single person from this office who is involved in the case directly. That includes me, in case you were wondering! So I want to know who he's talking to and I want their balls on a platter!" Logan and Farris both smiled as they looked down, but Neill still caught the gesture, "You guys think this is funny?! We'll see how funny you think it is when the media is roasting you over an open fire after losing the case." He turned to Gordon who had just been frozen in place since giving Neill the news. Gordon tried to mollify his boss, "We're trying to find out precisely that as we speak. I'm confident before we'll know who it is he's been talking to before too long, at least about this case." Neill seemed to settle a bit, but was still angry, "You better hope so. I'm serious Lucas, I want their balls when you find out who it is." Lucas nodded and left. He had wanted to ask his boss what he'd like to have on the platter if it was a woman that was talking to Garcia, but he thought better of it and just left without saying anything. Neill got back to the business at hand, "Well, it is what it is, now they know. Melanie, where are we with our expert witnesses?" Farris looked down at the open manila folder in front of her, "We have experts for just about every aspect of the science they are most likely to use. Anthropologists, archaeologists, paleoneurologists, psychiatrists and at least five other disciplines." Neill was visibly taken aback, "That's a lot of experts to prepare for, so we're going to need to have other people in the office handling some of it. Get Diaz from the human trafficking unit, Marchowski and Thompson from organized crime. All of them have had a lot of experience with expert witnesses and they can prepare ours for when the defense cross-examines them. I want the two of you to concentrate on coming up with the cross for their witnesses. By the time you are done with their experts the jury should be thinking they're just a bunch of crackpots capitalizing on a high-profile case." Logan and Farris looked at each other as if to ask 'Do you tell him or do I'; neither one of them was looking forward to this case having Neill looking over their shoulder and they really weren't looking forward to telling him when they thought he was wrong about something. It was Melanie Farris that finally spoke up, "Um, sir, we believe it may be risky to just discount their experts. We've looked into all of their backgrounds and they all check out as serious researchers at the top of their field. Perhaps it would be more effective to go forward with the assumption that their findings are correct and simply attacking their conclusions. We don't need for them to be crackpots to win the case, sir, we just need to show the jury that as accomplished as the expert are, they are human beings that can and have made mistakes." Neill let her finish and then shook his head while a wry smile spread across his face as he turned and looked directly at Bart Logan, "I see, and is this point of view shared by Logan." Bart Logan was definitely not as bold or seasoned as Melanie Farris was, but he very much shared the point of view so he nodded and chose to just go with a simple 'yes sir'. Neill nodded, put his hands on his waist and began to pace as he laid into his deputies, "Are you both crazy? Do I need to find two other deputies to handle this case? Anything short of taking apart their witnesses gives credence to this bullshit theory of theirs and credence is something we absolutely cannot give the defense. Not in any way." Farris's eyes were focused on a point on the floor as she listened. Neill had a point, but it was one that both she and Bart Logan had already explored and discounted. She had told herself she wouldn't respond to Neill, not matter what he said. She wasn't able to contain herself, however, "We actually started with that strategy in mind, sir, but after going through each of the witnesses' backgrounds we realized it just wouldn't be possible." Neill shook his head emphatically, "Nonsense, any witness can be taken apart by a good litigator, any witness. I don't care what their backgrounds are; this theory is ridiculous, so all we have to do is show the jury just how ridiculous it is. And, don't forget we also have very solid witnesses who will be testifying to that fact. So we go after the witnesses and we don't go after Loomis himself. Public sympathy is a powerful thing, especially because of what he'd been through. We stick with the law and we destroy the science and we'll be golden. This one is a slam dunk guys, it's an amazing opportunity to win the highest profile case this city, this country for god's sake, has ever seen." Now both Melanie and Bart were now looking down at the table they were seated around. Neither one of them responded to Neill, but they were both thinking along the same lines. They were both thinking 'if it was that easy it would be you handling the case', but they knew it didn't matter whether they said something or not. Neill's mind was made up. "You're both new at these high-profile cases, so I'll overlook your fumble this once, but one is all you get. All right let's go over our expert witness list." Farris and Logan nodded and came around to the side of the table Neill was at to look at the list. Neither was willing to let Neill know that they both thought the decision to pursue murder one and only murder one, was a huge mistake.

At the same time Neill was coming down on his deputies, Steven Loomis was gathering his thoughts at the law offices of Max Zeidler and Drew Willis, his two principal defense attorneys. They had been going over expert witness testimony all day for almost two weeks, grilling every single potential expert witness in every conceivable way. They even had two litigators that had been senior prosecuting attorneys for the US Attorney's office do the cross examinations. Both were brutal litigators who had well-deserved reputations for ripping expert witnesses to shreds. Steven looked out the window of the boardroom he had parked himself in. Even this high up he could see where the media was parked all over the city. They had basically erected a temporary, mobile city around the building and wherever they could find a place near the building. Initially he had wondered whether he had made the right choice going with such a large law firm, but now he was truly thankful he had decided as he had. Their resources were amazing and the legal talent was absolutely top notch. Willis was new to the firm, but was an experienced litigator who had established, maintained and grown his own small law firm before making the decision to take Max Zeidler up on his offer to come onboard. With offices in ten countries, forty-one partners and more than 300 associates, the law firm of Corliss, Zeidler and Kirk was large law firm even by New York standards. Art Goodman, the CEO of Global Intelligence Consultants (GIC), the security assessment and consulting firm that Steven worked for as an executive vice-president, had referred Steven to them. He was widely believed to be the most likely successor to Goodman before all of this. General Art Goodman, Marine Corps (Ret.) was used to getting his way and he had gotten his way in this instance as well. It had not been much of a decision for Steven to make, he had not considered what lawyer he would eventually ask to represent him, so when the General suggested Zeidler and explained that his firm was on retainer and that they billed GIC about $10 million dollars a year, Steven agreed to call them. Of course he'd had to wait until the right time to actually reach out to the lawyers. He had to get square with his family first, to make sure they were covered, really covered. He knew he was at risk of going away for a long time, maybe for life, and before he could make that kind a decision he needed to make sure they would be okay no matter what happened to him. He was still not used to the level of media attention his case was getting. The truth was that none of them were, not even Zeidler who had litigated countless, extremely high profile trials. He could see the media stationed around just about every open spot for three square blocks around the office, five square blocks around the courthouse and two square blocks around his house. It was an uncharacteristic move by the media that they listened when Steven had asked them to take it easy and give him and his family some room to breathe. He thought that perhaps some of the people who were providing security for him had spoken to a few members of the media and suggested they might want to give Loomis some space. His children were at his in-laws' house where media was also parked everywhere. In contrast to New York, however, Queensbury, a small town in Vermont, could be easily covered and controlled by the security teams that were covering them. One team was very obvious and public, the other team was never seen, never heard, but they were covering all the blind spots that no security detail every covered. Both teams were made up of people that Steven and the General knew well.

The boardroom he was in was a corner room, so he actually had two wall-length windows. He walked to the other window and looked over another part of the city, it was just about the same as the other side because the media was also parked everywhere. Steven knew how important these strategy and preparation sessions were; how important it was to prepare every expert witness, how important it was to prepare himself for being cross-examined and he was doing his best to do that and make sure his family was safe, but there was one thing that was getting in the way and by now he knew it was not going to change. Nigel Barlow, doctor Nigel Barlow, neuropsychologist, profiling consultant, scientist and the single most significant threat to humanity he had ever believed there could or would be. Steven had met with Barlow after Riche's shooting because of the man's insistence and, truth be told, because he had been a bit stir-crazy after being confined to his house for over a week. He had also done it because he believed Barlow was a scientist looking into the same science that Steven was actually researching at the time. Thirty seconds into their conversation, Steven knew that Barlow was all the things he had believed he was and far, far more. Barlow had reached out to Steven because he had wanted more information about Riche, about what Steven had seen and experienced at the warehouse where Riche had brought all his victims, including Steven' daughter Tracy. He wasn't looking for science, he was looking for the things that could not be captured in a report, the things that made every single person, CSIs, police officers, everyone in that warehouse first shiver and then completely nauseous. When Steven had let Barlow know that he knew what he was after, Barlow had completely dropped his sham and let Steven know exactly what he was after and exactly what he was. He had been doing the same research all right, except that his purposes had been quite different from those of every other scientist working on the science. Barlow had basically been alienated and excommunicated by the mainstream scientific community because he was thought to be unstable and even dangerous. He wanted to observe the subjects of the research in action, while they were on the hunt, regardless of what that meant for the person being hunted. Now, twenty years later, Barlow had established, developed and grown a network of individuals who he believed fit into the subspecies he and the other scientists had identified, Homo sapiens predaer or homo predator. Steven had not been the same since that meeting and what happened a few days after it. He had asked Cecil and Thurman Meeks, two operators he knew well to look into the guy's background, where he was from, how much money he had, everything they could possibly find to help paint a full picture of the man. While Steven had been waiting for them to get back to him, Barlow had managed to knock Steven out with a shot of tranquilizer administered by a very skilled operative, taken him to a nondescript motel in New Jersey and let him know under no uncertain terms that he would leave Steven and his family alone, but he would expect the same courtesy from Steven. He had to agree to leave Barlow alone and let him go do whatever it was he did with no interference. He had let Steven know that if he found that someone was trying to look into his business again, all bets would be off and his family would be the first to feel it. The fact that he had gotten the jump on Steven and that he had been able to register that two very skilled operators were looking into his business, let Steven know that the man had the resources and access to the talent and technology necessary to make that threat and carry through with it. So, here he was, preparing for trial and leaving Barlow alone, but he was never too far from Steven's mind. He was also thinking about Diana, almost certainly not her real name, and what she had warned him about. If there was anyone who knew what Barlow was capable of, it was Diana. She had been the operative that Barlow had used to deliver the shot that knocked Steven out. She was clearly Special Forces, whether from the US or elsewhere she was spec ops. He believed she was most likely Mossad. Her accent, her demeanor and the Star of David around her neck, made it almost certain that she was trained by the famed Israeli agency, their version of the CIA. She'd told him she was talking to him because she decided she did not want to be a part of whatever Barlow was planning. She had explained she had done a few jobs for Barlow in the past and that she did not know too much because everything the man did was compartmentalized. It made sense to Steven, that's how you had to develop effective, complex operations, by compartmentalizing and making sure each element could function independently of any other element. He wasn't sure whether he believed everything the woman had said, but it had sounded solid to Steven.

He had told his lawyers about what happened with Barlow because he believed that they could also be affected by what happened from that day forward, but he had told no one about Diana. He hadn't told his lawyers, he hadn't told the General and he hadn't told his wife. Well, he had placed a couple of calls earlier today to finally remedy that, at least the part about Barlow. He still wasn't sure about what to say, if anything, about Diana. Since his encounter with Barlow, he had been really off in everything he did and he knew it was because he knew he should have told his wife what happened and he didn't. She might not understand that the reason he had done that was because she was simply not ready to hear it. That had changed now. Now she was almost back to herself and they had fallen into a rhythm, as much of a rhythm as the situation allowed for, so he knew it was time. He also knew it was time to tell the General. Goodman had done more for Steven and his family than anyone else in every sense. He was footing the bill for his defense, which would be well over a million dollars; he had covered the bail so Steven could wait for trial at his house instead of sitting in jail and more important than everything else, he had been there for Steven, emotionally, like a father would have been. The General was a father figure for Steven, who had grown up without a father. From the time Steven had arrived at GIC to the present, Goodman had taken a deep personal interest in Steven, his family and his career and throughout everything he done nothing but help all of them. So yeah, the time had come for Steven to come clean about everything; almost everything, in any case.

Nigel Barlow was thousands of miles away in Colorado. He had left New York immediately after his fact-finding session with Harvey Lynch. It had proven to be a waste of time, but it had served as a release for him, which made it not a complete waste of time. When he arrived, everything he had requested was ready. All his files had been encrypted and loaded into twenty-two separate jump drives, each representing one year of his work. He had then had his lawyers prepare documents to provide clear and minutely detailed instructions as to how his operations and his property were to be utilized. He had named various directors, each dedicated to a specific part of his enterprises, each one of them would be handed one of the drives on the table. None had any influence or authority over another. They were to function independently only reporting in to the law firm to access funds, communicate with Barlow and to continue to expand their reach, his reach. He had been crafting this structure over decades and now finally felt that it was time to truly implement what he had been planning all along. After a few years of doing his work, Barlow had realized that he would simply not be able to do everything himself, not if the work was to reach as far as Barlow intended it to reach. After some more time had passed, he realized that he needed to set things up in such a way that the work would continue, regardless of what happened to him and so for the next thirteen years he had begun to set things up. Over that time he had established distinct areas that he wanted to take his work to. Politics, entertainment, media, energy, military were among some of his principal areas of interest. Within each of them there were sub areas of interest. Within entertainment there was content development, production or talent. Talent was his guilty pleasure. He had many accomplished and quite famous performers in various areas that he was able to consult, all in the pursuit of his one original objective, of course. Likewise there were sub areas within politics, foreign policy, funding, elections, etc. They were all organized this way. Sometimes the different areas of interest would overlap. Politics and finance was a perfect example, energy and military was another and so on. He had kept meticulous records of all his work. Contacts, relationship to each, influence or financial worth, it was all in his files. He had read everything there was to read about J. Edgar Hoover. He felt a kinship with the former head of the FBI. They were both men whose life was dedicated to locating, cataloging and using information to influence individuals that he had an interest in. That had included JFK and his brother Bobby, the Attorney General at the time. His filing system was based on his research of how Hoover had set up his confidential files. He had also become a master at using that information the way Hoover had used it when he had been alive, gathering the inner most secrets of those in power and then applying pressure. Or sending others to apply it. Hoover had almost certainly been a Prime Force, one of the new species, Barlow was certain. Smart, ruthless, keenly aware of those with influence and how to utilize them should he ever need to. Never married, perhaps a homosexual, but that was nothing of consequence to any of his subjects. They satisfied their needs and desires as they saw fit, whether it was with a man or a woman was of no importance. Only when procreating would that play a role in their choice of partner. Barlow paused, put all the documents aside and left the drives on the desk where he had been sitting as he walked over to the massive window with the breathtaking view of the Rockies. That was an area where he really felt he had not made sufficient progress. The rise of a new species depended on the ability of that species to adapt and procreate. Without procreation history would look upon the new species as a random mutation, something that over time became extinct because nature had not intended for them to be alive in the first place. He couldn't be too hard on himself, however, because he knew how difficult it was to find and nurture and guide one of them, let alone trying to find two of them and to get them to breed with each other. He had made some valiant efforts early on, utilizing genetic matching and a variety of other standardized tests to determine how suitable a woman was for some of his younger projects. There had even been a couple of instances where he had actually needed a suitable male. In almost every instance, however, their offspring appeared to be completely human, a remarkable human, but human nonetheless. Almost every instance. There were five offspring out there that showed incredible promise. He had maintained close contact with their parents and been apprised of every step of their education. He would be taking over their education very soon. He smiled at the thought. To be able to work with them from a young age was his dream, one of the things he had really hoped to be able to do at the outset. Still, five was far too low a number for what he now knew he would have to do. He had looked into Riche and what he had done because he had learned to look for certain elements in the situations he heard about and he thought that what had been happening in New York had the feel of something he might be interested in. But, before he could learn any more about Riche and what he had done, Steven Loomis had stepped in. Barlow had been initially disappointed when he had learned about what had happened to Riche, but fate had richly rewarded him for his work and persistence with Loomis. What a fascinating turn of events that had been! There was something about Loomis, something that went beyond his training and experience as a Special Forces commander that Barlow could sense in the man. A certain intellectual flow just under the surface, something Barlow had sensed before in others, but in a very different context. Still, after the Riche incident, after Loomis had done what he had done, things had changed dramatically. The true objectives of Barlow's entire body of work had been remarkably crystallized for him in the past few months. Everything he had worked for, all he risks, the ridicule he had endured from those he had once called colleagues had been all worth it. He had built something much, much more significant than he had ever dared hope for. His reach, the level and sophistication of the understanding he had been able to acquire, were also far more than he had ever hoped for. He smiled as he looked upon the sun going down, bouncing off the snow on the mountains and had to smile. He was thinking about the technology available when he had begun, particularly the technology that helped to map the human brain and its function, it had been almost medieval in comparison to what he had at his disposal now. Genetics, robotics, all of it had been just the lore of science fiction when he had begun his work. But, if he was forced to choose the one technology that had made most of his work possible, there was no question. The Internet had made it possible to reach beyond his own borders, to obtain information on those he was interested in, to search for instances that might lead him to find what he was looking for. If he were to chart his progress the graph would look fairly flat over the first sixteen years, especially during the time he had tried to do things their way. Those had been wasted years. Then, when the Internet had really taken off for him in the late 90s, the graph would pitch up dramatically and when social media took hold, it would once again pitch up. As he made it back to the desk where the drives were, he wondered what the next technological advancement would be that would put another spike up on the graph. Perhaps the gene sequencing work going on in the Netherlands or the stem cell work in Japan. It didn't matter, whatever it was he would be among the first to know. He reviewed the documents that his attorneys had given him. It all looked in order. The door to his study opened and his valet led Lon Crawford, one of his attorneys, a more junior one at the firm, into the room. Barlow stayed seated and motioned to the chair in front of his desk. "Thank you Cole." Cole nodded and left. "Mr. Crawford, I wasn't expecting you this evening." Crawford remained standing, "I know, but we might have a problem with one of the corporations you want us to set up in Belize." Barlow's eyebrows rose, "Oh? What problem would that be?" Cole shifted on his feet. He was clearly uncomfortable with what he had to say, "Well, it seems that the Department of Defense has an issue with the use of some of the technology you want to use. They insist it is classified and that the kind of fabrication you are looking to do could turn it to, uh, well they say that it's not meant for…see the thing is…" Barlow was tired and wanted to simply to have dinner and go to bed, "Spit it out Lon, I don't want to sit here all night while you grow some testicles." Lon took a breath and spit it out, "They say that it can be weaponized. The man that came to the firm said that it can be used to deliver both chemical and biological weapons." Barlow smiled. His elbows were on his desk and he was tapping the tips of the fingers of one hand against the tips of the fingers of the other, "Hmmm. That is unexpected, indeed. I wonder who it was that spoke to the DoD about the technology. We have kept out procurement of that technology very quiet and we've hired experts from other countries and vetted them out thoroughly about the project, so I am truly perplexed as to who it could have been." He picked up the documents he had been reviewing and handed them to Crawford, "These are fine. Move forward with everything and leave the documents for the Belize project with me. I'll take care of it." Crawford nodded. He knew Barlow would in fact take care of it. Lon wasn't too familiar with Barlow's business; he had been with the firm for just over a year and only knew he paid the firm hundreds of thousands of dollars each year. He didn't know why, but the old bastard gave him the willies. He took the documents Barlow handed him, turned around and walked to the door. Before he was able to leave, Barlow called out to him from his desk, "Oh, and Lon?" The young man turned around. Barlow had a thin smile on his face, but his eyes were ice cold, "Tell Brian Drake the next time he has one of his underlings come to give me news like these, I will be…displeased." Lon shuddered without knowing why, nodded and left.

On his way home, Steven tried to prepare for what he was about to do. He thought he knew what he wanted to say, but the truth was that like everything else related to the past six months, he was having to figure things out as he went along. He could not have prepared for any of it. He was still introspective enough to know that part of what he was dealing with was a deep sense of guilt. It hadn't been his intention to bring his family into a world that none of them were even aware of before Tracy had gone missing, but that's exactly what had happened. Even so, there were some things that had helped him to feel better. One of the biggest ironies about that was the role the media had played in all of it. Initially he had been incredibly mortified with all the coverage, which he saw growing every single day. Now, with some time to let things fall into a routine, he was thankful for their coverage. His lawyers had explained to him that whatever evidence they would not be able to get in for the jury to consider, the media would have no problem putting in front of almost every potential juror in New York. It made sense; he knew that there was around the clock coverage in multiple channels, which meant that finding a juror that had not heard anything about the case would be practically impossible. The media had also helped keep him feel better about his family's safety. He believed that as long as the world's attention was firmly planted on his case, his family would be safe. It would be virtually impossible for anyone, regardless of their resources or their connections, to get to his family undetected. The attention would be there through the trial and most likely for some time after that, but it would not be there forever. If what Diana and Barlow himself had said about the type of individual that might have an interest in him or his family was true, they would most definitely wait until things died down and the world's attention was no longer on the Loomis family before making a move. That gave Steven a few months, at least, to decide what the best solution would be. One of the first things he knew Beth would want to know would be whether her parents were going to be in any danger once it was all over. He did not know what the answer was, but what he did know is that after he explained the scope of what they were facing, it would be very easy for her to make that decision on her own. Neither one of her parents had brothers or sisters. Lucy, her mother, was an only child and Tom had been one of three children, but his two brothers had died years before. One had died in the Vietnam War and the other one had died of lung cancer after three decades of a three-pack-a-day habit.

When they arrived at Steven's building the same trucks that had been there in the morning were there that evening as were the reporters and photographers belonging to the trucks. Steven saw with some satisfaction that they looked exhausted and appeared to be wrapping up their coverage for the evening. He could not imagine how frustrating it would be to have to sit out in the cold, under rain, snow, waiting for something that might, but would most likely not happen. Steven and Lou, his driver and bodyguard, got out in front of the building where another security team had already ensured that what few photographers and reporters were there did not get in their way. Benny, the building's doorman, was already holding the door open for them. Steven was first through the door, "Thanks Benny." The young man smiled and shook his head, "No problem Mr. Loomis. Man, those assholes just don't give up. Would you believe some of them actually tried to bribe me to let them up? They offered me $250 bucks to let them up.   I told them to go fuck themselves. Unbelievable. " Steven squeezed his shoulder as he walked past him to the elevator, "I appreciate it Benny. Did Beth go out today?" Benny knew it wasn't about Steven keeping tabs on his wife, although he had plenty of other people in the building who did in fact keep very close tabs on their spouses and bribed Benny with all kinds of swag to keep them informed. He shook his head, "No, not while I've been here. But the older man that came by yesterday is upstairs now. He got here about a half an hour ago." Steven stopped in his tracks, "The man who was here last night?" Benny realized he might have made a serious mistake, "Hey, that's alright, isn't it Mr. Loomis? I mean I called your wife before I let him up. She said it'd be fine. I told her who it was and she said if it was the same man as last night to let him up. She didn't hesitate or nothin'." Steven could see the man was thinking he might have made a serious mistake, "That's fine Benny, you did the right thing. He's one of the good guys." Clearly relieved, Benny went back to his post. Steven bid goodbye to Lou who was as tired as he looked. Another team would take over for the overnight shift and Lou would be back for him in the morning. While he was in the elevator Steven wondered what the old man needed. He wondered whether maybe Beth had called him, but decided that was not likely. The General would have called Steven to let him know. Whatever he wanted to speak to Steven about he also wanted Beth there. He walked through the door, took the gun from his lower back and placed it in the same drawer he had put it in before. He walked into the living room where Beth and the General were sitting. The old man had his customary tumbler filled with 18-year-old Scotch and Beth had a small cup with what he thought would be Earl Grey tea. He threw his overcoat on a chair, loosened his tie and worked out of his suit jacket all as he moved further into the living room. Beth and

Goodman stood up and she came over to greet him, "Hey you. We were getting worried. I told Art you'd be here more than an hour ago." He hugged and kissed her and walked over to shake he General's hand as he explained why he was late, "I know babe. We're trying to narrow down our list of witnesses. I had no idea we had that many potential experts. I only spoke to two of them, but Max and Drew's staff have found almost a dozen more that could be great for us." Steven and Goodman sat down, Beth walked over to the kitchen, "Can I get you something to drink?" Steven turned to answer, "A glass of ice cold tea would be great." She smiled, "Coming up." Once she was out of earshot, he turned back to the General, "I'm surprised you're here. I'm glad as hell you are, but I'm surprised." That caught the old man off guard, "Glad as hell? Just in general or because you needed to talk to me." Steven paused to take the glass from Beth, who went to go back to the kitchen before he stopped her, "Hold on, sit down honey, I need to talk to you." A puzzled expression took over her face as she complied and sat down next to him. He turned back to the General and answered his question, "Both actually. I'm glad as hell that you're here because it always feels great to see friends, real friends when things are tough, but I am also glad you are here because I wanted to talk to you and you saved me the call." Now both Beth and Goodman had puzzled expressions on their faces. They both waited for Steven to continue. For his part Steven had thought that they would barrage him with questions about what he needed to talk to them about. It would have made it easier for him to just dole out answers to questions, but when neither one asked anything he realized he was going to have to do this cold. He began by explaining his research, how he had come upon dozens and dozens of scientists and researchers doing work on what he now thought of as 'his' science. He explained how it had been difficult to ascertain which ones were involved in serious research and which ones were simply opportunists looking to make a buck off his case. He had never spoken to either of them in detail about the process he had followed to find the science had had found. He then went on to tell them about his admin, Stephanie's, call about a Dr. Barlow and how insistent the man had been on seeing him. By that point he had been going a bit stir crazy, he explained, and was maybe just looking for a good excuse to get out of the house. He had also thought that maybe Barlow was one of the scientists who were doing serious research and maybe he thought Steven could help his work in some way. He continued and told them about that first meeting, how he had felt something off with the man. He went on to explain how the meeting had progressed and saw as both Beth and the General both tensed up and worried expressions took over from puzzlement. Steven went on, not waiting for them to ask any questions. Now that he was rolling he didn't want to stop. He explained about the Twins and what he had asked them to do. He had been looking directly at Goodman as he had explained that part of his story and finally felt that he needed to pause. He had to explain to both of them why he had kept quiet, "I know I should have told you, but at that point I didn't really know much about Barlow. When I asked the Twins to look into the man I was expecting them to come back and simply tell me the guy was some wacko involved in some creepy cases. I never expected for it to come to anything." He meant for this explanation to be for both of them, but kept his eyes on the General because he knew that while telling his wife might have been a good idea, telling the General should have been a given. No going back now. It happened, he made a mistake and was now explaining to both why he had made it. "It's no excuse, I know. You two are the people I trust most in this world and not telling you was killing me, especially after what happened next." Now Beth's face went from worried to scared, "What do you mean 'what happened next'? What happened next??" Steven looked at her and held her hand. He could tell she was getting overwhelmed with all of it and wanted to reassure her as he explained the really difficult part of his story. It wasn't lost on him that Art Goodman's expression hadn't changed. He never flinched when Steven had made reference to what had happened after he sent the Twins to look into Barlow. He wondered whether that was because he had learned to keep a poker face over decades of tough negotiations or because of something else. Steven continued his story explaining his encounter with the woman holding the packages, his being knocked out in the car and waking up in the motel room. Goodman simply listened, but Beth was clearly getting more and more upset as he went on. He squeezed her hand as he continued to signal her to let him finish. That squeeze let her know he would explain as much as she needed him to explain, but not now. The squeeze had been their 'not now' signal to each other for more years than he could remember. They had both come to use it in that fashion countless times over the years and Steven had never been more appreciative of that private signal than he was as he went on with the story. There were things he needed to tell his wife and his wife only. He told both of them that he had believed Barlow when he said he would leave him and his family alone if Steven returned the courtesy. He had wanted to make that clear to Beth so she could at least know they were not in any imminent danger. He already knew that Goodman would be thinking far beyond the immediate danger. A man did not get to the rank of general without having a keen strategic mind and Goodman's was keener than most. Steven went on to explain how he had tasked security teams to keep an eye on his family in Vermont and on his place here in New York. He was relieved when he saw, when he felt, Beth exhale. Once again, a half a lifetime of being together allowed them to communicate some of the most important things without saying a word. He imagined it was the same with most solid marriages. Two people joined at the heart didn't need words to communicate and with that exhale Beth had let him know she was okay. She would probably take him to the woodshed over not telling her and he would have a lot of explaining to do, but now he knew she would be okay in the end. He had gotten through the really tough part. He finished the story by explaining that he intended to do precisely as Barlow had requested. He would focus on his trial and protecting his family from it and the media coverage as much as possible. Once again, he reiterated that he believed Barlow when he had said he would leave him and his family alone. He went on to say, for Beth's benefit more than anything else, that he believed that the media's, the world's attention, really, would serve to keep his family safe. Now he did stop. He wanted to let both of them catch up and process everything he had just told them and he knew each would do so at their own pace. Goodman would be much further along than Beth in that regard, but he wasn't worried about him. Steven got up and went to put some ice in his drink, "Can I get you another drink Art? Babe, can I get you anything?" Both shook their heads, but didn't say anything. When Steven came back to sit down it was Beth who spoke first, "I guess the first thing I want to know is that the kids and my parents are safe. They are, aren't they?" It broke Steven's heart to see the pleading look on her face. It also broke his heart that she had gotten so used to the surreal quality of everything that had happened in their life in the past couple of months that she took his story in stride. She didn't break down or come unhinged, something that would have almost certainly happened before Tracy had gone missing. Steven couldn't imagine what a wife, any other wife, would say if her husband came home and told her that some sick bastard had knocked him out and taken him to a motel in New Jersey where he warned the man to stay away. Forget about what happened to Tracy or what he had done to Riche, that type of story would serve to send any other wife into a panic and almost certainly into a nervous breakdown. But now Steven understood, she had spent almost her entire adult life with him living with an almost daily uncertainty about what he was doing and where he was. She knew how dangerous his job was, how he would never be called into anything that didn't require the best and most experienced and deadly operators in the US military. It was no wonder that divorce rate among Navy SEALs was rumored to be over 80%. He couldn't imagine what it was for those that were a part of that most elite fraternity, DEVGRU or SEAL Team six, but it had to be higher than 80%. And yet here she was, through it all, through all those years and through all the missions, here she was. In a singular moment of clarity Steven came to realize that destiny or fate or God or whatever it was that decided such things had chosen them for this because they were equipped to handle it. He seemed to recall a saying from church about God placing problems and challenges only in front of those who were able to handle them. Wherever it was he had heard it didn't matter, what mattered was that it could not be truer than it was right then and there, with him sitting next to his wife. He smiled at her, gave her a kiss on her forehead and answered her question, "They are babe, they are absolutely safe. The people watching over them are serious operators. I know all of them. You've met some of them, in fact. You know the Twins, Cecil and Thurman right?" She nodded. She had met them a couple of times while they had served under her husband and again at some function or other while Steven was at GIC. Two very attractive black men in their late thirties or early forties. She remembered them being very intimidating, but very professional and well mannered. Identical except that one wore a goatee and the other one did not. She seemed to remember thinking the same thing about most of the people her husband worked with. She knew what it took to become a SEAL and what it took to be chosen to be a part of Team six. You were invited to try for the team only after years of combat experience in one of the other SEAL teams. The country was only now finding out what she had known for almost two decades, that these men were truly the best of the best. She considered the irony of the fact that some of the things she had resented about her husband's chosen profession were now things that gave her great comfort. The men watching over her family were trained to see what others didn't, to anticipate what others didn't and to take out any and all threats without hesitation. Most of them spoke several languages and all had to have above average IQs. They were experts at becoming experts of whatever it was they were tasked with and if they had been tasked with watching over her family she was certain that by now they knew her parents' and her children's routine by heart. They had scouted out their lake house, the town it was in and every other potential location where they thought a threat could come from. All of it served to make her feel, as her husband did, that their family was safe. Still, she had some questions she wanted answered, "Okay. What now? What are we supposed to do now? God, Steven, why now? Why did this happen to us now, when everything else is going on?" Steven could have pointed out how it was all connected, how one thing had led to another, but he didn't want to do that because he knew in the end the common thread, the connection between every one of the things that had happened to them after Tracy was found, was him, his decisions. He could sense she was starting to panic and needed him to bring sense to it all, as he had done many times before. He didn't disappoint her, "Really, nothing, nothing besides what we were doing already. I'm going to concentrate on the trial and on working with my lawyers to put the best case forward. Obviously we have to be more vigilant now, but we were already pretty cautious and aware before any of this happened. Like I said, it's ironic but having the media everywhere helps us in this case. Think about anyone trying to come or go without being noticed by the media, it would be virtually impossible. And if they did get past the media, think about them trying to get past the security teams in place, it would be literally impossible." He knew that was technically not true, but she needed the reassurance. She took this last comment and mulled it over. She got up and headed to the kitchen, "I have to get dinner going." Steven nodded, held on to her hand as she walked away and pulled it to his lips before she walked away. Once she was in the kitchen and out of earshot, he waited to hear from the General. The old man was most definitely turning things over in his head. Steven had seen the same expression of concentration countless times before. When he finally spoke, the old man almost knocked him out of his chair, "I already knew." He saw no expression other than deep concentration and heard no tone of recrimination. He waited for him to explain what he meant. "I already knew about all of it, the meeting with Barlow at your office, the thing in New Jersey and I even know about your little side trip to Little Italy to talk to that woman. That's what I came here to talk to you about. I came by last night, but I couldn't wait for you to get home. I'm glad I didn't have to ask you, that you did it on your own." Steven's mouth hung open for a half a second and then it shut. He hung his head and shook it slowly. He should have known. There had been an instant flash of resentment at the fact that Cecil and Thurman had told the General about Barlow and, he assumed, everything else that he had asked them to keep in confidence. But the feeling had quickly been replaced by a realization and acceptance of the fact that deep down inside he had always known that Art Goodman would somehow find out about everything, whether it had been the Twins or not didn't really matter, he would have found out some other way. How many times had Steven been completely baffled by the man's ability to get information that he had thought was simply impossible to get. Yeah, he should have known from the beginning. When he finally looked up at the old man there was a sideways grin on his face, "I should have known. Did know, actually, I think I always knew you'd find out somehow." The General returned the grin and nodded, "Well, it is what it is. The question is what do you want to do now?" Steven didn't need to think about it, "Nothing. Exactly what I said to

Beth. I certainly can't do anything about Barlow right now." Goodman nodded, "I understand. I noticed you didn't tell Beth about your meeting in Little Italy." Steven shook his head, "What for? To tell her what she's already heard about Barlow? She doesn't need to be convinced about how dangerous the man is, trust me. That's what Diana, that's the woman who I met with, was trying to do. She was trying to warn me about how far his reach extends and how many resources he has at his disposal." The old man held up his hands, "Hey, I'm not saying you should have told her. Fact is I think it was the right thing to do. What I meant was what do you want to do in the long term?" Steven hadn't really thought about that. He was busy with his trial and with keeping his family safe for its duration. His only long-term goal was to get through it without going to prison for the rest of his life. If he ended up going to prison whatever plans he might have would be moot. "I have to beat this charge, there's no two ways about it. Before Barlow came along I felt that even if I lost I would have accomplished what I set out to do." Goodman went to say something, but Steven raised his hand and kept going, "I'm not saying I was throwing in the towel. I told you before, I'm nobody's martyr. I've always planned to defend myself with everything I have. I'm just saying that back then going to prison would have been what I imagine going to prison is for most. Losing their family, their job, their life. It would have crushed me, but I could have moved on. Now that I understand what Barlow is and how far it goes, I'm not so sure. My family's safety is above everything else and if I went to prison I would go crazy worrying about them, but it would be doable because I have you and Beth's parents and everyone else that is behind me to protect them. What about all those other people, the ones who don't have anybody protecting them? The ones who are victimized and preyed upon every day? They have enough trying to keep safe from human predators, what about when these things come knocking? I keep thinking about the families of the other girls that Riche took. What have things been like for them? Their lives destroyed, their little girls gone." Now the General did interrupt him, "Wait a minute son, you can't put all of that on your shoulders, nobody can. We, humanity, know the dangers out there and we do our best to protect ourselves. It was that way when we lived in caves and it's that way now. No one man is ever going to be able to step up for humanity. Many have tried and lost their minds in the process." Steven shook his head in frustration, "I know that Art, I'm not diluted. But one thing that Barlow has made clear for me is that these things, these predators, have been in the shadows for a long time. They've done what they've done and preyed upon people completely unnoticed this entire time. We hear of disappearances and we put up our posters and eventually people just let it go, never knowing what happened and why. There are wars and riots and murders and we are fed what the media deems we should be fed and they are guided and moved by those in power. Don't get me wrong, I'm sure most wars and riots and every other form of uprising are exactly what we understand it to be, but now I know that there are some that are something else. There are some that were designed by others with a different agenda." The General now took on a look of open skepticism, "You're telling me that there are wars that are engineered by one of these things, these predators for their own amusement?" Steven leaned closer, "c'mon Art, do you really think it would be that hard? We've seen it done many times around the world. That's our business. Mad geniuses convincing people to go to war over their own personal agenda, to commit suicide for god's sake! World war II, Uganda, Rwanda, hell North Korea, it happens all the time. You think that it couldn't be done by one of these things?" Goodman mulled it over. It didn't take long; he had seen it with his own two eyes for more decades than he cared to remember. Steven went on, "I'm not trying to be humanity's savior, but I would be lying to you if I didn't say that I do feel a sense of responsibility. Barlow let me know that with all of this, with the trial, the media, all of it, they would come out from the shadows, maybe not too many of them, but some. He let me know that they've been operating in the shadows because they feel powerful; knowing what they are and having the world think they're just human gives them that power. That is how Barlow has been able to do everything he's been able to do. What do you think a senator or a CEO who has grown up believing they are freaks or psychopaths does when Barlow soothes them and lets them know that they're not freaks, that they're nature's next iteration? That they were designed to be what they are? Can you imagine their relief, their sense of empowerment and purpose? It's no wonder they're willing to shell out as much as they need to for him or to given him the access of power that he has. But now that I have brought the world's attention to them some of them are going to resent being 'outed' and they're going to come looking for the one who did it. It's not them I'm worried about, though, I told you I know we're covered. It's the ones who relish the world being aware of them and who might take to doing things that are more brazen and deadly in order to own what they are that worry me." Goodman nodded thoughtfully. Everything that Steven had said made sense and he knew it. He had the experience that only having lived through wars and watching men die because of one man's madness could bring. He still tried to bring Steven back to his original point, however, "Okay, I get it. What do you want to do about your family? I'm talking about tactics now, not the end game." Steven had thought about that, "I think Beth is fine here. She's being watched 24/7 by two rotating teams. They've got our place under electronic surveillance as well. Anyone points a parabolic mic or tries to put fiber optics in from anywhere and we'll know. They're all people you know." Steven smiled before moving on, "What am I talking about, you probably helped the Twins pick the teams." Goodman simply nodded. "So I don't need to tell you Beth's parents' place is also very well covered. I also wasn't making it up when I told Beth that having the media camped out everywhere was going to be helpful to us. I'm pretty comfortable with the situation right now, as comfortable as I can be anyways. That's why I am able to give my attention to preparing for the trial." Goodman now stood up to pace, a habit that Steven had also picked up over the years, "Okay, so we're set tactically. I think it would be a good idea to begin planning for what happens after the trial right now. We need to figure out how to keep your family safe in the long term. That's priority number one. What you decide to do after that's accomplished is up to you. I agree, you have to beat these charges no matter what. I've been doing some research and I've talked to Max. He feels, and I agree, that even if you are convicted you would almost certainly not be sentenced to life in prison. I'm not saying that to blow smoke up your ass and make you feel better. I'm saying it to put things into perspective. Even if you lose the trial, there will be an after for you. So, we'll concentrate on keeping your family safe for now and figure out how to make it permanent after the trial. The rest we can play by ear." Steven had heard that phrase countless times over the years. Whether he was talking to a president in one of the areas they operated or to his troops or to the janitor, he had the power to break things down into bits that could be digested and tackled. Everything in life came with an ever-present dose of uncertainty, however, and Goodman had the wisdom to understand that some things you just couldn't plan for until you knew more. This was the perfect illustration of that very point. Both men looked into each other's eyes. As always, some of the deepest thoughts were communicated in these looks. Steven could see how much the old man truly cared about him and his family. And he could see how worried he had been and would continue to be for some time. Goodman could see that Steven, his best executive and the closest thing to a son he would ever have, was tired and worried, but still all there. It gave him immense comfort to see that in Steven's eyes. The General had been afraid that the loss of his daughter and the subsequent pressure of what he had done and what he was facing had served to erode the spirit that had endeared him so much to Steven. He'd seen many men, good men, beaten down over time, plodding along because they had been trained to never give in, but no longer with the spark in their eyes that had let him know they were different, that they might go on to be great in time. That spark was still very much alive in Steven. Of course he would worry about him, he looked not just physically tired, but emotionally weary and that concerned the General. But a tired body and soul could be revived with rest, deep rest, as long as the spark was still there. They were about to get up to join Beth when Steven reached out and pulled him back down, "Listen, General, I need you to help me with Beth. She's going to need support through this and I might not be able to give it to her when she needs it. She believes me when I tell her things will be okay, that we're safe. I've always proved it to her. But this, this is different. I know she believes me, but she's still going to worry. She respects you almost as much as she respects her father and that's saying something. She needs to hear that we're going to be okay from someone else besides her parents and me. Someone who knows it for a fact and isn't trying to just make her feel better. " The General smiled a gentle smile, "I understand. My Kristy was the same way. Every time I'd leave on a deployment she's get that look, a look that said exactly that: 'I believe you when you say things will be fine, but I'm still going to worry.'" Steven saw deep sadness in the man's eyes. Goodman had lost his wife five years ago and still mourned her sometimes. They had been high school sweethearts and gotten married when they had both been 20 years old. They had never had any kids. Steven had never learned why and his boss hadn't offered. After two seconds of that far away, sad look, Goodman looked back at him, "Of course I'll be there. You don't ever have to ask. You may still not know this, Steven, but you and Beth and the kids are family to me." Steven squeezed the man's hand, "I do know it Art. Now, more than ever, I know it."